THE BENEDICTION OF BROTHER CADFAEL

·ELLIS PETERS·

THE BENEDICTION
· OF ·
BROTHER CADFAEL

THE MYSTERIOUS PRESS
New York · Tokyo · Sweden
Published by Warner Books

 A Time Warner Company

 Mysterious Press books are published by
Warner Books, Inc., 1271 Avenue of the Americas, New York, NY 10020.

Ⓦ A Time Warner Company

Printed in the United States of America
First printing: November 1992
10 9 8 7 6 5 4 3 2 1

Library of Congress Cataloging-in-Publication Data

Peters, Ellis, 1913–
    [Morbid taste for bones]
    The benediction of Brother Cadfael / Ellis Peters.
        p.   cm.
    Contents: A morbid taste for bones — Cadfael country / R. Talbot
and R. Whiteman — One corpse too many.
    ISBN 0-89296-449-9
    1. Cadfael, Brother (Fictitious character)—Fiction. 2. Great
Britain—History—Stephen, 1135–1154—Fiction. 3. Detective and
mystery stories, English. 4. Shrewsbury (England)—History—
Fiction. 5. Shropshire (England)—Pictorial works. I. Peters,
Ellis, 1913– One corpse too many. 1992. II. Talbot, Rob, 1958–
Cadfael country. Selections. 1992. III. Title.
PR6031.A49M67 1992
823′.912—dc20   91-50965
                                                            CIP

Contents

Introduction

I was born and bred in Shropshire and have never yet found any sound reason for leaving it, except perhaps for the pleasure of coming back to it again, after forays into regions otherwise delightful in themselves but no substitute for home. Or perhaps that can be extended into a further reason. What do they know of Shropshire that only Shropshire know? Travel sharpens the senses as well as broadening the mind, and gives an added savour to favourite food abstained from for a while, like Easter after Lent.

But I also have a toehold over the border, by courtesy of one Welsh grandmother, and feel the tension that Housman sensed between Wales and England, centred, logically enough, in the almost-island of Shrewsbury, frequently Welsh in its early history, frequently fought over from both sides, drawing its trade from both sides and, up to half a century ago, probably hearing as much Welsh as English in its streets and markets. By whatever name – Pengwern, Scrobbesbyrig, Shrewsbury, Salop – it has always been a regional capital to the Middle March of Wales, and no ground in the kingdom has been more tramped over by armies, coveted by chieftains, ravaged by battles, sung by poets and celebrated in epics of legend and tragedy.

This central March, both sides of the border, is my home ground, and since I have always preferred to set my writings in the places I know best and value most, it has also been the scene of most of my books, and the homeland I have handed on to Brother Cadfael, Welshman of Gwynedd, crusader, seaman and monk of Shrewsbury Abbey, a late *conversus* to the cloistered life.

Brother Cadfael arose naturally, as central figure in the first novel of the sequence, based on the actual early history of Shrewsbury's Benedictine abbey, and has survived to undertake a pilgrimage through the entire local and national history of the town and region during the anarchy of the twelfth century. There is an inherent difficulty in having a monk as protagonist in such a chronicle, since his vows included one of stability, and that meant being content to stay within the enclave itself, unless sent out on official business and at the abbot's orders, which allows his creator only a limited canvas. But the great abbeys had lands, granges, churches and fisheries, scattered fairly widely, and were committed to a certain amount of administration and management accordingly, and there were plenty of occasions for sending brothers out upon lawful business. With his modest acquired skills in medicine and the use of herbs, Cadfael enlarged his field legitimately from Lichfield and Elford in the east to Tregeiriog and Gwytherin in the west, and from Oswestry in the north to Ludlow and Clee in the south, besides his forays into the villages closer to home.

Words can convey, on occasion, very vivid visual images of place and weather and season, and landscapes familiar and well loved tend to accentuate the pictorial quality in the writing. But still there is ample room for another dimension, and the camera, in sensitive hands and with an inspired eye guiding it, can provide its own additional poetry and radiance. Place, time, weather, dawn and dark, bursting of bud and fall of leaf, bird and beast and flower, sunlight and mist and cloud, cloister and church, river and mill and field, look for them all within the covers of this book,

and even after eight centuries you may find yourself, now and then, seeing the Marches very much as Cadfael saw them, perhaps thinking the same thoughts and experiencing the same contemplative pleasure that illuminated his chosen lot in life. The works and signs of man's activity have suffered more from time than have woodland and hedgerow, but even so the long continuity of human occupation is there to be seen in the worn stone of church and castle and the shaping of field and village; and the unbroken thread of life and worship persists in the very soil, and reminds us that we are the custodians of this earth, the inheritors of its history and the trustees of its future.

It is my hope that Robin Whiteman's meticulous text and Rob Talbot's beautiful photographs may give you as much pleasure as, in preparation, they have already given me. And that even after another eight centuries our descendants will still find indestructible beauty and awe and wonder in Cadfael Country.

Ellis Peters.

A MORBID TASTE FOR BONES

A MORBID TASTE FOR BONES

Chapter One

n the fine, bright morning in early May when the whole sensational affair of the Gwytherin relics may properly be considered to have begun, Brother Cadfael had been up long before Prime, pricking out cabbage seedlings before the day was aired, and his thoughts were all on birth, growth and fertility, not at all on graves and reliquaries and violent deaths, whether of saints, sinners or ordinary decent, fallible men like himself. Nothing troubled his peace but the necessity to take himself indoors for Mass, and the succeeding half-hour of chapter, which was always liable to stray over by an extra ten minutes. He grudged the time from his more congenial labours out here among the vegetables, but there was no evading his duty. He had, after all, chosen this cloistered life with his eyes open, he could not complain even of those parts of it he found unattractive, when the whole suited him very well, and gave him the kind of satisfaction he felt now, as he straightened his back and looked about him.

He doubted if there was a finer Benedictine garden in the whole kingdom, or one better supplied with herbs both good for spicing meats, and also invaluable as medicine. The main orchards and lands of the Shrewsbury abbey of Saint Peter and Saint Paul lay on the northern side of the road, outside the monastic enclave, but here, in the enclosed garden within the walls, close to the abbot's fishponds and the brook that worked the abbey mill, Brother Cadfael ruled unchallenged. The herbarium in particular was his kingdom, for he had built it up gradually through the fifteen years of labour, and added to it many exotic plants of his own careful raising, collected in a roving youth that had taken him as far afield as Venice, and Cyprus and the Holy Land. For Brother Cadfael had come late to the monastic life, like a battered ship settling at last for a quiet harbour. He was well aware that in the first years of his vows the novices and lay servants had been wont to point him out to one another with awed whisperings.

"See that brother working in the garden there? The thickset fellow who rolls from one leg to the other like a sailor? You wouldn't think to look at him, would you, that he went on crusade when he was young? He was with Godfrey de Bouillon at Antioch, when the Saracens surrendered it. And he took to the seas as a captain when the king of Jerusalem ruled all the coast of the Holy Land, and served against the corsairs ten years! Hard to believe it now, eh?"

Brother Cadfael himself found nothing strange in his wide-ranging career, and had forgotten nothing and regretted nothing. He saw no contradiction in the delight he had taken in battle and adventure and the keen pleasure he now found in quietude. Spiced, to be truthful, with more than a little mischief when he could get it, as he liked his victuals well-flavoured, but quietude all the same, a ship becalmed and enjoying it. And probably the youngsters who eyed him with such curiosity also whispered that in a life such as he had led there must have been some encounters with women, and not all purely chivalrous, and what sort of grounding was that for the conventual life?

They were right about the women. Quite apart from Richildis, who had not unnaturally tired of waiting for his return after ten years, and married a solid yeoman with good prospects in the shire, and no intention of flying off to the wars, he remembered other ladies, in more lands than one, with whom he had enjoyed encounters pleasurable to both parties, and no harm to either. Bianca, drawing water at the stone well-head in Venice—the Greek boat-girl Arianna—Mariam, the Saracen widow who sold spices and fruit in Antioch, and who found him man enough to replace for a while the man she had lost. The light encounters and the grave, not one of them had left any hard feelings behind. He counted that as achievement enough, and having known

them was part of the harmonious balance that made him content now with this harboured, contemplative life, and gave him patience and insight to bear with these cloistered, simple souls who had put on the Benedictine habit as a life's profession, while for him it was a timely retirement. When you have done everything else, perfecting a conventual herb-garden is a fine and satisfying thing to do. He could not conceive of coming to this stasis having done nothing else whatever.

Five minutes more, and he must go and wash his hands and repair to the church for Mass. He used the respite to walk the length of his pale-flowered, fragrant inner kingdom, where Brother John and Brother Columbanus, two youngsters barely a year tonsured, were busy weeding and edge-trimming. Glossy and dim, oiled and furry, the leaves tendered every possible variation on green. The flowers were mostly shy, small, almost furtive, in soft, sidelong colours, lilacs and shadowy blues and diminutive yellows, for they were the unimportant and unwanted part, but for ensuring seed to follow. Rue, sage, rosemary, gilvers, gromwell, ginger, mint, thyme, columbine, herb of grace, savoury, mustard, every manner of herb grew here, fennel, tansy, basil and dill, parsley, chervil and marjoram. He had taught the uses even of the unfamiliar to all his assistants, and made plain their dangers, too, for the benefit of herbs is in their right proportion, and over-dosage can be worse than the disease. Small of habit, modest of tint, close-growing and shy, his herbs called attention to themselves only by their disseminated sweetness as the sun rose on them. But behind their shrinking ranks rose others taller and more clamorous, banks of peonies grown for their spiced seeds, and lofty, pale-leaved, budding poppies, as yet barely showing the white or purple-black petals through their close armour. They stood as tall as a short man, and their home was the eastern part of the middle sea, and from that far place Cadfael had brought their ancestors in the seed long ago, and raised and cross-bred them in his own garden, before ever he brought the perfected progeny here with him to make medicines against pain, the chief enemy of man. Pain, and the absence of sleep, which is the most beneficent remedy for pain.

The two young men, with habits kilted to the knee, were just straightening their backs and dusting the soil from their hands, as well aware as he of the hour. Brother Columbanus would not for the world have let slip one grain of his duties, or countenanced such a backsliding in any of his fellows. A very comely, well-made, upstanding young fellow he was, with a round, formidable, Norman head, as he came from a formidable, aristocratic Norman family, a younger son despatched to make his way in the monastic ranks as next-best to inheriting the land. He had stiff, up-standing yellow hair and full blue eyes, and his modest demeanour and withdrawn pallor tended to obscure the muscular force of his build. Not a very comfortable colleague, Brother Columbanus, for in spite of his admirable body equipment he had some while since proved that he had a mental structure of alarming sensitivity, and was liable to fits of emotional stress, crises of conscience, and apocalyptic visions far removed from the implications of his solid skull. But he was young and idealistic, he had time to get over his self-torments. Brother Cadfael had worked with him for some months, and had every hope for him. He was willing, energetic, and

almost too eager to please. Possibly he felt his debt to his aristocratic house too nearly, and feared a failure that would reflect on his kin. You cannot be of high Norman blood, and not excel! Brother Cadfael felt for any such victims as found themselves in this trap, coming as he did, of antique Welsh stock without superhuman pretensions. So he tolerated Brother Columbanus with equanimity, and doctored his occasional excesses philosophically. The juice of the paynim poppies had quieted Columbanus more than once when his religious fervour prostrated him.

Well, at any rate there was no nonsense of that kind with the other one! Brother John was as plain and practical as his name, a square young man with a snub nose and an untamable ring of wiry russet curls round his tonsure. He was always hungry, and his chief interest in all things that grew in gardens was whether they were eatable, and of agreeable flavour. Come autumn he would certainly find a way of working his passage into the orchards. Just now he was content to help Brother Cadfael prick out early lettuces, and wait for the soft fruits to come into season. He was a handsome, lusty, good-natured soul, who seemed to have blundered into this enclosed life by some incomprehensible error, and not yet to have realised that he had come to the wrong place. Brother Cadfael detected a lively sense of mischief the fellow to his own, but never yet given its head in a wider world, and confidently expected that some day this particular red-crested bird would certainly fly. Meantime, he got his entertainment wherever it offered, and found it sometimes in unexpected places.

"I must be in good time," he said, unkilting his gown and dusting his hands cheerfully on his seat. "I'm reader this week." So he was, Cadfael recalled, and however dull the passages they chose for him in the refectory, and innocuous the saints and martyrs he would have to celebrate at chapter, John would contrive to imbue them with drama and gusto from his own sources. Give him the beheading of Saint John the Baptist, and he would shake the foundations.

"You read for the glory of God and the saints, brother," Columbanus reminded him, with loving reproof and somewhat offensive humility, "not for your own!" Which showed either how little he knew about it, or how false he could be, one or the other.

"The blessed thought is ever in my mind," said Brother John with irrepressible zest, and winked at Cadfael behind his colleague's back, and set off enthusiastically along the aisles of shrubs towards the abbot's gate and the great court. They followed him more demurely, the slender, fair, agile youth and the squat, barrel-chested, bandy-legged veteran of fifty-seven. Was I ever, wondered Cadfael, rolling with his powerful seaman's gait beside the other's long, supple strides, as young and earnest as this? It cost him an effort to recall that Columbanus was actually fully twenty-five, and the sprig of a sophisticated and ambitious house. Whose fortunes, surely, were not founded wholly on piety?

This third Mass of the day was non-parochial and brief, and after it the Benedictine brothers of the abbey of Shrewsbury filed in procession from the choir into the chapter-house, and made their way to their stalls in due order, Abbot Heribert leading. The abbott was old, of mild nature and pliant, a gentle grey ascetic very wishful of peace and harmony around him. His figure was unimpressive, though his face was beguiling in its anxious sweetness. Novices and pupils were easy in his presence, when they could reach it, which was by no means always easy, for the extremely impressive figure of Prior Robert was liable to loom between.

Prior Robert Pennant of mixed Welsh and English blood, was more than six feet tall, attenuated and graceful, silver-grey hair at fifty, blanched and beautiful of visage, with long, aristocratic features and lofty marble brow. There was no man in the midland shires would look more splendid in a mitre, superhuman in height and authority, and there was no man in England better aware of it, or more determined to prove it at the earliest opportunity. His very motions, sweeping across the chapter-house to his stall, understudied the pontificate.

After him came Brother Richard the sub-prior, his antithesis, large, ungainly, amiable and benevolent, of a good mind, but mentally lazy. Doubtful if he would ever become prior when Robert achieved his end, with so many ambitious and industrious younger men eyeing the prospect of advancement, and willing to go to a great deal of trouble to secure it.

After Richard came all the other brothers in their hierarchies. Brother Benedict the sacristan, Brother Anselm the precentor, Brother Matthew the cellarer, Brother Dennis the hospitaller, Brother Edmund the infirmarer, Brother Oswald the almoner, Brother Jerome, the prior's clerk, and Brother Paul, master of the novices, followed by the commonalty of the convent, and a very flourishing number they made. Among the last of them Brother Cadfael rolled to his own chosen corner, well to the rear and poorly lit, half-concealed behind one of the stone pillars. Since he held no troublesome parchment office, he was unlikely to be called upon to speak in chapter upon the various businesses of the house, and when the matter in hand was dull into the bargain it was his habit to employ the time to good account by sleeping, which from long usage he could do bolt upright and undetected in his shadowy corner. He had a sixth sense which alerted him at need, and brought him awake instantly and plausibly. He had even been known to answer a question pat, when it was certain he had been asleep when it was put to him.

On this particular May morning he remained awake long enough to enjoy Brother John's extraction of the last improbable ounce of drama from the life of some obscure saint whose day fell on the morrow, but when the cellarer began to expound a complicated matter of a legacy partly to the altar of Our Lady, partly to the infirmary, he composed himself to slumber. After all, he knew that most of the remaining time, once a couple of minor malefactors had been dealt with, would be given to Prior Robert's campaign to secure the relics and patronage of a powerful saint for the monastery. For the past few months very little else had been discussed. The prior had had it on his mind, in fact, ever since the Cluniac house of Wenlock had rediscovered, with great pride and jubilation, the tomb of their original foundress, Saint Milburga, and installed her bones triumphantly on their altar. An alien priory, only a few miles distant, with its own miracle-working saint, and the great Benedictine house of Shrewsbury as empty of relics as a plundered almsbox! It was more than Prior Robert could stomach. He had been scouring the borderlands for a spare saint now for a year or more, looking hope-fully towards Wales, where it was well known that holy men and women had been common as mushrooms in autumn in the past, and as little regarded. Brother Cadfael had no wish to hear the latest of his complaints and urgings. He slept.

The heat of the sun rebounded from honed new facets of pale, baked rock, scorching his face, as the floating arid dust burned his throat. From where he crouched with his fellows in cover he could see the long crest of the wall, and the steel-capped heads of the guards on the turrets glittering in the fierce light. A landscape carved out of reddish stone and fire, all deep gullies and sheer cliffs, with never a cool green leaf to temper it, and before him the object of all his journeyings, the holy city of Jerusalem, crowned with towers and domes within its white walls. The dust of battle hung in the air, dimming the clarity of battlement and gate, and the hoarse shouting and clashing of armour filled his ears. He was waiting for the trumpet to sound the final assault, and keeping well in cover while he waited, for he had learned to respect the range of the short, curly Saracen bow. He saw the banners surge forward out of hiding, streaming on the burning wind. He saw the flash of the raised trumpet, and braced himself for the blare.

The sound that brought him leaping wide-awake out of his dream was loud enough and stirring enough, but not the brazen blast of a trumpet, nor was he launched from his still-ness towards the triumphant storming of Jerusalem. He was back in his stall in the dark corner of the chapter-house, and starting to his feet as alertly as the rest, and with the same consternation and alarm. And the shriek that had awakened him was just subsiding into a series of rending moans and broken cries that might have been of extreme pain or extreme ecstasy. In the open space in the centre of the chapter-house Brother Columbanus lay on his face, threshing and jerking like a landed fish, beating his forehead and his palms against the flagstones, kicking and flailing with long, pale legs bared to the knee by his contortions, and barking out of him those extraordinary sounds of shattering physical excitement, while the nearest of the brothers hovered in helpless shock, and Prior Robert with lifted hands exhorted and exclaimed.

Brother Cadfael and Brother Edmund, the infirmarer, reached the victim together, kneeled over him one on either side, and restrained him from battering his brains out against the stones of the floor, or dislocating his joints in the flailings. "Falling sickness!" said Brother Edmund tersely, and wedged the thick cord of Columbanus' girdle between his teeth, and a fold of his habit with it, to prevent him from biting his tongue.

Brother Cadfael was less certain of the diagnosis, for these were not the grunting, helpless noises of an epileptic in an attack, but such as might be expected from a hysterical woman in a frenzy. But at least the treatment stopped half the noise, and even appeared to diminish the vigour of the convulsions, though they resumed again as soon as the restraining grip on him was loosed.

"Poor young man!" fluttered Abbot Heribert, hovering in the background. "So sudden, so cruel an affliction! Handle him gently! Carry him to the infirmary. We must pray for his restoration."

Chapter broke up in some disorder. With the help of Brother John, and certain others of a practical turn of mind, they got Brother Columbanus securely but comfortably swathed in a sheet, confining arms and legs so that he would do himself no injury, wedged his teeth apart with a wooden spit instead of the cloth, on which he might have gagged and choked, and carried him on a shutter to the infirmary, where they got him into bed, and secured him there with bandages round breast and thighs. He moaned and gurgled and heaved still, but with weakening force, and when they had managed to get a draught of Brother Cadfael's poppy-juice into him his moans subsided into pitiful mutterings, and the violence of his struggles against his confinement grew feebler.

"Take good care of him," said Prior Robert, frowning anxiously over the young man's bed. "I think someone should be constantly by to watch over him, in case the fit comes again. You have your other sick men to attend to, you cannot sit by his side day and night. Brother Jerome, I put this sufferer in your charge, and excuse you from all other duties while he needs you."

"Willingly," said Brother Jerome, "and prayerfully!" He was Prior Robert's closest associate and most devoted hanger-on, and an inevitable choice whenever Robert required strict obedience and meticulous reporting, as might well be the case where a brother of the house succumbed to what might elsewhere be whispered abroad as a fit of madness.

"Stay with him in particular during the night," said the prior, "for in the night a man's resistance falters, and his bodily evils may rise against him. If he sleeps peacefully, you may rest also, but remain close, in case he needs you."

"He'll sleep within the hour," said Cadfael confidently, "and may pass into natural sleep well before night. God willing, he may put this off before morning."

For his part, he thought Brother Columbanus lacked sufficient work for both mind and body, and took his revenge for his deprivation in these excesses, half-wilful, half-involuntary, and both to be pitied and censured. But he retained enough caution to reserve a doubt with every conviction. He was not sure he knew any of his adopted brothers well enough to judge with certainty. Well, Brother John— yes, perhaps! But inside the conventual life or outside, cheerful, blunt, extrovert Brother Johns are few and far between.

Brother Jerome appeared at chapter next morning with an exalted countenance, and the air of one bursting with momentous news. At Abbot Heribert's mild reproof for leaving his patient without permission, he folded his hands meekly and bowed his head, but lost none of his rapt assurance.

"Father, I am sent here by another duty, that seemed to me even more urgent. I have left Brother Columbanus sleeping, though not peacefully, for even his sleep is tormented. But two lay-brothers are watching by him. If I have done wrong, I will abide it humbly."

"Our brother is no better?" asked the abbot anxiously.

"He is still deeply troubled, and when he wakes he raves. But, Father, this is my errand! There is a sure hope for him! In the night I have been miraculously visited. I have come to tell you what divine mercy has instructed me. Father, in the small hours I fell into a doze beside Brother Columbanus' bed, and had a marvellously sweet dream."

By this time he had everyone's attention, even Brother Cadfael was wide awake. "What,

another of them?" whispered Brother John wickedly into his ear. "The plague's spreading!"

"Father, it seemed to me that the wall of the room opened, and a great light shone in, and through the light and radiating the light there came in a most beautiful young virgin, and stood beside our brother's bed, and spoke to me. She told me that her name was Winifred, and that in Wales there is a holy spring, that rose to the light where she suffered martyrdom. And she said that if Brother Columbanus bathed in the water of that well, he would surely be healed, and restored at once to his senses. Then she uttered a blessing upon our house, and vanished in a great light, and I awoke."

Through the murmur of excitement that went round the chapter-house, Prior Robert's voice rose in reverent triumph: "Father Abbot, we are being guided! Our quest for a saint has drawn to us this sign of favour, in token that we should persevere."

"Winifred!" said the abbot doubtfully. "I do not recall clearly the story of this saint and martyr. There are so many of them in Wales. Certainly we ought to send Brother Columbanus to her holy spring, it would be ingratitude to neglect so clear an omen. But exactly where is it to be found?"

Prior Robert looked round for the few Welshmen among the brothers, passed somewhat hurriedly over Brother Cadfael, who had never been one of his favourites, perhaps by reason of a certain spark in his eye, as well as his notoriously worldly past, and lit gladly upon Old Brother Rhys, who was virtually senile but doctrinally safe, and had the capacious if capricious memory of the very old. "Brother, can you tell us the history of this saint, and where her well is to be found?"

The old man was slow to realise that he had become the centre of attention. He was shrunken like a bird, and toothless, and used to a tolerant oblivion. He began hesitantly, but warmed to the work as he found all eyes upon him.

"Saint Winifred, you say, Father? Everybody knows of Saint Winifred. You'll find her spring by the name they gave the place, Holywell, it's no great way in from Chester. But she's not there. You won't find her grave at Holywell."

"Tell us about her," coaxed Prior Robert, almost fawning in his eagerness. "Tell us all her story."

"Saint Winifred," declaimed the old man, beginning to enjoy his hour of glory, "was the only child of a knight named Tevyth, who lived in those parts when the princes were yet heathens. But this knight and all his household were converted by Saint Beuno, and made him a church there, and gave him houseroom. The girl was devoted even above her parents, and pledged herself to a virgin life, hearing Mass every day. But one Sunday it happened that she was sick, and stayed at home when all the rest of the household went to church. And there came to the door the prince of those parts. Cradoc, son of the king, who had fallen in love with her at a distance. For this girl was very beautiful. *Very* beautiful!" gloated Brother Rhys, and licked his lips loudly. Prior Robert visibly recoiled, but refrained from stopping the flow by reproof. "He pleaded that he was hot and parched from hunting," said Brother Rhys darkly, "and asked for a drink of water, and the girl let him in and gave him to drink. Then," he shrilled, hunching himself in his voluminous habit and springing erect with a vigour nobody present

would have credited, "he pressed his suit upon her, and grappled her in his arms. *Thus!*" The effort was almost too much for him, and moreover, the prior was eyeing him in alarm; he subsided with dignity. "The faithful virgin put him off with soft words, and escaping into another room, climbed from a window and fled towards the church. But finding that she had eluded him, Prince Cradoc took horse and rode after, and overtaking her just within sight of the church, and dreading that she would reveal his infamy, struck off her head with his sword."

He paused for the murmur of horror, pity and indignation, and got it, with a flurry of prayerfully-folded hands, and a tribute of round eyes.

"Then thus piteously she came by her death and beatitude?" intoned Brother Jerome enthusiastically.

"Not a bit of it!" snapped Brother Rhys. He had never liked Brother Jerome. "Saint Beuno and the congregation were coming out of the church, and saw what had passed. The saint drew a terrible curse upon the murderer, who at once sank to the ground, and began to melt like wax in a fire, until all his body had sunk away into the grass. Then Saint Beuno fitted the head of the virgin onto her neck, and the flesh grew together, and she stood up alive, and the holy fountain sprang up on the spot where she arose."

They waited, spellbound, and he let them wait. He had lost interest after the death.

"And afterwards?" insinuated Prior Robert. "What did the saint do with her restored life?"

"She went on a pilgrimage to Rome," said Brother Rhys indifferently, "and she attended at a great synod of saints, and was appointed to be prioress over a community of virgin sisters at Gwytherin, by Llanrwst. And there she lived many years, and did many miracles in her lifetime. If it should be called her lifetime? She was once dead already. When she died a second time, that was where it befell." He felt nothing concerning this residue of life, he offered it with a shrug. The girl had had her chance with Prince Cradoc, and let is slip, obviously her natural bent was to be prioress of a nest of virgins, and there was nothing more to be told about her.

"And she is buried there at Gwytherin?" persisted the prior. "And her miracles continued after death?"

"So I have heard. But it's a long time," said the old man, "since I've heard her name mentioned. And longer since I was in those parts."

Prior Robert stood in the circle of sunlight that filtered between the pillars of the chapter-house, drawn to his full imposing height, and turned a radiant face and commanding eyes upon Abbot Heribert.

"Father, does it not seem to you that our reverent search for a patron of great power and sanctity is being divinely guided? This gentle saint has visited us in person, in Brother Jerome's dream, and beckoned us to bring our afflicted brother to her for healing. Shall we not hope, also, that she will again show us the next step? If she does indeed receive our prayers and restore Brother Columbanus to health of body and mind, may we not be encouraged to hope that she will come in person and dwell among us? That we may humbly beg the church's sanction to take up her blessed relics and house them fittingly here in Shrewsbury? To the great glory and lustre of our house!"

"And of Prior Robert!" whispered Brother John in Cadfael's ear.

"It certainly seems that she has shown us singular favour," admitted Abbot Heribert.

"Then, Father, have I your leave to send Brother Columbanus with a safe escort to Holywell? This very day?"

"Do so," said the abbot, "with the prayers of us all, and may he return as Saint Winifred's own messenger, hale and grateful."

The deranged man, still wandering in mind and communing with himself in incoherent ravings, was led away out of the gatehouse on the first stage of his journey immediately after the midday meal, mounted on a mule, with a high, cradling saddle to give him some security from falling, in case the violent fit took him again, and with Brother Jerome and a brawny lay-brother one on either side, to support him at need. Columbanus looked about him with wide, pathetic, childlike eyes, and seemed to know nobody, though he went submissively and trustfully where he was led.

"I could have done with a nice little trip into Wales," said Brother John wistfully, looking after them as they rounded the corner and vanished towards the bridge over the Severn. "But I probably shouldn't have seen the right visions. Jerome will do the job better."

"Boy," said Brother Cadfael tolerantly, "you become more of an unbeliever every day."

"Not a bit of it! I'm as willing to believe in the girl's sanctity and miracles as any man. We know the saints have power to help and bless, and I'll believe they have the goodwill, too. But when it's Prior Robert's faithful hound who has the dream, you're asking me to believe in *his* sanctity, not hers! And in any case, isn't her favour glory enough? I don't see why they should want to dig up the poor lady's dust. It seems like charnel-house business to me, not church business. And you think exactly the same," he said firmly, and stared out his elder, eye to eye.

"When I want to hear my echo," said Brother Cadfael, "I will speak first. Come on, now, and get the bottom strip of ground dug, there are kale plants waiting to go in ."

The delegation to Holywell was gone five days, and came home towards evening in a fine shower of rain and a grand glow of grace, chanting prayers as the three entered the courtyard. In the midst rode Brother Columbanus, erect and graceful and jubilant, if that word could be used for one so humble in his gladness. His face was bright and clear, his eyes full of wonder and intelligence. No man ever looked less mad, or less likely to be subject to the falling sickness. He went straight to the church and gave thanks and praise to God and Saint Winifred on his knees, and from the altar all three went dutifully to report to the abbot, prior and sub-prior, in the abbot's lodging.

"Father," said Brother Columbanus, eager and joyous, "I have no skill to tell what has befallen me, for I know less than these who have cared for me in my delirium. All I know is that I was taken on this journey like a man in an ill dream, and went where I was taken, not knowing how to fend for myself, or what I ought to do. And suddenly I was like a man awakened out of that nightmare to a bright morning and a world of spring, and I was standing naked in the grass beside a well, and these good brothers were pouring water over me that healed as it touched. I knew myself and them, and only marvelled where I might be, and how I came there. Which they willingly

told me. And then we went, all, and many people of that place with us, to sing Mass in a little church that stands close by the well. Now I know that I owe my recovery to the intervention of Saint Winifred, and I praise and worship her from my heart, as I do God who caused her to take pity on me. The rest these brothers will tell."

The lay-brother was large, taciturn, weary—having done all the work throughout—and by this time somewhat bored with the whole business. He made the appropriate exclamations where needed, but left the narrative in the able hands of Brother Jerome, who told all with zest. How they had brought their patient to the village of Holywell, and asked the inhabitants for directions and aid, and been shown where the saint had risen living after her martyrdom, in the silver fountain that still sprang in the same spot, furnished now with a stone basin to hold its sacred flow. There they had led the rambling Columbanus, stripped him of habit, shirt and drawers, and poured the sacred water over him and instantly he had stood erect and lifted his hands in prayer, and given thanks for a mind restored. Afterwards he had asked them in wonder how he came there, and what had happened to him, and had been greatly chastened and exalted at his humbling and his deliverance, and most grateful to his patroness, by whose guidance he had been made whole.

"And, Father, the people there told us that the saint is indeed buried at Gwytherin, where she died after her ministry, and that the place where her body is laid has done many miracles. But they say that her tomb, after so long, is neglected and little thought of, and it may well be that she longs for a better recognition, and to be installed in some place where pilgrims may come, where she may be revered as is her due, and have room to enlarge her grace and blessing to reach more people in need."

"You are inspired, having been present at this miracle," said Prior Robert, tall and splendid with faith rewarded, "and you speak out what I have felt in listening to you. Surely Saint Winifred is calling us to rescue as she came to the rescue of Brother Columbanus. Many have need of her goodness as he had, and know nothing of her. In our hands she would be exalted as she deserves, and those who need her grace would know where to come and seek it. I pray that we may mount that expedition of faith to which she summons us. Father Abbot, give me your leave to petition the church, and bring this blessed lady home to rest here among us, and be our proudest boast. For I believe it is her will and her command."

"In the name of God," said Abbot Heribert devoutly, "I approve that project, and pray the blessing of heaven upon it!"

"He had it all planned beforehand," said Brother John over the bed of mint, between envy and scorn. "That was all a show, all that wonder and amazement, and asking who Saint Winifred was, and where to find her. He knew it all along. He'd already picked her out from those he's discovered neglected in Wales, and decided she was the one most likely to be available, as well as the one to shed most lustre on him. But it had to come out into the open by miraculous means. There'll be another prodigy whenever he needs his way smoothed for him, until he gets the girl here safely installed in the church, to his glory. It's a great enterprise, he means to climb high on

the strength of it. So he starts out with a vision, and a prodigious healing, and divine grace leading his footsteps. It's as plain as the nose on your face."

"And are you saying," asked Brother Cadfael mildly, "that Brother Columbanus is in the plot as well as Brother Jerome, and that falling fit of his was a fake, too? I should have to be very sure of my reward in heaven before I volunteered to break the paving with my forehead, even to provide Prior Robert with a miracle.

Brother John considered seriously, frowning. "No, that I don't say. We all know our meek white lamb is liable to the horrors over a penance scamped, and ecstasies over a vigil or a fast, and pouring ice-cold water over him at Holywell would be the very treatment to jolt him back into his right wits. We could just as well have tossed him in the fish-pond here! But of course *he*'d believe what they told him, and credit it all to the saint. Catch him missing such a chance! No, I wouldn't say he was a party to it—not knowingly. But he gave them the opportunity for a splendid demonstration of grace. You notice it was Jerome who was set to take care of him overnight! It takes only one man to be favoured with a vision, but it has to be the right man." He rolled a sprig of the young green leaves sadly between his palms, and the fragrance distilled richly on the early morning air. "And it will be the right men who'll accompany Prior Robert into Wales," he said with sour certainty. "You'll see!"

No doubt about it, this young man was hankering after a glimpse of the world again, and a breath of air from outside the walls. Brother Cadfael pondered, not only with sympathy for his young assistant, but also with some pleasurable stirrings of his own. So momentous an event in the otherwise even course of monastic life ought not to be missed. Besides the undoubted possibilities of mischief!

"True!" he said thoughtfully. "Perhaps we ought to take some steps to leaven the lump. Wales should not be left with the notion that Jerome is the best Shrewsbury can muster, that's very true."

"You have about as much chance of being invited as I," said Brother John with his customary bluntness. "Jerome is sure of his place. Prior Robert must have his right hand with him. And Columbanus, fool innocent, was the instrument of grace, and could be made to serve the same turn again. Brother Sub-Prior they have to take along, for form's sake. Surely we could think up some way of getting a foot in the door? They can't move for a few days yet, the carpenters and carvers are working hard on this splendid reliquary coffin they're going to take with them for the lady, but it will take them a while to finish it. Get your wits to work, brother! There isn't anything you couldn't do, if you've a mind! Prior or no prior!"

"Well, well, did I say you had no faith?" wondered Brother Cadfael, charmed and disarmed. "I might worm my own way in, there could be ways, but how am I to recommend a graceless rogue like you? What are you good at, to be taken along on such an errand?"

"I'm a good hand with mules," said Brother John hopefully, "and you don't think Prior Robert intends to go on foot, I suppose? Or to do the grooming and feeding and watering himself? Or the mucking-out? They'll need *somebody* to do the hard work and wait on them. Why not me?"

It was, indeed, something nobody as yet seemed to have thought of. And why take a lay-brother, if there was a cloister-brother, with a sweet voice in the Mass, willing to do the sweating into the bargain? And the boy deserved his outing, since he was willing to earn it the hard way. Besides, he might be useful before the end. If not to Prior Robert, to Brother Cadfael.

"We'll see," he said, and with that drove his mutinous protégé back to the work in hand. But after dinner, in the somnolent half-hour of sleep for the elders and play for the novices, he sought out Abbot Heribert in his study.

"Father Abbot, it is on my mind that we are undertaking this pilgrimage to Gwytherin without full consideration. First we must send to the bishop of Bangor, in whose see Gwytherin lies, for without his approval the matter cannot proceed. Now it is not essential to have a speaker fluent in Welsh there, since the bishop is obviously conversant with Latin. But not every parish priest in Wales has that tongue, and it is vital to be able to speak freely with the priest at Gwytherin, should the bishop sanction our quest. But most of all, the see of Bangor is wholly within the sovereignty of the king of Gwynedd, and surely his goodwill and permission are essential as those of the church. The princes of Gwynedd speak only Welsh, though they have learned clerks. Father Prior, certainly, has a smattering of Welsh, but..."

"That is very true," said Abbot Heribert, easily dismayed. "It is but a smattering. And the king's agreement is all-important. Brother Cadfael, Welsh is your first, best language, and has no mysteries for you. Could you...? The garden, I am aware...But with your aid there would be no problem."

"In the garden," said Brother Cadfael, "everything is well forward, and can manage without me ten days or more, and take no hurt. I should be glad indeed to be the interpreter, and lend my skills also in Gwytherin."

"Then so be it!" sighed the abbot in heartfelt relief. "Go with Prior Robert, and be our voice to the Welsh people. I shall sanction your errand myself, and you will have my authority."

He was old and human and gentle, full of experience, short on ambition, self-righteousness and resolution. There could have been two ways of approaching him concerning Brother John. Cadfael took the more honest and simple way.

"Father, there is a young brother concerning whose vocation I have doubts, but concerning whose goodness I have none. He is close to me, and I would that he might find his true way, for if he finds it he will not forsake it. But it may not be with us. I beg that I may take him with me, as our hewer of wood and drawer of water in this enterprise, to allow him time to consider."

Abbot Heribert looked faintly dismayed and apprehensive, but not unsympathetic. Perhaps he remembered long-ago days when his own vocation had suffered periods of storm.

"I should be sorry," he said, "to refuse a choice to any man who may be better fitted to serve God elsewhere. Which of us can say he has never looked over his shoulder? You have not," he questioned delicately, approaching the aspect that really daunted him, though with a cautiously dauntless face, "broached this matter to Prior Robert?"

"No, Father," said Brother Cadfael virtuously. "I thought it wrong to charge him with so small a responsibility, when he already carries one so great."

"Very proper!" agreed the abbot heartily. "It would be ill-done to distract his mind from his great purpose at this stage. I should say no word to him of the reason for adding this young man to the party. Prior Robert in his own unshaken certainty is apt to take an austere view of any man who looks back, once having set his hand to the plough."

"Yet, Father, we were not all cut out to be ploughmen. Some could be more useful labouring in other ways."

"True!" said the abbot, and warily smiled, pondering the recurring but often forgotten riddle of Brother Cadfael himself. "I have wondered, I confess... But never mind! Very well, tell me this young brother's name, and you shall have him."

Chapter Two

rior Robert's fine, frosty face momentarily registered displeasure and suspicion when he heard how his delegation was to be augmented. Brother Cadfael's gnarled, guileless-eyed self-sufficiency caused him discomfort without a word amiss or a glance out of place, as though his dignity were somehow under siege. Of Brother John he knew no particular evil, but the redness of his hair, the exuberance of his health and high spirits, the very way he put live blood back into old martyrdoms with his extravagant gusto in the reading, were all offensive in themselves, and jarred on the prior's aesthetic sensibilities. However, since Abbot Heribert had innocently decreed that they should join the party, and since there was no denying that a fluent Welsh speaker might become an urgent necessity at some stage, Prior Robert accepted the fiat without demur, and made the best of it.

They set out as soon as the fine reliquary for the saint's bones was ready, polished oak ornamented with silver, to serve as a proof what honours awaited Winifred in her new shrine. In the third week of May they came to Bangor, and told their story to Bishop David, who was sympathetic, and readily gave his consent to the proposed translation, subject only to the agreement of Prince Owain, who was regent of Gwynedd owing to the illness of the old king, his father. They ran the prince to earth at Aber, and found him equally obliging, for he not only gave the desired approval, but sent his one English-speaking clerk and chaplain to show them the best and quickest way to Gwytherin, and commend them and their errand to the parish priest there. Thus episcopally and royally blessed, Prior Robert led his party on the last stage of their journey, a little too easily convinced that his progress was being divinely smoothed, and would be so to its triumphant end.

They turned aside from the Conway valley at Llanrwst, climbing away from the river into forested hill country. Beyond the watershed they crossed the Elwy where it is young and small, and moved steadily south-eastwards through thick woods, over another ridge of high land, to descend once again into the upland valley of a little river, that provided some marshy water-meadows along its banks, and a narrow band of tilled fields, sloping and sturdy but protected by the forests, above these lush pastures. The wooded ridge on either hand ran in oblique folds, richly green, hiding the scattered house-steads. The fields were already planted, and here and there orchards flowered. Below them, where the woods drew back to leave an amphitheatre of green, there was a small stone church, whitewashed and shimmering, and a little wooden house beside it.

"You see the goal of your pilgrimage," said the chaplain Urien. He was a compact, neat, well-shaven personage, handsomely dressed and mounted, more of an ambassador than a clerk.

"That is Gwytherin?" asked Prior Robert.

"It is the church and priest's house of Gwytherin. The parish stretches for several miles along the river valley, and a mile or more from the Cledwen on either bank. We do not congregate in villages as you English do. Land good for hunting is plentiful, but good for tillage meagre. Every man lives where best suits him for working his fields and conserving his game."

"It is a very fair place," said the sub-prior, and meant it, for the fold on fold of well-treed hills beyond the river made a pattern of spring beauty in a hundred different greens, and the water-meadows were strung like a necklace of emeralds along the fringes of a necklace of silver and lapis-lazuli.

"Good to look at, hard to work," said Urien practically. "See, there's an ox-team on the far side trying to break a new strip, now all the rest are planted. Watch the beasts

strain at it, and you'll know how the higher ground weighs."

Across the river, some way below them and a great way off, the snaky curve of the furrows already won patterned the slope between cultivated fields and leaning trees, a dark brown writing upon the hillside, and on the higher furrow, as yet uncompleted, the oxen leaned into their yokes and heaved, and the ploughman behind them clung and dragged at the heavy share. Before the leading pair a man walked backwards, arms gently waving and beckoning, his goad only a wand, flourished for magic, not for its sting, his high, pure calls carried aloft on the air, cajoling and praising. Towards him the beasts leaned willingly, following his cries with all their might. The new-turned soil, greyish-brown and sluggish, heaved moist and fresh to light after the share.

"A harsh country," said Urien, as one assessing, not complaining, and set his horse moving downhill towards the church. "Come, I'll hand you over to Father Huw, and see you well-received."

They followed him by a green path that wound out of the hills, and soon lost its view of the valley between scattered, flowering trees. A wooden house or two showed among the woods, surrounded by small garden plots, and again vanished.

"Did you see?" said Brother John in Cadfael's ear, pacing beside the sumpter mule. "Did you see how the beasts laboured towards that fellow not to escape the goad, only to go where he willed, only to please him? And such labour! That I should like to learn!"

"It's labour for man as well as beast," said Brother Cadfael.

"But for free goodwill! They wanted to go

with him, to do what he wanted them to do. Brother, could devoted disciples do more? Do you tell me he takes no delight in what he does?"

"No man nor God who sees his faithful delight to serve him," said Brother Cadfael patiently and carefully, "but he knows delight. Hush, now, we're barely here, there'll be time to look round us."

They were down in the little arena of grass and vegetable plots, clear of the trees. The stone church with its tiny turret and tinier bell visible within shone blindingly white, bluish-white against all the lush green. And out of the cabbage-patch, freshly planted, in the lee of the wooden cabin, rose a small, square man in a brown sackcloth gown hoisted to the knees, thick brown legs sturdy under him, and a thicket of curly brown hair and beard half-concealing a brown, broad, wondering face round two large, dark-blue eyes. He came out hastily, scrubbing his hands on his skirts. At close quarters his eyes were larger, bluer and more astonished than ever, and as timid as the mild eyes of a doe.

"Good-day to you, Father Huw," said Urien, reining in before him, "I've brought you distinguished guests from England, upon important church business, and with the blessing of prince and bishop."

When they had ridden into the clearing the priest had certainly been the only man in sight, but by the time Urien had ended his greeting a score of silent, sudden figures had appeared from nowhere, and made a wary and curious half-circle about their pastor. By the distracted look in Father Huw's eyes he was busy reckoning up in some alarm how many of these strangers his modest hut could fittingly house, and where to bestow the rest

of them, and how much food there was in his larder to make a meal for so many, and where he could best commander whatever extra was needed. But no question of not extending a welcome. Guests were sacrosanct, and must not even be questioned on the proposed length of their stay, however ruinous.

"My poor household is at the reverend fathers' disposal," he said, "and whatever powers I have to serve them, also. You come fresh from Aber?"

"From Aber," said Urien, "from Prince Owain, and I must rejoin him there tonight. I am only the herald for these Benedictine brothers, who come on a holy errand, and when I have explained their case to you, then I leave them in your hands." He presented them by name, Prior Robert first. "And have no fear when I have left, for Brother Cadfael here is a man of Gwynedd himself, and speaks Welsh as well as you do."

Huw's look of harassed apprehension was immediately eased, but in case he should be in any doubt, Cadfael favoured him with a rapid brotherly greeting in the promised language, which gratifyingly produced the identical look of slight distrust and insecurity in Prior Robert's normally assured grey eyes.

"You are welcome to this poor house you honour," said Huw, and ran a quick eye over the horses and mules and their loads, and without hesitation called a couple of names over his shoulder. A shaggy-headed elder and a sunburned boy of about ten came forward readily in answer. "Ianto, help the good brother water the beasts, and put them in the little paddock to graze, until we see how best to stable them. Edwin, run and tell Marared we have guests, and help her bring water and wine."

They ran to do his bidding, and several of the others who had gathered, brown, bare-legged men, slender dark women and half-naked children, drew nearer, conferred softly among themselves, and the women slipped away to their own cooking-fires and bake-ovens to bring whatever they could to contribute to Gwytherin's hospitality.

"While it's so fine and mild," said Huw, standing aside to wave them into the little enclosure of his garden, "it may please you best to sit in the orchard. I have benches and table there. Through the summer I live out of doors. Time enough to go within and light fires when the days draw in and the nights grow cold."

His holding was tiny and his living poor enough but he took good care of his fruit-trees and was a diligent gardener, Brother Cadfael noted with approval. And for one who seemed, unlike many of the parish priests of the Celtic persuasion, to be celibate, and happily so, he had the bare little house and grounds in very neat order, and could produce from his own store, or his parishioners' shared stock, clean wooden trenchers and good bread to put on them, and plain but presentable drinking-horns for his raw red wine. He performed all the ceremonies due from a host with humble dignity. The boy Edwin returned with a lively old woman, Huw's neighbour, bringing food and drink. And all the while that the visitors sat there in the sun, various of the people of Gwytherin, scattered though the parish might be, found occasion to walk past the wattle fence of the orchard and examine the party carefully, though without seeming to do so. It was not every day, or every year, indeed, that they had so momentous a visitation. Every soul in the parish would know before evening not only that monks from Shrewsbury were guests at Huw's house, but also how many they were, what they looked like, what fine horses and handsome mules they had, and most probably what they had come for, into the bargain. But the eyeing and the listening were done with perfect courtesy and discretion.

"And now, since Master Urien has to return to Aber," said Huw, when they had eaten and were sitting at ease, "it might be well if he would tell me in what particular I can serve the brothers of Shrewsbury, so that he may be assured we understand each other before he leaves us. And whatever is in my competence I will surely do."

Urien told the story as he had heard it, and Prior Robert elaborated at such length that Brother John, growing bored and restless, let his eyes stray to take stock of the occasional figures that passed along the fence, with alert ears and shy but sharp eyes. His interest and curiosity were somewhat less discreet than theirs. And there were some very handsome girls among them! The one passing now, for instance, her step graceful and slow—she knew she was watched!—and her hair a great, heavy braid over her shoulder, the colour of polished oak, a light, silken brown, even with silvery dashes in it like the grain of oak...

"And the bishop has given his consent to your proposal?" asked Huw, after a long minute of silence, and in a voice that suggested wonder and doubt.

"Both bishop and prince have sanctioned it." Prior Robert was uneasy at the very hint of a hitch at this stage. "The omens have surely not misled us? Saint Winifred is here? She lived out her restored life here, and is buried in this place?"

Huw owned that it was so, with so curious an intonation of caution and reluctance that Cadfael decided he was trying to recall exactly where the lady was to be found, and wondering in what state her grave would be discovered, after all this time since last he had so much as thought of it.

"She is here, in this cemetery?" The little white-washed church gleamed provocatively in the sunshine.

"No, not here." Some relief this time, he did not have to reveal her whereabouts immediately. "This church is new since her time. Her grave is in the old burial-ground of the wooden church on the hill, a mile or more from here. It is long disused. Yes, certainly the omens favour your plans, and beyond question the saint is here in Gwytherin. But..."

"But?" said Prior Robert with displeasure. "Both prince and bishop have given us their blessing, and commended our cause to you. Moreover, we have heard, and they have agreed, that the saint in her stay here among you has been much neglected, and may well wish to be received where greater honour will be paid to her."

"In my church," said Huw humbly, "I have never heard that the saints desired honour for themselves, but rather to honour God rightly. So I do not presume to know what Saint Winifred's will may be in this matter. That you and your house should desire to honour *her* rightly, that is another matter, and very proper. But.... This blessed virgin lived out her miraculously restored life in this place, and no other. Here she died for the second time, and here is buried, and even if my people have neglected her, being human and faulty, yet they always knew that she was here among them, and at a pinch they could rely

on her, and for a Welsh saint I think that counts for much. Prince and bishop—both of whom I reverence as I ought—may not altogether understand how my flock will feel, if their holiest girl is to be dug up out of her grave and taken away into England. It may matter little to the crown and the crozier, a saint is a saint wherever her relics rest. But I tell you plainly, the people of Gwytherin are not going to like it at all!"

Brother Cadfael, stirred to an atavistic fervour of Welshness by this homely eloquence, snatched the initiative from Urien at this point, and translated with the large declamation of the bards.

In full spate, he turned his eyes away from the distracting faces, to light upon one even more distracting. The girl with the light-oak sheen on her hair was again passing the fence, and had been so charmed by what she heard, and the vehemence of its delivery, that for a moment she forgot to keep moving, and stood there at gaze, apple-blossom face radiant and rose-leaf lips laughing. And with the same satisfaction with which she gazed at Cadfael, Brother John gazed at her. Cadfael observed both, and was dazzled. But the next moment she caught herself up in a hasty alarm, and blushed beautifully, and swept away out of sight. Brother John was still gaping long after she had vanished.

"It is hardly important, surely?" said Prior Robert with ominous mildness. "Your bishop and your prince have made their views plain. The parishioners need not be consulted."

That, too, Cadfael interpreted, Urien choosing to remain neutral and mute.

"Impossible!" said Huw firmly, knowing himself on secure ground. "In such a grave matter affecting the whole parish, nothing can be done without calling together the assembly of the free men, and putting the case to them fully and publicly. Doubtless the will of prince and bishop will prevail, but even so, these must be put to the people before they can say yes or no to them. I shall call such an assembly tomorrow. Your case can only be vindicated absolutely by public acceptance."

"He says truly," said Urien, holding the prior's austere and half affronted eyes. "You will do well to get the goodwill of Gwytherin, however many blessings you already have. They respect their bishop, and are very content with their king and his sons. I doubt if you need grudge the delay."

Prior Robert accepted both the warning and the reassurance, and felt the need of a period of quietude in which to review his strategy and prepare his persuasions. When Urien rose to take his leave, his errand punctiliously completed, the prior also rose, half a head taller than the tallest there, and folded his long white hands in submissive resignation.

"We have yet two hours or more to Vespers," he said, eyeing the angle of the sun. "I should like to withdraw into your church and spend some while in meditation, and prayer for right guidance. Brother Cadfael, you had better remain with Father Huw, and help him in any arrangements he needs to make, and you, Brother John, bestow the horses as he directs, and see them cared for. The rest will join me in intercession, that we may conduct this enterprise rightly."

He swept away, elongated and silvery and majestic, and had to stoop his head to enter under the low round arch of the church door. Brother Richard, Brother Jerome, Brother Columbanus vanished within on his heels.

Not all the time they were together there would be spent in prayer. They would be considering what arguments would be most likely to carry the day with Father Huw's free assembly, or what oblique ecclesiastical threats daunt them into submission.

Brother John looked after the lofty silver head until it stooped with accurate dignity just low enough to pass under the stone, and let out something between a sigh and an arrested gurgle of laughter, as though he had been praying for a miscalculation. What with the journey, and the exercise, and the outdoor living, he looked ruddier and healthier and more athletic than ever.

"I've been hoping all this while for a chance to get my leg over that dapple-gray," he said. "Richard rides him like a badly-balanced woolsack. I hope Father Huw's stabling is a mile or more away."

Father Huw's plans for them, it seemed, involved two of the nearer and more prosperous members of his flock, but even so, in the scattered Welsh way, their houses were dispersed in valley and forest.

"I shall give up my own house to the prior and sub-prior, of course," he said, "and sleep in the loft above my cow. For the beasts, my grazing here is too small, and I have no stable, but Bened the smith has a good paddock above the water-meadows, and stabling with a loft, if this young brother will not mind being lodged the better part of a mile from his fellows. And for you and your two companions, Brother Cadfael, there is open house half a mile from here through the woods, with Cadwallon, who has one of the biggest holdings in these parts."

Brother Cadfael considered the prospect of being housed with Jerome and Columbanus, and found it unattractive. "Since I am the only one among us who has fluent Welsh," he said diplomatically, "I should remain close to Prior Robert's side. With your goodwill, Huw, I'll share your loft above the cow-byre, and be very comfortable there."

"If that's your wish," said Huw simply, "I shall be glad of your company. And now I must set this young man on his way to the smithy."

"And I," said Cadfael, "if you don't need me along with you—and yonder boy will make himself understood in whatever language, or none!—will go a piece of the way back with Urien. If I can pick up an acquaintance or so among your flock, so much the better, for I like the look of them and their valley."

Brother John came out from the tiny paddock leading the two tall horses, the mules following on leading reins. Huw's eyes glowed almost as bright as John's, caressing the smooth lines of neck and shoulder.

"How long it is," he said wistfully, "since I was on a good horse!"

"Come on, then, Father," urged Brother John, understanding the look if not the words, "up with you! Here's a hand, if you fancy the roan. Lead the way in style!" And he cupped a palm for the priest's lifted foot, and hoisted him, dazed and enchanted, into the saddle. Up himself on the grey, he fell in alongside, ready if the older man should need a steadying hand, but the brown knees gripped happily. He had not forgotten how. "Bravely!" said John, hugely laughing. "We shall get on famously together, and end up in a race!"

Urien, checking his girth, watched them ride away out of the gentle bowl of the clearing "There go two happy men," he said thoughtfully.

"More and more I wonder," said Cadfael, "how that youngster ever came to commit himself to the monastic life."

"Or you, for instance?" said Urien, with his toe in the stirrup. "Come, if you want to view the ground, we'll take the valley way a piece, before I leave you for the hills."

They parted at the crest of the ridge, among the trees but where a fold of the ground showed them the ox-team still doggedly labouring at a second strip, continuing the line of the first, above the richer valley land. Two such strips in one day was prodigious work.

"Your prior will be wise," said Urien, taking his leave, "to take a lesson from yonder young fellow. Leading and coaxing pays better than driving in these parts. But I need not tell you—a man as Welsh as myself."

Cadfael watched him ride away gently along the cleared track until he vanished among the trees. Then he turned back towards Gwytherin, but went steeply downhill towards the river, and at the edge of the forest stood in green shadow under an oak tree, gazing across the sunlit meadows and the silver thread of river to where the team heaved and strained along the last furrow. Here there was no great distance between them, and he could see clearly the gloss of sweat on the pelts of the oxen, and the heavy curl of the soil as it heeled back from the share. The ploughman was dark, squat and powerful, with a salting of grey in his shaggy locks, but the ox-caller was tall and slender, and the curling hair that tossed on his neck and clung to his moist brow was as fair as flax. He managed his backward walking without a glance behind, feeling his way light-footed and gracefully, as if he had eyes in the back of his heels. His voice was hoarse and tired with long use now, but still clear and merry, more effective than any goad, as he cajoled his weary beasts along the final furrow, calling and luring and praising, telling them they had done marvels, and should get their rest and their meed for it, that in moments now they would be going home, and he was proud of them and loved them, as if he had been talking to Christian souls. And the beasts heaved and leaned, throwing their weight into the yokes and keeping their eyes upon him, and plainly would do anything in their power to please him. When the plough curved to the end and halted, and the steaming oxen stood with lowered heads, the young man came and flung an arm over the neck of the near leader, and scrubbed with brisk knuckles in the curly hair on the other's brow, and Cadfael said aloud: "Bravely! But, my friend, how did *you* stray into Wales?"

Something small, round and hard dropped rustling through the leaves above him, and hit him neatly in the middle of his weather-beaten tonsure. He clapped a hand to his crown, and said something unbecoming his habit. But it was only one of last year's oak-balls, dried out by a winter's weathering to the hardness of a pebble. He looked up into the foliage above his head, already thick and turning rich green from its early gold, and it seemed to him that the tremor of leaves where there was no wind required more explanation than the accidental fall of one small remnant of a dead year. It stilled very quickly, and even its stillness, by contrast, seemed too careful and aware. Cadfael removed himself a few yards, as if about to walk on, and doubled round again behind the next barrier of bushes to see if the bait had been taken.

A small bare foot, slightly strained with moss and bark, reached down out of the branches to a toe-hold on the trunk. Its fellow, stretched at the end of a long, slim leg, swung clear, as the boy prepared to drop. Brother Cadfael, fascinated, suddenly averted his eyes in haste, and turned his back, but he was smiling, and he did not, after all, withdraw, but circled his screen of bushes and reappeared innocently in view of the bird that had just flown down out of its nest. No boy, as he had first supposed, but a girl, and a most personable girl, too, now standing decorously in the grass with her skirts nobly disposed round her, and even the small bare feet concealed.

They stood looking at each other with candid curiosity, neither at all abashed. She might have been eighteen or nineteen years old, possibly younger, for there was a certain erect assurance about her that gave her the dignity of maturity even when newly dropped out of an oak tree. And for all her bare feet and mane of unbraided dark hair, she was no villein girl. Everything about her said clearly that she knew her worth. Her gown was of fine homespun wool, dyed a soft blue, and had embroidery at neck and sleeves. No question but she was a beauty. Her face was oval and firm of feature, the hair that fell in wild waves about her shoulders was almost black, but black with a tint of dark and brilliant red in it where the light caught, and the large, blacklashed eyes that considered Brother Cadfael with such frank interest were of almost the same colour, dark as damsons, bright as the sparkles of mica in the river pebbles.

"You are one of the monks from Shrewsbury,"

she said with certainty. And to his astonishment she said it in fluent and easy English.

"I am," said Cadfael. "But how did you come to know all about us so soon? I think you were not among those who made it their business to walk along Huw's garden fence while we were talking. There was one very young girl, I remember, but not a black lass like you."

She smiled. She had an enchanting smile, sudden and radiant. "Oh, that would be Annest. But everybody in Gwytherin knows by now all about you, and what you've come for. Father Huw is right, you know," she warned seriously, "we shan't like it at all. Why do you want to take Saint Winifred away? When she's been here so long, and nobody ever paid any attention to her before? It doesn't seem neighbourly or honest to me."

It was an excellent choice of words, he thought, and marvelled how a Welsh girl came by it, for she was using English as if she had been born to it, or come to it for love.

"I question the propriety of it myself, to be truthful," he agreed ruefully. "When Father Huw spoke up for his parish, I confess I found myself inclining to his side of the argument."

That made her look at him more sharply and carefully than before, frowning over some sudden doubt or suspicion in her own mind. Whoever had informed her had certainly witnessed all that went on in Father Huw's garden. She hesitated a moment, pondering, and then launched at him unexpectedly in Welsh: "You must be the one who speaks our language, the one who translated what Father Huw said." It seemed to trouble her more than was reasonable. "You do know Welsh! You understand me now."

"Why, I'm as Welsh as you, child," he admitted mildly, "and only a Benedictine in my middle years, and I haven't forgotten my mother-tongue yet, I hope. But I marvel how you've come to speak English as well as I do myself, here in the heart of Rhos."

"Oh, no," she said defensively, "I've only learned a very little. I tried to use it for you, because I thought you *were* English. How was I to know you'd be just *that* one?" Now why should his being bilingual cause her uneasiness? he wondered. And why was she casting so many rapid, furtive glances aside towards the river, brightly glimpsed through the trees? Where, as he saw in a glance just as swift as hers, the tall, fair youngster who was no Welshman, and was certainly the finest ox-caller in Gwynedd, had broken away from his placidly-drinking team, and was wading the river thigh-deep towards this particular tall oak, in a flurry of sparkling spray. The girl had been ensconced in this very tree, whence, no doubt, she had a very good view of the ploughing. And came down as soon as it was finished! "I'm shy of my English," she said, pleading and vulnerable. "Don't tell anyone!"

She was wishing him away from here, and demanding his discretion at the same time. His presence, he gathered, was inconvenient.

"I've known the same trouble myself," he said comfortably, "when first I tried getting my tongue round English. I'll never call your efforts into question. And now I'd better be on my way back to our lodgings, or I shall be late for Vespers."

"God go with you, then, Father," she said, radiant and relieved.

"And with you, my child."

He withdrew by a carefully chosen route that evaded any risk of bumping into the fair young man. And she watched him go for a long moment, before she turned eagerly to meet the ox-caller as he came splashing through the shallows and climbed the bank. Cadfael thought that she was perfectly aware how much he had observed and understood, and was pleased by his reticence. Pleased and reassured. A Welsh girl of status, with embroidery along the hems of her gown, had good need to go softly if she was meeting an outlander, a man landless and rootless here in a clan society, where to be without place in a kinship was to be without the means of living. And yet a very pleasing, comely young man, good at his work and feeling for his beasts. Cadfael looked back, when he was sure the bushes covered him, and saw the two of them draw together, still and glad, not touching, almost shy of each other. He did not look back again.

Now what I really need here, he thought as he walked back towards the church of Gwytherin, is a good, congenial acquaintance, someone who knows every man, woman and child in the parish, without having to carry the burden of their souls. A sound drinking companion with good sense is what I need.

Chapter Three

e found not one of what he wanted, but three at one stroke, after Compline that evening, when he walked back with Brother John in the twilight to the smithy and croft at the edge of the valley fields. Prior Robert and Brother Richard had already withdrawn for the night into Huw's house, Jerome and Columbanus were on their way through the woods to Cadwallon's holding, and who was to question whether Brother Cadfael had also gone to his pallet in the priest's loft, or was footloose among the gossips of Gwytherin? The lodging arrangements were working out admirably. He had never felt less inclined for sleep at this soft evening hour, nor was anyone going to rouse them at midnight here for Matins. Brother John was delighted to introduce him into the smith's household, and Father Huw favoured the acquaintance for his own reasons. It was well that others besides himself should speak for the people of the parish, and Bened the smith was a highly respected man, like all of his craft, and his words would carry weight.

There were three men sitting on the bench outside Bened's door when they arrived, and the mead was going round as fast as the talk. All heads went up alertly at the sound of their steps approaching, and a momentary silence marked the solidarity of the local inhabitants. But Brother John seemed already to have made himself welcome, and Cadfael cast them a greeting in Welsh, like a fisherman casting a line, and was accepted with something warmer than the strict courtesy the English would have found. Annest with the light-brown, sunflecked hair had spread word of his Welshness far and wide. Another bench was pulled up, and the drinking-horns continued their circling in a wider ring. Over the river the light was fading gradually, the dimness green with the colours of meadow and forest, and threaded through with the string of silver water.

Bened was a thickset, muscular man of middle years, bearded and brown. Of his two companions the younger was recognisable as the ploughman who had followed the ox-team that day, and no wonder he was dry after such labour. And the third was a grey-headed elder with a long, smoothly-trimmed beard and fine, sinewy hands, in an ample homespun gown that had seen better days, perhaps on another wearer. He bore himself as one entitled to respect, and got it.

"Padrig, here, is a good poet and a fine harpist," said Bened, "and Gwytherin is lucky to have him staying a while among us, in Rhisiart's hall. That's away beyond Cadwallon's place, in a forest clearing, but Rhisiart has land over this way, too, both sides the river. He's the biggest landowner in these parts. There are not many here entitled to keep a harp, or maybe we'd be honoured with more visits from travelling bards like Padrig. I have a little harp myself—I have that privilege—but Rhisiart's is a fine one, and kept in use, too. I've heard his girl play on it sometimes."

"Women cannot be bards," said Padrig with tolerant scorn. "But she knows how to keep it tuned, and well looked after, that I will say. And her father's a patron of the arts, and a generous, open-handed one. No bard goes away disappointed from his hall, and none ever leaves without being pressed to stay. A good household!"

"And this is Cai, Rhisiart's ploughman. No doubt you saw the team cutting new land, when you came over the ridge today."

"I did and admired the work," said Cadfael heartily. "I never saw better. A good team you had there, and a good caller, too."

"The best," said Cai without hesitation. "I've worked with a good many in my time, but never known one with the way Engelard has with the beasts. They'd die for him. And as good a hand with all cattle, calving or sick or what you will. Rhisiart would be a sorry man if ever he lost him. Ay, we did a good day's work today."

"You'll have heard from Father Huw," said Cadfael, "that all the free men are called to the church tomorrow after Mass, to hear what our prior is proposing. No doubt we shall see Rhisiart there."

"See and hear him," said Cai, and grinned. "He speaks his mind. An open-hearted, open-natured man, with a temper soon up and soon down, and never a grudge in him, but try and move him when his mind's made up, and you're leaning on Snowdon."

"Well, a man can but hold fast to what he believes right, and even the opponent he baulks should value him for that. And have his sons no interest in the harp, that they leave it to their sister?"

"He has no sons," said Bened. "His wife is dead, and he never would take another, and there's only this one girl to follow him."

"And no male heir anywhere in his kinship? It's rare for a daughter to inherit."

"Not a man on his side the family at all," said Cai, "and a pity it is. The only near kin is her mother's brother, and he has no claim, and is old into the bargain. The greatest match anywhere in this valley, is Sioned, and young men after her like bees. But God willing, she'll be a contented wife with a son on her knee long before Rhisiart goes to his fathers."

"A grandson by a good man, and what could any lord want more." said Padrig, and emptied the jug of mead and passed the horn along. "Understand me, I'm not a Gwytherin man myself, and have no right to give a voice one way or the other. But if I may say a word my friends won't say for themselves—you having your duty to your prior as Cai has to his lord, or I to my art and my patrons—don't look for an easy passage, and don't take offence if your way is blocked. Nothing personal to you! But where the free men of

Wales see no fair dealing, they won't call it by fair names, and they won't stand aside."

"I should be sorry if they did," said Cadfael. "For my part, the ending I want is the fair ending, leaving no man with a just grievance. And what of the other lords we can expect to see there? Of Cadwallon we've heard, two of our brothers are enjoying his hospitality. And his lands are neighbour to Rhisiart's?"

"It's a fair piece beyond to Rhisiart's hall, on through the forest. But they're neighbours, boundary to boundary, yes, and friends from youth. A peaceable man, Cadwallon, he likes his comfort and his hunting. His way would be to say yes to whatever bishop and prince commend, but then, his way normally is also to say yes to Rhisiart. For that matter," owned Bened, tilting the last drop from the horn, "I know no more than you what either of them will have to say in this matter. For all I know they'll accept your omens and bless your errand. If the free voice goes with your prior, then Saint Winifred goes home with you, and that's the end of it."

It was the end of the mead, too, for that night.

"Bide the night here," said Bened to Padrig, when the guests rose to walk home, "and we'll have a little music before you leave tomorrow. My small harp needs to be played, I've kept it in fettle for you."

"Why, so I will, since you're so kind," said Padrig, and weaved his way gently into the house with his host. And Cai and Brother Cadfael, taking their leave, set off companionably shoulder to shoulder, to make their way back to Father Huw's house, and thence in courtesy a measure of the way through the woods towards Rhisiart's hall before they parted.

"I would not say more nor plainer," said Cai confidingly, "while Bened was present, nor in front of Padrig, for that matter, though he's a good fellow—so are they both!—but a traveller, not a native. This Sioned, Rhisiart's girl.... The truth is, Bened would like to be a suitor for her himself, and a good, solid man he is, and a girl might well do worse. But a widower, poor soul, and years older than the lass, and a poor chance he has. But you haven't seen the girl!"

Brother Cadfael was beginning to suspect that he had indeed seen the girl, and seen more than any here had ever been allowed to see. But he said nothing.

"A girl like a squirrel! As swift, as sudden, as black and as red! If she had nothing, they'd still be coming from miles around, and she will have lands any man might covet even if she squinted! And there's poor Bened, keeping his own counsel and feeding on his own silence, and still hoping. After all, a smith is respected in any company. And give him his due, it isn't her heritage he covets. It's the girl herself. If you'd seen her, you'd know. In any case," said Cai, sighing gustily for his friend, "her father has a favourite for son-in-law already, and has all along. Cadwallon's lad has been in and out of Rhisiart's hall, and made free with Rhisiart's servants and hawks and horses, ever since he could run, and grown up with the girl. And he's sole heir to the neighbouring holding, and what could suit either father better? They've had it made up between them for years. And the children seem ideally matched, they know each other through and through, like brother and sister."

"I doubt if I'd say that made for an ideal match," said Brother Cadfael honestly.

"So Sioned seems to think, too," said Cai

drily. "So far she's resisted all pressures to accept this lad Peredur. And mind you, he's a very gay, lively well-looking young fellow, spoiled as you please, being the only one, but show me a girl round here who wouldn't run if he lifted his finger—all but this girl! Oh, she likes him well enough, but that's all. She won't hear of marriage yet, she's still playing the heartfree child."

"And Rhisiart bears with her?" asked Cadfael delicately.

"You don't know him, either. He dotes on her, and well he may, and she reveres him, and well *she* may, and where does that get any of us? He won't force her choice. He never misses a chance to urge how suitable Peredur is, and she never denies it. He hopes, if he bides his time, she'll come round."

"And will she?" asked Brother Cadfael, responding to something in the ploughman's voice. His own was milder than milk.

"No accounting," said Cai slowly, "for what goes on in a girl's head. She may have other plans of her own. A bold, brave one she is, clever and patient at getting her own way. But what that may be, do I know? Do you? Does any man?"

"There may be one man who does," said Brother Cadfael with guileful disinterest.

If Cai had not risen to that bait, Cadfael would have let well alone then, for it was no business of his to give away the girl's secrets, when he had stumbled upon them himself only by chance. But he was no way surprised when the ploughman drew meaningfully close against his arm, and jabbed a significant elbow into his ribs. A man who had worked closely with the young ox-caller as he had must surely have noted a few obvious things by now. This afternoon's purposeful bee-line across the meadows and through the water to a certain well-grown oak would be enough in itself for a sharp man. And as for keeping his mouth shut about it, it was pretty plain that his sympathies were with his work-mate.

"Brother Cadfael, you wouldn't be a talking man, not out of turn, and you're not tied to one side or the other in any of our little disputes here. No reason *you* shouldn't know. Between you and me, she *has* got a man in her eye, and one that wants her worse than Bened does, and has even less chance of ever getting her. You remember we were talking of my fellow on the team, Engelard? A good man with cattle, worth plenty to his lord, and Rhisiart knows it and values him fairly on it. But the lad's an *alltud*—an outlander!"

"Saxon?" asked Cadfael.

"The fair hair. Yes, you saw him today. The length and slenderness of him too. Yes, he's a Cheshire man from the borders of Maelor, on the run from the bailiffs of Earl Ranulf of Chester. Oh, not for murder or banditry or any such! But the lad was simply the most outrageous deer-poacher in the earldom. He's a master with the short bow, and always stalked them afoot and alone. And the bailiff was after his blood. Nothing for him to do, when he was cornered on the borders, but run for it into Gwynedd. And he daren't go back, not yet, and you know what it means for a foreigner to want to make a living in Wales."

Cadfael knew indeed. In a country where every native-born man had and knew his assured place in a clan kinship, and the basis of all relationships was establishment on the land, whether as free lord or villein partner in a village community, the man from outside, owning no land here, fitting into no place, was deprived of the very basis of living. His only means of establishing himself was by getting some overlord to make compact with him, give him house-room and a stake in the land, and employ him for whatever skills he could offer. For three generations this bargain between them was revocable at any time, and the outlander might leave at the fair price of dividing his chattels equally with the lord who had given him the means of acquiring them.

"I do know. So Rhisiart took this young man into his service and set him up in a croft?"

"He did. Two years ago now, a little more. And neither of them has had any call to regret it. Rhisiart's a fair-minded master, and gives credit where it's due. But however much he respects and values him, can you see a Welsh lord ever letting his only daughter go to an *alltud*?"

"Never!" agreed Cadfael positively. "No chance of it! It would be against all his laws and customs and conscience. His own kinship would never forgive it."

"True as I'm breathing!" sighed Cai ruefully. "But you try telling that to a proud, stubborn young fellow like Engelard, who has his own laws and rights from another place, where his father's lord of a good manor, and carries every bit as much weight in his feudal fashion as Rhisiart does here."

"Do you tell me he's actually spoken for her to her father?" demanded Cadfael, astonished and admiring.

"He has, and got the answer you might expect. No malice at all, but no hope either. Yes, and stood his ground and argued his case just the same. And comes back to the subject every chance that offers, to remind Rhisiart

he hasn't given up, and never will. I tell you what, those two are two of a kind, both hot-tempered, both obstinate, but both as open and honest as you'll find anywhere, and they've a great respect for each other that somehow keeps them from bearing malice or letting this thing break them apart. But every time this comes up, the sparks fly. Rhisiart clouted Engelard once, when he pushed too hard, and the lad came within an ace of clouting back. What would the answer to that have been? I never knew it happen with an *alltud*, but if a slave strikes a free man he stands to lose the hand that did it. But he stopped himself in time, though I don't think it was fear that stopped him—he knew he was in the wrong. And what did Rhisiart do, not half an hour later, but fling back and ask his pardon! Said he was an insolent, unreasonable, unWelsh rascal, but he should not have struck him. There's a battle going on all the time between those two, and neither of them can get any peace, but let any man say a word against Rhisiart in Engelard's hearing, and he'll get it back down his throat with a fist behind it. And if one of the servants ever called down Engelard, thinking to curry favour with Rhisiart, he'd soon get told that the *alltud's* an honest man and a good worker, worth ten of the likes of his backbiters. So it goes! And I can see no good end to it."

"And the girl?" said Cadfael. "What does she say to all this?"

"Very little, and very softly. Maybe at first she did argue and plead, but if so it was privately with her father alone. Now she's biding her time, and keeping them from each other's throat as best she can."

And meeting her lover at the oak tree, thought Cadfael, or any one of a dozen other private places, wherever his work takes him. So that's how she learned her English, all through those two years while the Saxon boy was busy learning Welsh from her, and that's why, though she was willing to pass the time of day in his own language with a visiting monk, she was concerned about having betrayed her accomplishment to a Welsh-speaking stranger, who might innocently blurt it abroad locally. She'd hardly want to let slip how often she's been meeting Engelard in secret, if she's biding her time, and keeping father and lover from each other's throat till she can get her own way with them. And who's to say which of the three will give way first, where all look immovable?

"It seems you've your own troubles here in Gwytherin, let alone what we've brought with us." he said, when he parted from Cai.

"God resolves all given time," said Cai philosophically and trudged away into darkness. And Cadfael returned along the path with the uncomfortable feeling that God, nevertheless, required a little help from men, and what he mostly got was hindrance.

All the free men of Gwytherin came to the meeting next day, and their womenfolk and all the villein community came to the Mass beforehand. Father Huw named the chief among them softly to Brother Cadfael as they made their appearance. He had seldom had such a congregation.

"Here is Rhisiart, with his daughter and his steward, and the girl's waiting-woman."

Rhisiart was a big, bluff, hearty-looking man of about fifty, high-coloured and darkhaired, with a short, grizzled beard, and bold features that could be merry or choleric, fierce or jovial, but were far too expressive ever to

be secretive or mean. His stride was long and impetuous, and his smile quick in response when he was greeted. His dress hardly distinguished him from any of the other free landholders who came thronging into the church, being plain as any, but of good homespun cloth. To judge from his bright face, he came without prejudice, willing to listen, and for all his thwarted family plans, he looked an expansively happy man, proud and fond of his daughter.

As for the girl, she followed at his heels modestly, with poised head and serene eyes. She had shoes on for this occasion, and her hair was brushed and braided into a burnished dark coil on her neck, and covered with a linen coif, but there was no mistaking her. This was the urchin of the oak tree, and the greatest heiress and most desirable prize in marriage in all this countryside.

The steward was an older man, grey-headed and balding, with a soft, good-humoured face. "He is Rhisiart's kinsman by marriage," whispered Huw, "his wife's elder brother."

"And the other girl is Sioned's tirewoman?" No need to name her, he already knew her name. Dimpled and smiling, Annest followed her friend with demure little steps into the church, and the sun stroked all the bright, silvery grain in the sheaf of her pale hair. "She is the smith's niece," said Father Huw helpfully. "A good girl, she visits him often since he buried his wife, and bakes for him."

"Bened's niece?" Brother John pricked his ears, and looked after the shapely waist and glowing hair with fascinated eyes, no doubt hoping there would be a baking day before they had to leave Gwytherin. The lodging arrangements had certainly been inspired, though whether by an angel or an imp remained to be seen.

"Lower your eyes, brother," said Jerome chidingly. "It is not seemly to look so straightly upon women."

"And how did he know there were women passing," whispered Brother John rebelliously, "if his own eyes were so dutifully lowered?"

Brother Columbanus, at least, was standing as prescribed in the presence of females, with pale hands prayerfully folded, and lofty eyelids lowered, his gaze upon the grass.

"And here comes Cadwallon now," said Father Huw. "These good brothers already know him, of course. And his lady. And his son Peredur."

So this young man, loping after his parents with the long, springy gait of a yearling roebuck, was the chosen husband for Sioned, the lad she liked well enough, and had known familiarly all her life, but was in no way inclined to marry. It occurred to Cadfael that he had never asked how the groom felt about the situation, but it needed only a glimpse of Peredur's face when he caught sight of Sioned to settle the matter. Here was a tangle. The girl might have worn out in mere liking all her inclination to love, but the boy certainly had not. At sight of her his face paled, and his eyes took fire.

The parents were ordinary enough, comfortable people grown plump from placid living, and expecting things to go smoothly still as they always had. Cadwallon had a round, fleshy, smiling face, and his wife was fat, fair and querulous. The boy cast back to some more perilous ancestor. The spring of his step was a joy to watch. He was not above middle height, but so well-proportioned that he looked tall. His dark hair was cut short, and curled crisply all over his head. His chin was shaven clean, and all the bones of his face were as bold and elegant as his colouring was vivid, with russet brushings of sun on high cheekbones, and a red, audacious, self-willed mouth. Such a young person might well find it hard to bear that another, and an alien at that, should be preferred to him. He proclaimed in his every movement and glance that everything and everyone in his life had responded subserviently to his charm, until now.

At the right moment, when the church was full, Prior Robert, tall and imposing and carefully groomed, swept in through the tiny sacristy and took his place, and all the Shrewsbury brothers fell into line and followed on his heels. The Mass began.

In the deliberations of the free assembly of the parish, of course, the women had no part. Neither had the villeins, though they had their indirect influence through those of their friends who were free. So while the free men lingered after the Mass, the rest dispersed, moving away with slow dignity, and not too far, just far enough to be discreetly out of sight and earshot, but handy to detect what was passing by instinct, and confirm it as soon as the meeting broke up.

The free men gathered in the open before the church. The sun was already high, for it was little more than an hour to noon. Father Huw stood up before the assembly, and gave them the gist of the matter, as it had been presented to him. He was the father of this flock, and he owed his people truth, but he also owed his church fealty. He told them what bishop and prince had answered to the request from Shrewsbury, reverently presented, and with many proofs. Which proofs he left to Robert to deliver.

The prior had never looked holier or more surely headed for sainthood himself. He had always a sense of occasion, and beyond a doubt it had been his idea to hold the meeting here in the open, where the sun could gild and illuminate his other-worldly beauty. It was Cadfael's detached opinion that he did himself more than justice, by being less overbearing than might have been expected. Usually he overdid things, this time he got it right, or as right as something only equivocally right in itself can be got.

"They're not happy!" whispered Brother John in Cadfael's ear, himself sounding far from sad about it. There were times when even Brother John could be humanly smug. And indeed, those Welsh faces ranged round them were singularly lacking in enthusiasm for all these English miracles performed by a Welsh saint. Robert at his best was not exactly carrying his audience.

They swayed and murmured, and eyed one another, and again turned as one man to eye him.

"If Owain ap Griffith wills it, and the bishop gives his blessing, too," began Cadwallon hesitantly, "as loyal sons of the church, and true men of Gwynedd, we can hardly..."

"Both prince and bishop have blessed our errand," said the prior loftily.

"But the girl is here, in Gwytherin," said Rhisiart abruptly. He had the voice that might have been expected from him, large, melodious and deep, a voice that sang what it felt, and waited for thought afterwards, to find that the thought had been there already in the feeling. "Ours, not Bishop David's! Not Owain ap Griffith's! She lived out her life here, and never said a word about wanting to leave us. Am I to believe easily that she wants to leave us now, after so long? Why has she never told us? Why?"

"She has made it clear to us," said the prior, "by many manifestations, as I have told you."

"But never a word to *us*," cried Rhisiart, roused. "Do you call that courtesy? Are we to believe that, of a virgin who chose to make her home here among us?"

They were with him, his assurance had fired their smouldering reluctance. They cried out from a dozen directions at once that Saint Winifred belonged to Gwytherin, and to no other place.

"Do you dare tell me," said Prior Robert, high and clear, "that you have visited her? That you have committed your prayers to her? That you have invoked the aid of this blessed virgin, and given her the honour that is her due? Do you know of any reason why she should desire to remain here among you? Have you not neglected even her grave?"

"And if we have," said Rhisiart with blithe conviction, "do you suppose the girl wonders at it? You have not lived here among us. She did. You are English, she was Welsh, she knew us, and was never so moved against us that she withdrew or complained. We know she is there, no need to exclaim or make any great outcry. If we have needs, she knows it, and never asks that we should come with prayers and tears, knocking our knees on the ground before her. If she grudged a few brambles and weeds, she would have found a means to tell us. Us, not some distant Benedictine house in England!"

Throats were opening joyfully, shouting where they had muttered. The man was a poet and a preacher, match for any Englishman. Brother Cadfael let loose his bardic blood, and rejoiced silently. Not even because it was Prior Robert recoiling into marble rage under Welsh siege. Only because it was a Welsh voice that cried battle.

"And do you deny," thundered Robert, stretching his ascetic length to its loftiest, "the truth of those omens and miracles I have declared to you, the beckoning that led us here?"

"No!" said Rhisiart roundly. "I never doubted you believed and had experienced these portents. But portents can arise, miracles can be delivered, either from angels or devils. If these are from heaven, why have we not been instructed? The little saint is here, not in England. She owes us the courtesy of kinsmen. Dare you say she is turned traitor? Is there not a church in Wales, a Celtic church such as she served? What did she know of yours? I do not believe she would speak to you and not to us. You have been deceived by devils! Winifred never said word!"

A dozen voices took up the challenge, hallooing applause for their most articulate spokesman, who had put his finger on the very pulse of their resentment. Even the very system of bishoprics galled the devout adherents of the old, saintly Celtic church, that had no worldly trappings, courted no thrones, but rather withdrew from the world into the blessed solitude of thought and prayer. The murmur became a subdued rumbling, a thunder, a roar. Prior Robert, none too wisely, raised his commanding voice to shout them down.

"She said no word to you, for you had left her forgotten and unhonoured. She has turned to us for recognition, when she could get none from you."

"That is not true," said Rhisiart, "though you in your ignorance may believe it. The saint is a good Welshwoman, and knows her countrymen. We are not quick in respect to rank or riches, we do not doff and bow and scrape when any man flaunts himself before us. We are blunt and familiar even in praise. What we value we value in the heart, and this Welsh girl knows it. She would never leave her own unfurnished, even if we have neglected to trim her grave. It is the spirit that leans to us, and is felt by us as guardian and kin. But these bones you come hunting are also hers. Not ours, not yours! Until she tells us she wills to have them moved, here they stay. We should be damned else!"

It was the bitterest blow of Prior Robert's life to know that he had met his match and overmatch in eloquence and argument, here in a half-barbaric Welsh landholder, no great lord, but a mere squireling elevated among his inferiors to a status he barely rated, at least in Norman eyes. It was the difference between them that Robert thought in hierarchies, and Rhisiart thought in blood-ties, high and low of one mind and in one kinship, and not a man among them aware of inferiority, only of his due place in a united family.

The thunder was one voice now, demanding and assured, but it was one man who had called it into being. Prior Robert, well aware that a single adversary confronted him, subdued his angry tones, and opted for the wisdom of the dove, and the subtlety of single combat. He raised his long, elegant arms, from which the wide sleeves of his habit fell free, and smiled on the assembly, turning the smile at its most compelling and fatherly upon Rhisiart.

"Come Brother Cadfael, say this for me to

the lord Rhisiart, that it is all too easy for us, who have the same devotion at heart, to disagree about the means. It is better to speak quietly, man to man, and avoid the deformation of anger. Lord Rhisiart, I beg you to come apart with me, and let us debate this matter in quietude, and then you shall have liberty to speak out what you will. And having had my say fairly with you, I will say no word further to challenge what you have to impart to your people."

"That is fair and generous," said Rhisiart promptly to this offer, and stood forward with ingenuous pleasure from the crowd, which parted to let him through.

"We will not take even the shadow of dissension into the church," said Prior Robert. "Will you come with us into Father Huw's house?" All those bright, sullen, roused eyes followed them in through the low doorway, and clung there to wait for them to come forth again. Not a man of the Welsh moved from his place. They trusted the voice that had spoken for them hitherto to speak for them still.

In the small, wood-scented room, dark after the brightness of the day outside, Prior Robert faced his opponent with a calm and reasonable face.

"You have spoken well," he said, "and I commend your faith, and the high value you set on the saint, for so do we value her highly. And at her own wish, for so we believe, we have come here, solely to serve her. Both church and state are with us, and you know better than I the duty a nobleman of Wales owes to both. But I would not willingly leave Gwytherin with a sense of grievance, for I do know that by Saint Winifred's departure

Gwytherin's loss is great. That we own, and I would wish to make due reparation."

"Reparation to Gwytherin?" repeated Rhisiart, when this was translated to him. "I do not understand how . . ."

"And to you," said Robert softly and matter-of-factly, "if you will withdraw your opposition, for then I feel sure all your fellows will do the same, and sensibly accept what bishop and prince decree."

It occurred to Cadfael as he interpreted this, even before the prior began the slow, significant motion of one long hand into the breast of his habit, that Robert was about to make the most disastrous miscalculation of his life. But Rhisiart's face remained dubious and aloof, quite without understanding, as the prior drew from his bosom a soft leather bag drawn up with a cord at the neck, and laid it on the table, pushing it gently across until it rested against Rhisiart's right hand. Its progress over the rough boards gave out a small chinking sound. Rhisiart eyed it suspiciously, and lifted uncomprehending eyes to stare at the prior. "I don't understand you. What is this?"

"It is yours," said Robert, "if you will persuade the parish to agree to give up the saint."

Too late he felt the unbelieving coldness in the air, and sensed the terrible error he had made. Hastily he did his best to recover some of the ground lost. "To be used as you think best for Gwytherin—a great sum . . ." It was useless. Cadfael let it lie in silence.

"Money!" said Rhisiart in the most extraordinary of tones, at once curious, derisory and revolted. He knew about money, of course, and even understood its use, but as an aberration in human relations. In the rural parts of

Wales, which indeed were almost all of Wales, it was hardly used at all, and hardly needed. Provision was made in the code for all necessary exchange of goods and services, nobody was so poor as to be without the means of living, and beggars were unknown. The kinship took care of its helpless members, and every house was open as of right. The minted coins that had seeped in through the marches were a pointless eccentricity. Only after a moment of scornful wonder did it occur to Rhisiart that in this case they were also a mortal insult. He snatched away his hand from the affronting touch, and the blood surged into his face darkly red, suffusing even the whites of his eyes.

"Money? You dare offer to *buy* our saint? To buy *me*? I was in two minds about you, and about what I ought to do, but now, by God, I know what to think! You had your omens. Now I have mine."

"You mistake me!" cried the prior, stumbling after his blunder and seeing it outdistance him at every breath. "One cannot buy what is holy, I am only offering a gift to Gwytherin, in gratitude and compensation for their sacrifice—"

"Mine, you said it was," Rhisiart reminded him, glowing copper bright with dignified rage. "Mine, if I *persuaded*...! Not a gift! A bribe! This foolish stuff you hoard about you more dearly far than your reputations, don't think you can use it to buy my conscience. I know now that I was right to doubt you. You have said your say, now I will say mine to those people without, as you promised me I should, without hindrance."

"No, wait!" The prior was in such agitation that he actually reached out a hand and caught his opponent by the sleeve. "Do nothing in haste! You have mistaken my meaning indeed, and if I was wrong even to offer an alms to Gwytherin, I am sorry for it. But do not call it—"

Rhisiart withdrew himself angrily from the detaining clasp, and cut off the protest curtly, wheeling on Cadfael. "Tell him he need not be afraid. I should be ashamed to tell my people that a prior of Shrewsbury tried to corrupt me with a bribe. I don't deal in that kind of warfare. But where I stand—that they shall know, and you, too." And he strode out from them, and Father Huw put out a warning hand to prevent any of them from attempting to impede or follow him.

"Not now! He is hot now. Tomorrow something may be done to approach him, but not now. You must let him say what he will."

"Then at least let's put in an appearance," said the prior, magnificently picking up what pieces he could of the ruin he had created; and he swept out into the sunlight and took his stand close to the door of the church, with all his fellow-monks dutifully following on his heels, and stood with erect head and calmly folded hands, in full view, while Rhisiart thundered his declaration to the assembled people of Gwytherin.

"I have listened to what these men from Shrewsbury have had to say to me, and I have made my judgment accordingly, and now I deliver it to you. I say that so far from changing my views, I am confirmed a thousand times that I was right to oppose the sacrilege they desire. I say that Saint Winifred's place is here among us, where she has always belonged, and that it would be mortal sin to let her be taken away to a strange place, where not even the prayers would be in a tongue she knows, where foreigners not worthy to draw near her would be her only company. I pledge my opposition to the death, against any attempt to move her bones, and I urge upon you the same duty. And now this conference is ended."

So he said, and so it was. There could be no possible way of prolonging it. The prior was forced to stand with marble face and quiet hands while Rhisiart strode away towards the forest path, and all the assembly, in awed and purposeful silence, melted away mysteriously in all directions after his departure, so that within minutes all that green, trodden arena was empty.

Chapter Four

**Y**ou should have told me what you intended," said Father Huw, timidly reproachful. "I could have told you it was folly, the worst possible. What attraction do you think money has for a man like Rhisiart? Even if he was for sale, and he is not, you would have had to find other means to purchase him. I thought you had taken his measure, and were proposing to plead to him the sorry plight of English pilgrims, who have no powerful saints of their own, and are sadly in need of such a protectress. He would have listened to something that entreated of his generosity."

"I am come with the blessing of church and sovereign," said the prior fiercely, though the repetition was beginning to pall even on him. "I cannot be repudiated at the will of a local squire. Has my order no rights here in Wales?"

"Very few," said Cadfael bluntly. "My people have a natural reverence, but it leans towards the hermitage, not the cloister."

The heated conference went on until Vespers, and poisoned even Vespers with its bitterness, for there Prior Robert preached a fearful sermon detailing all the omens that Winifred desired above all things to remove to the sanctity of Shrewsbury, and issuing her prophetic denunciation against all who stood in the way of her translation. Terrible would be her wrath visited on those who dared resist her will. Thus Prior Robert approached the necessary reconciliation with Rhisiart. And though Cadfael in translating toned down the threat as much as he dared, there were some among the congregation who understood enough English to get the full drift of it. He knew by their closed, mute faces. Now they would go away to spread the word to those who had not been present, until everyone in Gwytherin knew that the prior had bidden them remember what befell Prince Cradoc, whose very flesh watered away into the ground like rain, so that he vanished utterly, as to the body expunged out of the world, as to the soul, the fearful imagination dared not guess. So also it might happen to those who dared offend against Winifred now.

Father Huw, harried and anxious, cast about him as honestly as he could for a way of pleasing everybody. It took him most of the evening to get the prior to listen, but from sheer exhaustion a calm had to set in at last.

"Rhisiart is not an impious man—"

"Not impious!" fluted Brother Jerome, appealing to heaven with uplifted eyes. "Men have been excommunicated for less!"

"Then men have been excommunicated for no evil at all," said Huw sturdily, "and truly I think they sometimes have. No, I say he is a decent, devout man, open-handed and fair, and had a right to resent it when he was misunderstood and affronted. If he is ever to withdraw his opposition, it must be you, Father Prior, who make the first approach to him, and upon a different footing. Not in person first, I would not ask or advise it. But if I were to go to him, perhaps with Brother Cadfael here, who is known to be a good Welshman himself, and ask him to forget all that has been said and done, and come with an open mind to begin the discussion over again, I think he would not refuse. Moreover, the very act of seeking him out would disarm him, for he has a generous heart. I don't say he would necessarily change his mind—it would depend on how he is handled this time—but I do say he would listen."

"Far be it from me," said Prior Robert loftily, "to pass over any means of saving a soul from perdition. I wish the man no ill, if he tempers his offences. It is not a humiliation to stoop to deliver a sinner."

"O wondrous clemency!" intoned Brother Jerome. "Saintly generosity towards the ill-doer!"

Brother John flashed a narrow, glittering glance, and shifted one foot uneasily, as if restraining an impulse to kick. Father Huw, desperate to preserve his stock of goodwill with prince, bishop, prior and people alike, cast him a warning look, and resumed hurriedly: "I will go to Rhisiart tonight, and ask him to dine here at my house tomorrow. Then if we can come to terms between us, another assembly can be called, so that all may know there is peace."

"Very well!" said the prior, after consideration. In that way he need never actually admit any guilt on his part, or apologise for any act of his, nor need he enquire too closely what Huw might have to say on his behalf. "Very well, do so, and I hope you may succeed."

"It would be a mark of your status, and the importance of this gesture," suggested Cadfael with an earnest face, "if your messengers went mounted. It's not yet dark, and the horses would be better for exercise."

"True," said the prior, mildly gratified. "It would be in keeping with our dignity and lend weight to our errand. Very well, let Brother John bring the horses."

"Now that's that I call a friend!" said Brother John heartily, when they were all three in the saddle, and safely away into the early dusk under the trees, Father Huw and John on the two tall horses, Brother Cadfael on the best of the mules. "Ten more minutes, and I should have earned myself a penance that would have lasted a month or more, and now here we are in the best company around, on a decent errand, and enjoying the quiet of the evening."

"Did I ever say word of your coming with us?" said Cadfael slyly. "I said the horses would add lustre to the embassage, I never went so far as to say *you* would add any."

"I go with the horses. Did you ever hear of

an ambassador riding without a groom? I'll keep well out of the way while you confer, and play the dutiful servant. And by the by, Bened will be doing his drinking up there at the hall tonight. They go the rounds, and it's Cai's turn."

"And how did you learn so much," wondered Cadfael, "without a word of Welsh?"

"Oh, they knock their meaning into me somehow, and I into them. Besides, I have several words of Welsh already, and if we're held up here for a while I shall soon learn a great many more, if I can get my tongue round them. I could learn the smith's art, too. I lent him a hand at the forge this morning."

"You're honoured. In Wales not everyone can be a smith."

Huw indicated the fence that had begun to run alongside them on the right. "Cadwallon's holding. We have a mile of forest to go yet to Rhisiart's hall."

It was still no more than dusk when they emerged into a large clearing, with ploughed and planted strips surrounding a long stockade fence. The smell of wood-smoke drifted on the air, and glimmer of torches lit the open doorway of the hall. Stables and barns and folds clung to the inner side of the fence, and men and women moved briskly about the evening business of a considerable household.

"Well, well!" said the voice of Cai the ploughman, from a bench under the eaves of one of the byres. "So you've found your way by nose to where the mead is tonight, Brother Cadfael." And he moved up obligingly to make room, shoulder to shoulder with Bened. "Padrig's making music within, and from all I hear it may well be war music, but he'll be with us presently. Sit yourself down, and welcome. Nobody looks on you as the enemy."

There was a third with them already, a long man seated in deeper shadow, his legs stretched well out before him at ease, and his hair showing as a primrose pallor even in the dimness. The young outlander, Engelard, willingly gathered up his long limbs and also moved to share the bench. He had a quick, open smile vivid with white teeth.

"We've come expressly to halt the war," said Brother Cadfael as they dismounted, and a groom of the household came running to take their bridles. "Father Huw has the peace in hand, I'm only an assessor to see fair play. And, sadly, we'll be expected back with an answer as soon as we've spoken with your lord. But if you'll take charge of Brother John while we deal, he'll be grateful. He can speak English with Engelard, a man should practise his own tongue when he can."

But Brother John, it appeared, had at that moment completely lost the use of his tongue in any language, for he stood at gaze, and let the reins be taken from his hands like a man in a dream. Nor was he looking at Engelard, but towards the open doorway of the hall, from which a girl's figure had issued, and was crossing gaily towards the drinkers under the eaves, a large jug carried in both hands. The lively brown eyes flickered over the visitors, took in Cadfael and the priest with easy friendliness, and opened wide upon Brother John, standing like a very lifelike statue, all thorny russet hair, weather-burned cheeks and wild, admiring eyes. Cadfael looked where Annest's eyes were looking, and approved a very upstanding, ruggedly-built, ingenuous, comely young fellow, maybe two or three years older than the girl. The Benedictine habit, kilted to the knee for riding and forgotten now, looked as much like a working Welsh tunic as made no matter, and the tonsure, however well a man (or a girl!) knew it was there, was invisible behind the burning bush of curls.

"Thirsty people you are, then!" said Annest, still with one eye upon Brother John, and set down her pitcher on the bench beside Cai, and with a flick of her skirts and a wave of her light-brown mane, sat down beside it, and accepted the horn Bened offered her. Brother John stood mute and enchanted.

"Come on, then, lad," said Bened, and made a place for him between himself and Cai, only one remove from where the girl sat delicately sipping. And Brother John, like a man walking in his sleep, though perhaps with rather more zestful purpose, strode forward towards the seat reserved for him.

"Well, well!" said Cadfael silently to himself, and left the insoluble to the solver of all problems, and with Father Huw moved on into the hall.

"I will come," said Rhisiart, shut into a small chamber apart with his visitors. "Of course I will come. No man should refuse another his say. No man can be sure he will not belie himself and do himself less than justice, and God forbid I should refuse anyone his second chance. I've often spoken in haste myself, and been sorry after, and said so, as your prior has said so now." He had not, of course, nor had Huw claimed, in so many words, that he had. Rather he had expressed his own shame and regret, but if Rhisiart attributed these to Prior Robert, Huw was desperate enough to let him continue in the delusion. "But I tell you this, I expect little from this meeting. The gap between us is too wide. To you I can say what I have not said to

any who were not there, because I am ashamed. The man offered me money. He says now he offered it to Gwytherin, but how is that possible? Am I Gwytherin? I am a man like other men, I fill my place as best I can, but remain one only. No, he offered the purse to me, to take back my voice against him. To persuade my own people to go along with his wishes. I accept his desire to talk to me again, to bring me to see this matter as he sees it. But I cannot forget that he saw it as something he could buy with money. If he wishes to change me, that must change, and be shown to be changed. As for his threats, for threats they are, and I approve you for reporting them faithfully, they move me not at all. My reverence for our little saint is the equal of his or any man's. Do you think she does not know it?"

"I am sure she does," said Father Huw.

"And if all they want is to honour and adore her rightly, why can they not do so here, where she lies? Even dress her grave, if that is what disturbs them, that we've let it run wild?"

"A good question," said Brother Cadfael. "I have asked it myself. The sleep of saints should be more sacred and immune even than the sleep of ordinary men."

Rhisiart looked him over with those fine, challenging eyes, a shade or two lighter than his daughter's, and smiled. "Howbeit, I will come, and my thanks for all your trouble. At the hour of noon, or a little after, I will come to your dinner, and I will listen faithfully to whatever may be said to me."

There was a good laughter echoing from end to end of the bench under the eaves, and it was tempting to join the drinkers, at least for one quick cup, as Cai demanded. Bened had got up to replenish his horn from the pitcher, and Brother John, silent and flushed but glowingly happy, sat with no barrier between him and the girl, their sleeves all but touching when she leaned curiously closer, her hair dropping a stray lock against his shoulder.

"Well, how have you sped?" asked Cai, pouring mead for them. "Will he come and talk terms with your prior?"

"He'll come," said Cadfael. "Whether he'll talk terms I doubt. He was greatly affronted. But he'll come to dine, and that's something."

"The whole parish will know it before ever you get back to the parsonage," said Cai. "News runs faster than the wind in these parts, and after this morning they're all building on Rhisiart. I tell you, if he changed his tune and said amen, so would they. Not for want of their own doubts and waverings, but because they trust him. He took a stand, and they know he won't leave it but for good reason. Sweeten him, and you'll get your way."

"Not my way," said Cadfael. "I never could see why a man can't reverence his favourite saint without wanting to fondle her bones, but there's great rivalry for such relics among the abbeys these days. A good mead, this, Cai."

"Our Annest here brewed it," said Bened, with tolerant pride in his niece, and clapped a hand fondly on her shoulder. "And only one of her skills! She'll be a treasure for some man when she weds, but a sad loss to me."

"I might bring you a good smith to work with you," said the girl, dimpling. "Where's the loss then?"

It was deep dusk, and with all the longing they felt to linger, they had to be away. Huw was fidgety, thinking of Prior Robert's rising impatience, his tall figure pacing the garden and looking out for the first glimpse of his messengers returning. "We should be off. We shall be looked for. Come, brother, make your farewells."

Brother John rose reluctantly but dutifully. The groom was leading the horses forward, an arm under each arching neck. With composed face but glowing eyes Brother John said his general goodnight and blessing. In careful but resounding Welsh!

The echo swept the riders away towards the gate on a wave of laughter and goodwill, in which the girl's light voice soared gaily, and Engelard's hearty English "God go with you!" balanced the tongues.

"And who taught you that between evening and dark?" asked Brother Cadfael with interest, as they entered the deep green twilight under the trees. "Bened or Cai?"

"Neither," said Brother John, contentedly pondering a deep private satisfaction.

Small use asking how she had managed it, she having no English and he no Welsh, to determine what the phrase was she was drumming into him. There was a kind of language at work here that made short shrift on interpreters.

"Well, you can fairly claim the day hasn't been wasted," owned Cadfael generously, "if something's been learned. And have you made any other discoveries to add to that?"

"Yes," said Brother John, placidly glowing. "The day after tomorrow is baking-day at Bened's."

"You may rest and sleep, Father Prior," said Huw, fronting the tall, pale forehead gallantly with his low, brown one. "Rhisiart has said he will come, and he will listen. He was gracious and reasonable. Tomorrow at noon or soon after he will be here."

Prior Robert certainly loosed a cautious, suppressed sigh of relief. But he required more before they could all go away and sleep. Richard loomed at his shoulder, large, benign and anxious.

"And is he sensible of the wrong-mindedness of his resistance? Will he withdraw his opposition?"

In the dimness where the candle-light barely reached, Brothers Jerome and Columbanus trembled and hoped, for while doubt remained they had not been permitted to remove to their rest at Cadwallon's house. Anxious eyes appealed, reflecting the light.

Father Huw hedged, wanting his own sleep. "He offers friendly interest and faithful consideration. I asked no more."

Brother Cadfael said bluntly: "You will need to be persuasive, and sincere. *He* is sincere. I am no way convinced that he can be lightly persuaded." He was tired of nursing wounded vanities, he spoke out what was in his mind. "Father Prior, you made your mistake with him this morning. You will need a change of heart, *his or yours*, to undo that damage."

Prior Robert made his dispositions as soon as Mass was over next morning, and with some care.

"Only Brother Sub-Prior and I, with Father Huw, and Brother Cadfael as interpreter, will sit at table together. You, Brother John, will make yourself useful to the cooks, and do whatever is needed, and you may also see to Father Huw's cattle and chickens. And you two, Brother Jerome, Brother Columbanus, I

have a special mission for you. Since we are about Saint Winifred's business, I would have you go and spend the hours while we deliberate in vigil and prayer, imploring her aid to bring the obdurate to reason, and our errand to a successful conclusion. Not in the church here, but in her own chapel in the old graveyard where she is buried. Take your food and your measure of wine with you, and go there now. The boy Edwin will show you the way. If we prevail upon Rhisiart, as with her aid I trust we may, I will send to release you. But continue your intercessions until I do send word."

They scattered dutifully, John, cheerfully enough, to tend the fire for Marared, and fetch and carry as she directed. The old woman, long widowed and her own sons grown, preened herself at having a strapping young fellow to keep her company, and Cadfael reflected that John might well be favoured with the best bits before the meal ever came to table. As for Jerome and Columbanus, he saw them set out with the boy, bread and meat wrapped in napkins in the breasts of their habits, and Columbanus carrying the flask with their ration of wine, and a small bottle of spring water for himself.

"It is very little to offer," he said meekly, "but I will touch nothing but water until our cause has prevailed."

"More fool he," said Brother John blithely, "for he may well be swearing off wine for life!"

It was a fine spring morning, but capricious as May can be. Prior Robert and his attendants sat in the orchard until they were driven indoors by a sharp and sparkling shower that lasted almost half an hour. It was then approaching noon, the time when Rhisiart should join them. He would have a wet walk by the short path through the forest. Or perhaps he had waited for the sun's return at Cadwallon's house, which was on his way. Making allowances for that, they thought little of it when another half-hour passed, and he did not put in an appearance. But when he was an hour late for the meeting, and still no sign of him, Prior Robert's face grew both grim and cautiously triumphant.

"He has heard the warning I issued against his sin, and he fears to come and face me," he said.

"He had heard the warning, indeed," said Father Huw heavily, "but I saw no signs of fear in him. He spoke very firmly and calmly. And he is a man of his word. I don't understand this, it is not like him."

"We will eat, but frugally," said the prior, "and give him every chance of keeping his promise, if something has happened to delay him. So it may, to any man. We will wait until it is time to prepare for Vespers."

"I'll walk as far as Cadwallon's house," offered Brother Richard, "for the way is all one to that point, and see if I can meet with him, or get word if he's on his way."

He was gone more than an hour and a half, and came back alone. "I went beyond, some way along the ride, but saw no sign of him. On my way back I asked at Cadwallon's gate, but no one had seen him pass. I feared he might have walked by the short path while I was taking the other road."

"We'll wait for him until Vespers, and no longer," said the prior, and by then his voice was growing grimly confident, for now he did not expect the guest to come, and the enemy would have put himself in the wrong, to Prior Robert's great gain. Until Vespers, therefore, they waited, five hours after the appointed time. The people of Gwytherin could hardly say Rhisiart had been written off too hastily.

"So it ends," said the prior, rising and shaking out his skirts like one shaking off a doubt or an incubus. "He has turned tail, and his opposition will carry no weight now with any man. Let us go!"

The sunlight was still bright but slanting over the green bowl where the church stood, and a number of people were gathering for the service. And out of the deeper green shadow where the forest path began, came, not Rhisiart, but his daughter, sailing gallantly out into the sunlight in a green gown, with her wild hair tamed and braided, and a linen coif over it, Sioned in her church-going person, with Peredur on her heels, his hand possessively cupping her elbow, though she paid little heed to that attention. She saw them issuing in a silent procession from Huw's gate, and her eyes went from person to person, lingering on Cadfael who came last, and again looking back with a small frown, as though one face was missing from the expected company.

"Where is my father?" she asked, her wide eyes surprised but not yet troubled. "Is he not still here with you? Have I missed him? I rode as far as Cadwallon's house, and he was on foot, so if he has left more than an hour ago he may well be home by now. I came to bear him company to church and go back with him afterwards."

Prior Robert looked down at her in some wonder, the first flickering uneasiness twitching his nostrils. "What is she saying? Do you tell me that the lord Rhisiart set out to come to our meeting?"

"Of course!" said Sioned, amazed. "He had said he would."

"But he did not come," said Robert. "We've waited for him since noon, and we've seen no sign of him. Brother Sub-Prior went a part of the way to see if he could meet with him, but in vain. He has not been here."

She caught the meaning of that without Cadfael's services. Her eyes flashed from face to face, distrustful and ready for anger. "Are you telling me truth? Or have you hidden him away under lock and key until you can get Winifred out of her grave and away to Shrewsbury? He was all that stood in your way. And you have threatened him!"

Peredur closed his fingers anxiously on her arm, and drew her against his side. "Hush, you must not say such things. These brothers would not lie to you."

"At what hour," asked Cadfael, "did your father set out this morning?"

She looked at him, and was a little reassured. The ring of silent onlookers drew nearer, listening attentively, ready to take her part if she needed an army.

"A good hour before noon. He was going first to the fields in the clearing, so he would be coming here by the shortest way, cutting through a quarter of a mile of forest to the usual path. He had plenty of time to be here before noon. As far as the clearing Engelard would be with him, he was going beyond, to the byres over the hill. There are two cows there ready to drop their calves."

"We are telling you truly, child," said Father Huw, his voice as grave and anxious as her own, "we waited for him, and he never came."

"What can have happened to him? Where can he be?"

"He will have crossed with us and gone home," urged Peredur, hovering unhappily at her shoulder. "We'll ride back, we shall surely find him there before us."

"No! Why should he turn back, and never come to the dinner? And if he did, why so late? He would have been home long before I dressed my hair and set out to meet him, if he had changed his mind. And besides, he never would."

"I think," said Father Huw, "that my whole parish has some interest in this matter, and we had better put off everything else, even the services of the church, until we have found Rhisiart and assured ourselves that all's well with him. Truly this may be no more than a tangle of mistiming and misunderstanding, but let's resolve it first, and wonder about it afterwards. There are enough of us here. Let's send out in parties along all the roads he may have taken, and Sioned shall show us where she thinks his short cut from the upland fields would bring him to the path. He could not well meet with any dangerous beasts in these woods, but he may have had a fall, an injury that has halted or slowed him. Father Prior, will you join with us?"

"With all my heart," said Prior Robert, "and so will we all."

The less active among them were sent along the open ride, with orders to scatter on either side and comb the surroundings as they went, while the more athletic took the narrow foot-path beyond Cadwallon's stockade. The woods here were not yet close-set, there was thick, springy grass under the trees, and no dense undergrowth. They spread out into a half-circle, moving along within a few paces of one another, Sioned pressing purposefully forward up the path with set lips and fixed eyes, Peredur with every evidence of desperate affection following close and murmuring agitated urgings into her unheeding ears. Whether he believed in his own reassurances or not, out of all question he was a young man fathoms deep in love, and ready to do anything to serve and protect Sioned, while she saw in him nothing but the boy from the next holding, and tiresome at that.

They were perhaps half a mile beyond Cadwallon's enclosure when Father Huw suddenly plucked at Brother Cadfael's sleeve.

"We have forgotten Brother Jerome and Brother Columbanus! The hill of the chapel is off to the right here, no great way. Ask Prior Robert, should we not send and call them to join us?"

"I had indeed forgotten," admitted the prior. "Yes, by all means send someone. Best one of your parishioners, they'll all know the way."

One of the young men swerved aside obediently between the trees, and ran. The slow-moving scythe swept on into deeper forest.

"About here," said Sioned, halting, "he would have come down from the clearing. If we go obliquely to the right here, and spread out as before, we shall be covering his likely way."

The ground rose, the trees grew closer, the undergrowth thicker. They began to thread the encroaching bushes, having to part company by a few yards, losing sight momentarily of their neighbours. They had gone thus only a short way when Bened the smith, crashing through bushes at Brother Cadfael's left hand, uttered a great shout of discovery and dismay, and everyone in the wavering line halted and shook to the sound.

Cadfael turned towards the cry, thrusting through thorn-branches, and came out in a narrow oval of grass surrounded every way with thick bushes, through which a used track no wider than a man's shoulders clove, the long way of the oval. Just where he must have brushed through into the clear space, Rhisiart lay on his back, his right hip hollowing the grass under him, shoulders flattened to the ground and arms spread wide. His legs were drawn up under him with bent knees, the left leg crossed over the right. His short, defiant beard pointed at the sky. So, and at the very same slanting angle, did the feathered flight of the arrow that jutted out from under the cage of his ribs.

Chapter Five

rom both sides they gathered, drawn to the smith's call, breaking through bushes like the running of a startled herd of deer, and halting appalled round the oval where the body lay. Cadfael went on his knees, and looked for any sign of breath within the drawnback lips, any pulse in the stretched throat or rise and fall of the pierced breast, but there was none. And for that first moment he was the only one who moved within the open space of grass, and what he did was done in strange, too-intense silence, as though everyone round him held his breath.

Then everything broke out at once in noise and motion. Sioned clawed through the screening circle and saw her father's body, and uttered a great shriek that was more of fury even than of grief, and flung herself forward. Peredur caught her by the wrist and pulled her round into his arms, one hand cupped behind her head to press her face into his shoulder, but she shrieked again, and struck out at him with all her strength, and breaking loose, hurled herself to her knees facing Cadfael, and reached out to embrace her father's body. Cadfael leaned across to ward her off, his hand braced into the grass under Rhisiart's right armpit.

"No! Touch nothing! Not yet! Let him alone, he has things to tell us!"

By some intuitive quickness of mind that had not deserted her even at this moment, she obeyed the tone first, and awakened to the words immediately after. Her eyes questioned him, widening, and slowly she sat back in the grass, and drew her hands together in her lap. Her lips shaped the words after him silently: "—things to tell us!" She looked from his face into the face of the dead man. She knew he was dead. She also knew that the dead speak, often in thunder. And she came of proud Welsh stock to which the blood-feud is sacred, a duty transcending even grief.

When those following gathered closer, and one reached to touch, it was she who spread her arm protectively over the body, and said with authority: "No! Let him be!"

Cadfael had drawn back his arm, and for a moment wondered what troubled him about the palm he had lifted from the grass beside Rhisiart's breast. Then he knew. Where he knelt the grass was perceptibly damp from the morning's sharp shower, he could feel the cling of the habit when he shifted his knee. Yet under the outflung right arm the grass was dry, his hand rose from it with no hint of moisture, no scent of rain. He touched again, ran his fingers up and down alongside Rhisiart's right flank. He was down to the knee before he felt the dampness and stirred the green fragrance. He felt outwards, the width of the body, to find the same signs. Strange! Very strange! His mind recorded and forbore to wonder then, because there were other things to be observed, and all manner of dangers were falling in upon all manner of people.

The tall shape looming at his back, motionless and chill, could be none other than Prior Robert, and Prior Robert in a curious state of exalted shock, nearer to Brother Columbanus' ecstatic fit than he had ever been before or would ever be again. The high, strained voice asked, over the shuddering quietness of Sioned's tearless sobs: "He is dead?"

"Dead," said Cadfael flatly, and looked into Sioned's wide, dry eyes and held them, promising something as yet undefined. Whatever it was, she understood it and was appeased, for he was Welsh, too, he knew about the blood-feud. And she was the only heir, the only close kin, of a murdered man. She had a task far above sorrow.

The prior's voice soared suddenly, awed and exalted. "Behold the saint's vengeance! Did I not say her wrath would be wreaked upon all those who stood in the way of her desire? Tell them what I am saying! Tell them to look well at the fulfilment of my prophecy, and let all other obdurate hearts take warning. Saint Winifred has shown her power and her displeasure."

There was hardly any need for translation, they had the sense of it already. A dozen of those standing close shrank warily away, a dozen voices muttered hurried submission. Not for worlds would they stand in the saint's way.

"The impious man reaps what he sows," declaimed Robert. "Rhisiart had his warning, and did not heed it."

The most timorous were on their knees by then, cowed and horrified. It was not as if Saint Winifred had meant very much to them, until someone else wanted her, and Rhisiart stated a prior claim on behalf of the parish. And Rhisiart was dead by violence, struck down improbably in his own forests.

Sioned's eyes held Cadfael's, above her father's pierced heart. She was a gallant girl, she said never a word, though she had words building up in her ripe for saying, spitting, rather, into Prior Robert's pallid, aristocratic, alabaster face. It was not she who suddenly spoke out. It was Peredur.

"I don't believe it!" He had a fine, clear, vehement voice that rang under the branches. "What, a gentle virgin saint, to take such vengeance on a good man? Yes, a good man, however mistaken! If she had been so pitiless as to want to slay—and I do not believe it of her! —what need would she have of arrows and bows? Fire from heaven would have done her will just as well, and shown her power better. You are looking at a murdered man, Father Prior. A man's hand fitted that arrow, a man's hand drew the bow, and for a man's reason. There must have been others who had a grudge against Rhisiart, others whose plans he was obstructing, besides Saint Winifred. Why blame this killing on her?"

This forthright Welsh sense Cadfael translated into English for Robert's benefit, who had caught the dissenting tone of it, but not the content. "And the young man's right. This arrow never was shot from heaven. Look at the angle of it, up from under his ribs into the heart. Out of the earth, rather! A man with a short bow, on his knee among the bushes? True, the ground slopes, he may even have been lower than Rhisiart, but even so…"

"Avenging saints may make use of earthly instruments," said Robert overbearingly.

"The instrument would still be a murderer," said Cadfael. "There is law in Wales, too. We shall need to send word to the prince's bailiff."

Bened had stood all this time darkly gazing, at the body, at the very slight ooze of blood round the wound, at the jutting shaft with its trimmed feathers. Slowly he said: "I know this arrow. I know its owner, or at least the man whose mark it bears. Where young men are living close together in a household, they mark their own with a distinctive sign, so that there can be no argument. See the tip of the feathering on one side, dyed blue." It was as he said, and at the mention of it several there drew breath hard, knowing the mark as well as he knew it.

"It's Engelard's," said Bened outright, and three or four hushed voices bore him out.

Sioned raised her stricken face, shocked into a false, frozen calm that suddenly melted and crumbled into dread and anger. Rhisiart was dead, there was nothing she could do now for him but mourn and wait, but Engelard was alive and vulnerable, and an outlander, with no kinship to speak for him. She rose abruptly, slender and straight, turning her fierce eyes from face to face all round the circle.

"Engelard is the most trustworthy of all my father's men, and would cut off his own drawing hand rather than loose against my father's life. Who dares say this is his work?"

"I don't say so," said Bened reasonably. "I do say this is marked as his arrow. He is the best shot with the short bow in all this countryside."

"And everybody in Gwytherin knows," spoke up a voice from among the Welshmen, not accusing, only pointing out facts, "that he has quarrelled often and fiercely with Rhisiart, over a certain matter at issue between them."

"Over me," said Sioned harshly. "Say what you mean! I, of all people, know the truth best. Better than you all! Yes, they have had high words many times, on this one matter, and only this, and would have had more, but for all that, these two have understood each other, and neither one of them would ever have done the other harm. Do you think the prize fought over does not get to know the risks to herself and both the combatants? Fight they did, but they thought more highly of each other than either did of any of you, and with good reason."

"Yet who can say," said Peredur in a low voice, "how far a man may step aside even from his own nature, for love?"

She turned and looked at him with measuring scorn. "I thought you were his friend!"

"So I am his friend," said Peredur, paling but steadfast. "I said what I believe of myself, no less than of him."

"What is this matter of one Engelard?" demanded Prior Robert, left behind in this exchange. "Tell me what they are saying." And when Cadfael had done so, as tersely as possible: "It would seem that at least this young man must be asked to account for his movements this day," decreed Robert, appropriating an authority to which he had no direct right here. "It may be that others have been with him, and can vouch for him. But if not..."

"He set out this morning with your father," said Huw, distressfully eyeing the girl's fixed and defiant face. "You told us so. They went together as far as the cleared fields. Then your father turned to make his way down to us, and Engelard was to go a mile beyond, to the byres where the cows were in calf. We must send out and ask if any man has seen your father since he parted from Engelard. Is there any who can speak to that?"

There was a silence. The numbers gathered about them were growing steadily. Some of the slower searchers from the open ride had made their way up here without news of their own, to find the matter thus terribly resolved. Others, hearing rumours of the missing man, had followed from the village. Father Huw's messenger came up behind with Brother Columbanus and Brother Jerome from the chapel. But no one spoke up to say he had seen Rhisiart that day. Nor did any volunteer word of having encountered Engelard.

"He must be questioned," said Prior Robert, "and if his answers are not satisfactory, he must be held and handed over to the bailiff. For it's clear from what has been said that this man certainly had a motive for wishing to remove Rhisiart from his path."

"Motive?" blazed Sioned, burning up abruptly as a dark and quiet fire suddenly spurts flame. Instinctively she recoiled into Welsh, though she had already revealed how well she could follow what was said around her in English, and the chief reason for her reticence concerning her knowledge had been cruelly re-

moved. "Not so strong a motive as *you* had, Father Prior! Every soul in this parish knows what store you set upon getting Saint Winifred away from us, what glory it will be to your abbey, and above all, to you. And who stood in your way but my father? *Yours,* not the saint's! Show me a better reason for wanting him dead! Did any ever wish to lift hand against him, all these years! Until *you* came here with your quest for Winifred's relics? Engelard's disagreement with my father was constant and understood, yours was new and urgent. Our need could wait, we're young. Yours could not wait. And who knew better than you at what hour my father would be coming through the forest to Gwytherin? Or that he would not change his mind?"

Father Huw spread a horrified hand to hush her long before this, but she would not be hushed. "Child, child, you must not make such dreadful accusations against the reverend prior, it is mortal sin."

"I state facts, and let them speak," snapped Sioned. "Where's the offence in that? Prior Robert may point out the facts that suit him, I showed you the others, those that do not suit him. My father was the sole obstacle in his path, and my father has been removed."

"Child, I tell you every soul in this valley knew that your father was coming to my house, and the hour of his coming, and many would know all the possible ways, far better than any of these good brethren from Shrewsbury. The occasion might well suit another grudge. And you must know that Prior Robert has been with me, and with Brother Richard and Brother Cadfael here, ever since morning Mass." And Father Huw turned in agitated supplication to Robert, wringing his hands. "Father Prior, I beg you, do not hold it against the girl that she speaks so wildly. She is in grief—a father lost.... You cannot wonder if she turns on us all."

"I say no word of blame," said the prior, though coldly. "I gather she is casting doubts upon myself and my companions, but doubtless, you have answered her. Tell the young woman, in my name, that both you and others here can witness for my own person, for all this day I have been within your sight."

Grateful for at least one certainty, Huw turned to repeat as much to Sioned yet again, but she blazed back with biting promptness and force, forgetting all restraints in the need to confront Robert face to face, without the tedious intervention of interpreters. "So you may have been, Father Prior," she flashed in plain English. "In any case I don't see *you* as likely to make a good bowman. But a man who would try to buy my father's compliance would be willing and able to buy some more pliable person to do even this work for him. You still had your purse! Rhisiart spurned it!"

"Take care!" thundered Robert, galled beyond the limits of his arduous patience. "You put your soul in peril! I have borne with you thus far, making allowances for your grief, but go no further along this road!"

They were staring upon each other like adversaries in the lists before the baton falls, he very tall and rigid and chill as ice, she light and ferocious and very handsome, her coif long ago lost among the bushes, and her sheaves of black hair loose on her shoulders. And at that moment, before she could spit further fire, or he threaten more imminent damnation, they all heard voices approaching from higher up among the woods, a man's voice and a girl's in quick, concerned exchanges, and coming rapidly nearer with a light threshing of branches, as though they had caught the raised tones and threatening sounds of many people gathered here improbably deep in the forest, and were hurrying to discover what was happening.

The two antagonists heard them, and their concentration on each other was shaken and disrupted. Sioned knew them, and a fleeting shadow of fear and desperation passed over her face. She glanced round wildly, but there was no help. A girl's arm parted the bushes above the oval where they stood, and Annest stepped through, and stood in astonishment, gazing round at the inexplicable gathering before her.

It was the narrowness of the track—no more than the shadow of a deer-path in the grass—and the abruptness with which she had halted that gave Sioned her one chance. She took it valiantly. "Go back home, Annest," she said loudly. "I am coming with company. Go and prepare for guests, quickly, you'll have little time." Her voice was high and urgent. Annest had not yet lowered her eyes to the ground, and grass and shadows veiled Rhisiart's body.

The effort was wasted. Another hand, large and gentle, was laid on Annest's shoulder while she hesitated, and moved her aside. "The company sounds somewhat loud and angry," said a man's voice, high and clear, "so, with your leave, Sioned, we'll all go together."

Engelard put the girl aside between his hands, as familiarly and serenely as a brother might have done, and stepped past her into the clearing.

He had eyes for no one but Sioned, he walked towards her with the straight gait of a proprietor, and as he came he took in her stiff erectness, and fixed face of fire and ice and despair, and his own face mirrored everything he saw in her. His brows drew together, his smile, taut and formidable to begin with, vanished utterly, his eyes burned bluer than cornflowers. He passed by Prior Robert as though he had not even been there, or not alive, a stock, a dead tree by the path. He put out his hands, and Sioned laid her hands in them, and for an instant closed her eyes. There was no frowning him away now, he was here in the midst, quite without defences. The circle, not all inimical but all hampering, was closing round him.

He had her by the hands when he saw Rhisiart's body.

The shock went into him as abruptly as the arrow must have gone into Rhisiart, stopping him instantly. Cadfael had him well in view, and saw his lips part and whisper soundlessly: "Christ aid!" What followed was most eloquent. The Saxon youth moved with loving slowness, shutting both Sioned's hands into one of his, and with his freed right hand stroked softly over her hair, down temple and cheek and chin and throat, all with such mastered passion that she was soothed, as he meant, while he had barely stopped shaking from the shock.

He folded an arm about her, holding her close against his side, and slowly looked all round the circle of watching faces, and slowly down at the body of his lord. His face was bleakly angry.

"Who did this?"

He looked round, seeking the one who by rights should be spokesman, hesitating between Prior Robert, who arrogated to himself authority wherever he came, and Father Huw, who was known and trusted here. He repeated his demand in English, but neither of them answered him, and for a long moment neither did anyone else. Then Sioned said, with clear, deliberate warning: "There are some here are saying that *you* did."

"I?" he cried, astonished and scornful rather than alarmed, and turned sharply to search her face, which was intent and urgent.

Her lips shaped silently: "Run! They're blaming you!"

It was all she could do, and he understood, for they had such a link between them that meanings could be exchanged in silence, in a look. He measured with a quick glance the number of his possible enemies, and the spaces between them, but he did not move. "Who accuses me?" he said. "And on what ground? It seems to me I might rather question all of you, whom I find standing here about my lord's dead body, while I have been all day out with the cows, beyond Bryn. When I got home Annest was anxious because Sioned had not returned, and the sheep boy told her there was no service at Vespers at the church. We came out to look for you, and found you by the noise you were making among you. And I ask again, and I will know before ever I give up: *Who did this?*"

"We are all asking that," said Father Huw. "Son, there's no man here has accused you. But there are things that give us the right to question you, and a man with nothing on his conscience won't be ashamed or afraid to answer. Have you yet looked carefully at the arrow that struck Rhisiart down? Then look at it now!"

Frowning, Engelard drew a step nearer, and looked indeed, earnestly and bitterly at the dead man, only afterwards at the arrow. He saw the flutter of deep blue, and gasped.

"This is one of mine!" He looked up with

wild suspicion at them all. "Either that, or someone has copied my mark. But no, this is mine, I know the trim, I fletched it new only a week or so ago."

"He owns it his?" demanded Robert, following as best he could. "He admits it?"

"Admit?" flashed Engelard in English. "What is there to admit? I *say* it! How it was brought here, who loosed it, I know no more than you do, but I know the shaft for mine. God's teeth!" he cried furiously, "do you think if I had any hand in this villainy I should leave my mark flaunting in the wound? Am I fool as well as outlander? And do you think I would do anything to harm Rhisiart? The man who stood my friend and gave me the means of living here when I'd poached myself out of Cheshire?"

"He refused to consider you as a suitor for his daughter," Bened said almost reluctantly, "whatever good he did for you otherwise."

"So he did, and according to his lights, rightly so. And I know it, knowing as much as I've learned of Wales, and even if I did smart under it, I knew he had reason and custom on his side. Never has he done anything I could complain of as unfair to me. He stood much arrogance and impatience from me, come to that. There isn't a man in Gwynedd I like and respect more. I'd as soon have cut my own throat as injured Rhisiart."

"He knew and knows it," said Sioned, "and so do I."

"Yet the arrow is yours," said Huw unhappily. "And as for reclaiming or disguising it, it may well have been that speedy flight after such an act would be more important."

"If I had planned such an act,," said Engelard, "though God forbid I should ever have to imagine a thing so vile, I could as easily have done what some devil has done now to me, and used another man's shaft."

"But, son, it would be more in keeping with your nature," the priest pursued sadly, "to commit such a deed without planning, having with you only your own bow and arrows. Another approach, another quarrel, a sudden wild rage! No one supposes this was plotted beforehand."

"I had no bow with me all this day. I was busy with the cattle, what should I want with a bow?"

"It will be for the royal bailiff to enquire into all possible matters concerning this case," said Prior Robert, resolutely reclaiming the dominance among them. "What should be asked at once of this young man is where he has been all this day, what doing, and in whose company."

"In no man's company. The byres behind Bryn are in a lonely place, good pasture but apart from the used roads. Two cows dropped their calves today, one around noon, the second not before late afternoon, and that was a hard birth, and gave me trouble. But the young things are there alive and on their legs now, to testify to what I've been doing."

"You left Rhisiart at his fields along the way?"

"I did, and went straight on to my own work. And have not seen him again until now."

"And did you speak with any man, there at the byres? Can anyone testify as to where you were, at any time during the day?" No one was likely to try and wrest the initiative from Robert now. Engelard looked round him quickly, measuring chances. Annest came forward silently, and took her stand beside Sioned. Brother John's roused, anxious eyes followed her progress, and approved the loyalty which had no other way of expressing itself.

"Engelard did not come home until half an hour ago," she said stoutly.

"Child," said Father Huw wretchedly, "where he was not does not in any way confirm where he says he was. Two calves may be delivered far more quickly than he claims, how can we know, who were not there? He had time to slip back here and do this thing, and be back with his cattle and never noticed. Unless we can find someone who testifies to having seen him elsewhere, at whatever time this deed may have been done, then I fear we should hold Engelard in safe-keeping until the prince's bailiff can take over the charge for us."

The men of Gwytherin hovered, murmuring, some convinced, many angry, for Rhisiart had been very well liked, some hesitant, but granting that the outlander ought to be held until his innocence was established or his guilt proved. They shifted and closed, and their murmur became one of consent.

"It is fair," said Bened, and the growl of assent answered him.

"One lone Englishman with his back to the wall," whispered Brother John indignantly in Cadfael's ear, "and what chance will he have, with nobody to bear out what he says? And plain truth, for certain! Does he act or speak like a murderer?"

Peredur had stood like a stock all this while, hardly taking his eyes from Engelard's face but to gaze earnestly and unhappily at Sioned. As Prior Robert levelled an imperious arm at Engelard, and the whole assembly closed in slowly in obedience, braced to lay hands on him, Peredur drew a little further back at the edge of the trees, and Cadfael saw him catch Sioned's eye, flash her a wild, wide-eyed look,

and jerk his head as though beckoning. Out of her exhaustion and misery she roused a brief, answering blaze, and leaned to whisper rapidly in Engelard's ear.

"Do your duty, all of you," commanded Robert, "to your laws and your prince and your church, and lay hold of this man!"

There was one instant of stillness, and then they closed in all together, the only gap in their ranks where Peredur still hung back. Engelard made a long leap from Sioned's side, as though he would break for the thickest screen of bushes, and then, instead, caught up a dead, fallen bough that lay in the grass, and whirled it about him in a flailing circle, laying two unwary elders flat, and sending others reeling back out of range. Before they could reassemble, he had changed direction, leaped over one of the fallen, and was clean through the midst of them, arming off the only one who almost got a grip on him, and made straight for the gap Peredur had left in their ranks. Father Huw's voice, uplifted in vexed agitation, called on Peredur to halt him, and Peredur sprang to intercept his flight. How it happened was never quite clear, though Brother Cadfael had a rough idea, but at the very moment when his outstretched hand almost brushed Engelard's sleeve, Peredur stepped upon a rotten branch in the turf, that snapped under his foot and rolled, tossing him flat on his face, half-blinded among the bushes. And winded, possibly, for certainly he made no move to pick himself up until Engelard was past him and away.

Even then it was not quite over, for the nearest pursuers on either side, seeing how the hunt had turned, had also begun to run like hares, on courses converging with the fugitive's at the very edge of the clearing.

From the left came a long-legged villein of Cadwallon's, with a stride like a greyhound, and from the right Brother John, his habit flying, his sandalled feet pounding the earth mightily. It was perhaps the first time Brother John had ever enjoyed Prior Robert's whole-hearted approval. It was certainly the last.

There was no one left in the race but these three, and fleet though Engelard was, it seemed that the long-legged fellow would collide with him before he could finally vanish. All three were hurtling together for a shattering collision, or so it seemed. The villein stretched out arms as formidably long as his legs. So, on the other side, did Brother John. A great hand closed on a thin fold of Engelard's tunic from one side. Brother John bounded exuberantly in from the other. The prior sighed relief, expecting the prisoner to be enfolded in a double embrace. And Brother John, diving, caught Cadwallon's villein round the knees and brought him crashing to the ground, and Engelard, plucking his tunic out of the enemy's grasp, leaped into the bushes and vanished in a receding susurration of branches, until silence and stillness closed over the path of his withdrawal.

Half the hunt, out of excitement rather than any real enmity, streamed away into the forest after the quarry, but half-heartedly now. They had little chance of capturing him. Probably they had no great desire to do anything of the kind, though once put to it, hounds must follow a scent. The real drama remained behind in the clearing. There, at least, justice had one clear culprit to enjoy.

Brother John unwound his arms from his victim's knees, sat up in the grass, fended off placidly a feeble blow the villein aimed at him, and said in robust but incomprehensible English: "Ah, let well alone, lad! What did he ever do to you? But faith, I'm sorry I had to fetch you down so heavily. If you think you're hard-done-to, take comfort! I'm likely to pay dearer than you."

He looked round him complacently enough as he clambered to his feet and dusted off the debris of leaves and twigs that clung to his habit. There stood Prior Robert, not yet unfrozen from the shock of incredulous disillusionment, tall and stiff and grey, a Norman lordling debating terrible penalties for treason. But there, also, stood Sioned, tired, distraught, worn out with passion, but with a small, reviving glow in her eyes, and there was Annest at her elbow, an arm protectively round her waist, but her flower-face turned towards John. Not much use Robert thundering and lightning, while she so smiled and blossomed, beaming her gratitude and admiration.

Brother Richard and Brother Jerome loomed like messengers of doom, one at either elbow. "Brother John, you are summoned. You are in gross offence."

He went with them resignedly. For all the threatening thunder-bolts he had never felt freer in his life. And having now nothing to lose but his own self-respect, he was sturdily determined not to sacrifice that.

"Unfaithful and unworthy brother," hissed Prior Robert, towering in terrible indignation, "what have you done? Do not deny what we have all witnessed. You have not merely connived at the escape of a felon, you have frustrated the attempt of a loyal servant to arrest him. You felled that good man deliberately, to let Engelard go free. Traitor against church and law, you have put yourself beyond the pale. If there is anything you can say in your defence, say it now."

"I thought the lad was being harried beyond reason, on very suspect suspicion," said Brother John boldly. "I've talked with Engelard, I've got my own view of him, a decent, open soul who'd never do violence to any man by stealth, let alone Rhisiart, whom he liked and valued high. I don't believe he has any part in this death, and what's more, I think he'll not go far until he knows who had, and God help the murderer then! So I gave him his chance, and good luck to him!"

The two girls, their heads close together in women's solidarity, interpreted the tone for themselves, if they lacked the words, and glowed in silent applause. Prior Robert was helpless, though he did not know it. Brother Cadfael knew it very well.

"Shameless!" thundered Robert, bristling until even his suave purity showed knife-edged with affront. "You are condemned out of your own mouth, and a disgrace to our order. I have no jurisdiction here as regards Welsh law. The prince's bailiff must resolve this crime that cries for vengeance here. But where my own subordinates are concerned, and where they have infringed the law of this land where we are guests, there two disciplines threaten you, Brother John. As to the sovereignty of Gwynedd, I cannot speak. As to my own discipline, I can and do. You are set far beyond mere ecclesiastical penance. I consign you to close imprisonment until I can confer with the secular authority here, and I refuse to you, meanwhile, all the comforts and consolations of the church." He looked about him and took thought, brooding. Father Huw hovered miserably, lost in this ocean of complaints and accusations. "Brother Cadfael,

ask Father Huw where there is a safe prison, where he can be held."

This was more than Brother John had bargained for, and though he repented of nothing, like a practical man he did begin to look round to weigh up the chances of evading the consequences. He eyed the gaps in the ring as Engelard had done, braced his sturdy feet well apart, and flexed his shoulders experimentally, as though he had thoughts of elbowing Brother Richard smartly in the belly, kicking the legs from under Jerome, and making a dash for freedom. He stopped himself just in time when he heard Cadfael report sedately: "Father Huw suggests there is only one place secure enough. If Sioned is willing to allow her holding to be used, a prisoner could be safe enough there."

At this point Brother John unaccountably lost interest in immediate escape.

"My house is at Prior Robert's disposal," said Sioned in Welsh, with appropriate coldness, but very promptly. She had herself well in hand, she made no more lapses into English. "There are storehouses and stables, if you wish to use them. I promise I shall not go near the prisoner, or hold the key to his prison myself. Father Prior may choose his guard from among my people as he sees fit. My household shall provide him his living, but even that charge I shall give to someone else. If I undertook it myself I fear my impartiality might be doubted, after what has happened."

A good girl, Cadfael thought, translating this for Robert's benefit rather less than for John's. Clever enough to step resolutely round any actual lies even when she was thus wrung by one disaster after another, and generous enough to think for the wants and wishes of others. The someone else who would be charged with seeing Brother John decently housed and fed was standing cheek to cheek with her mistress as she spoke, fair head against dark head. A formidable pair! But they might not have found this unexpected and promising path open to them but for the innocence of celibate parish priests.

"That may be the best plan," said Prior Robert, chilly but courteous, "and I thank you for your dutiful offer, daughter. Keep him straitly, see he has what he needs for life, but no more. He is in great peril of his soul, his body may somewhat atone. If you permit, we will go before and bestow him securely, and let your uncle know what has happened, so that he may send down to you and bring you home. I will not intrude longer on a house of mourning."

"I will show you the way," said Annest, stepping demurely from Sioned's side.

"Hold him fast!" warned the prior, as they massed to follow her uphill through the woods. Though he might have seen for himself, had he looked closely, that the culprit's resignation had mellowed into something very like complacency, and he stepped out as briskly as his guards, a good deal more intent on keeping Annest's slender waist and lithe shoulders in sight than on any opportunity for escape.

Well, thought Cadfael, letting them go without him, and turning to meet Sioned's steady gaze, God sort all! As doubtless he is doing, now as ever!

The men of Gwytherin cut young branches and made a green litter to carry Rhisiart's body home. Under the corpse, when they lifted it, there was much more blood than about the frontal wound, though the point of

the arrow barely broke through skin and clothing. Cadfael would have liked to examine tunic and wound more closely, but forbore because Sioned was there beside him, stiffly erect in her stony grief, and nothing, no word or act that was not hieratic and ceremonial, was permissible then in her presence. Moreover, soon all the servants of Rhisiart's household came down in force to bring their lord home, while the steward waited at the gate with bards and mourning women to welcome him back for the last time, and this was no longer an enquiry into guilt, but the first celebration of a great funeral rite, in which probing would have been indecent. No hope of enquiring further tonight. Even Prior Robert had acknowledged that he must remove himself and his fellows reverently from a mourning community in which they had no rights.

When it was time to raise the litter and its burden, now stretched out decently with his twisted legs drawn out straight and his hands laid quietly at his sides, Sioned looked round for one more to whom she meant to confide a share in this honourable load. She did not find him.

"Where is Peredur? What became of him?"

No one had seen him go, but he was gone. No one had had attention to spare for him after Brother John had completed what Peredur had begun. He had slipped away without a word, as though he had done something to be ashamed of, something for which he might expect blame rather than thanks. Sioned was a little hurt, even in her greater hurt, at his desertion.

"I thought he would have wanted to help me bring my father home. He was a favourite with him, and fond of him. From a little boy he was in and out of our house like his own."

"He maybe doubted his welcome," said Cadfael, "after saying a word that displeased you concerning Engelard."

"And doing a thing afterwards that more than wiped that out?" she said, but for his ears only. No need to say outright before everyone what she knew very well, that Peredur had contrived a way out for her lover. "No, I don't understand why he should slink away without a word, like this." But she said no more then, only begged him with a look to walk with her as she fell in behind the litter. They went some distance in silence. Then she asked, without looking aside at him: "Did my father yet tell you those things he had to tell?"

"Some," said Cadfael. "Not all."

"Is there anything I should do, or not do? I need to know. We must make him seemly tonight." By the morrow he would be stiff, and she knew it. "If you need anything from me, tell me now."

"Keep me the clothes he's wearing, when you take them off him, and take note for me where they're damp from this morning's rain, and where they're dry. If you notice anything strange, remember it. Tomorrow, as soon as I can, I'll come to you."

"I must know the truth," she said. "You know why."

"Yes, I know. But tonight sing him and drink to him, and never doubt but he'll hear the singing."

"Yes," she said, and loosed a great, renewing sigh. "You are a good man. I'm glad you're here. You do not believe it was Engelard."

"I'm as good as certain it was not. First and best, it isn't in him. Lads like Engelard hit out in passion, but with their fists, not with weapons. Second, if it had been in his scope, he'd have made a better job of it. You saw the angle of the arrow. Engelard, I judge, is the breadth of three fingers taller than your father. How could he shoot an arrow under a man's rib-cage who is shorter than he, even from lower ground? Even if he kneeled or crouched in the undergrowth in ambush, I doubt if it could be done. And why should it ever be tried? No, this is folly. And to say that the best shot in all these parts could not put his shaft clean through his man, at any distance there where he could see him? Not more than fifty yards clear in any direction. Worse folly still, why should a good bowman choose such a blind tangled place? They have not looked at the ground, or they could not put forward such foolishness. But first and last and best, that young man of yours is too open and honest to kill by stealth, even a man he hated. And he did not hate Rhisiart. You need not tell me, I know it."

Much of what he had said might well have been hurtful to her, but none of it was. She went with him every step of that way, and flushed and warmed into her proper, vulnerable girlhood at hearing her lover thus accepted.

"You've said no word in wonder," she said, "that I have not been more troubled over what has become of Engelard, and where he is gone to earth now."

"No," said Cadfael, and smiled. "You know where he is, and how to get in touch with him whenever you need. I think you two have two or three places better for secrecy than your oak tree, and in one of them Engelard is resting now, or soon will be. You seem to think he'll be safe enough. Tell me nothing, unless you need a messenger, or help."

"You can be my messenger, if you will, to another," she said. They were emerging from the forest at the edge of Rhisiart's home fields, and Prior Robert stood tall and grim and noncommittal aside from their path, his companions discreetly disposed behind him, his hands, features, and the angle of his gently bowed head all disposed to convey respect for death and compassion for the bereaved without actually owning to forgiveness of the dead. His prisoner was safely lodged, he was waiting only to collect the last stray from his flock, and make an appropriately impressive exit. "Tell Peredur I missed him from among those my father would have liked to carry him home. Tell him what he did was generous, and I am grateful. I am sorry he should ever have doubted it."

They were approaching the gate, and Uncle Meurice, the steward, came out to meet them with his kindly, soft-lined face quaking and shapeless with shock and distress.

"And come tomorrow," said Sioned on an almost soundless breath, and walked away from him alone, and entered the gateway after her father's body.

Chapter Six

ioned's message might not have been delivered so soon, for it would not have been any easy matter to turn aside at Cadwallon's house, without a word of request or excuse to Prior Robert; but in the dimness of the woods, a little above the holding, Cadfael caught a glimpse of a figure withdrawing from them, with evident intent, some fifty yards into cover, and knew it for Peredur. He had not expected to be followed, for he went only far enough to be secure from actual encounter on the path, and there sat down moodily on a fallen trunk, his back against a young tree that leaned with him, and kicked one foot in the litter of last year's leaves. Cadfael asked no permission, but went after him.

Peredur looked up at the sound of other feet rustling the beech-mast, and rose as if he would have removed further to avoid speech, but then gave up the thought, and stood mute and unwelcoming, but resigned.

"I have a word to you," said Brother Cadfael mildly, "from Sioned. She bade me to tell you that she missed you when she would gladly have asked you to lend a shoulder for her father's bier. She sends you word that what you did was generous, and she is grateful."

Peredur stirred his feet uneasily, and drew a little back into deeper shadow.

"There were plenty of her own people there," he said, after a pause that seemed awkward rather than sullen. "She had no need of me."

"Oh, there were hands enough, and shoulders enough," agreed Cadfael, "nevertheless, she missed you. It seems to me that she looks upon you as one having a forward place among her own people. You have been like a brother to her from children, and she could do well with a brother now."

The stiffness of Peredur's young body was palpable even in the green dusk, a constraint that crippled even his tongue. He got out, with a bitter spurt of laughter: "It was not her brother that I wanted to be."

"No, that I understand. Yet you behaved like one, towards her and towards Engelard, when it came to the testing."

What was meant to comfort and compliment appeared, instead, to hurt. Peredur shrank still deeper into his morose stillness. "So she feels she has a debt to me, and wants to pay it but not for my sake. She does not want *me*."

"Well," said Cadfael equably, "I have delivered her message, and if you'll go to her she'll convince you, as I cannot. There was another would have wanted you there, if he could have spoken."

"Oh, hush!" said Peredur, and jerked his head aside with a motion of sudden pain. "Don't say more...."

"No, pardon me, I know this is a grief to you, as well as to her. She said so. 'He was a favourite with him,' she said, 'and fond of him—'"

The boy gave a sharp gasp, and turning with blundering haste, walked away rapidly through the trees, deeper into the wood, and left Brother Cadfael to return very thoughtfully to his companions, with the feel of that unbearably tender spot still wincing under his probing finger.

"You and I," said Bened, when Cadfael walked down to the smithy after Compline, "must do our drinking alone tonight, my friend. Huw has not yet come down from Rhisiart's hall, and Padrig will be busy singing the dead man till the small hours. Well that he was there at this time. A man's all the better for being sung to his grave by a fine poet and harpist, and it's a great thing for his children to remember. And Cai—Cai we shan't

be seeing down here much for a while, not until the bailiff comes to take his prisoner off his hands."

"You mean Brother John has *Cai* for his gaoler?" asked Cadfael, enlightened.

"He volunteered for the job. I fancy that girl of mine ran and prompted him, but he wouldn't need much prodding. Between them, Brother John will be lying snug enough for a day or two. You need not worry about him."

"Nothing was further from my mind," said Cadfael. "And it's Cai who keeps the key on him?"

"You may be sure. And what with Prince Owain being away in the south, as I hear he is, I doubt if sheriff or bailiff will have much time to spare for a small matter of insubordination in Gwytherin." Bened sighed heavily over his horn, filled this time with coarse red wine. "It grieves me now that ever I spoke up and called attention to the blue on the feathers, at least in front of the lass. But someone would have said it. And it's truth that now, with only her Uncle Meurice as guardian, she could have got her own way. She twists him round her finger, he wouldn't have stood in her road. But now I misdoubt me, no man would be such a fool as to leave his private mark on a dead man for all to see. Not unless he was disturbed and had to take to his heels. All it needed was the corner clipping, how long does that take if you've a knife on you? No, it's hard to understand. And yet it could be so!"

By his deep gloom there was more on Bened's mind than that. Somewhere within, he was in abysmal doubt whether he had not spoken up in the hope of having a better chance with Sioned himself if his most favoured rival was removed. He shook his head sadly. "I was glad when he broke clear as he did, but I'll be satisfied if he makes his way back to Cheshire after this alarm. And yet it's hard to think of him as a murderer."

"We might give our minds to that, if you're willing," said Cadfael, "for you know the people of these parts better than I do. Let's own it, the girl's suspicion, that she spoke out to Prior Robert's face, will be what many a one here is thinking, whether he says it or not. Here are we come into the place and starting a great contention, chiefly with this one lord—no need to argue who's in the right—and there he stands as the one obstacle to what we've come for, and suddenly he's dead, murdered. What's more natural than to point the finger at us, all of us?"

"It's blasphemy even to consider such a charge against such reverend brothers," said Bened, shocked.

"Kings and abbots are also men, and can fall to temptation. So how do we all stand in regard to this day's doings? All six of us were together or close within sight of one another until after Mass. Then Prior Robert, Brother Richard and I were with Father Huw, first in the orchard, and when it rained, half an hour before noon, in the house. None of the four of us could have gone into the forest. Brother John, too, was about the house and holding, Marared can vouch for him as well as we. The only one who left, before we all came forth for Vespers and set off to search for Rhisiart, was Brother Richard, who offered to go and see if he could meet with him or get word of him, and was gone perhaps an hour and a

half, and came back empty-handed. From an hour after noon he was gone, and into the forest, too, for what it's worth, and makes no claim to have spoken with anyone until he enquired at Cadwallon's gate on his way back, which would be nearing half past two. I must speak with the gate-keeper, and see if he bears that out. Two of us are left, but not unaccounted for. Brother Jerome and Brother Columbanus were sent off to keep vigil together at Saint Winifred's chapel, to pray for a peaceful agreement. We all saw them set off together, and they'd be in the chapel and on their knees long before ever Rhisiart came down towards the path. And there they stayed until Father Huw's messenger went to fetch them to join us. Each of them is warranty for the other."

"I said so," said Bened, reassured. "Holy men do not murder."

"Man," said Cadfael earnestly, "there are as holy persons outside orders as ever there are in, and not to trifle with truth, as good men out of the Christian church as most I've met within it. In the Holy Land I've known Saracens I'd trust before the common run of the crusaders, men honourable, generous and courteous, who would have scorned to haggle and jostle for place and trade as some of our allies did. Meet every man as you find him, for we're all made the same under habit or robe or rags. Some better made than others, and some better cared for, but on the same pattern all. But there it is. As far as I can see, only one of us, Brother Richard, had any chance at all to be in the neighbourhood when Rhisiart was killed, and of all of us he makes the least likely murderer. So we're forced to look if the ground is not wide open for others, and Saint Winifred only an opportunity and an excuse. Had Rhisiart any enemies around Gwytherin? Some who might never have moved against him if we had not blown up this storm and put the temptation in their way?"

Bened considered gravely, nursing his wine. "I wouldn't say there's a man anywhere who has not someone to wish him ill, but it's a far cry from that to murder. Time was when Father Huw himself came up against Rhisiart over a patch of land both claimed, and tempers ran high, but they settled it the proper way, by witness from the neighbours, and there's been no malice after. And there have been lawsuits— did you ever hear of a Welsh landholder without one or two lawsuits in hand? One with Rhys ap Cynan over a disputed boundary, one over some beasts that strayed. Nothing to make lasting bad blood. We thrive on suits at law. One thing's true, with the interest you've roused here, every soul for miles around knew that Rhisiart was due at Father Huw's parsonage at noon. No limit at all, there, on who might have decided to waylay him on the road."

That was as far as they could get. The field was wide, wide enough still to include Engelard, however persuaded Cadfael might be that he was incapable of such an act. Wide enough to enfold even neighbours like Cadwallon, villeins from the village, servants of the household.

But not, surely, thought Brother Cadfael, making his way back to Huw's loft in the green and fragrant dark, not that strange young man who had been a favourite of Rhisiart, and fond of him, and in and out of his house like a son from childhood? The young man who had said of Engelard, and of himself, that a man might step far aside even from his own nature, for love, and then, presumably for love, had opened a way for Engelard to escape, as Cadfael had seen for himself. And who was now avoiding Sioned's gratitude and affection, either because it was not love, and love was the only thing he wanted from her, or for some darker reason. When he flung away in silence into the forest he had had the look of one pursued by a demon. But surely not *that* demon? So far from furthering his chances, Rhisiart's death robbed him of his most staunch ally, who had waited patiently and urged constantly, to bring his daughter to the desired match in the end. No, whichever way a man looked at him, Peredur remained mysterious and disturbing.

Father Huw did not come back from Rhisiart's house that night. Brother Cadfael lay alone in the loft, and mindful that Brother John was locked up somewhere in Sioned's barns, and there was no one to prepare food, got up in good time and went to do it himself, and then set off to Bened's paddock to see the horses, who were also left without a groom. It suited him better to be out and working in the fresh morning than cooped up with Prior Robert, but he was obliged to return in time for chapter, which the prior had decreed should be held daily as at home, however brief the business they had to transact here.

They met in the orchard, the five of them, Prior Robert presiding in as solemn dignity as ever. Brother Richard read out the saints to be celebrated that day and the following day. Brother Jerome composed his wiry person into his usual shape of sycophantic reverence, and made all the appropriate responses. But it seemed to Cadfael that Brother Columbanus looked unusually withdrawn and troubled, his full blue eyes veiled. The contrast between his athletic build and fine, autocratic head, and his meek and anxious devoutness of feature and bearing, was always confusing to the observer, but that morning his extreme preoccupation with some inward crisis of real or imagined sin made it painful to look at him. Brother Cadfael sighed, expecting another falling fit like the one that had launched them all on this quest. Who knew what this badly-balanced half-saint, half-idiot would do next?

"Here we have but one business in hand," said Prior Robert firmly, "and we shall pursue it as in duty bound. I mean to press more resolutely than ever for our right to take up the relics of the saint, and remove them to Shrewsbury. But we must admit, at this moment, that we have not so far been successful in carrying the people with us. I had great hopes yesterday that all would be resolved. We made every reverent preparation to deserve success...."

At this point he was interrupted by an audible sob from Brother Columbanus, that drew all eyes to that young man. Trembling and meek, he rose from his place and stood with lowered eyes and folded hands before Robert.

"Father Prior, alas, *mea culpa!* I am to blame! I have been unfaithful, and I desire to make confession. I came to chapter determined to cleanse my bosom and ask penance, for my backsliding is the cause of our continued distresses. May I speak?"

I knew there was something brewing, thought Brother Cadfael, resigned and disgusted. But at least without rolling on the ground and biting the grass, this time!

"Speak out," said the prior, not unkindly. "You have never sought to make light of your failings, I do not think you need fear our too harsh condemnation. You have been commonly your own sternest judge." So he had, but that, well handled, can be one way of evading and forestalling the judgements of others.

Brother Columbanus sank to his knees in the orchard turf. And very comely and aristocratic he looked, Cadfael admitted, again admiring with surprise the compact grace and strength of his body, and the supple flow of his movements.

"Father, you sent me with Brother Jerome, yesterday, to keep vigil in the chapel, and pray earnestly for a good outcome, in amity and peace. Father, we came there in good time, before eleven, as I judge, and having eaten our meal, we went in and took our places, for there are prayer-desks within, and the altar is kept clean and well-tended. Oh, Father, my will to keep vigil was good, but the flesh was weak. I had not been half an hour kneeling in prayer, when I fell asleep on my arms on the desk, to my endless shame. It is no excuse that I have slept badly and thought much since we came here. Prayer should fix and purify the mind. I slept, and our cause was weakened. I must have slept all the afternoon, for the next thing I remember is Brother Jerome shaking me by the shoulder and telling me there was a messenger calling us to go with him."

He caught his breath, and a frantic tear rolled down his cheek, circling the bold, rounded Norman bone. "Oh, do not look askance at Brother Jerome, for he surely never knew I had been sleeping, and there is no blame at all to him for not observing and reporting my sin. I awoke as he touched me, and arose and went with him. He thought me as earnest in prayer as he, and knew no wrong."

Nobody, probably, had thought of looking askance at Brother Jerome until then, but Cadfael was probably the quickest and most alert, and the only one who caught the curious expression of apprehension, fading rapidly into complacency, that passed over Brother Jerome's normally controlled countenance. Jerome had not been pursuing the same studies as Cadfael, or he would have been far from complacent. For Brother Columbanus in his self-absorbed innocence had just removed all certainty that Jerome had spent the previous noon and afternoon motionless in Saint Winifred's chapel, praying for a happy solution. His only guarantor had been fast asleep throughout. He could have sauntered out and gone anywhere he chose.

"Son," said Prior Robert, in an indulgent voice he would certainly never have used to Brother John, "your fault is human, and frailty is in our nature. And you redeem your own error, in defending your brother. Why did you not tell us of this yesterday?"

"Father, how could I? There was no opportunity, before we learned of Rhisiart's death. Thus burdened, how could I burden you further at that time? I kept it for this chapter, the right place for erring brothers to receive their penance, and make their abasement. As I do abase myself, as all unworthy the vocation I chose. Speak out sentence on me, for I desire penance."

The prior was opening his lips to give judgment, patiently enough, for such devout submission and awareness of guilt disarmed him, when they were distracted by the clap of the wooden bar of the garden gate, and there was Father Huw himself advancing across the grass towards them, hair and beard even more disordered than usual, and his eyes heavy and resolved and calm.

"Father Prior," he said, halting before them, "I have just come from holding council with Cadwallon, and Rhys, and Meurice, and all the men of substance in my parish. It was the best opportunity, though I'm sad indeed about the cause. They all came to the mourning for Rhisiart. Every man there knew how he had been struck down, and how such a fate was prophesied. . . ."

"God forbid," said Prior Robert hastily, "that I should threaten any man's death. I said that Saint Winifred would be revenged in her own time on the man who stood in the way and did her offence, I never said word of killing."

"But when he was dead you did claim that this was the saint's vengeance. Every man there heard it, and most believed. I took this chance of conferring with them again in the matter. They do not wish to do anything that is against the will of heaven, nor to give offence to the Benedictine order and the abbey of Shrewsbury. They do not think it right or wise, after what has happened, even to put any man, woman or child of Gwytherin in peril. I am commissioned, Father Prior, to tell you that they withdraw all opposition to your plans. The relics of Saint Winifred are yours to take away with you."

Prior Robert drew a great breath of triumph

and joy, and whatever will he might have had to deal even the lightest punishment left him in an instant. It was everything he had hoped for. Brother Columbanus, still kneeling, cast up his eyes radiantly towards heaven and clasped his hands in gratitude, and somehow contrived to look as though he had brought about this desired consummation himself, the deprivation caused by his unfaithfulness compensated in full by this reward of his penitence. Brother Jerome, just as determined to impress prior and priest with his devotion, threw up his hands and uttered a reverent Latin invocation of praise to God and the saints.

"I am certain," said Prior Robert magnanimously, "that the people of Gwytherin never wished to offend, and that they have done wisely and rightly now. I am glad, for them as for my abbey, that we may complete our work here and take our leave in amity with you all. And for your part in bringing about this good ending, Father Huw, we are all grateful. You have done well for your parish and your people."

"I am bound to tell you," said Huw honestly, "that they are not at all happy at losing the saint. But none of them will hinder what you wish. If you so will, we will take you to the burial place today."

"We will go in procession after the next Mass," said the prior, unwonted animation lighting up his severe countenance now that he had his own way, "and not touch food until we have knelt at Saint Winifred's altar and given thanks." His eyes lit upon Brother Columbanus, patiently kneeling and gazing upon him with doglike eyes, still insistent upon having his sin recognised. Robert looked faintly surprised for a moment, as if he had

forgotten the young man's existence. "Rise, brother, and take heart, for you see that there is forgiveness in the air. You shall not be deprived of your share in the delight of visiting the virgin saint and paying honour to her."

"And my penance?" insisted the incorrigible penitent. There was a good deal of iron in Brother Columbanus's meekness.

"For penance you shall undertake the menial duties that fell to Brother John, and serve your fellows and their beasts until we return home. But your part in the glory of this day you shall have, and help to bear the reliquary in which the saint's bones are to rest. We'll carry it with us, and set it up before the altar. Every move we make I would have the virgin approve plainly, in all men's sight."

"And will you break the ground today?" asked Father Huw wearily. No doubt he would be glad to have the whole episode over and forgotten, and be rid of them all, so that Gwytherin could settle again to its age-old business, though short of one good man.

"No," said Prior Robert after due thought. "I wish to show forth at every stage our willingness to be guided, and the truth of what we have claimed, that our mission was inspired by Saint Winifred herself. I decree that there shall be three nights of vigil and prayer before the chapel altar, before ever we break the sod, to confirm to all that what we are doing is indeed right and blessed. We are six here, if you will join us, Father Huw. Two by two we will be watching nightlong in the chapel, and pray to be guided rightly."

They took up the silver-inlaid coffin made in implicit faith in Shrewsbury, and carried it in procession up through the woods, past Cadwallon's house, taking the right-hand path that led them obliquely away from the scene of Rhisiart's death, until they came to a small clearing on a hillside, ringed round on three sides by tall, thick clumps of hawthorn, then in snowy bloom. The chapel was of wood, dark with age, small and shadowy within, a tiny bell-turret without a bell leaning over the doorway. Round it the old graveyard lay spread like billowing green skirts, thick with herbs and brambles and tall grasses. By the time they reached this place they had a silent and ever-growing company of local inhabitants following them, curious, submissive, wary. There was no way of telling whether they still felt resentment. Their eyes were steady, observant and opaque, determined to miss nothing and give nothing away.

At the sagging wooden gate that still hung where the path entered, Prior Robert halted, and made the sign of the cross with large, grave gestures. "Wait here!" he said, when Huw would have led him forward. "Let us see if prayer can guide my feet, for I have prayed. You shall not show me the saint's grave. I will show it to you, if she will be my aid."

Obediently they stood and watched his tall figure advance with measured steps, as if he felt his way, the skirts of his habit sweeping through the tangles of grass and flowers. Without hesitation and without haste he made his way to a little, overgrown mound aligned with the east end of the chapel, and sank to his knees at its head.

"Saint Winifred lies here," he said.

Cadfael thought about it every step of the way, as he went up through the woods that afternoon to Rhisiart's hall. A man could count on Prior Robert to be impressive, but that little miracle had been a master-stroke. The breathless hush, the rippling outbreak of comment and wonder and awe among the men of Gwytherin were with him still. No question but the remotest villein hut and the poorest free holding in the parish would be buzzing with the news by now. The monks of Shrewsbury were vindicated. The saint had taken their prior by the hand and led him to her grave. No, the man had never before been to that place, nor had the grave been marked in any way, by a belated attempt to cut the brambles from it, for instance. It was as it had always been, and yet he had known it from all the rest.

No use at all pointing out, to a crowd swayed by emotion, that if Prior Robert had not previously been to the chapel, Brothers Jerome and Columbanus, his most faithful adherents, had, only the previous day, and with the boy Edwin to guide them, and what more probable than that one of them should have asked the child the whereabouts of the lady they had come all this way to find?

And now, with this triumph already establishing his claim, Robert had given himself three whole days and nights of delay, in which other, similar prodigies might well confirm his ascendancy. A very bold step, but then, Robert was a bold and resourceful man, quite capable of gambling his chances of providing further miracles against any risk of contrary chance refuting him. He meant to leave Gwytherin with what he had come for, but to leave it, if not fully reconciled, then permanently cowed. No scuttling away in haste with his prize of bones, as though still in terror of being thwarted.

But he could not have killed Rhisiart, thought Cadfael with certainty. That I know. Could he have gone so far as to procure...? He considered the possibility honestly, and discarded it. Robert he endured, disliked, and in a fashion admired. At Brother John's age he would have detested him, but Cadfael was old, experienced and grown tolerant.

He came to the gatehouse of Rhisiart's holding, a wattle hut shored into a corner of the palisade fence. The man knew him again from yesterday, and let him in freely. Cai came across the enclosed court to meet him, grinning. All grins here were somewhat soured and chastened now, but a spark of inward mischief survived.

"Have you come to rescue your mate?" asked Cai. "I doubt he wouldn't thank you, he's lying snug, and feeding like a fighting cock, and no threats of the bailiff yet. *She's* said never a word, you may be sure, and Father Huw would be in no hurry. I reckon we've a couple of days yet, unless your prior makes it his business, where it's none. And if he does, we have boys out will give us plenty of notice before any horseman reaches the gate. Brother John's in good hands."

It was Engelard's fellow-worker speaking, the man who knew him as well as any in this place. Clearly Brother John had established himself with his gaoler, and Cai's mission was rather to keep the threatening world from him, than to keep him from sallying forth into the world. When the key was needed for the right purpose, it would be provided.

"Take care for your own head," said Cadfael,

though without much anxiety. They knew what they were doing. "Your prince may have a lawyer's mind, and want to keep in with the Benedictines along the border."

"Ah, never fret! An escaped felon can be nobody's fault. And everybody's quarry and nobody's prize! Have you never hunted zealously in all the wrong places for something you desired not to find?"

"Say no more," said Cadfael, "or I shall have to stop my ears. And tell the lad I never even asked after him, for I know there's no need."

"Would you be wishing to have a gossip with him?" offered Cai generously. "He's lodged over yonder in a nice little stable that's clean and empty, and he gets his meals princely, I tell you!"

"Tell me nothing, for I might be asked," said Cadfael. "A blind eye and a deaf ear can be useful sometimes. I'll be glad to spend a while with you presently, but now I'm bound to *her.* We have business together."

Sioned was not in the hall, but in the small chamber curtained off at its end, Rhisiart's private room. And Rhisiart was private there with his daughter, stretched out straight and still on draped furs, on a trestle table, with a white linen sheet covering him. The girl sat beside him, waiting, very formally attired, very grave, her hair austerely braided about her head. She looked older, and taller, now that she was the lady-lord of this holding. But she rose to meet Brother Cadfael with the bright, sad, eager smile of a child sure now of counsel and guidance.

"I looked for you earlier. No matter, I'm glad you're here. I have his clothes for you. I did not fold them; if I had, the damp would have spread evenly through, and now, though they may have dried off, I think you'll still feel a difference." She brought them, chausses, tunic and shirt, and he took them from her one by one and felt at the cloth testingly. "I see," she said, "that you already know where to feel."

Rhisiart's hose, though partly covered by the tunic he had worn, were still damp at the back of the thighs and legs, but in front dry, though the damp had spread round through the threads to narrow the dry part to a few inches. His tunic was moist all down the back to the hem, the full width of his shoulders still shaped in a dark patch like spread wings, but all the breast of it, round the dark-rimmed slit the arrow had made, was quite dry. The shirt, though less definitely, showed the same pattern. The fronts of the sleeves were dry, the backs damp. Where the exit wound pierced his back, shirt and tunic were soaked in blood now drying and encrusted.

"You remember," said Cadfael, "just how he lay when we found him?"

"I shall remember it my life long," said Sioned. "From the hips up flat on his back, but his right hip turned into the grass, and his legs twisted, the left over the right, like...." She hesitated, frowning, feeling for her own half-glimpsed meaning, and found it. "Like a man who has been lying on his face, and heaves himself over in his sleep on to his back, and sleeps again at once."

"Or," said Cadfael, "like a man who has been taken by the left shoulder, as he lay on his face, and heaved over on to his back. After he was well asleep!"

She gazed at him steadily, with eyes hollow and dark like wounds. "Tell me all your thoughts. I need to know. I must know."

"First, then," said Brother Cadfael, "I call attention to the place where this thing happened. A close-set, thicketed place, with plenty of bushes for cover, but not more than fifty paces clear view in any direction. Is that an archer's ground? I think not. Even if he wished the body to be left in woodlands where it might lie undiscovered for hours, he could have found a hundred places more favourable to him. An expert bowman does not need to get close to his quarry, he needs room to draw on a target he can hold in view long enough for a steady aim."

"Yes," said Sioned. "Even if it could be believed of him that he would kill, that rules out Engelard."

"Not only Engelard, any good bowman, and if someone so incompetent as to need so close a shot tried it, I doubt if he could succeed. I do not like this arrow, it has no place here, and yet here it is. It has one clear purpose, to cast the guilt on Engelard. But I cannot get it out of my head that it has some other purpose, too."

"To kill!" said Sioned, burning darkly.

"Even that I question, mad though it may seem. See the angle at which it enters and leaves. And then see how the blood is all at the back, and not where the shaft entered. And remember all we have said and noted about his clothes, how they were wet behind, though he lay on his back. And how you yourself said it was the attitude of a man who had heaved himself over from lying on his face. And one more thing I found out yesterday, as I kneeled beside him. Under him the thick grass was wet. But all down by his right side, shoulder to hip and body-wide, it was bone-dry. There was a brisk shower yesterday morning, half an hour of rain. When that rain began, your father was lying on his face, already dead. How else could that patch of grass have remained dry, but sheltered by his body?"

"And then," said Sioned low but clearly, "as you say, he was taken by his left shoulder and heaved over on to his back. When he was well asleep. Deep asleep!"

"So it looks to me!"

"But the arrow entered his breast," she said. "How, then, could he fall on his face?"

"That we have to find out. Also why he bled behind, and not in front. But lie on his face he did, and that from before the rain began until after it ceased, or the grass beneath him could not have been dry. From half an hour before noon, when the first drops fell, until some minutes past noon, when the sun came out again. Sioned, may I, with all reverence look closely again now at his body?"

"I know no greater reverence anyone can pay to a murdered man," she said fiercely, "than to seek out by all possible means and avenge him on his murder. Yes, handle him if your must. I'll help you. No one else! At least," she said with a pale and bitter smile, "you and I are not afraid to touch him, in case he bleeds in accusation against us."

Cadfael was sharply arrested in the act of drawing down the sheet that covered Rhisiart's body, as though what she had said had put a new and promising idea into his head. "True! There are not many who do not believe in that trial. Would you say everyone here holds by it?"

"Don't your people believe it? Don't you?" She was astonished. Her eyes rounded like a child's.

"My cloister-brothers. . . . Yes, I dare say all

or most believe in it. I? Child, I've seen too many slaughtered men handled over and over after a battle by those who finish them off, and never known one of them gush fresh blood, once the life was out of him. But what I believe or don't believe is not to the point. What the murderer believes well may be. No, you have endured enough. Leave him now to me."

Nevertheless, she did not turn her eyes away, as Cadfael drew off the covering sheet. She must have anticipated the need to examine the body further, for as yet she had left him naked, unshrouded. Washed clean of blood, Rhisiart lay composed and at rest, a thick, powerful trunk brown to the waist, whiter below. The wound under his ribs, an erect slit, now showed ugly and torn, with frayed, bluish lips, though they had done their best to smooth the lacerated flesh together.

"I must turn him," said Cadfael. "I need to see the other wound."

She did not hesitate, but with the tenderness of a mother rather than a daughter she slipped an arm under her father's shoulders, and with her free hand flattened under him from the other side, raised the stiffened corpse until he lay on his right side, his face cradled in the hollow of her arm. Cadfael steadied the stretched-out legs, and leaned to peer closely at the wound high on the left side of the back.

"You would have trouble pulling out the shaft. You had to withdraw it frontally."

"Yes." She shook for a moment, for that had been the worst of the ordeal. "The tip barely broke the skin behind, we had no chance to cut it off. Shame to mangle him so, but what could we do? And yet all that blood!"

The steel point had indeed done little more than puncture the skin, leaving a small, blackened spot, dried blood with a bluish bruise round it. But there was a further mark there, thin and clear and faint. From the black spot the brown line of another upright slit extended, a little longer above the arrow-mark than below, its length in all about as great as the width of Cadfael's thumb-joint, and a faint stain of bruising extending it slightly at either end, beyond where the skin was broken. All that blood—though in fact it was not so very much, though it took Rhisiart's life away with it—had drained out of this thin slit, and not from the wound in his breast, though that now glared, and this lay closed and secret.

"I have done," said Cadfael gently, and helped her to lay her father at peace again. When they had smoothed even the thick mane of his hair, they covered him again reverently. Then Cadfael told her exactly what he had seen. She watched him with great eyes, and thought for some moments in silence. Then she said: "I did see this mark you speak of. I could not account for it. If you can, tell me."

"It was there his life-blood came out," said Cadfael. "And not by the puncture the arrow certainly made, but by a prior wound. A wound made, as I judge, by a long dagger, and a very thin and sharp one, no common working knife. Once it was withdrawn, the wound was nearly closed. Yet the blade passed clean through him. For it was possible, afterwards, to trace and turn that same thrust backwards upon itself, and very accurately, too. What we took for the exit wound is no

exit wound at all, but an entry wound. The arrow was driven in from the front after he was dead, to hide the fact that he was stabbed in the back. That was why the ambush took place in thick undergrowth, in a tangled place. That was why he fell on his face, and why, afterwards, he was turned on his back. And why the upward course of the arrow is so improbable. It never was shot from any bow. To *thrust* in an arrow is hard work, it was made to get its power from flight. I think the way was opened first with a dagger."

"The same that struck him down from behind," she said, white and translucent as flame.

"It would seem so. Then the arrow was inserted after. Even so he could not make it penetrate further. I mistrusted that shot from the first. Engelard could have put a shaft through a couple of oak boards and clean away at that distance. So could any archer worth his pay. But to thrust it in with your hands—no, it was a strong, lusty arm that made even this crude job of it. And at least he got the line right. A good eye, a sensitive hand."

"A devil's heart," said Sioned, "and Engelard's arrow! Someone who knew where to find them, and knew Engelard would not be there to prevent." But for all her intolerable burdens, she was still thinking clearly. "I have a question yet. Why did this murderer leave it so long between killing and disguising his kill? My father was dead before ever the rain came. You have shown it clearly. But he was not turned on his back to receive Engelard's arrow until after the rain stopped. More than half an hour. Why? Was his murderer startled away by someone passing close? Did he wait in the bushes to be sure Rhisiart was dead before he dared touch him? Or did he only think of this devilish trick later, and have to go and fetch the shaft for his purpose? Why so long?"

"That," said Cadfael honestly, "I do not know."

"What do we know? That whoever it was wished to pin this thing upon Engelard. Was that the whole cause? Was my father just a disposable thing, to get rid of Engelard? Bait to trap another man? Or did someone want my father disposed of, and only afterwards realise how easy, how convenient, to dispose of Engelard, too?"

"I know no more than you," said Cadfael, himself shaken. And he thought, and wished he had not, of that young man fretting his feet tormentedly among the leaves, and flinching from Sioned's trust as from a death-wound. "Perhaps whoever it was did the deed, and slipped away, and then paused to think, and saw how easy it might be to point the act away from himself, and went back to do it. All we are sure of is this, and, child, thank God for it. Engelard has been set up as a sacrificial victim, and is clear of all taint. Keep that at heart, and wait."

"And whether we discover the real murderer or not, if ever it should be needful you will speak out for Engelard?"

"That I will, with all my heart. But for now, say nothing of this to anyone, for *we* are still here, the troublers of Gwytherin's peace, and never think that I have set us apart as immaculate. Until we know the guilty, we do not know the innocent."

"I take back nothing," said Sioned firmly, "of what I said concerning your prior."

"Nevertheless, he could not have done it. He was not out of my sight."

"No, that I accept. But he buys men, and he is utterly set upon getting his saint, and now, as I understand, he had his will. It is a cause. And never forget, Welshmen, as well as Englishmen may be for sale. I pray not many. But a few."

"I don't forget," said Cadfael.

"Who is he? *Who?* He knows my father's movements. He knows where to lay hands on Engelard's arrows. He wants God knows what from my father's death, but certainly he wants to pin murder on Engelard. Brother Cadfael, who can this man be?"

"That, God willing," he said, "you and I between us will find out. But as at this moment, I cannot judge nor guess, I am utterly astray. What was done I see, but why, or by whom, I know no more than you. But you have reminded me how the dead are known to rebel against the touch of those who struck them down, and as Rhisiart has told us much, so he may tell us all."

He told her, then, of the three nights of prayer and vigil Prior Robert had decreed, and how all the monks and Father Huw, by turns, would share the duty. But he did not tell her how Columbanus, in his single-minded innocence and his concern for his own conscience, had added one more to those who had had the opportunity to lie in wait for her father in the forest. Nor did he admit to her, and hardly to himself, that what they had discovered here lent a sinister meaning to Columbanus's revelation. Jerome out hunting his man with bow and arrow was a most unlikely conception, but Jerome creeping up behind a man's back in thick cover, with a sharp dagger in hand....

Cadfael put the thought behind him, but it did not go far. There was a certain credibility about it that he did not like at all.

"Tonight and for two nights following, two of us will be keeping watch in the chapel from after Compline in the evening until Prime in the morning. All six of us can be drawn into the same trial, and not one can feel himself singled out. After that, we'll see. Now this," said Brother Cadfael, "is what you must do...."

Chapter
Seven

fter Compline, in the soft evening light, with the slanting sunset filtering through young viridian leaves, they went up, all six together, to the wooden chapel and the solitary graveyard, to bring their first pair of pilgrims to the vigil. And there, advancing to meet them in the clearing before the gate, came another procession, eight of Rhisiart's household officers and servants, winding down out of the woods with their lord's bier upon their shoulders, and their lord's daughter, now herself their lord, walking erect and dignified before them, dressed in a dark gown and draped with a grey veil, under which her long hair lay loose in mourning. Her face was calm and fixed, her eyes looked far. She could have daunted any man, even an abbot. Prior Robert baulked at sight of her. Cadfael was proud of her.

So far from checking at sight of Robert, she gave a slight spring of hope and purpose to her step, and came on without pause. Face to face with him at three paces distance, she halted and stood so still and quiet that he might have mistaken this for submission, if he had been fool enough. But he was not a fool, and he gazed and measured silently, seeing a woman, a mere girl, who had come to match him, though not yet recognising her as his match.

"Brother Cadfael," she said, without taking her eyes from Robert's face, "stand by me now and make my words plain to the reverend prior, for I have a prayer to him for my father's sake."

Rhisiart was there at her back, not coffined, only swathed and shrouded in white linen, every line of the body and face standing clear under the tight wrappings, in a cradle of leafy branches, carried on a wooden bier. All those dark, secret Welsh eyes of the men who bore him glowed like little lamps about a catafalque, betraying nothing, seeing everything. And the girl was so young, and so solitary. Prior Robert, even in his assured situation, was uneasy. He may have been moved.

"Make your prayer, daughter," he said.

"I have heard that you intend to watch three nights in reverence to Saint Winifred, before you take her hence with you. I ask that for the ease of my father's soul, if he has offended against her, which was never his intent, he may be allowed to lie those three nights before her altar, in the care of those who keep watch. I ask that they will spare one prayer for forgiveness and rest to his soul, one only, in a long night of prayer. Is that too much to ask?"

"It is a fair asking," said Robert, "from a loyal daughter." And after all, he came of a noble family, and knew how to value the ties of blood and birth, and he was not all falsity.

"I hope for a sign of grace," said Sioned, "all the more if you approve me."

There was no way that such a request could do anything but add lustre and glory to his reputation. His opponent's heiress and only child came asking his countenance and patronage. He was more than gratified, he was charmed. He gave his consent graciously, aware of more pairs of Gwytherin eyes watching him than belonged to Rhisiart's bearers. Scattered though the households were, apart from the villein community that farmed as one family, the woods were full of eyes now wherever the strangers went. A pity they had not kept as close a watch on Rhisiart when he was man alive!

They installed his green bier on the trestles before the altar, beside the reliquary that awaited Saint Winifred's bones. The altar was small and plain, the bier almost dwarfed it, and the light that came in through the narrow east window barely illuminated the scene even by morning sunlight. Prior Robert had brought altar-cloths in the chest, and with these the trestles were draped. There the party from Rhisiart's hall left their lord lying in state, and quietly withdrew on the way home.

"In the morning," said Sioned, before she went with them, "I shall come to say my thanks to those who have asked grace for my father during the night. And so I shall do each morning, before we bury him."

She made the reverence due to Prior Robert, and went away without another word, without so much as a glance at Brother Cadfael, drawing the veil close round her face.

So far, so good! Robert's vanity and self-interest, if not his compunction, had assured her of her chance, it remained to be seen what would come of it. The order of their watches had been decreed by Robert himself, in consultation with no one but Father Huw, who wished to be the first to spend the night opening his heart to the saint's influence, if she pleased to make her presence known. His partner was Brother Jerome, of whose obsequious attendance the prior occasionally grew weary, and Cadfael was thankful for the accidental choice that suited him best. That first morning, at least, no one would know what to expect. After that the rest would have due warning, but surely no way of evading the issue.

In the morning, when they went to the chapel, it was to find a fair number of the inhabitants of Gwytherin already gathered there, though unobtrusively, lurking in the edges of the woods and under the fragrant shadow of the hawthorn hedges. Only when the prior and his companions entered the chapel did the villagers emerge silently from cover and gather close, and the first of them to draw near was Sioned, with Annest at her elbow. Way was opened for the two girls, and the people of Gwytherin closed in after them, filling the doorway of the chapel and blocking off the early light, so that only the candles on the altar cast a pale glow over the bier where the dead man lay.

Father Huw got up from his knees somewhat creakily, leaning on the solid wood of the desk till he could get his old legs straightened and working again. From the other desk beside him Jerome rose briskly and supply. Cadfael thought suspiciously of devout watch-keepers who fell asleep as comfortably as possible on their folded arms, but at the moment that was of no importance. He would hardly have expected heaven to open and rain down roses of forgiveness at Jerome's request, in any case.

"A quiet watch," said Huw, "and all most calm. I was not visited by any great experience, but such hardly fall to humble parish priests. We have prayed, child, and I trust we have been heard."

"I am grateful," said Sioned. "And before you go, will you do one more kindness for me and mine? As you have all been sufferers in this trouble and dissension, will you show your own will to mercy? You have prayed for him, now I ask you to lay your hand, each of you, upon my father's heart, in token of reassurance and forgiveness."

The people of Gwytherin, still as trees in the doorway, but live as trees, too, and all eyes as a tree is all leaves, made never a sound, and missed never a move.

"Gladly!" said Father Huw, and stepped to the bier and laid his rough hand gently on the stilled heart, and by the wagging of his beard his lips were again moving in silent intercession. All eyes turned upon Brother Jerome, for Brother Jerome was hesitating.

He did not look greatly disturbed, but he did look evasive. The face he turned upon Sioned was benevolent and sweet, and having bestowed on her the obligatory glance of compassion, he modestly lowered his eyes before her as was prescribed, and turned to look trustfully at Prior Robert.

"Father Huw holds the cure of this parish, and is subject to one discipline, but I to another. The lord Rhisiart surely carried out his religious duties faithfully, and I feel with him. But he died by violence, unconfessed and unshriven, and such a death leaves the health of his soul in doubt. I am not fit to pronounce in this case. I have prayed, but blessing is not for me to dispense without authority. If Prior Robert feels it is justified, and gives me leave, I will gladly do as I am asked."

Along this devious path Cadfael followed him with some amazement and considerable doubt. If the prior had himself authorised the death, and sent his creature out to accomplish it, Jerome could not have turned the threat back on his superior more neatly. On the other hand, knowing Jerome, this could as well be his way of flattering and courting, at this opportunity as at every other. And if Robert graciously gave his leave, did he suppose that would protect him, as having plainly handed on the guilt and the threat where they truly belonged, and leave him free to touch his victim with impunity? It would have mattered less if Cadfael had firmly believed that the murdered bleed when the murderer touches, but what he believed was very different, simply that the belief was general among most people, and could drive the guilty, when cornered, to terror and confession. That very terror and stress might even produce some small effusion of blood, though he doubted it. He was beginning to think that Jerome doubted it, too.

The watching eyes had changed their quarry, and hung heavily upon the prior. He frowned, and considered gravely for some moments, before he gave judgment. "You may do what she wishes, with a good conscience. She is asking only for forgiveness, which is every man's to give, not for absolution."

And Brother Jerome, gratefully acknowledging the instruction, stepped readily to the bier, and laid his hand upon the swathed heart without a tremor. No spurt of red showed through the shroud to accuse him. Complacently he followed Prior Robert out of the chapel, the others falling in behind, and the silent, staring people fell back from the doorway and let them pass.

And where, thought Cadfael following, does that leave us? Is he quite hardy about the ordeal, not believing in it at all, or does he feel he has passed the guilt to the guilty, whatever his own part in it, and is therefore out of danger? Or had he no part in it at all, and was all this to no purpose? He is quite narrow enough to refuse the girl a kindness, unless he could turn it to his own credit and advantage.

Well, we shall see tomorrow, reasoned Cadfael, what Robert will do when he's asked for his own forgiveness, instead of being generous with another man's.

However, things did not turn out quite as he had expected. Prior Robert had certainly elected to take that night's watch himself, along with Brother Richard. But as the two were on their way to the chapel, and passing by Cadwallon's holding, the prior was hailed by the gateman, and Cadwallon himself came hastening out to intercept him, with a burly, handsomely-dressed Welshman in a short riding tunic at his heels.

The first Cadfael knew of it was when the prior came striding back into Huw's garden with the stranger beside him, just at the hour when he should have been sinking to his knees in the sombre chapel with its tiny lights, to keep nightlong company with his dead man, in a confrontation which might yet produce fruitful evidence. But here he was, just in time to prevent Cadfael from slipping away to Bened's smithy to exchange the news of the day, and share a cup of wine. And plainly not seriously displeased at having his night's vigil disrupted, either.

"Brother Cadfael, we have a visitor, and I shall require your services. This is Griffith ap Rhys, Prince Owain's bailiff in Rhos. Cadwallon sent to him concerning the death of the lord Rhisiart, and I must make my own statement to him, and discuss what is to be done. He will be enquiring of all those who may have witness to deliver, but now he requires that I shall render my account first. I have had to send Brother Richard on to the chapel without me."

Jerome and Columbanus had been about to set out for their own beds in Cadwallon's house, but they lingered dutifully at hearing this. "I will go in your place, Father Prior," offered Jerome devotedly, certain he would be refused.

"No, you have had one sleepless night." (Had he? In that dim interior there was no being sure, even if Father Huw had been a suspicious man. And Jerome was not the kind to wear himself out needlessly.) "You must get your rest."

"I would gladly take your place, Father Prior," offered Columbanus just as ardently.

"You have your turn tomorrow. Beware, brother, of taking too much to yourself, of arrogance in the guise of humility. No, Brother Richard will keep the vigil alone tonight. You may wait, both, until you have given your witness as to what you did and saw the day before yesterday, and then leave us, and get your proper sleep."

That was a long tedious session, and greatly fretted Brother Cadfael, who was obliged to fall back on his own conception of truth, not, indeed, by translating falsely, but by adding his own view of those things that had happened in the forest by Rhisiart's body. He did not suppress anything Robert said, but he severed plain fact from supposition, the thing observed from the conclusion leaped to, on his own authority. Who was there with Welsh enough to challenge him, except Griffith ap Rhys himself? And that experienced and sceptical officer soon proved himself not only a quick and agile listener, but a very shrewd dissector of feelings and motives, too. He was, after all, Welsh to the bone, and Welsh bones were at the heart of this tangle. By the time he had dealt with Columbanus and Jerome, those two faithful watchers of whom one had turned out to be a treasonous sleeper-on-duty (though neither they nor Prior Robert saw fit to mention that lapse!), Cadfael was beginning to feel he could rely on the good sense of the prince's bailiff, and need not have gone to so much trouble to suppress most of what he himself knew and was about. Better so, though, he decided finally, for what he most needed now was time, and a day or two saved buy sending Griffith all round the parish after evidence might see the satisfactory conclusion of his own enquiries. Official justice does not dig deep, but regards what comes readily to the surface, and draws conclusions accordingly. A nagging doubt now and then is the price

it pays for speedy order and a quiet land. But Cadfael was not prepared to let the nagging doubt occur in the person of either Engelard or Brother John. No, better go his own way to the end, and have a finished case to present to bailiff and prince.

So there was nothing at all for Sioned to do, when she came the next morning, but to ask Brother Richard, that large, lazy, kindly man who willed peace and harmony all round him, for his personal pity towards her father, and his benediction in the laying on of hands. Which he gave willingly and guilelessly, and departed still in ignorance of what he had done, and what he had been absolved from doing.

"I missed you," said Bened, briefly visited between Mass and dinner. "Padrig came down for a while, we were talking over the old days, when Rhisiart was younger. Padrig's been coming here a good many years now. He knows us all. He asked after you."

"Tell him we'll share a cup one of these days, here or there. And say I'm about Rhisiart's business, if that's any comfort."

"We're getting used to you," said Bened, stooping to his fire, where a sinewy boy was bending into the bellows. "You should stay, there'd be a place for you."

"I've got my place," said Cadfael. "Never fret about me. I chose the cowl with both eyes open. I knew what I did."

"There are some I can't reconcile with you," said Bened, with the iron in hand for the shoe that waited.

"Ah, priors and brothers come and go, as mixed as the rest of men, but the cloister remains. Now, there are some who did lose their way, I grant you," said Cadfael, "mostly young things who mistook a girl's 'no' for the end of the world. Some of them might make very useful craftsmen, if ever they broke free. Always supposing they were free men, and could get entry to, say, the smith's mystery...."

"He has a good arm and wrist on him, that one," said Bened reflectively, "and knows how to jump and do as he's bid when the man bidding knows his business. That's half the craft. If he hasn't let Rhisiart's killer loose on the world, then there isn't an outlander would be more welcome here. But that I don't yet know, though the poor girl up yonder may think she does. How if she's wrong? Do *you* know?"

"Not yet," owned Cadfael. "But give us time, and we shall know."

On this third day of Brother John's nominal captivity he found himself more closely confined. The word had gone round that the bailiff was in the parish and asking questions everywhere concerning the circumstances of Rhisiart's death, and it was known that he had had a lengthy session with the prior at Father Huw's parsonage, and must certainly have been urged and admonished as to his duty to take action also in the matter of Brother John's crime. Not that John had any complaints as to his lodging, his food or his company; he had seldom been so completely content. But for two days, with brief intervals when caution had seemed advisable, he had been out from dawn to dusk about the holding, lending a hand with the cattle, replenishing the wood-pile, fetching and carrying, planting out in the vegetable garden, and had had neither time nor inclination to worry about his situation. Now that he was hustled out of

sight, and sat idle in the stable, the realities fretted even John, and the want of Welsh, or of Brother Cadfael to supply the want, was a frustration no longer so easy to bear. He did not know what Cadfael and Sioned were up to, he did not know what was happening to Saint Winifred, or to Prior Robert and his fellows, and above all he did not know where Engelard was, or how he was to be extricated from the tangle of suspicion roused against him. Since his instinctive gesture of solidarity, John took a proprietorial interest in Engelard, and wanted him safe, vindicated, and happy with his Sioned.

But Sioned, true to her word, did not come near him, and there was no one else in the holding who could talk to him freely. Simple things could be conveyed, but there was no way of communicating to him everything he wanted and needed to know. There was he, willing but useless, wondering and fretting how his friends were faring, and quite unable to do anything to aid them.

Annest brought his dinner, and sat by him while he ate, and the same want of words troubled her. It was all very well teaching him simple words and phrases in Welsh by touching the thing she meant, but how to set about pouring out to him, as she would have liked, all that was happening at the chapel, and what the village was saying and thinking? The helplessness of talking at all made their meetings almost silent, but sometimes they did speak aloud, he in English, she in Welsh, saying things because they could not be contained, things that would be understood by the other only in some future day, though the tone might convey at least the sense of friendship, like a kind of restrained caress. Thus they conducted two little monologues which yet were an exchange and a comfort.

Sometimes, though they did not know it, they were even answering each other's questions.

"I wonder who she was," said Annest, soft and hesitant, "that one who drove you to take the cowl? Sioned and I, we can't help wondering how a lad like you ever came to do it." Now if he had known Welsh, she could never have said that to him.

"How did I ever come to think that Margery such a beauty!" marvelled John. "And take it so hard when she turned me down? But I'd never really seen beauty then—I'd never seen *you*!"

"She did us all a bad turn," said Annest, sighing, "whoever she was, driving you into that habit for life!"

"Dear God," said John, "to think I might have married her! At least she did me that much of a favour, with her 'no.' There's only the matter of a cowl between you and me, not a wife." And that was the first moment when he had entertained the dazzling idea that escape from his vows might be possible at all. The thought caused him to turn his head and look with even closer and more ardent attention at the fair face so close to his. She had smooth, rounded, apple-blossom cheeks, and delicate, sun-glossed bones, and eyes like brook-water in the sun over bright pebbles, glittering, polished, crystal-clear.

"Do you still fret after her?" wondered Annest in a whisper. "A conceited ninny who hadn't the wit to know a good man when she saw one?" For he was indeed a very well-grown, handy, handsome, good-humoured young fellow, with his long, sturdy legs and his big, deft hands, and his bush of russet curls, and the girl who thought herself too good for him must have been the world's fool. "I hate her!" said Annest, leaning unwarily towards him.

The lips that tantalised him with soft utterances he could not understand were only a little way from his own. He resorted in desperation to a kind of sign-language that needed no interpreter. He hadn't kissed a girl since Margery, the draper's daughter, threw him over when her father became bailiff of Shrewsbury, but it seemed he hadn't forgotten how. And Annest melted into his arms, where she fitted a great deal better than his too-hasty vows had ever fitted him.

"Oh, Annest!" gasped Brother John, who had never in his life felt less like a brother, "I think I love you!"

Brother Cadfael and Brother Columbanus walked up through the woodland together, to keep the third night of prayer. The evening was mild and still but overcast, and under the trees the light grew dusky green. Until the last moment it had remained a possibility that Prior Robert, having missed his chosen night of duty, might elect to be present on this last occasion, but he had said no word, and to tell the truth, Cadfael was beginning to wonder if that long session with the bailiff had really been necessary at all, or whether the prior had welcomed it as an alternative to keeping the night-watch and facing Sioned with her request in the morning. Not necessarily a proof of any guilt on his part, beyond the guilt of still wishing to refuse grace to Rhisiart, without actually having to do so face to face with his daughter. For whatever virtues might be found in Prior Robert, humility was not one, nor magnanimity. He was invariably sure of his own rightness, and where it was challenged he was not a forgiving man.

"In this quest and this vigil, brother," said Columbanus, his long young steps keeping easy pace with Cadfael's seaman's roll, "we are greatly privileged. The history of our abbey will record our names, and brothers in the generations to come will envy us."

"I have already heard," said Cadfael drily, "that Prior Robert is proposing to write a life of Saint Winifred, and complete it with the story of this translation to Shrewsbury. You think he'll record the names of *all* his companions?" Yours, however, he thought, he well might mention, as the afflicted brother who first fell sick and was sent to Holywell to be cured. And Jerome's, who had the dream that took you there. But mine, I feel sure, will remain a silence, and so much the better!

"I have a fault to atone for," recalled Columbanus devoutly, "having betrayed my trust once in this same chapel, I, who most of all should have been faithful." They were at the decrepit gate, the tangle of the graveyard before them, threaded by a narrow path just discernible through the long grass. "I feel a holy air reaching out to me," said the young man, quivering, his face uplifted and pale. "I am drawn into a light. I believe we are approaching a wonder, a miracle of grace. Such mercy to me, who fell asleep in betrayal of her service!" And he led the way to the open door, his stride lengthening in eagerness, his hands extended as if to clasp a mistress rather than make obeisance before a saint. Cadfael followed morosely but resignedly, used to these uncomfortable ardours, but not looking forward to being confined in so small a chapel with them overnight. He had

thinking as well as praying to do, and Columbanus was not conducive to either activity.

Inside the chapel the air was heavy with the scent of old wood, and the spices and incense of the draperies on which the reliquary lay, and the faint, aromatic aura of years of dust and partial disuse. A small oil-lamp burned with a dark yellow flame on the altar, and Cadfael went forward and lit the two altar candles from it, and set them one on either side. Through the narrow east window the fragrance of the falling may-blossom breathed freshness on a very light breeze, causing the flames to flicker for a few minutes. Their faint, dancing radiance glanced from every near surface, but did not reach the corners of the roof, or fix the walls in place. They were in a narrow cavern of brown, wood-scented darkness, with a dim focus of light before them, that shone on an empty coffin and an uncoffined body, and just showed them the rough outlines of the two prayer-desks drawn up side by side at a little distance from the catafalque. Rhisiart lay nearer to them, the black and silver bulk of the reliquary like a low wall shading him from the altar lights.

Brother Columbanus bowed humbly low to the altar, and took his place at the desk on the right. Brother Cadfael settled solidly at the one on the left, and with practised movements sought and found the best place for his knees. Stillness came down on them gently. He composed himself for a long watch, and said his prayer for Rhisiart, not the first he had said for him. Great darkness and constant, feeble light, the slow flowing of time from far beyond his conception to far beyond his power to follow, the solitude about him and the troubled and peopled world within, all these settled into their perpetual pattern, a steady rhythm as perfect as sleep. He thought no more of Columbanus, he forgot that Columbanus existed. He prayed as he breathed, forming no words and making no specific requests, only holding in his heart, like broken birds in cupped hands, all those people who were in stress or in grief because of this little saint, for if he suffered like this for their sake, how much more must she feel for them?

The candles would last the night, and by instinct he traced time by the rate at which they dwindled, and knew when it was near to midnight.

He was thinking of Sioned, to whom he had nothing but himself to offer in the morning, this pietistic innocent being essentially nothing, and Cadfael himself by no means enough, when he heard the faintest and strangest of sounds issuing from the prie-dieu on his right, where Columbanus leaned in total absorption. Not now with face hidden on his linked hands, but uplifted and strained upwards into what light could reach him, and faint though it was, it conjured his sharp profile into primrose pallor. His eyes were wide open and staring beyond the chapel wall, and his lips open and curved in ecstasy, and singing, a mere thread of Latin chant in praise of virginity. It was barely audible, yet clear as in a dream. And before Cadfael was fully aware of what he heard, he saw the young man thrust himself upwards, holding by the desk, and stand upright before the altar. The chant ceased. Suddenly he reared himself erect to his tallest, drawing back his head as though he would see through the roof into a spring night full of stars, and

spreading out his arms on either side like a man stretched on a cross. He gave a great, wordless cry, seemingly both of pain and triumph, and fell forward full-length on the earthen floor, crashing to the ground stiffly, arms still outspread, body stretched to the very toes, and lay still, his forehead against the trailing fringe of the altar-cloth that spilled from beneath Rhisiart's body.

Cadfael got up in a hurry and went to him, torn between anxiety and alarm on one hand, and disgusted resignation on the other. Exactly what was to be expected of the idiot, he thought with exasperation, even as he was on his knees feeling at the prone brow, and adjusting a fold of the altar drapery under it to ease the position of nose and mouth, turning the young man's head to one side so that he could breathe freely. I should have recognised the signs! Never an opportunity but he can produce a devotional fit or a mystic ecstasy to order. One of these days he'll be drawn into that light of his, and never come back. Yet I've noticed he can fall flat on his face without hurting himself, and go into pious convulsions over his visions or his sins without ever hurling himself against anything sharp or hard, or even biting his tongue. The same sort of providence that takes care of drunken men looks out for Columbanus in his throes. And he reflected at the back of his mind, and tartly, that there ought somewhere to be a moral in that, lumping all excesses together.

No convulsions this time, at any rate. He had simply seen whatever he had seen, or thought he had seen, and fallen down before it in this destroying rapture. Cadfael shook him by the shoulder gently, and then more sharply, but he was rigid and unresponsive.

His forehead was cool and smooth, his features, very dimly seen, yet looked serene, composed, if anything, in a gentle and joyful peace. But for the rigidity of body and limbs, and that unnatural attitude as though he lay stretched on a cross, he might have been asleep. All Cadfael had been able to do by way of easing him was to turn his head so that he lay on his right cheek, pillowed on the draperies. When he tried to bend the right arm and turn the young man more comfortably on his side, the joints resisted him, so he let well enough alone.

And now, he thought, what am I supposed to do? Abandon my watch and go down and fetch the prior with help for him? What could they do for him that I cannot do here? If I can't rouse him, then neither could they. He'll come out of it when the right time comes, and not before. He's done himself no injury, his breathing is steady and deep. His heart beats strongly and regularly, he has no fever. Why interfere with a man's peculiar pleasures, if they're doing him no harm? It isn't cold here, and he can have one of these altar-cloths for blanket, a fancy that ought to please him. No, we came to watch out the night together, and so we will, I here on my knees as is due, and he wherever he may be at this moment in his dreams.

He covered Columbanus, adjusted the cloths to cushion his head, and went back to his own prie-dieu. But whatever this visitation had done for Columbanus, it had shattered all possibility of thought or concentration for Cadfael. The more he tried to focus his mind whether upon his duty of prayer and meditation, or the urgent need to consider where Sioned stood now, and what more could be done, the more was he drawn to look again at the prone body, and listen again to make sure it still breathed as evenly as ever. What should have been a profitable night hung heavy upon him, wasted as worship, useless as thought, as long and dreary and tedious a night as he had ever passed.

The first dove-grey softening of the darkness came as a blessing, bringing release at least within sight. The narrow space of sky seen through the altar window changed from grey to pale, clear green, from green to saffron, from saffron to gold, a cloudless morning, the first sunray piercing through the slit and falling on the altar, the reliquary, the shrouded body, and then striking like a golden sword across the chapel, leaving Columbanus in darkness. Still he lay rigid, yet breathing deeply and softly, and no touch or word could reach him.

He was in the same condition when Prior Robert came with his fellows, and Sioned with Annest in attendance, and all the people from the village and the nearby holdings, silent and watchful as before, to see the end of this three-night vigil.

Sioned was the first to enter, and the dimness within, after the brightness without, made her blind for a moment, so that she halted in the doorway until her eyes should grow accustomed to the change. Prior Robert was close behind her when she saw the soles of Brother Columbanus's sandals upturned before her, just touched by the sunray from the window, while the rest of him lay still in shadow. Her eyes widened in wonder and horror, and before Cadfael could rise and turn to reassure her she had uttered a sharp cry: "What is it? Is he dead?"

The prior put her aside quickly, and strode

past her, and was brought up short with his foot on the hem of Columbanus' habit.

"What happened here? Columbanus! Brother!" He stooped and laid his hand upon a rigid shoulder. Columbanus slept and dreamed on, unmoved and unmoving. "Brother Cadfael, what does this mean? What has befallen him?"

"He is not dead," said Cadfael, putting first things first, "nor do I think he is in any danger. He breathes like a man peacefully sleeping. His colour is good, he is cool to the touch, and has no injury. Simply, at midnight he suddenly stood up before the altar, and spread out his arms and fell forward thus in trance. He has lain all night like this, but without distress or agitation."

"You should have called us to his aid," said the prior, shaken and dismayed.

"I had also a duty," said Cadfael shortly, "to remain here and keep the vigil I was sent to keep. And what could have been done for him more than I have done, in giving him a pillow for his head and a cover against the chill of the night? Nor, I think, would he have been grateful if we had carried him away before the appointed time. Now he has kept his own watch faithfully, and if we cannot rouse him we may bear him away to his bed, without doing violence to his sense of duty."

"There is something in that," said Brother Richard earnestly, "for you know that Brother Columbanus has several times been visited and favoured by visions, and it might have been a great wrong to take him away from the very place where such blessings befell him. An offence, perhaps, against the saint herself, if she was pleased to reveal herself to him. And if that is so, then he will awake when the time is right that he should, and it might do him great harm to try and hasten the hour."

"It is true," said the prior, a little reassured, "that he seems at peace, and has a good colour, and no sign of trouble or pain. This is most strange. Is it possible that this young brother will be the occasion of another such prodigy as when his affliction first drew us to Saint Winifred?"

"He was the instrument of grace once," said Richard, "and may be so again. We had better carry him down to his bed at Cadwallon's house, and keep him quiet and warm, and wait. Or had we not better take him to Father Huw's parsonage, so that he may be close to the church? It may be that his first need will be to give thanks."

With a heavy altar-cloth and their girdles they made a sling in which to carry Columbanus, lifting him from the floor, stiff as a branch, even his extended arms still rigid. They laid him on his back in their improvised litter, and he suffered whatever they did to him, and made no sound or sign. A few of the watching natives, moved and awed by the spectacle, came forward to lend a hand in carrying him down through the forest to Huw's house. Cadfael let them go. He turned to look at Sioned, as she was looking at him, with dubious and speculative eyes.

"Well, I, at least," he said, "am in my right senses, and can and will do what you have asked of me." And he stepped to Rhisiart's side, and laid his hand upon the dead man's heart, and signed his forehead with a cross.

She walked beside him as they followed the slow procession down towards the village.

"What more can we do? If you know of anything, only tell me. We have not been favoured so far. And today is to be his burial."

"I know it," said Cadfael, and brooded. "As for this affair in the night, I'm torn two ways. I should think it possible it was all planned, to reinforce our cause with another miracle, but for two things. To me Prior Robert's amazement and concern, however I look at them, seem to be true and not false. And Columbanus has shown these strange properties before, and the way they overtake him is violent and perilous, and it's hard to believe he is feigning. A tumbler at a fair, making his living by playing the devil with his own body, could not outdo Columbanus when the fit comes on him. I am not able to judge. I think there are some who live on a knife-edge in the soul, and at times are driven to hurl themselves into the air, at the mercy of heaven or hell which way to fall."

"All I know," said Sioned, burning darkly red like a slow torch, "is that my father whom I loved is murdered, and I want justice on the murderer, and I do not want a blood price. There is no price I will accept for Rhisiart's blood."

"I know, I know!" said Cadfael. "I am as Welsh as you. But keep a door open to pity, as who knows when you or I may need it! And have you spoken with Engelard? And is all well with him?"

She quivered and flushed and softened beside him, like a frost-blighted flower miraculously revived by a southern wind. But she did not answer. There was no need.

"Ah, you'll live!" said Brother Cadfael, satisfied. "As he'd want you to. Even if he did set his face against, like a proper Welsh lord. You'd have got your way in the end, you were right about that. And listen, I have thought of two things you should yet do. We must try whatever we can. Don't go home now. Let Annest take you to Bened's smithy to rest, and the both of you come to Mass. Who knows what we may learn once our half-fledged saint regains his senses? And then, also, when you bury your father, make certain Peredur comes with *his* father. He might try to avoid else, if he's eluded you this far, but if you ask him, he cannot refuse. I am still in more minds than one, and none of them very clear, concerning Master Peredur."

Chapter Eight

t was the little brazen bell ringing for Mass that penetrated Brother Columbanus' enchanted sleep at last. It could not be said that it awoke him, rather it caused him to open his closed eyes, quiver through all his frozen members, flex his stiff arms, and press his re-quickened hands together over his breast. Otherwise his face did not change, nor did he seem to be aware of those who were gathered anxiously about the bed on which he lay. They might not have been there at all. All Brother Columbanus responded to was the bell, the first call to worship. He stirred and sat up. He rose from the bed, and stood firmly on his feet. He looked radiant, but still private and apart.

"He is preparing to take his usual place with us," said the prior, moved and awed. "Let us go, and make no attempt yet to rouse him. When he has given thanks he'll come back to us, and speak out what he has experienced."

And he led the way to the church, and as he had supposed, Columbanus fell into his usual place as the youngest in the attendant brotherhood now that John was disgraced, and followed modestly, and modestly took part in the service, still like a man in a dream.

The church was full as it would hold, and there were more people clustered outside the doorway. The word had gone round already that something strange and wonderful had happened at Saint Winifred's chapel, and revelations might very well follow at Mass.

Not until the end did any further change occur in the condition of Brother Columbanus. But when the prior, slowly and expectantly, as one turning a key and almost confident of entry, took the first step towards the doorway, suddenly Columbanus gave a great start, and uttered a soft cry, staring wonderingly about him at all these known faces. His own visage came to life, smiling. He put out a hand as if to arrest the prior's departure, and said in a high voice: "Oh, Father, I have been so blessed, I have known such bliss! How did I come here, when I know I was elsewhere, and translated out of night's darkness into so glorious a light? And surely this is again the world I left! A fair world enough, but I have been in a fairer, far beyond any deserts of mine. Oh, if I could but tell you!"

Every eye was upon him, and every ear stretched to catch his least word. Not a soul left the church, rather those without crowded in closer.

"Son," said Prior Robert, with unwontedly respectful kindness, "you are here among your brothers, engaged in the worship of God, and there is nothing to fear and nothing to regret, for the visitation granted you was surely meant to inspire and arm you to go fearless through an imperfect world, in the hope of a perfect world hereafter. You were keeping night watch with Brother Cadfael at Saint Winifred's chapel— do you remember that? In the night something befell you that drew your spirit for a time away from us, out of the body, but left that body unharmed and at rest like a child asleep. We brought you back here still absent from us in the spirit, but now you are here with us again, and all is well. You have been greatly privileged."

"Oh, greatly, far more than you know," sang Columbanus, glowing like a pale lantern. "I am the messenger of such goodness, I am the instrument of reconciliation and peace. Oh, Father.... Father Huw...brothers...let me speak out here before all, for what I am bidden to tell concerns all."

Nothing, thought Cadfael, could have stopped him, so plainly did his heavenly embassage override any objection mere prior or priest might muster. And Robert was proving surprisingly compliant in accepting this transfer of authority. Either he already knew that the voice from heaven was about to say something entirely favourable to his plans and conducive to his glory, or else he was truly

impressed, and inclining heart and ear to listen as devoutly as any man there present.

"Speak freely, brother," he said, "let us share your joy."

"Father, at the hour of midnight as I knelt before the altar I heard a sweet voice crying my name, and I arose and went forward to obey the call. What happened to my body then I do not know, you tell me it was lying as if asleep when you came. But it seemed to me that as I stepped towards the altar there was suddenly a soft, golden light all about it, and there rose up, floating in the midst of the light, a most beautiful virgin, who moved in a miraculous shower of white petals, and distilled most sweet odours from her robe and from her long hair. And this gracious being spoke to me, and told me that her name was Winifred, and that she was come to approve our enterprise, and also to forgive all those who out of mistaken loyalty and reverence had opposed it hitherto. And then, oh, marvellous goodness!—she laid her hand on Rhisiart's breast, as his daughter has begged us to do in token of our mere personal forgiveness, but she in divine absolution, and with such perfection of grace, I cannot describe it."

"Oh, son," said Prior Robert in rapture, riding over the quivering murmurs that crossed the church like ripples on a pool, "you tell a greater wonder than we dared hope. Even the lost saved!"

"It is so! And, Father, there is more! When she laid her hand on him, she bade me speak out to all men in this place, both native and stranger, and make known her merciful will. And it is this 'Where my bones shall be taken out of the earth,' she said, 'there will be an open grave provided. What I relinquish, I may bestow. In this grave,' said Winifred, 'let Rhisiart be buried, that his rest may be assured, and my power made manifest.'"

"What could I do," said Sioned, "but thank him for his good offices, when he brought divine reassurance for my father's weal? And yet it outrages me, I would rather have stood up and said that I am not and never have been in the least doubt that my father is in blessedness this moment, for he was a good man who never did a mean wrong to anyone. And certainly it's kind of Saint Winifred to offer him the lodging she's leaving, and graciously forgive him, but—forgiveness for what? Absolution for what? She might have praised him while she was about it, and said outright that he was justified, not forgiven."

"Yet a very ambassadorial message," admitted Cadfael appreciatively, "calculated to get us what we came for, assuage the people of Gwytherin, make peace all round—"

"And to placate me, and cause me to give up the pursuit of my father's murderer," said Sioned, "burying the deed along with the victim. Except that I will not rest until I know."

"—and shed reflected glory upon Prior Robert, I was going to say. And I wish I knew which mind conceived the idea!"

They had met for a few hurried minutes at Bened's smithy, where Cadfael had gone to borrow mattock and spade for the holy work now to be undertaken. Even a few of the men of Gwytherin had come forward and asked to have a share in breaking the sacred earth, for though they were still reluctant to lose their saint, if it was her will to leave them they had no wish to cross her. Prodigious things were happening, and they intended to be in receipt

of her approval and blessing rather than run the risk of encountering her arrows.

"It seems to me most of the glory is falling, rather, on Brother Columbanus of late," said Sioned shrewdly. "And the prior took it meekly, and never made any attempt to filch it back from him. That's the one thing that makes me believe he may be honest."

She had said something that caused Cadfael to pause and look attentively at her, scrubbing dubiously at his nose. "You may well be right. And certainly this story is bound to go back to Shrewsbury with us, and spread through all our sister houses, when we come home with our triumph. Yes, Columbanus will certainly have made himself a great name for holiness and divine favour in the order."

"They say an ambitious man can make a grand career in the cloister," she said. "Maybe he's busy laying the foundations, a great step up towards being prior himself when Robert becomes abbot. Or even abbot, when Robert supposes *he's* about to become abbot! For it's not *his* name they'll be buzzing round the shires as the visionary the saints use to make their wants known."

"That," agreed Cadfael, "may not even have dawned on Robert yet, but when the awe of the occasion passes it will. And he's the one who's pledged to write a life of the saint, and complete it with the account of this pilgrimage. Columbanus may very well end up as an anonymous brother who happened to be charged with a message to the prior from his patroness. Chroniclers can edit names out as easily as visionaries can noise them abroad. But I grant you, this lad comes of a thrusting Norman family that doesn't put even its younger sons into the Benedictine habit to spend their lives doing menial work like gardening."

"And we're no further forward," said Sioned bitterly.

"No. But we have not finished yet."

"But as I see it, this is devised to be an ending, to close this whole episode in general amity, as if everything was resolved. But everything is *not* resolved! Somewhere in this land there is a man who stabbed my father in the back, and we're all being asked to draw a veil over that and lose sight of it in the great treaty of peace. But I want that man found, and Engelard vindicated, and my father avenged, and I won't rest, or let anyone else rest, until I get what I want. And now tell me what I am to do."

"What I've already told you," said Cadfael. "Have all your household party and friends gathered at the chapel to watch the grave opened, and make sure that Peredur attends."

"I've already sent Annest to beg him to come," said Sioned. "And then? What have I to say or do to Peredur?"

"That silver cross you wear round your neck," said Cadfael. "Are you willing to part with it in exchange for one step ahead towards what you want to know?"

"That and all the rest of the valuables I own. You know it."

"Then this," said Cadfael, "is what you will do...."

With prayers and psalms they carried their tools up to the tangled graveyard by the chapel, trimmed back the brambles and wild flowers and long grass from the little mound of Winifred's grave, and reverently broke the sod. By turns they laboured, all taking a share in the work for the merit to be acquired. And most of Gwytherin gathered round the place in the course of the day, all work left at a standstill in the fields and crofts, to watch the end of this contention. For Sioned had spoken truly. She and all her household servants were there among the rest, in mourning and massed to bring out Rhisiart's body for burial when the time came, but this funeral party had become, for the time being, no more than a side-issue, an incident in the story of Saint Winifred, and a closed incident at that.

Cadwallon was there, Uncle Meurice was there, and Bened, and all the other neighbours. And there at his father's elbow, withdrawn and brooding, stood young Peredur, by the look of him wishing himself a hundred leagues away. His thick dark brows were drawn together as though his head ached, and wherever his brown eyes wandered, it was never towards Sioned. He had crept here reluctantly at her express asking, but he could not or would not face her. The bold red mouth was chilled and pale from the tension with which it was tightened against his teeth. He watched the dark pit deepen in the grass, and breathed hard and deep, like a man containing pain. A far cry from the spoiled boy with the long, light step and the audacious smile, who so plainly had taken it for granted that the world was his for the wooing. Peredur's demons were at him within.

The ground was moist but light, not hard to work, but the grave was deep. Gradually the diggers sank to the shoulders in the pit, and by mid-afternoon Brother Cadfael, shortest of the party, had almost disappeared from view when he took his final turn in the depths. No one dared to doubt openly if they were in the right place, but some must have been wondering. Cadfael, for no good reason that he could see, had no doubts at all. The girl was here. She had lived many years as an abbess after her brief martyrdom and miraculous restoration, yet he thought of her as that devout, green girl, in romantic love with celibacy and holiness, who had fled from Prince Cradoc's advances as from the devil himself. By some perverse severance of the heart in two he could feel both for her and for the desperate lover, so roughly molten out of the flesh and presumably exterminated in the spirit. Did anyone every pray for him? He was in greater need than Winifred. In the end, perhaps the only prayers he ever benefited by were Winifred's prayers. She was Welsh, and capable of detachment and subtlety. She might well have put in a word for him, to reassemble his liquefied person and congeal it again into the shape of a man. A chastened man, doubtless, but still the same shape as before. Even a saint may take pleasure, in retrospect, in having been once desired.

The spade grated on something in the dark, friable soil, something neither loam nor stone. Cadfael checked his stroke instantly at its suggestion of age, frailty and crumbling dryness. He let the blade lie, and stooped to scoop away with his hands the cool, odorous, gentle earth that hid the obstruction from him. Dark soil peeled away under his fingers from a slender, pale, delicate thing, the gentle dove-grey of pre-dawn, but freckled with pitted points of black. He drew out an arm-bone, scarcely more than child size, and stroked away the clinging earth. Islands of the same soft colouring showed below, grouped loosely together. He did not want to break any of them. He hoisted the spade and tossed it out of the pit.

"She is here. We have found her. Softly, now, leave her to me."

Faces peered in upon him. Prior Robert

gleamed in silvery agitation, thirsting to plunge in and dredge up the prize in person, but deterred by the clinging darkness of the soil and the whiteness of his hands. Brother Columbanus at the brink towered and glittered, his exalted visage turned, not towards the depths where this fragile virgin substance lay at rest, but rather to the heavens from which her diffused spiritual essence had addressed him. He displayed, no doubt of it, an aura of distinct proprietorship that dwarfed both prior and sub-prior, and shone with its full radiance upon all those who watched from the distance. Brother Columbanus meant to be, was, and knew that he was, memorable in this memorable hour.

Brother Cadfael kneeled. It may even have been a significant omen that at this moment he alone was kneeling. He judged that he was at the feet of the skeleton. She had been there some centuries, but the earth had dealt kindly, she might well be whole, or virtually whole. He had not wanted her disturbed at all, but now he wanted her disturbed as little as might be, and delved carefully with scooping palms and probing, stroking finger-tips to uncover the whole slender length of her without damage. She must have been a little above medium height, but willowy as a seventeen-year-old girl. Tenderly he stroked the earth away from round her. He found the skull, and leaned on stretched arms, fingering the eye-sockets clear, marvelling at the narrow elegance of the cheek-bones, and the generosity of the dome. She had beauty and fineness in her death. He leaned over her like a shield, and grieved.

"Let me down a linen sheet," he said, "and some bands to raise it smoothly. She shall not come out of here bone by bone, but whole woman as she went in."

"They handed a cloth down to him, and he spread it beside the slight skeleton, and with infinite care eased her free of the loose soil, and edged her by inches into the shroud of linen, laying the disturbed arm-bone in its proper place. With bands of cloth slung under her she was drawn up into the light of day, and laid tenderly in the grass at the side of her grave.

"We must wash away the soil-marks from her bones," said Prior Robert, gazing in reverent awe upon the prize he had gone to such trouble to gain, "and wrap them afresh."

"They are dry and frail and brittle," warned Cadfael impatiently. "If she is robbed of this Welsh earth she may very well crumble to Welsh earth herself in your hands. And if you keep her here in the air and the sun too long, she may fall to dust in any case. If you are wise, Father Prior, you'll wrap her well as she lies, and get her into the reliquary and seal her from the air as tight as you can, as quickly as you can."

That was good sense, and the prior acted on it, even if he did not much relish being told what to do so brusquely. With hasty but exultant prayers they brought the resplendent coffin out to the lady, to avoid moving her more than they must, and with repeated swathings of linen bound her little bones carefully together, and laid her in the coffin. The brothers who made it had realised the need for perfect sealing to preserve the treasure, and taken great pains to make the lid fit down close as a skin, and line the interior with lead. Before Saint Winifred was carried back into the chapel for the thanksgiving Mass the lid was closed upon her, the catches secured, and

at the end of the service the prior's seals were added to make all fast. They had her imprisoned, to be carried away into the alien land that desired her patronage. All the Welsh who could crowd into the chapel or cling close enough to the doorway to catch glimpses of the proceedings kept a silence uncannily perfect, their eyes following every move, secret eyes that expressed no resentment, but by their very attention, fixed and unwavering, implied an unreconciled opposition they were afraid to speak aloud.

"Now that this sacred duty is done," said Father Huw, at once relieved and saddened, "it is time to attend to the other duty which the saint herself has laid upon us, and bury Rhisiart honourably, with full absolution, in the grave she has bequeathed to him. And I call to mind, in the hearing of all, how great a blessing is thus bestowed, and how notable an honour." It was as near as he would go to speaking out his own view of Rhisiart, and in this, at least, he had the sympathy of every Welshman there present.

That burial service was brief, and after it six of Rhisiart's oldest and most trusted servants took up the bier of branches, a little wilted now but still green, and carried it out to the graveside. The same slings which had lifted Saint Winifred waited to lower Rhisiart into the same bed.

Sioned stood beside her uncle, and looked all round her at the circle of her friends and neighbours, and unclasped the silver cross from her neck. She had so placed herself that Cadwallon and Peredur were close at her right hand, and it was simple and natural to turn towards them. Peredur had hung back throughout, never looking at her but when he was sure she was looking away, and when she swung round upon him suddenly he had no way of avoiding.

"One last gift I want to give to my father. And I would like you, Peredur, to be the one to give it. You have been like a son to him. Will you lay this cross on his breast, where the murderer's arrow pierced him? I want it to be buried with him. It is my farewell to him here, let it be yours, too."

Peredur stood dumbstruck and aghast, staring from her still and challenging face to the little thing she held out to him, in front of so many witnesses, all of whom knew him, all of whom were known to him. She had spoken clearly, to be heard by all. Every eye was on him, and all recorded, though without understanding, the slow draining of blood from his face, and his horror-stricken stare. He could not refuse what she asked. He could not do it without touching the dead man, touching the very place where death had struck him.

His hand came out with aching reluctance, and took the cross from her. To leave her thus extending it in vain was more than he could stand. He did not look at it, but only desperately at her, and in her face the testing calm had blanched into incredulous dismay, for now she believed she knew everything, and it was worse than anything she had imagined. But as he could not escape from the trap she had laid for him, neither could she release him. It was sprung, and now he had to fight his way out of it as best he could. They were already wondering why he made no move, and whispering together in concern at his hanging back.

He made a great effort, drawing himself together with a frantic briskness that lasted only a moment. He took a few irresolute steps towards the bier and the grave, and then baulked like a frightened horse, and halted again, and that was worse, for now he stood alone in the middle of the circle of witnesses, and could go neither forward nor back. Cadfael saw sweat break in great beads on his forehead and lip.

"Come, son," said Father Huw kindly, the last to suspect evil, "don't keep the dead waiting, and don't grieve too much for them, for that would be sin. I know, as Sioned has said, he was like another father to you, and you share her loss. So do we all."

Peredur stood quivering at Sioned's name, and at the word "father," and tried to go forward, and could not move. His feet would not take him one step nearer to the swathed form that lay by the open grave. The light of the sun on him, the weight of all eyes, bore him down. He fell on his knees suddenly, the cross still clutched in one hand, the other spread to hide his face.

"He cannot!" he cried hoarsely from behind the shielding palm. "He cannot accuse me! I am not guilty of murder! What I did was done when Rhisiart was already dead!"

A great, gasping sigh passed like a sudden wind round the clearing and over the tangled grave, and subsided into a vast silence. It was a long minute before Father Huw broke it, for this was his sheep, not Prior Robert's, a child of his flock, and hitherto a child of grace, now stricken into wild self-accusation of some terrible sin not yet explained, but to do with violent death.

"Son Peredur," said Father Huw firmly, "you have not been charged with any ill-doing by any other but yourself. We are waiting only for you to do what Sioned has asked of you, for her asking was a grace.

Therefore do her bidding, or speak out why you will not, and speak plainly."

Peredur heard, and ceased to tremble. A little while he kneeled and gathered his shattered composure about him doggedly, like a cloak. Then he uncovered his face, which was pale, despairing but eased, no longer in combat with truth but consenting to it. He was a young man of courage. He got to his feet and faced them squarely.

"Father I come to confession by constraint, and not gladly, and I am as ashamed of that as of what I have to confess. But it is not murder. I did not kill Rhisiart. I found him dead."

"At what hour?" asked Brother Cadfael, wholly without right, but nobody questioned the interruption.

"I went out after the rain stopped. You remember it rained." They remembered. They had good reason. "It would be a little after noon. I was going up to the pasture our side of Bryn, and I found him lying on his face in that place where afterwards we all saw him. He was dead then, I swear it! And I was grieved, but also I was tempted, for there was nothing in this world I could do for Rhisiart, but I saw a way...." Peredur swallowed and sighed, bracing his forehead against his fate, and went on. "I saw a means of ridding myself of a rival. Of the favoured rival. Rhisiart had refused his daughter to Engelard, but Sioned had not refused him, and well I knew there was no hope for me, however her father urged her, while Engelard was there between us. Men might easily believe that Engelard should kill Rhisiart, if—if there was some proof...."

"But *you* did not believe it," said Cadfael, so softly that hardly anyone noticed the inter-ruption, it was accepted and answered with-out thought.

"No!" said Peredur almost scornfully. "I knew him, he never would!"

"Yet you were willing he should be taken and accused. It was all one to you if it was death that removed him out of your way, so he was removed."

"No!" said Peredur again, smouldering but aware that he was justly lashed. "No, not that! I thought he would run, take himself away again into England, and leave us alone, Sioned and me. I never wished him worse than that. I thought, with him gone, in the end Sioned would do what her father had wished, and marry me. I could wait! I would have waited years...."

He did not say, but there were two there, at least, who knew, and remembered in his fa-vour, that he had opened the way for Engelard to break out of the ring that penned him in, and deliberately let him pass, just as Brother John, with a better conscience, had frustrated the pursuit.

Brother Cadfael said sternly: "But you went so far as to steal one of this unfortunate young man's arrows, to make sure all eyes turned on him."

"I did not steal it, though no less discredit to me that I used it as I did. I was out with Engelard after game, not a week earlier, with Rhisiart's permission. When we retrieved our arrows, I took one of his by error among mine. I had it with me then."

Peredur's shoulders had straightened, his head was up, his hands, the right still holding Sioned's cross, hung gently and resignedly at his sides. His face was pale but calm. He had got the worst of it off his back, after what he had borne alone these last days confession and penance were balm.

"Let me tell the whole of it, all the thing I did, that has made me a monster in my own eyes ever since. I will not make it less than it was, and it was hideous. Rhisiart was stabbed in the back, and the dagger withdrawn and gone. I turned him over on his back, and I turned that wound back to front, and I tell you, my hands burn now, but I did it. He was dead, he suffered nothing. I pierced my own flesh, not his. I could tell the line of the wound, for the dagger had gone right through him, though the breast wound was small. I took my own dagger, and opened the way for Engelard's arrow to follow, and I thrust it through and left it standing in him for witness. And I have not had one quiet moment, night or day," said Peredur, not asking pity, rather grateful that now his silence was broken and his infamy known, and nothing more to hide, "since I did this small, vile thing, and now I am glad it's out, whatever becomes of me. And at least grant me this, I did not make my trap in such a way as to accuse Engelard of shooting a man in the back! I knew him! I lived almost side by side with him since he came here a fugitive, we were of an age, we could match each other. I have liked him, hunted with him, fought with him, been jealous of him, even hated him because he was loved where I was not. Love makes men do terrible things," said Peredur, not pleading, marvelling, "even to their friends."

He had created, all unconsciously, a tremendous hush all about him, of awe at his blasphemy, of startled pity for his desolation, of chastened wonder at their own misconceivings. The truth fell like thunder, subduing them all. Rhisiart had not been shot down with an arrow, but felled from behind at close quarters, out of thick cover, a coward's killing. Not saints, but men, deal in that kind of treachery.

Father Huw broke the silence. In his own providence, where no alien dignitaries dared intrude, he grew taller and more secure in his gentle, neighbourly authority. And great violence had been done to what he knew to be right, and great requital was due from the sinner, and great compassion due to him.

"Son Peredur," he said, "you stand in dire sin, and cannot be excused. Such violation of the image of God, such misuse of a clean affection—for such I know you had with Rhisiart—and such malice towards an innocent man—for such you proclaimed Engelard—cannot go unpunished."

"God forbid," said Peredur humbly, "that I should escape any part of what is due. I want it! I cannot live with myself if I have only this present self to live with!"

"Child, if you mean that, then give yourself into my hands, to be delivered up both to secular and religious justice. As to the law, I shall speak with the prince's bailiff. As to the penance due before God, that is for me as your confessor, and I require that you shall wait my considered judgment."

"So I will, Father," said Peredur. "I want no unearned pardon. I take penance willingly."

"Then you need not despair of grace. Go home now, and remain withindoors until I send for you."

"I will be obedient to you in all things. But I have one prayer before I go." He turned slowly and faced Sioned. She was standing quite still where the awful dread had fallen upon her, her hands clutched to her cheeks, her eyes fixed in fascination and pain upon the boy who had grown up as her playfellow. But the rigidity had ebbed out of her, for though he called himself a monster, he was not, after all, the monster she had briefly thought him. "May I now do what you asked of me? I am not afraid now. He was a fair man always. He won't accuse me of more than my due."

He was both asking her pardon and saying his farewell to any hope he had still cherished of winning her, for now that was irrevocably over. And the strange thing was that now he could approach her, even after so great an offence, without constraint, almost without jealousy. Nor did her face express any great heat or bitterness against him. It was thoughtful and intent.

"Yes," she said, "I still wish it." If he had spoken the whole truth, and she was persuaded that he had, it was well that he should take his appeal to Rhisiart, in a form every man there would acknowledge. In otherworldly justice the body would clear him of the evil he had not committed, now that confession was made of what he had.

Peredur went forward steadily enough now, ·sank to his knees beside Rhisiart's body, and laid first his hand, and then Sioned's cross, upon the heart he had pierced, and no gush of blood sprang at his touch. And if there was one thing certain, it was that here was a man who did believe. He hesitated a moment, still kneeling, and then, feeling a need rather to give thanks for this acceptance than to make any late and unfitting display of affection, stooped and kissed the right hand that lay quiet over the left on Rhisiart's breast, their clasped shape showing through the close shroud. That done, he rose and went firmly away by the downhill path towards his father's house. The people parted to let him through in a great silence, and Cadwallon, starting out of a trance of unbelieving misery, lurched forward in haste and went trotting after his son.

Chapter Nine

The evening was drawing in by the time they had buried Rhisiart, and it was too late for Prior Robert and his companions to take their prize and leave at once for home, even if it had been a seemly thing to do, after all that had happened. Some ceremony was due to the community the saint was leaving, and the houses that had offered hospitality freely even to those who came to rob them.

"We will stay this night over, and sing Vespers and Compline in the church with you, and give due thanks," said the prior. "And after Compline one of us will again watch the night through with Saint Winifred, as is only proper. And should the prince's bailiff require that we stay longer, we will do as he asks. For there is still the matter of Brother John, who stands in contempt of the law, to our disgrace."

"At present," said Father Huw deprecatingly, "the bailiff is giving his attention to the case of Rhisiart's murder. For though we have suffered many revelations in that matter, you see that we are no nearer knowing who is guilty. What we have seen today is one man who certainly is innocent of the crime, whatever his other sins may be."

"I fear," said Prior Robert with unwonted humility, "that without ill intent we have caused you great grief and trouble here, and for that I am sorry. And greatly sorry for the parents of that sinful young man, who are suffering, I think, far worse than he, and without blame."

"I am going to them now," said Huw. "Will you go on ahead, Father Prior, and sing Vespers for me? For I may be delayed some time. I must do what I can for this troubled household."

The people of Gwytherin had begun to drift away silently by many paths, vanishing into the woods to spread the news of the day's happening to the far corners of the parish. In the long grass of the graveyard, trampled now by many feet, the dark, raw shape of Rhisiart's grave made a great scar, and two of his men were filling in the earth over him. It was finished. Sioned turned towards the gate, and all the rest of her people followed.

Cadfael fell in beside her as the subdued, straggling procession made its way home towards the village.

"Well," he said resignedly, "it was worth trying. And we can't say it got us nothing. At least we know now who committed the lesser crime, if we're very little nearer knowing who committed the greater. And we know why there were two, for they made no sense, being one and the same. And at any rate, we have shaken the devil off that boy's back. Are you quite revolted at what he did? As *he* is?"

"Strangely," said Sioned, "I don't believe I am. I was too sick with horror, that short time while I thought him the murderer. After that, it was simple relief that he was not. He has never gone short of anything he wanted, you see, until he wanted me."

"It was a real wanting," said Brother Cadfael, remembering long-past hungers of his own. "I doubt if he'll ever quite get over it, though I'm pretty sure he'll make a sound marriage, and get handsome children like himself, and be fairly content. He grew up today, she won't be disappointed, whoever she may be. But she'll never be Sioned."

Her tired, woeful, discouraged face had softened and warmed, and suddenly she was smiling beside him, faintly but reassuringly. "You are a good man. You have a way of reconciling people. But no need! Do you think I did not see how he dragged himself painfully to this afternoon's business, and has gone striding away with his head up to embrace his punishment? I might really have loved him a little, if there had been no Engelard. But only a little! He may do better than that."

"You are a fine girl," said Brother Cadfael heartily. "If I had met you when I was thirty years younger, I should have made Engelard sweat for his prize. Peredur should be thankful even for such a sister. But we're no nearer knowing what we want and need to know."

"And have we any more shafts left to loose?" she asked ruefully. "Any more snares to set? At least we've freed the poor soul we caught in the last one."

He was silent, glumly thinking.

"And tomorrow," she said sadly, "Prior Robert will take his saint and all his brothers, and you with them, and set out for home, and I shall be left with nobody to turn to here. Father Huw is as near a saint himself, in his small, confused way, as ever Winifred was, but no use to me. And Uncle Meurice is a gentle creature who knows about running a manor, but nothing about anything else, and wants no trouble and no exertion. And Engelard must go on hiding, as well you know. Peredur's plot against him is quite empty now, we all know it. But does that prove he did not kill my father, after a raging quarrel?"

"In the back?" said Cadfael, unguardedly indignant.

She smiled. "All that proves is that you know him! Not everyone does. Some will be saying at this moment, perhaps, after all…that Peredur may have been right without even knowing it."

He thought about it and was dismayed, for no question but she was right. What, indeed, did it prove if another man had wished to burden him with the guilt? Certainly not that the guilt was *not* his. Brother Cadfael confronted his own voluntarily assumed responsibility, and braced himself to cope with it.

"There is also Brother John to be considered," said Sioned. It may well be that Annest, walking behind, had prodded her.

"I have not forgotten Brother John," agreed Cadfael.

"But I think the bailiff well may have done. He would shut his eyes or look the other way, if Brother John left for Shrewsbury with the rest of you. He has troubles enough here, what does he want with alien trouble?"

"And if Brother John should seem to him to have left for Shrewsbury, he would be satisfied? And ask no questions about one more outlander taken up by a patron here?"

"I always knew you were quick," said Sioned, brown and bright and animated, almost herself again. "But would Prior Robert pursue him still, when he hears he's gone from custody? I don't see him as a forgiving man."

"No, nor he is, but how would he set about it? The Benedictine order has no real hold in Wales. No, I think he'd let it ride, now he has what he came for. I'm more concerned for Engelard. Give me this one more night, child, and do this for me! Send your people home, and stay the night over with Annest at Bened's croft, and if God aids me with some new thought—for never forget God is far more deeply offended even than you or I by this great wrong!—I'll come to you there."

"We'll do that," said Sioned. "And you'll surely come."

They had slowed to let the cortège move well ahead of them, so that they could talk freely. They were approaching the gatehouse of Cadwallon's holding, and Prior Robert and his companions were far in front and had passed by the gate, bent upon singing Vespers in good time. Father Huw, issuing forth in haste and agitation in search of help, seemed relieved rather than dismayed to find only Cadfael within call. The presence of Sioned checked him to a decent walk and a measured tone, but did nothing to subdue the effect of his erected hair and frantic mien.

"Brother Cadfael, will you spare some minutes for this afflicted household? You have some skills with medicines, you may be able to advise...."

"His mother!" whispered Sioned in immediate reassurance. "She weeps herself into a frenzy at everything that crosses her. I knew this would set her off. Poor Peredur, he has his penance already! Shall I come?"

"Better not," he said softly, and moved to meet Father Huw. Sioned was, after all, the innocent cause of Peredur's fall from grace, she would probably be the last person calculated to calm his mother's anguish. And Sioned understood him so, and went on, and left the matter to him, so calmly that it was clear she expected no tragic results from the present uproar. She had known Cadwallon's wife all her life, no doubt she had learned to treat her ups and downs as philosophically as Cadfael did Brother Columbanus' ecstasies and excesses. He never really hurt himself in his throes, either!

"Dame Branwen is in such a taking," fluttered Father Huw distractedly, steering Cadfael in haste towards the open door of the hall. "I fear for her wits. I've seen her upset before, and hard enough to pacify, but now, her only child, and such a shock.... Really, she may do herself an injury if we cannot quiet her."

Dame Branwen was indeed audible before they even entered the small room where husband and son were trying to soothe her, against a tide of vociferous weeping and lamentation that all but deafened them. The lady, fat and fair and outwardly fashioned only for comfortable, shallow placidity, half-sat, half-lay on a couch, throwing her substantial person about in extravagant distress, now covering her silly, fond face, now throwing her arms abroad in sweeping gestures of desolation and despair, but never for one moment ceasing to bellow her sorrow and shame. The tears that flowed freely down her round cheeks and the shattering sobs that racked her hardly seemed to impede the flow of words that poured out of her like heavy rain.

Cadwallon on one side and Peredur on the other stroked and patted and comforted in vain. As often as the father tried to assert himself she turned on him with wild reproaches, crying that he had no faith in his own son, or he could never have believed such a terrible thing of him, that the boy was bewitched, under some spell that forced false confession out of him, that he ought to have stood up for him before everybody and prevented the tale from being accepted so lightly, for somewhere there was witchcraft in it. As often as Peredur tried to convince her he had told the truth, that he was willing to make amends, and she must accept his word, she rounded on him with fresh outbursts of tears, screaming that her own son had brought dreadful disgrace upon himself and her, that she wondered he dare come near her, that she would never be able to lift up her head again, that he was a monster. . . .

As for poor Father Huw, when he tried to assert his spiritual authority and order her to submit to the force of truth and accept her son's act with humility, as Peredur himself had done in making full confession and offering full submission, she cried out that she had been a God-fearing and law-abiding woman all her life, and done everything to bring up her child in the same way, and she could not now accept his guilt as reflecting upon her.

"Mother," said Peredur, haggard and sweating worse than when he faced Rhisiart's body,

"nobody blames you, and nobody will. What I did I did, and it's I who must abide the consequence, not you. There isn't a woman in Gwytherin won't feel for you."

At that she let out a great wail of grief, and flung her arms about him, and swore that he should not suffer any grim penalties, that he was her own boy, and she would protect him. And when he extricated himself with fading patience, she screamed that he meant to kill her, the unfeeling wretch, and went off into peals of ear-piercing, sobbing laughter.

Brother Cadfael took Peredur firmly by the sleeve, and hauled him away to the back of the room. "Show a little sense, lad, and take yourself out of her sight, you're fuel to her fire. If nobody marked her at all she'd have stopped long ago, but now she's got herself into this state she's past doing that of her own accord. Did our two brothers stop in here, do you know, or go on with the prior?"

Peredur was shaking and tired out, but responded hopefully to this matter-of-fact treatment. "They've not been here, or I should have seen them. They must have gone on to the church."

Naturally, neither Columbanus nor Jerome would dream of absenting himself from Vespers on such a momentous day.

"Never mind, you can show me where they lodge. Columbanus brought some of my poppy syrup with him, in case of need, the phial should be there with his scrip, he'd hardly have it on him. And as far as I know, he's had no occasion to use it, his cantrips here in Wales have been of a quieter kind. We can find a use for it now."

"What does it do?" asked Peredur, wide-eyed.

"It soothes the passions and kills pain—either of the body or the spirit."

"I could use some of that myself," said Peredur with a wry smile, and led the way out to one of the small huts that lined the stockade. The guests from Shrewsbury had been given the best lodging the house afforded, with two low brychans, and a small chest, with a rush lamp for light. Their few necessaries occupied almost no space, but each had a leather scrip to hold them, and both of these dangled from a nail in the timber wall. Brother Cadfael opened first one, and then the other, and in the second found what he was seeking.

He drew it out and held it up to the light, a small phial of greenish glass. Even before he saw the line of liquid in it, its light weight had caused him to check and wonder. Instead of being full to the stopper with the thick, sweet syrup, the bottle was three-quarters empty.

Brother Cadfael stood stock-still for a moment with the phial in his hand, staring at it in silence. Certainly Columbanus might at some time have felt the need to forestall some threatening spiritual disturbance but Cadfael could recall no occasion when he had said any word to that effect, or shown any sign of the rosy, reassuring calm the poppies could bring. There was enough gone from the bottle to restore serenity three times over, enough to put a man to sleep for hours. And now that he came to think back, there had been at least one occasion when a man had slept away hours of the day, instead of keeping the watch he was set to keep. The day of Rhisiart's death Columbanus had failed of his duty, and confessed as much with heartfelt penitence. Columbanus, who had the syrup in his possession, and knew its use....

"What must we do?" asked Peredur, uneasy in the silence. "If it tastes unpleasant you'll have trouble getting her to drink it."

"It tastes sweet." But there was not very much of it left, a little reinforcement with something else soothing and pleasant might be necessary. "Go and get a cup of strong wine, and we'll see how that goes down."

They had taken with them a measure of wine that day, he remembered, the ration for the two of them, when they set off for the chapel. Columbanus had drawn and carried it. And a bottle of water for himself, since he had made an act of piety of renouncing wine until their mission was accomplished. Jerome had done well, getting a double ration.

Brother Cadfael stirred himself out of his furious thoughts to deal with the immediate need. Peredur hurried to do his bidding, but brought mead instead of wine.

"She's more likely to drink it down before she thinks to be obstinate, for she likes it better. And it's stronger."

"Good!" said Cadfael. "It will hide the syrup better. And now, go somewhere quiet, and harden your heart and stop your ears and stay out of her sight, for it's the best thing you can do for her, and God knows the best for yourself, after such a day. And leave agonising too much over your sins, black as they are, there isn't a confessor in the land who hasn't heard worse and never turned a hair. It's a kind of arrogance to be so certain you're past redemption."

The sweet, cloying drink swirled in the cup, the syrup unwinding into it in a long spiral that slowly melted and vanished. Peredur with shadowy eyes watched and was silent.

After a moment he said, very low: "It's strange! I never could have done so shabbily by anyone I hated."

"Not strange at all," said Cadfael bluntly, stirring his potion. "When harried, we go as far as we dare, and with those we're sure of we dare go very far, knowing where forgiveness is certain."

Peredur bit his lip until it was biddable. "*Is it certain?*"

"As tomorrow's daylight, child! And now be off out of my way, and stop asking fool questions. Father Huw will have no time for you today, there's more important business waiting."

Peredur went like a docile child, startled and comforted, and wherever he hid himself, he did it effectively, for Cadfael saw no more of him that evening. He was a good lad at heart, and this wild lunge of his into envy and meanness had brought him up short against an image of himself that he did not like at all. Whatever prayers Huw set him by way of penance were likely to hit heaven with the irresistible fervour of thunderbolts, and whatever hard labour he was given, the result was likely to stand solid as oak and last for ever.

Cadfael took his draught, and went back to where Dame Branwen was still heaving and quivering with uncontrollable sobs, by this time in genuine distress, exhausted by her efforts but unable to end them. He took advantage of her sheer weariness to present the cup to her as soon as he reached her side, and with abrupt authority that acted on her before she could muster the fibre of stubbornness.

"Drink this!" And automatically she drank it, half of it going down out of pure surprise, the second half because the first had taught her how dry and sore her throat was from all its exertions, and how smooth was the texture and how sweet the taste of this brew. The

very act of swallowing it broke the frightening rhythm of the huge sighs that had convulsed her almost worse than the sobbing. Father Huw had time to mop his brow with a fold of his sleeve before she was able to resume her complaints. Even then, by comparison with what had gone before, they sounded half-hearted.

"We women, we mothers, we sacrifice our lives to bringing up children, and when they're grown they reward us by bringing disgrace upon us. What did I ever do to deserve this?"

"He'll do you credit yet," said Cadfael cheerfully. "Stand by him in his penance, but never try to excuse his sin, and he'll think the better of you for it."

That went by her like the wind sighing at the time, though she may have remembered it later. Her voice declined gradually from its injured self-justification, dwindled into a half-dreamy monologue of grief, and took on at length a tone of warm and drowsy complacency, before it lapsed into silence. Cadwallon breathed deep and cautiously, and eyed his advisers.

"I shall call her women and get her to bed," said Cadfael. "She'll sleep the night through, and it'll do her nothing but good." And you more good still, he thought but did not say. "Let your son rest, too, and never say another word about his trouble but by the way, like any other daily business, unless he speaks up first. Father Huw will take care of him faithfully."

"I will," said Huw. "He's worth our efforts."

Dame Branwen went amiably where she was led, and the house was wonderfully quiet. Cadfael and Huw went out together, pursued as far as the gate by Cadwallon's distracted gratitude. When they were well away from the holding, at the end of the stockade, the quietness of the dusk came down on them softly, a cloud descending delicately upon a cloud.

"In time for supper, if not for Vespers," said Huw wearily. "What should we have done without you, Brother Cadfael? I have no skill at all with women, they confuse me utterly. I marvel how you have learned to deal with them so ably, you, a cloistered brother."

Cadfael thought of Bianca, and Arianna, and Mariam, and all the others, some known so briefly, all so well.

"Both men and women partake of the same human nature, Huw. We both bleed when we're wounded. That's a poor, silly woman, true, but we can show plenty of poor, silly men. There are women as strong as any of us, and as able." He was thinking of Mariam—or was it of Sioned? "You go to supper, Huw, and hold me excused, and if I can be with you before Compline, I will. I have some business first at Bened's smithy."

The empty phial swung heavily in the pocket in his right sleeve, reminding him. His mind was still busy with the implications. Before ever he reached Bened's croft he had it clear in his mind what must be done, but was no nearer knowing how to set about it.

Cai was with Bened on the bench under the eaves, with a jug of rough wine between them. They were not talking, only waiting for him to appear, and there could be no reason for that, but that Sioned had told them positively that he would.

"A fine tangle it turns out," said Bened, shaking his grizzled head. "And now you'll be off and leave us holding it. No blame to you, you have to go where your duty is. But what are we to do about Rhisiart when you're

gone? There's more than half this parish thinks your Benedictines have killed him, and the lesser half thinks some enemy here has taken the chance to blame you, and get clean away into cover. We were a peaceful community until you came, nobody looked for murder among us."

"God knows we never meant to bring it," said Cadfael. "But there's still tonight before we go, and I haven't shot my last bolt yet. I must speak with Sioned. We've things to do, and not much time for doing them."

"Drink one cup with us before you go in to her," insisted Cai. "That takes no time at all, and is a powerful aid to thought."

They were seated all together, three simple, honest men, and the wine notably lower in the jug, when someone turned in at the gate, light feet came running in great haste along the path, and suddenly there was Annest confronting them, skirts flying and settling about her like wings folding, her breath short and laboured, and excitement and consternation in her face. And ready to be indignant at the very sight of them sitting peacefully drinking wine.

"You'd better stir yourselves," she said, panting and sparkling. "I've been along to Father Huw's house to see what's going on there—Marared and Edwin between them have been keeping an eye open for us. Do you know who's there taking supper with the Benedictines? Griffith ap Rhys, the bailiff! And do you know where he's bound, afterwards? Up to our house, to take Brother John to prison!"

They were on their feet fast enough at this news, though Bened dared to question it. "He can't be there! The last I heard of him he was at the mill."

"And that was this morning, and I tell you now he's eating and drinking with Prior Robert and the rest. I've seen him with my own eyes, so don't tell me he can't be there. And here I find you sitting on your hams drinking, as though we had all the time in the world!"

"But *why* in such a hurry tonight?" persisted Bened. "Did the prior send for him, because he's wanting to be away tomorrow?"

"The devil was in it! He came to Vespers just by way of compliment to Father Huw, and who should he find celebrating instead but Prior Robert, and the prior seized on it as just the chance he wanted, and has hung on to him and persuaded him Brother John must be taken in charge tonight, for he can't leave without knowing he's safely in the hands of the law. He says the bailiff should deal with him for the secular offence of hindering the arrest of a criminal, and when he's served his penalty he's to be sent back to Shrewsbury to answer for his defiance of discipline, or else the prior will send an escort to fetch him. And what could the bailiff do but fall in with it, when it was put to him like that? And here you sit—!"

"All right, girl, all right," said Cai placatingly. "I'm off this minute, and Brother John will be out of there and away to a safe place before ever the bailiff gets near us. I'll take one of your ponies, Bened...."

"Saddle another for me," said Annest with determination. "I'm coming with you."

Cai went off at a jogtrot to the paddock, and Annest, drawing breath more easily now that the worst was told, drank off the wine he had left in his cup, and heaved a huge, resolute sigh.

"We'd better be out of here fast, for that young brother who looks after the horses now will be coming down after supper to get them. The prior means to be there to see John safe bound. 'There's time yet before Compline,' he said. He was complaining of wanting you, too, to interpret for him, they were managing lamely with only Latin between them. Dear God, what a day it's been!"

And what a night, thought Cadfael, it's still likely to be. "What else was going on there?" he asked. "Did you hear anything that might give me a light? For heaven knows I need one!"

"They were debating which one of them should watch the night through at the chapel. And that same young fair one, the one who has visions, up and prayed it might be him. He said he'd been unfaithful to his watch once, and longed still to make amends. And the prior said he might. That much I understood myself. All the prior's thinking about seems to be making all the trouble he can for John," said Annest resentfully, "or I should think he might have sent somebody else instead. That young brother—what is it you call him?"

"Columbanus," said Brother Cadfael.

"That's him, Columbanus! He begins to put on airs as if he *owned* Saint Winifred. I don't want her to go away at all, but at least it was the prior who first thought of it, and now if there's a halo for anybody it's shifted to this other fellow's head."

She did not know it, but she had indeed given Cadfael a light, and with every word she said it burned more steadily. "So he's to be the one who watches the night through before the altar—and alone, is he?"

"So I heard." Cai was coming with the ponies, at a gay trot out of the meadow. Annest rose eagerly and kilted her gown, knotting her girdle tightly about the broad pleat she drew up over her hips. "Brother Cadfael, you don't think it wrong of me to love John? Or of him to love me? I don't care about the rest of them, but I should be sorry if *you* thought we were doing something wicked."

Cai had not bothered with a saddle for himself, but had provided one for her. Quite simply and naturally Brother Cadfael cupped his hands for her foot, to give her a lift on to the pony's broad back, and the fresh scent of her linen and the smooth coolness of her ankle against his wrists as she mounted made one of the best moments of that interminably long and chaotic day. "As long a I may live, girl," he said, "I doubt if I shall ever know two creatures with less wickedness between them. He made a mistake, and there should be provision for everybody to make one fresh start. I don't think he's making any mistake this time."

He watched her ride away, setting an uphill pace to which Cai adapted himself goodhumouredly. They had a fair start, it would be ten minutes or more yet before Columbanus came to fetch the horses, and even then he had to take them back to the parsonage. It might be well to put in an appearance and go with Robert dutifully to interpret his fulminations, too, in which case there was need of haste, for he had now a great deal to say to Sioned, and this night's moves must be planned thoroughly. He withdrew into the croft as soon as Annest and Cai were out of sight, and Sioned came out of the shadows eagerly to meet him.

"I expected Annest to be here before you. She went to find out what's happening at Father Huw's. I thought best to stay out of sight. If people think I'm away home, so much the better. You haven't seen Annest?"

"I have, and heard all her news," said Cadfael, and told her what was in the wind, and where Annest was gone. "Never fear for John, they'll be there well ahead of any pursuit. We have other business, and no time to waste, for I shall be expected to ride with the prior, and it's as well. I should be there to see fair play. If we manage our business as well as I fancy Cai and Annest will manage theirs, before morning we may know what we want to know."

"You've found out something," she said with certainty. "You are changed. You are sure!"

He told her briefly all that had happened at Cadwallon's house, how he had brooded upon it without enlightenment as to how it was to be used, and how Annest in innocence had shown him. Then he told her what he required of her.

"I know you can speak English, you must use it tonight. This may be a more dangerous trap than any we've laid before, but I shall be close by. And you may call in Engelard, too, if he'll promise to stay close in cover. But, child, if you have any doubts or fears, if you'd rather let be, and have me try some other way, say so now, and so be it."

"No," she said, "no doubts and no fears. I can do anything. I dare do anything."

"Then sit down with me, and learn your part well, for we haven't long. And while we plan, can I ask you to bring me some bread and a morsel of cheese? For I've missed my supper."

Prior Robert and Brother Richard rode into Rhisiart's yard with the prince's bailiff between them, his two henchmen and Brother Cadfael close behind, at about half past seven, in a mild twilight, with all the unhurried ceremony of the law, rather as if Griffith ap Rhys held his commission from Saint Benedict, and not from Owain Gwynedd. The bailiff was, in fact, more than a little vexed at this unfortunate encounter, which had left him no alternative but to comply with Robert's demands. An offence against Welsh law was alleged, and had been reported to him, and he was obliged to investigate it, where, considering the circumstances, he would much have preferred to pack all the Benedictine delegation back to Shrewsbury, and let them sort out their own grudges there, without bothering a busy man who had plenty of more important things on his mind. Unhappily Cadwallon's villein, the long-legged fellow who had been brought down by Brother John, had given vociferous evidence in support of the accusation, or it would have been easier to ignore it.

There was no one on duty at the gate, which was strange, and as they rode in, a number of people seemed to be running hither and thither in a distracted way, as if something unforeseen had happened, and confused and conflicting orders were being given from several authorities at once. No groom ran to attend to them, either. Prior Robert was displeased. Griffith ap Rhys was mildly and alertly interested. When someone did take notice of them, it was a very handsome young person in a green gown, who came running with her skirts gathered in her hands, and her light-brown hair slipping out of its glossy coil to her shoulders.

"Oh, sirs, you must excuse us this neglect, we've been so disturbed! The gate-keeper was called away to help, and all the grooms are hunting.... But I'm ashamed to let our troubles cast a shadow over our hospitality. My lady's resting, and can't be disturbed, but I'm at your service. Will it please you light down? Shall I have lodgings made ready?"

"We don't propose to stay," said Griffith ap Rhys, already suspecting this artless goodwill, and approving the way she radiated it. "We came to relieve you of a certain young malefactor you've had in hold here. But it seems you've suffered some further calamity, and we should be sorry to add to your troubles, or disturb your lady, after the grievous day she's endured."

"Madam," said Prior Robert, civilly but officiously, "you are addressing the prince's bailiff of Rhos, and I am the prior of Shrewsbury abbey. You have a brother of that abbey in confinement here, the royal bailiff is come to relieve you of his care."

All of which Cadfael duly and solemnly translated for Annest's benefit, his face as guileless as hers.

"Oh, sir!" She opened her eyes wide and curtseyed deeply to Griffith and cursorily to the prior, separating her own from the alien. "It's true we had such a brother here a prisoner...."

"Had?" said Robert sharply, for once detecting the change of tense.

"Had?" said Griffith thoughtfully.

"He's gone, sir! You see what confusion he's left behind. This evening, when his keeper took him his supper, this brother struck him down with a board torn loose from the manger in this prison, and dropped the bolt on him and slipped away. It was some time before we knew. He must have climbed the wall, you see it is not so high. We have men out now looking for him in the woods, and searching everywhere here within. But I fear he's clean gone!"

Cai made his entrance at the perfect time, issuing from one of the barns with shaky steps, his head wreathed in a white cloth lightly dabbled with red.

"The poor man, the villain broke his head for him! It was some time before he could drag himself to the door and hammer on it, and make himself heard. There's no knowing how far the fellow may have got by now. But the whole household is out hunting for him."

The bailiff, as in duty bound, questioned Cai, but gently and briefly, questioned all the other servants, who ran to make themselves useful and succeeded only in being magnificently confusing. And Prior Robert, burning with vengeful zeal, would have pressed them more strenuously but for the bailiff's presence and obvious prior right, and the brevity of the time at his disposal if he was to get back for Compline. In any case, it was quite clear that Brother John was indeed over the wall and clean gone. Most willingly they showed the place where he had been confined, and the manger from which he had ripped the board, and the board itself, artistically spattered at one end with spots of Cai's gore, though it may, of course, have been pigment borrowed from the butcher.

"It seems your young man has given us all the slip," said Griffith, with admirable serenity for a man of law who has lost a malefactor. "There's nothing more to be done here. They could hardly expect such violence from a Benedictine brother, it's no blame to them."

With considerable pleasure Cadfael translated that neat little stab. It kindled a spark in the speaking eyes of the young person in green, and Griffith did not miss it. But to challenge it would have been folly. The clear brown eyes would have opened wide enough and deep enough to drown a man in their innocence. "We'd best leave them in peace to mend their broken mangers and broken heads," said Griffith, "and look elsewhere for our fugitive."

"The wretch compounds his offences," said Robert, furious. "But I cannot allow his villainy to disrupt my mission. I must set out for home tomorrow, and leave his capture to you."

"You may trust me to deal properly with him," said Griffith drily, "when he is found." If he laid the slightest of emphasis on the "when", no one appeared to remark it but Cadfael and Annest. By this time Annest was quite satisfied that she liked this princely official, and could trust him to behave like a reasonable man who is not looking for trouble, or trying to make it for others as harmless as himself.

"And you will restore him to our house when he has purged his offences under Welsh law?"

"When he has done so," said Griffith, decidedly with some stress this time on the "when", "you shall certainly have him back."

With that Prior Robert had to be content, though his Norman spirit burned at being deprived of its rightful victim. And on the ride back he was by no means placated by Griffith's tales of the large numbers of fugitive outlaws who had found no difficulty in living wild in these forests, and even made friends among the country people, and been accepted into families, and even into respectability at last. It galled his orderly mind to think of insubordination mellowing with time and being tolerated and condoned. He was in no very Christian mood when he swept into Father Huw's church, only just in time for Compline.

They were all there but Brother John, the remaining five brethren from Shrewsbury and a good number of the people of Gwytherin, to witness the last flowering of Brother Columbanus' devotional gift of ecstasy, now dedicated entirely to Saint Winifred, his personal patroness who had healed him of madness, favoured him with her true presence in a dream, and made known her will through him in the matter of Rhisiart's burial. For at the end of Compline, rising to go to his self-chosen vigil, Columbanus turned to the altar, raised his arms in a sweeping gesture, and prayed aloud in a high, clear voice that the virgin martyr would deign to visit him once more in his holy solitude, in the silence of the night, and reveal to him again the inexpressible bliss from which he had returned so reluctantly to this imperfect world. And more, that this time, if she found him worthy of translation out of the body, she would take him up living into that world of light. Humbly he submitted his will to endure here below, and do his duty in the estate assigned him, but rapturously he sent his desire soaring to the timber roof, to be uplifted out of the flesh, transported through death without dying, if he was counted ready for the assumption.

Everyone present heard, and trembled at such virtue. Everyone but Brother Cadfael, who was past trembling at the arrogance of man, and whose mind, in any case, was busy and anxious with other, though related, matters.

Chapter Ten

rother Columbanus entered the small, dark, woodscented chapel, heavy with the odours of centuries, and closed the door gently behind him, without latching it. There were no candles lighted, tonight, only the small oil-lamp upon the altar, that burned with a tall, unwavering flame from its floating wick. That slender, single turret of light cast still shadows all around, and being almost on a level with the bier of Saint Winifred, braced on trestles before it, made of it a black coffin shape, only touched here and there with sparkles of reflected silver.

Beyond the capsule of soft golden light all was darkness, perfumed with age and dust. There was a second entrance, from the minute sacristy that was no more than a porch beside the altar, but no draught from that or any source caused the lamp-flame to waver even for an instant. There might have been no storms of air or spirit, no winds, no breath of living creature, to disturb the stillness.

Brother Columbanus made his obeisance to the altar, briefly and almost curtly. There was no one to see, he had come alone, and neither seen nor heard any sign of another living soul in the graveyard or the woods around. He moved the second prayer-desk aside, and set the chosen one squarely in the centre of the chapel, facing the bier. His behavior was markedly more practical and moderate than when there were people by to see him, but did not otherwise greatly differ. He had come to watch out the night on his knees, and he was prepared to do so, but there was no need to labour his effects until morning, when his fellows would come to take Saint Winifred in reverent procession on the first stage of her journey. Columbanus padded the prie-dieu for his knees with the bunched skirts of his habit, and made himself as comfortable as possible with his gowned arms broadly folded as a pillow for his head. The umber darkness was scented and heavy with the warmth of wood, and the night outside was not cold. Once he had shut out the tiny, erect tower of light and the few bright surfaces from which it was reflected, the drowsiness he was inviting came stealing over him in long, lulling waves until it washed over his head, and he slept.

It seemed, after the fashion of sleep, no time at all before he was startled awake, but in fact it was more than three hours, and midnight was approaching, when his slumbers began to be strangely troubled with a persistent dream that someone, a woman, was calling him by name low and clearly, and over and over and over and over again: "Columbanus.... Columbanus..." with inexhaustible and relentless patience. And he was visited, even in sleep, by a sensation that this woman had all the time in the world, and was willing to go on calling for ever, while for him there was no time left at all, but he must awake and be rid of her.

He started up suddenly, stiff to the ends of fingers and toes, ears stretched and eyes staring wildly, but there was the enclosing capsule of mild darkness all about him as before, and the reliquary dark, too, darker than before, or so it seemed, as if the flame of the lamp, though steady, had subsided, and was now more than half hidden behind the coffin. He had forgotten to check the oil. Yet he knew it had been fully supplied when last he left it, after Rhisiart's burial, and that was only a matter of hours ago.

It seemed that all of his senses, hearing had been the last to return to him, for now he was aware, with a cold crawling of fear along his skin, that the voice of his dream was still with him, and had been with him all along, emerging from dream into reality without a break. Very soft, very low, very deliberate, not a whisper, but the clear thread of a voice, at once distant and near, insisting unmistakably: "Columbanus . . . Columbanus . . . Columbanus, what have you done?"

Out of the reliquary the voice came, out of the light that was dwindling even as he stared in terror and unbelief.

"Columbanus,Columbanus, my false servant, who blasphemes against my will and murders my champions, what will you say in your defence to Winifred? Do you think you can deceive me as you deceive your prior and your brothers?"

Without haste, without heat, the voice issued forth from the darkening apse of the altar, so small, so terrible, echoing eerily out of its sacred cave.

"You who claim to be my worshipper, you have played me false like the vile Cradoc, do you think you will escape his end? I never wished to leave my resting-place here in Gwytherin. Who told you otherwise but your own devil of ambition? I laid my hand upon a good man, and sent him out to be my champion, and this day he has been buried here, a martyr for my sake. The sin is recorded in heaven, there is no hiding-place for you. Why," demanded the voice, cold, peremptory and menacing in its stillness, "have you killed my servant Rhisiart?"

He tried to rise from his knees, and it was as if they were nailed to the wood of the prie-dieu. He tried to find a voice, and only a dry croaking came out of his stiff throat. She could not be there, there was no one there! But the saints go where they please, and reveal themselves to whom they please, and sometimes terribly. His cold fingers clutched at the desk, and felt nothing. His tongue, like an unplaned splinter of wood, tore the roof of his mouth when he fought to make it speak.

"There is no hope for you but in confession, Columbanus, murderer! Speak! Confess!"

"No!" croaked Columbanus, forcing out

words in frantic haste. "I never touched Rhisiart! I was here in your chapel, holy virgin, all that afternoon, how could I have harmed him? I sinned against you, I was faithless, I slept.... I own it! Don't lay a greater guilt on me...."

"It was not you who slept," breathed the voice, a tone higher, a shade more fiercely, "liar that you are! Who carried the wine? Who poisoned the wine, causing even the innocent to sin? Brother Jerome slept, not you! *You* went out into the forest and waited for Rhisiart, and struck him down."

"No...no, I swear it!" Shaking and sweating, he clawed at the desk before him, and could get no leverage with his palsied hands to prise himself to his feet and fly from her. How can you fly from beings who are everywhere and see everything? For nothing mortal could possibly know what this being knew. "No, it's all wrong, I am misjudged! I was asleep here when Father Huw's messenger came for us. Jerome shook me awake.... The messenger is witness...."

"The messenger never passed the doorway. Brother Jerome was already stirring out of his poisoned sleep, and went to meet him. As for you, you feigned and lied, as you feign and lie now. Who was it brought the poppy syrup? Who was it knew its use? You were pretending sleep, you lied even in confessing to sleep, and Jerome, as weak as you are wicked, was glad enough to think you could not accuse him, not even seeing that you were indeed accusing him of worse, of *your* act, of *your* slaying! He did not know you lied, and could not charge you with it. But *I* know, and I do charge you! And my vengeance loosed upon Cradoc may also be loosed upon you, if you lie to me but once more!"

"No!" he shrieked, and covered his face as though she dazzled him with lightnings, though only a thin, small, terrible sound threatened him. "No, spare! I am not lying! Blessed virgin, I have been your true servant...I have tried to do your will...I know nothing of this! I never harmed Rhisiart! I never gave poisoned wine to Jerome!"

"Fool!" said the voice in a sudden loud cry. "Do you think you can deceive *me*? *Then what is this?*"

There was a sudden silvery flash in the air before him, and something fell and smashed with a shivering of glass on the floor just in front of the desk, spattering his knees with sharp fragments and infinitesimal, sticky drops, and at the same instant the flame of the lamp died utterly, and black darkness fell.

Shivering and sick with fear, Columbanus groped forward along the earth floor, and slivers of glass crushed and stabbed under his palms, drawing blood. He lifted one hand to his face, whimpering, and smelled the sweet, cloying scent of the poppy syrup, and knew that he was kneeling among the fragments of the phial he had left safe in his scrip at Cadwallon's house.

It was no more than a minute before the total darkness eased, and there beyond the bier and the altar the small oblong shape of the window formed in comparative light, a deep, clear sky, moonless but starlit. Shapes within the chapel again loomed very dimly, giving space to his sickening terror. There was a figure standing motionless between him and the bier.

It took a little while for his eyes to accustom themselves to the dimness, and assemble out of it this shadowy, erect pallor, a woman lost in obscurity from the waist down, but head and shoulders feebly illuminated by the starlight from the altar window. He had not seen her come, he had heard nothing. She had appeared while he was dragging his torn palm over the shards of glass, and moaning as if at the derisory pain. A slender, still form swathed from head to foot closely in white, Winifred in her grave clothes, long since dust, a thin veil covering her face and head, and her arm outstretched and pointing at him.

He shrank back before her, scuffling abjectly backwards along the floor, making feeble gestures with his hands to fend off the very sight of her. Frantic tears burst out of his eyes, and frantic words from his lips.

"It was for you! It was for you and for my abbey! I did it for the glory of our house! I believed I had warranty—from you and from heaven! He stood in the way of God's will! He would not let you go. I meant only rightly when I did what I did!"

"Speak plainly," said the voice, sharp with command, "and say out what you did."

"I gave the syrup to Jerome—in his wine—and when he was asleep I stole out to the forest path, and waited for Rhisiart. I followed him. I struck him down. . . . Oh, sweet Saint Winifred, don't let me be damned for striking down the enemy who stood in the way of blessedness. . . ."

"Struck in the back!" said the pale figure, and a sudden cold gust of air swept over her and shuddered in her draperies, and surging across the chapel, blew upon Columbanus and chilled him to the bone. As if she had touched him! And she was surely a pace nearer, though he had not seen her move. "Struck in the back, as mean cowards and traitors do! Own it! Say it all!"

"In the back!" babbled Columbanus, scram-bling back from her like a broken animal, until his shoulders came up against the wall, and he could retreat no farther. "I own it. I confess it all! Oh, merciful saint, you know all, and I cannot hide from you! Have pity on me! Don't destroy me! It was all for you, I did it for you!"

"You did it for yourself," charged the voice, colder than ice and burning like ice. "You who would be master of whatever order you enter, you with your ambitions and strata-gems, you setting out wilfully to draw to yourself all the glory of possessing me, to work your way into the centre of all achieve-ments, to show as the favourite of heaven, the paragon of piety, to elbow Brother Richard out of his succession to your prior, and if you could, the prior out of his succession to your abbot. You with your thirst to become the youngest head under a mitre in this or any land! I know you, and I know your kind. There is no way too ruthless for you, provid-ing it leads to power."

"No, no!" he panted, bracing himself back against the wall, for certainly she was advanc-ing upon him, and now in bitter, quiet fury, jetting menace from her outstretched finger-tips. "It was all for you, only for you! I believed I was doing your will!"

"My will to evil?" the voice rose into a piercing cry, sharp as a dagger. "My will to murder?"

She had taken one step too many. Colum-banus broke in frenzied fear, clawed himself upright by the wall, and struck out with both hands, beating at her blindly to fend her off from touching, and uttering thin, babbling cries as he flailed about him. His left hand caught in her draperies and dragged the veil from her face and head. Dark hair fell round her shoulders. His fingers made contact with the curve of a smooth, cool cheek, cool, but not cold, smooth with the graceful curves of firm young flesh, where in his sick horror he had expected to plunge his hand into the bony hollows of a skull.

He uttered a scream that began in frantic terror and ended in soaring triumph. The hand that had shrunk from contact turned suddenly to grasp hold, knotting strong fingers in the dark tangle of hair. He was very quick, Columbanus. It took him no more than the intake of a breath to know he had a flesh-and-blood woman at the end of his arm, and scarcely longer to know who she must be, and what she had done to him, with this intolerable trap in which she had caught him. And barely another breath to consider that she was here alone, and to all appearances had set her trap alone, and if she survived he was lost, and if she did not survive, if she vanished—there was plenty left of the night!—he was safe, and still in command of all this expedition, and inheritor of all its glory.

It was his misfortune that Sioned was almost as quick in the uptake as he. In a darkness in which vision hardly helped or hindered, she heard the great, indrawn breath that released him from the fear of hell and heaven together; and felt the wave of animal anger that came out from him like a foul scent, almost as sickening as the odour of his fear. She sprang back from it by instinct, and repeated the lunge of intent, dragging herself out of his grasp at the price of a few strands of hair. But his clawing hand, cheated, loosed the fragments and caught again at the linen sheet that draped her, and that would not tear so easily. She swung round to her left, to put as much distance as she could between her body and his right hand, but she saw him lunge into the breast of his habit, and saw the brief, sullen flash of the steel as he whipped it out and followed her swing, hacking into dimness. The same dagger, she thought, swooping beneath its first blind stab, that killed my father.

Somewhere a door had opened fully on the night, for the wind blew through the chapel suddenly, and sandalled feet thudded in with the night air, a thickset, powerful body driving the draught before it. A loud voice thundered warning. Brother Cadfael erupted into the chapel from the sacristy like a bolt from a crossbow, and drove at full speed into the struggle.

Columbanus was in the act of striking a second time, and with his left hand firmly clutching the linen sheet wound about Sioned's body. But she was whirling round away from him to unloose those same folds that held her, and the blow that was meant for her heart only grazed painfully down her left forearm. Then his grip released her, and she fell back against the wall, and Columbanus was gone, hurtling out at the door in full flight, and Brother Cadfael was embracing her with strong, sustaining arms, and upbraiding her with a furious, bracing voice, while he held her in a bear's hug, and felt at her as tenderly and fervently as a mother.

"For God's sake, fool daughter, why did you get within his reach? I *told* you, keep the bier between you and him...!"

"Get after him," shouted Sioned wrathfully, "do you want him clean away? I'm sound enough, go get *him*! He killed my father!"

They headed for the door together, but Cadfael was out of it first. The girl was strong, vigorous and vengeful, a Welshwoman to the heart, barely grazed, he knew the kind. The wind of action blew her, she felt no pain and was aware of no effusion of blood, blood she wanted, and with justification. She was close on his heels as he rolled like a thunderbolt down the narrow path through the graveyard towards the gate. The night was huge, velvet, sewn with stars, their veiled and delicate light barely casting shadows. All that quiet space received and smothered the sound of their passage, and smoothed the stillness of the night over it.

Out of the bushes beyond the graveyard wall a man's figure started, tall, slender and swift, leaping to block the gateway. Columbanus saw him, and baulked for a moment, but Cadfael was running hard behind him, and the next instant the fugitive made up his mind and rushed on, straight at the shadow that moved to intercept him. Hard on Cadfael's heels, Sioned suddenly shrieked: "Take care, Engelard! He has a dagger!"

Engelard heard her, and swerved to the right at the very moment of collision, so that the stroke meant for his heart only ripped a fluttering ribbon of cloth from his sleeve. Columbanus would have bored his way past at speed, and run for the cover of the woods, but Engelard's long left arm swept round hard into the back of his neck, sending him off-balance for a moment, though he kept his feet, and Engelard's right fist got a tight grip on the flying cowl, and twisted. Half-strangled, Columbanus whirled again and struck out with the knife, and this time Engelard was ready for the flash, and took the thrusting wrist neatly in his left hand. They swayed and wrestled together, feet braced in the grass, and they were very fairly matched if both had been armed. That unbalance was soon amended.

Engelard twisted at the wrist he held, ignoring the clawing of Columbanus' free hand at his throat, and the numbed fingers opened at last and let the dagger fall. Both lunged for it, but Engelard scooped it up and flung it contemptuously aside into the bushes, and grappled his opponent with his bare hands. The fight was all but over. Columbanus hung panting and gasping, both arms pinned, looking wildly round for a means of escape and finding none.

"Is this the man?" demanded Engelard.

Sioned said: "Yes. He has owned to it."

Engelard looked beyond his prisoner then for the first time, and saw her standing in the soft starlight that was becoming to their accustomed eyes almost as clear as day. He saw her dishevelled and bruised and gazing with great, shocked eyes, her left arm gashed and bleeding freely, though the cut was shallow. He saw smears of her blood dabbling the white sheet in which she was swathed. By starlight there is little or no colour to be seen but everything that Engelard saw at that moment was blood-red. This was the man who had murdered in coward's fashion Engelard's well-liked lord and good friend—whatever their differences!—and now he had tried to kill the daughter as he had killed the father.

"You dared, you dared touch her!" blazed Engelard in towering rage. "You worthless cloister rat!" And he took Columbanus by the throat and hoisted him bodily from the ground, shook him like the rat he had called him, cracked him in the air like a poisonous snake, and when he had done with him, flung him down at his feet in the grass.

"Get up!" he growled, standing over the wreckage. "Get up now, and I'll give you time to rest and breathe, and then you can fight a man to the death, without a dagger in your hand, instead of writhing through the undergrowth and stabbing him in the back, or carving up a defenceless girl. Take your time, I can wait to kill you till you've got your breath."

Sioned flew to him, breast to breast, and held him fast in her arms, pressing him back. "No! Don't touch him again! I don't want the law to have any hold on *you,* even the slenderest."

"He tried to kill you—you're hurt...."

"No! It's nothing...only a cut. It bleeds, but it's nothing!"

His rage subsided slowly, shaking him. He folded his arms round her and held her to him, and with a disdainful but restrained jab of a toe urged his prostrate enemy again: "Get up! I won't touch you. The law can have you, and welcome!"

Columbanus did not move, not by so much as the flicker of an eyelid or the twitching of a finger. All three of them stood peering down at him in sudden silence, aware how utterly still he was, and how rare such stillness is among living things.

"He's foxing," said Engelard scornfully, "for fear of worse, and by way of getting himself pitied. I've heard he's a master at that."

Those who feign sleep and hear themselves talked of, usually betray themselves by some exaggeration of innocence. Columbanus lay in a stillness that was perfectly detached and indifferent.

Brother Cadfael knelt down beside him, shook him by the shoulder gently, and sat back with a sharp sigh at the broken movement of the head. He put a hand inside the breast of the habit, and stooped to the parted lips and wide nostrils. Then he took the head between his hands, and gently turned and tilted it. It rolled back, as he released it, into a position so improbable that they knew the worst even before Cadfael said, quite practically: "You'd have waited a long time for him to get his breath back, my friend. You don't know your own strength! His neck is broken. He's dead."

Sobered and shocked, they stood dumbly staring down at what they had hardly yet recognised for disaster. They saw a regrettable accident which neither of them had ever intended, but which was, after all, a kind of justice. But Cadfael saw a scandal that could yet wreck their young lives, and others, too, for without Columbanus alive, and forced by two respected witnesses to repeat his confession, how strong was all their proof against him? Cadfael sat back on his heels, and thought. It was startling to realise, now that the unmoved silence of the night came down on them again, how all this violence and passion had passed with very little noise, and no other witnesses. He listened, and no stirring of foot or wing troubled the quiet. They were far enough away from any dwelling, not a soul had been disturbed. That, at least, was time gained.

"He can't be dead," said Engelard doubtfully. "I barely handled him at all. Nobody dies as easily as that!"

"This one did. And now what's to be done? I hadn't bargained for this." He said it not complainingly, but as one pointing out that further urgent planning would now be necessary, and they had better keep their minds flexible.

"Why, what can be done?" To Engelard it was simple, though troublesome. "We shall have to call up Father Huw and your prior, and tell them exactly what's happened. What else can we do? I'm sorry to have killed the fellow, I never meant to, but I can't say I feel any *guilt* about it." Nor did he expect any blame. The truth was always the best way. Cadfael felt a reluctant affection for such innocence. The world was going to damage it sooner or later, but one undeserved accusation had so far failed even to bruise it, he still trusted men to be reasonable. Cadfael doubted if Sioned was so sure. Her silence was anxious and foreboding. And her grazed arm was still oozing blood. First things first, and they might as well be sensibly occupied while he thought.

"Here, make yourself useful! Help me get this carrion back into the chapel, out of sight. And, Sioned, find his dagger, we can't leave that lying about to bear witness. Then let's get that arm of yours washed and bound up. There's a stream at the back of the hawthorn hedge, and of linen we've plenty."

They had absolute faith in him, and did his bidding without question, though Engelard, once he had assured himself that Sioned was not gravely hurt, and had himself carefully and deftly bandaged her scratch, returned to his dogged opinion that their best course was to tell the whole story, which could hardly cast infamy upon anyone but Columbanus. Cadfael busied himself with flint and tinder until he had candles lighted, and the lamp refilled, from which he himself had drained a judicious quantity of oil before Sioned took her place under the draperies of the saint's catafalque.

"You think," he said at length, "that because you've done nothing wrong, and we've all of us banded together to expose a wrong, that the whole world will be of the same opinion, and honestly come out and say so. Child, I know better! The only proof we have of Columbanus' guilt is his confession, which both of us here heard. Or rather, the only proof we had, for we no longer have even that. Alive, we two could have forced the truth out of him a second time. Dead, he's never going to give us that satisfaction. And without that, our position is vulnerable enough. Make no mistake, if we accuse him, if this fearful scandal breaks, to smirch the abbey of Shrewsbury, and all the force of the Benedictine order, backed here by the bishop and the prince, take my word for it, all the forces of authority will band together to avert the disaster, and nobody, much less a friendless outlander, will be allowed to stand in the way. They simply can't afford to have the acquisition of Saint Winifred called in question and brought to disrepute. Rather than that, they'll call this an outlaw killing by a desperate man, a fugitive already, wanted for another crime, and trying to escape both together. A pity," he said, "I ever suggested that Sioned should call you in to wait in reserve, in case we had trouble. But none of this is your fault, and I won't have you branded with it. I made the plot, and I must unravel it. But give up all idea of going straight to Father Huw, or the bailiff, or anyone else, with the true story. Far better use the rest of this night to rearrange matters to better advantage. Justice can be arrived at by more routes than one."

"They wouldn't dare doubt Sioned's word," said Engelard stoutly.

"Fool boy, they'd say that Sioned, for love's sake, might go as far aside from her proper nature as Peredur did. And as for me, my influence is small enough, and I am not interested in protecting only myself, but as many of those in this coil as I can reach. Even my prior, who is arrogant and rigid, and to tell the truth, sometimes rather stupid, but not a murderer and not a liar. And my order, which has not deserved Columbanus. Hush, now, and let me think! And while I do, you can be clearing away the remains of the syrup bottle. This chapel must be as neat and quiet tomorrow as before we ever brought our troubles into it."

Obediently they went about removing the traces of the night's alarms, and let him alone until he should have found them a way through the tangle.

"And I wonder, now," he said at length, "what made you improve on all the speeches I made for you, and put such fiery words into Saint Winifred's mouth? What put it into your head to say that you'd never wanted to leave Gwytherin, and did not want it now? That Rhisiart was not merely a decent, honest man, but your chosen champion?"

She turned and looked at him in astonishment and wonder. "Did I say that?"

"You did, and very well you delivered it, too. And very proper and apt it sounded, but I think we never rehearsed it so. Where did you get the words?"

"I don't know," said Sioned, puzzled. "I don't remember what I did say. The words seemed to come freely of themselves, I only let them flow."

"It may be," said Engelard, "that the saint was taking her chance when it offered. All these strangers having visions and ecstasies, and interpreting them to suit themselves, yet nobody ever really asked Saint Winifred what *she* wanted. They all claimed they knew better than she did."

"Out of the mouths of innocents!" said Cadfael to himself, and pondered the road that was gradually opening before his mind's eye. Of all the people who ought to be left happy with the outcome, Saint Winifred should surely come first. Aim, he thought, at making everybody happy, and if that's within reach, why stir up any kind of unpleasantness? Take Columbanus, for instance! Only a few hours ago at Compline he prayed aloud before us all that if the virgin deemed him worthy, he might be taken up out of this world this very night, translated instantly out of the body. Well, that was one who got his wish! Maybe he'd have withdrawn his request if he'd known it was going to be taken up so literally, for its purpose was rather to reflect incomparable holiness upon him while he was still alive to enjoy it. But saints have a right to suppose that their devotees mean what they say, and bestow gifts accordingly. And if the saint has really spoken through Sioned, he thought— and who am I to question it?—if she really wants to stay here in her own village, which is a reasonable enough wish, well, the plot where she used to sleep has been newly turned today, no one will notice anything if it's turned again tonight.

"I believe," said Sioned, watching him with the first faint smile, wan but trusting, "you're beginning to see your way."

"I believe," said Cadfael, "I'm beginning to see *our* way, which is more to the point. Sioned, I have something for you to do, and you need not hurry, we have work to do here while you're away. Take that sheet of yours, and go and spread it under the may trees in the hedge, where they're beginning to shed, but not yet brown, Shake the bushes and bring us a whole cloud of petals. The last time she visited him, it was with wondrous sweet odours and a shower of white flowers. Bring the one, and we shall have the other."

Confidently, understanding nothing as yet, she took the linen sheet from which she had unwound herself as from a shroud, and went to do his bidding.

"Give me the dagger," said Cadfael briskly when she was gone. He wiped the blade on the veil Columbanus had torn from Sioned's head, and moved the candles so that they shone upon the great red seals that closed Winifred's reliquary. "Thank God he didn't bleed," he said. "His habit and clothes are unmarked. Strip him!"

And he fingered the first seal, nodded satisfaction at its fatness and the thinness and sharpness of the dagger, and thrust the tip of the blade into the flame of the lamp.

Long before daylight they were ready. They walked down all three together from the chapel towards the village, and separated at the edge of the wood, where the shortest path turned off uphill towards Rhisiart's holding.

Sioned carried with her the blood-stained sheet and veil, and the fragments of glass they had buried in the forest. A good thing the servants who had filled in Rhisiart's grave had left their spades on the scene, meaning to tidy the mound next day. That had saved a journey to borrow without leave, and a good hour of time.

"There'll be no scandal," said Cadfael, when they halted at the place where the paths divided. "No scandal, and no accusations. I think you may take him home with you, but keep him out of sight until we're gone. There'll be peace when we're gone. And you needn't fear that the prince or his bailiff will ever proceed further against Engelard, any more than against John. I'll speak a word in Peredur's ear, Peredur will speak it into the bailiff's ear, the bailiff will speak it into Owain Gwynedd's ear—Father Huw we'll leave out of it, no need to burden his conscience, the good, simple man. And if the monks of Shrewsbury are happy, and the people of Gwytherin are happy—for they'll hear the whisper fast enough—why should anyone want to upset such a satisfactory state of affairs, by speaking the word aloud? A wise prince—and Owain Gwynedd seems to me very wise—will let well alone."

"All Gwytherin," said Sioned, and shivered a little at the thought, "will be there in the morning to watch you take the reliquary away."

"So much the better, we want all the witnesses we can have, all the emotion, all the wonder. I am a great sinner," said Cadfael philosophically, "but I feel no weight. Does the end justify the means, I wonder?"

"One thing I know," she said. "My father can rest now, and that he owes to you. And I owe you that and more. When I first came down to you out of the tree—you remember? —I thought you would be like other monks, and not want to look at me."

"Child, I should have to be out of my wits, not to want to look at you. I've looked so attentively, I shall remember you all my life. But your love, my children, and how you manage it—with that I can't help you."

"No need," said Engelard. "I am an outlander, with a proper agreement. That agreement can be dissolved by consent, and I can be a free man by dividing all my goods equally with my lord, and now Sioned *is* my lord."

"And then there can no man prevent," said Sioned, "if I choose to endow him with half *my* goods, as is only fair. Uncle Meurice won't stand in our way. And it won't even be hard for him to justify. To marry an heiress to an outlander servant is one thing, to marry her to a free man and heir to a manor, even if it's in England and can't be claimed for a while, is quite another."

"Especially," said Cadfael, "when you already know he's the best hand with cattle in the four cantrefs."

It seemed that those two, at any rate, were satisfied. And Rhisiart in his honoured grave would not grudge them their happiness. He had not been a grudging man.

Engelard, no talker, said his thanks plainly and briefly when they parted. Sioned turned back impulsively, flung her arms round Cadfael's neck, and kissed him. It was their farewell, for he had thought it best to advise them not to show themselves at the chapel again. It was a wry touch that she smelled so heady and sweet with flowering may, and left so saintly a fragrance in his arms when she was gone.

On his way down to the parsonage Cadfael made a detour to the mill-pond, and dropped Columbanus's dagger into the deepest of the dark water. What a good thing, he thought, making for the bed he would occupy for no more than an hour or so before Prime, that the brothers who made the reliquary were such meticulous craftsmen, and insisted on lining it with lead!

Chapter Eleven

rior Robert arose and went to the first service of the day in so great content with his success that he had almost forgotten about the escape of Brother John, and even when he remembered that one unsatisfactory particular, he merely put it away in the back of his mind, as something that must and would be dealt with faithfully in good time, but need not cloud the splendour of this occasion. And it was indeed a clear, radiant morning, very bright and still, when they came from the church and turned towards the old graveyard and the chapel, and all the congregation fell in at their heels and followed, and along the way others appeared silently from every path, and joined the procession, until it was like some memorable pilgrimage. They came to Cadwallon's gatehouse, and Cadwallon came out to join them, and Peredur, who had hung back in strict obedience to his orders to remain at home until his penance was appointed, was kindly bidden forth by Father Huw, and even smiled upon, though as saint to sinner, by Prior Robert. Dame Branwen, if not still asleep, was no doubt recuperating after her vapours. Her menfolk were not likely to be very pressing in their invitations to her to go with them, and perhaps she was still punishing them by withdrawing herself. Either way, they were relieved of her presence.

The order of procession having only a loose form, brothers and villagers could mingle, and greet, and change partners as they willed. It was a communal celebration. And that was strange, considering the contention that had threatened it for some days. Gwytherin was playing it very cautiously now, intent on seeing everything and giving nothing away.

Peredur made his way to Cadfael's side, and remained there thankfully, though silently. Cadfael asked after his mother, and the young man coloured and frowned, and then smiled guiltily like a child, and said that she was very well, a little dreamy still, but placid and amiable.

"You can do Gwytherin and me a good service, if you will," said Brother Cadfael, and confided to his ear the work he had in mind to pass on to Griffith ap Rhys.

"So that's the way it is!" said Peredur, forgetting altogether about his own unforgivable sins.

His eyes opened wide. He whistled softly. "And that's the way you want it left?"

"That's the way it is, and that's the way I want it left. Who loses? And everyone gains. We, you, Rhisiart, Saint Winifred—Saint Winifred most of all. And Sioned and Engelard, of course," said Cadfael firmly, probing the penitent to the heart.

"Yes . . . I'm glad for them!" said Peredur, a shade too vehemently. His head was bent, and his eyelids lowered. He was not yet as glad as all that, but he was trying. The will was there. "Given a year or two longer, nobody's going to remember about the deer Engelard took. In the end he'll be able to go back and forth to Cheshire if he pleases, and he'll have lands when his father dies. And once he's no longer reckoned outlaw and felon he'll have no more troubles. I'll get your word to Griffith ap Rhys this very day. He's over the river at his cousin David's but Father Huw will give me indulgence if it's to go voluntarily to the law." He smiled wryly. "Very apt that I should be your man! I can unload my own sins at the same time, while I'm confiding to him what everyone must know but no one must say aloud."

"Good!" said Brother Cadfael, contented. "The bailiff will do the rest. A word to the prince, and that's the whole business settled."

They had come to the place where the most direct path from Rhisiart's holding joined with their road. And there came half the household from above, Padrig the bard nursing his little portable harp, perhaps bound for some other house after this leavetaking. Cai the ploughman still with an impressive bandage round his quite intact head, an artistic lurch to his gait, and a shameless gleam in his one exposed eye. No Sioned, no Engelard, no Annest, no John. Brother Cadfael, though he himself had given the orders, felt a sudden grievous deprivation.

Now they were approaching the little clearing, the woodlands fell back from them on either side, the narrow field of wild grass opened, and then the stone-built wall, green from head to foot, of the old graveyard. Small, shrunken, black, a huddled shape too tall for its base, the chapel of Saint Winifred loomed, and at its eastern end the raw, dark oblong of Rhisiart's grave scarred the lush spring green of the grass.

Prior Robert halted at the gate, and turned to face the following multitude with a benign and almost affectionate countenance, and through Cadfael addressed them thus:

"Father Huw, and good people of Gwytherin, we came here with every good intent, led, as we believed and still believe, by divine guidance, desiring to honour Saint Winifred as she had instructed us, not at all to deprive you of a treasure, rather to allow its beams to shine upon many more people as well as you. That our mission should have brought grief to any is great grief to us. That we are now of one mind, and you are willing to let us take the saint's relics away with us to a wider glory, is relief and joy. Now you are assured that we meant no evil, but only good, and that what we are doing is done reverently."

A murmur began at one end of the crescent of watchers, and rolled gently round to the other extreme, a murmur of acquiescence, almost of complacency.

"And you do not grudge us the possession of this precious thing we are taking with us? You do believe that we are doing justly, that we take only what had been committed to us?"

He could not have chosen his words better, thought Brother Cadfael, astonished and gratified, if he had known everything—or if I had written this address for him. Now if there comes an equally well-worded answer, I'll believe in a miracle of my own.

The crowd heaved, and gave forth the sturdy form of Bened, as solid and respectable and fit to be spokesman for his parish as any man in Gwytherin, barring, perhaps, Father Huw, who here stood in the equivocal position of having a foot in both camps, and therefore wisely kept silence.

"Father Prior," said Bened gruffly, "there's not a man among us now grudges you the relics within there on the altar. We do believe they are yours to take, and you take them with our consent home to Shrewsbury, where by all the omens they rightly belong."

It was altogether too good. It might bring a blush of pleasure, even mingled with a trace of shame, to Prior Robert's cheek, but it caused Cadfael to run a long, considering glance round all those serene, secretive, smiling faces, all those wide, honest, opaque eyes. Nobody fidgeted, nobody muttered, nobody, even at the back, sniggered. Cai gazed with simple admiration from his one visible eye. Padrig beamed benevolent bardic satisfaction upon this total reconciliation.

They knew already! Whether through some discreet whisper started on its rounds by Sioned, or by some earth-rooted intuition of their own, the people of Gwytherin knew, in essence if not in detail, everything there was to be known. And not a word aloud, not a word out of place, until the strangers were gone.

"Come, then," said Prior Robert, deeply gratified, "let us release Brother Columbanus from his vigil, and take Saint Winifred on the first stage of her journey home." And he turned, very tall, very regal, very silvery-fine, and paced majestically to the door of the chapel, with most of Gwytherin crowding into the graveyard after him. With a long, white, aristocratic hand he thrust the door wide and stood in the doorway.

"Brother Columbanus, we are here. Your watch is over."

He took just two paces into the interior, his eyes finding it dim after the brilliance outside, in spite of the clear light pouring in through the small east window. Then the dark-brown, wood-scented walls came clear to him, and every detail of the scene within emerged from dimness into comparative light, and then into a light so acute and blinding that he halted where he stood, awed and marvelling.

There was a heavy, haunting sweetness that filled all the air within, and the opening of the door had let in a small morning wind that stirred it in great waves of fragrance. Both candles burned steadily upon the altar, the small oil-lamp between them. The prie-dieu stood centrally before the bier, but there was no one kneeling there. Over altar and reliquary a snowdrift of white petals lay, as though a miraculous wind had carried them in its arms across two fields from the hawthorn hedge, without spilling one flower on the way, and breathed them in here through the altar window. The snowy sweetness carried as far as the prie-dieu, and sprinkled both it and the crumpled, empty garments that lay discarded there.

"Columbanus! What is this? He is not here!"

Brother Richard came to the prior's left shoulder, Brother Jerome to the right, Bened and Cadwallon and Cai and others crowded in after them and flowed round on either side to line the dark walls and stare at the marvel, nostrils widening to the drowning sweetness. No one ventured to advance beyond where the prior stood, until he himself went slowly forward, and leaned to look more closely at all that was left of Brother Columbanus.

The black Benedictine habit lay where he had been kneeling, skirts spread behind, body fallen together in folds, sleeves spread like wings on either side, bent at the elbow as though the arms that had left them had still ended in hands pressed together in prayer. Within the cowl an edge of white showed.

"Look!" whispered Brother Richard in awe. "His shirt is still within the habit, and look!—his sandals!" They were under the hem of the habit, neatly together, soles upturned, as the feet had left them. And on the book-rest of the prie-dieu, laid where his prayerful hands had rested, was a single knot of flowering may.

"Father Prior, all his clothes are here, shirt and drawers and all, one within another as he would wear them. As though—as though he had been lifted out of them and left them lying, as a snake discards its old skin and emerges bright in a new...."

"This is most marvellous," said Prior Robert. "How shall we understand it, and not sin?"

"Father, may we take up these garments? If there is trace or mark on them...."

There was none, Brother Cadfael was certain of that. Columbanus had not bled, his habit was not torn, nor even soiled. He had fallen only in thick spring grass, bursting irresistibly through the dead grass of last autumn.

"Father, it is as I said, as though he has been lifted out of these garments quite softly,

and let them fall, not needing them any more. Oh, Father, we are in the presence of a great wonder! I am afraid!" said Brother Richard, meaning the wonderful, blissful fear of what is holy. He had seldom spoken with such eloquence, or been so moved.

"I do recall now," said the prior, shaken and chastened (and that was no harm!), "the prayer he made last night at Compline. How he cried out to be taken up living out of this world, for pure ecstasy, if the virgin saint found him fit for such favour and bliss. Is it possible that he was in such a state of grace as to be found worthy?"

"Father, shall we search? Here, and without? Into the woods?"

"To what end?" said the prior simply. "Would he be running naked in the night? A sane man? And even if he ran mad, and shed the clothes he wore, would they be thus discarded, fold within fold as he kneeled, here in such pure order? It is not possible to put off garments thus. No, he is gone far beyond these forests, far out of this world. He has been marvellously favoured, and his most demanding prayers heard. Let us say a Mass here for Brother Columbanus, before we take up the blessed lady who has made him her herald, and go to make known this miracle of faith."

There was no knowing, Prior Robert being the man he was, at what stage his awareness of the use to be made of this marvel thrust his genuine faith and wonder and emotion into the back of his mind, and set him manipulating events to get the utmost glory out of them. There was no inconsistency in such behaviour. He was quite certain that Brother Columbanus had been taken up living out of this world, just as he had wished. But that being so, it was not only his opportunity, but his duty, to make the utmost use of the exemplary favour to glorify the abbey of Saint Peter and Saint Paul of Shrewsbury, and not only his duty, but his pleasure, to make use of the same to shed a halo round the head of Prior Robert, who had originated this quest. And so he did. He said Mass with absolute conviction, in the cloud of white flowers, the huddle of discarded garments at his feet. Almost certainly he would also inform Griffith ap Rhys, through Father Huw, of all that had befallen, and ask him to keep an alert eye open in case any relevant information surfaced after the brothers from Shrewsbury were gone. Brother Prior was the product of his faith and his birth, his training for sanctity and for arbitrary rule, and could shake off neither.

The people of Gwytherin, silent and observant, crowded in to fill the space available, made no sound, expressed no opinion. Their presence and silence passed for endorsement. What they really thought they kept to themselves.

"Now," said Prior Robert, moved almost to tears, "let us take up this blessed burden, and praise God for the weight we carry."

And he moved forward to offer his own delicate hands and frail shoulder, first of the devout.

That was Brother Cadfael's worst moment, for it was the one thing he had overlooked, But Bened, unwontedly quick at the right moment, called aloud: "Shall Gwytherin be backward, now peace is made?" and rolled forward with less stateliness and greater speed, and had a solid shoulder under the head end of the reliquary before the prior was able to reach it, and half a dozen of the smith's own powerful but stocky build took up the challenge with enthusiasm. Apart from Cadfael, the only monk of Shrewsbury who got a corner hoisted into his neck was Jerome, being of much the same height, and his was the sole voice that cried out in astonishment at the weight, and sagged under it until Bened shifted nearer and hefted most of the load from him.

"Your pardon, Father Prior! But who would have thought those slender little bones could weigh so heavily?"

Cadfael spoke up in hasty interpretation: "We are surrounded here by miracles, both small and great. Truly did Father Prior say that we thank God for the weight we carry. Is not this evidence of singular grace, that heaven has caused the weight of her worthiness to be so signally demonstrated?"

In his present state, at once humbled and exalted, Prior Robert apparently did not find the logic of this nearly as peculiar as did Brother Cadfael himself. He would have accepted and embraced anything that added to his own triumph. So it was on sturdy Gwytherin shoulders that the reliquary and its contents were hoisted out of the chapel and borne in procession down to the parsonage, with such brisk enthusiasm that it almost seemed the parish could hardly wait to get rid of them. It was Gwytherin men who fetched the horses and mules, and rigged a little cart, spread with cloths, on which the precious casket could be drawn home. Once installed on this vehicle, which, after all, cost little in materials or labour, given the smith's benevolent interest, the casket need not be unloaded until it reached Shrewsbury. Nobody wanted anything untoward to happen to it on the way, such as Brother Jerome crumpling under his end, and starting the joints by dropping it.

"But you we'll miss," said Cai regretfully, busy with the harness. "Padrig has a song in praise of Rhisiart you'd have liked to hear, and one more companionable drinking night would have been pleasant. But the lad sends you his thanks and his godspeed. He's only in hiding until the pack of you have gone. And Sioned told me to tell you from him, look out for your pear trees, for the winter moth's playing the devil with some of ours here."

"He's a good helper in a garden," Cadfael confirmed judicially. "A shade heavy-handed, but he shifts the rough digging faster than any novice I ever had under me. I shall miss him, too. God knows what I shall get in his place."

"A light hand's no good with iron," said Bened, standing back to admire the banded wheels he had contributed to the cart. "Deft, yes! Not light. I tell you what, Cadfael! I'll see you in Shrewsbury yet. For years I've had a fancy to make a great pilgrimage across England some day and get to Walsingham. I reckon Shrewsbury would be just about on my way."

At the last, when all was ready and Prior Robert mounted, Cai said in Cadfael's ear: "When you're up the hill, where you saw us ploughing that day, cast a look the other way. There's a place where the woods fall away, and an open hillock just before they close again. We'll be there, a fair gathering of us. And that's for you."

Brother Cadfael, without shame, for he had been up and busy all night and was very tired, annexed the gentler and cleverer of the two mules, a steady pad that would follow where the horses led, and step delicately on any ground. It had a high, supporting saddle, and he had not lost the trick of riding through his knees, even when asleep. The larger and heavier beast was harnessed to draw the cart, but the carriage was narrow yet stable, rode well even on a forest floor, and Jerome, no great weight, could still ride, either on the mule's back or the shafts and yoke. In any case, why trouble too much about the comfort of Jerome, who had concocted that vision of Saint Winifred in the first place, almost certainly knowing that the prior's searches in Wales had cast up this particular virgin as one most desirable, and most available? Jerome would have been courting Columbanus just as assiduously, if he had survived to oust Robert.

The cortège set forth ceremoniously, half of Gwytherin there to watch it go, and sigh immense relief when it was gone. Father Huw blessed the departing guests. Peredur, almost certainly, was away across the river, planting the good seed in the bailiff's mind. He deserved that his errand should be counted to his own credit. Genuine sinners are plentiful, but genuine penitents are rare. Peredur had done a detestable thing, but remained a very likeable young man. Cadfael had no serious fears for his future, once he was over Sioned. There were other girls, after all. Not many her match, but some not so very far behind.

Brother Cadfael settled himself well down in the saddle, and shook his bridle to let the mule know it might conduct him where it would. Very gently he dozed. It could not yet be called sleep. He was aware of the shifting light and shadow under the trees, and the fresh cool air, and movement under him, and a sense of something completed. Or almost completed, for this was only the first stage of the way home.

He roused when they came to the high ridge above the river valley. There was no team ploughing, even the breaking of new ground, was done. He turned his head towards the wooded uplands on his right, and waited for the opening vista between the trees. It was brief and narrow, a sweep of grass soaring to a gentle crest beyond which the trees loomed close and dark. There were a number of people clustered there on the rounded hillock, most of Sioned's household, far enough removed to be nameless to anyone who knew them less well than he. A cloud of dark hair beside a cap of flaxen, Cai's flaunting bandage shoved back like a hat unseated in a hot noon, a light brown head clasped close against a red thorn-hedge that looked very like Brother John's abandoned tonsure. Padrig, too, not yet off on his wanderings. They were all waving and smiling, and Cadfael returned the salute with enthusiasm. Then the ambulant procession crossed the narrow opening, and the woods took away all.

Brother Cadfael, well content, subsided into his saddle comfortably, and fell asleep.

Overnight they halted at Penmachno, in the shelter of the church, where there was hospitality for travellers. Brother Cadfael, without apology to any, withdrew himself as soon as he had seen to his mule, and continued his overdue sleep in the loft above the stables. He was roused after midnight by Brother Jerome in delirious excitement.

"Brother, a great wonder!" bleated Jerome, ecstatic. "There came a traveller here in great pain from a malignant illness, and made such outcry that all of us in the hostel were robbed of sleep. And Prior Robert took a few of the petals we saved from the chapel, and floated them in holy water, and gave them to this poor soul to drink, and afterwards we carried him out into the yard and let him kiss the foot of the reliquary. And instantly he was eased of his pain, and before we laid him in his bed again he was asleep. He feels nothing, he slumbers like a child! Oh, brother, we are the means of astonishing grace!"

"Ought it to astonish you so much?" demanded Brother Cadfael censoriously, malicious half out of vexation at being awakened, and half in self-defence, for he was considerably more taken aback than he would admit. "If you had any faith in what we have brought from Gwytherin, you should not be amazed that it accomplishes wonders along the way."

But by the same token he thought honestly, after Jerome had left him to seek out a more appreciative audience, *I should!* I do believe I begin to grasp the nature of miracles! For would it be a miracle, if there was any reason for it? Miracles have nothing to do with reason. Miracles contradict reason, they strike clean across mere human deserts, and deliver and save where they will. If they made sense, they would not be miracles, And he was comforted and entertained, and fell asleep again readily, feeling that all was well with a world he had always know to be peculiar and perverse.

Minor prodigies, most of them trivial, some derisory, trailed after them all the way to Shrewsbury, though how many of the crutches discarded had been necessary, and how many, even of those that were, had to be resumed shortly afterwards, how many of the speech impediments had been in the will rather than in the tongue, how many feeble tendons in the mind rather than in the legs, it was difficult to judge, not even counting all the sensation-seekers who were bound to bandage an eye or come over suddenly paralytic in order to be in with the latest cult. It all made for a great reputation that not only kept pace with them, but rushed ahead, and was already bringing in awestruck patronage in gifts and legacies to the abbey of Saint Peter and Saint Paul, in the hope of having dubious sins prayed away by a grateful saint.

When they reached the outskirts of Shrewsbury, crowds of people came out to meet them, and accompany the procession as far as the boundary church of Saint Giles, where the reliquary was to await the great day of the saint's translation to the abbey church. This could hardly take place without the blessing of the bishop, and due notice to all churches and religious houses, to add to the glory accruing. It was no surprise to Brother Cadfael that when the day came it should come with grey skies and squally rain, to leave room for another little miracle. For though it rained heavily on all the surrounding fields and countryside, not a drop fell on the procession, as they carried Saint Winifred's casket at last to its final resting-place on the altar of the abbey church, where the miracle-seekers immediately betook themselves in great numbers, and mostly came away satisfied.

In full chapter Prior Robert gave his account of his mission to Abbot Heribert. "Father, to my grief I must own it, we have come back only four, who went out from Shrewsbury six brethren together. And we return without both the glory and the blemish of our house, but bringing with us the treasure we set out to gain."

On almost all of which counts he was in error, but since no one was ever likely to tell him so, there was no harm done. Brother Cadfael dozed gently behind his pillar through the awed encomiums on Brother Columbanus, out of whom they would certainly have wished to make a new saint, but for the sad fact that they supposed all his relics but his discarded clothes to be for ever withdrawn from reach. Letting the devout voices slip out of his consciousness, Cadfael congratulated himself on having made as many people as possible happy, and drifted into a dream of a hot knife-blade slicing deftly through the thick wax of a seal without ever disturbing the device. It was a long time since he had exercised some of his more questionable skills, he was glad to be confirmed in believing that he had forgotten none of them, and that every one had a meritorious use in the end.

Chapter Twelve

t was more than two years later, and the middle of a bright June afternoon, when Brother Cadfael, crossing the great court from the fish-ponds, saw among the travellers arriving at the gate a certain thickset, foursquare, powerful figure that he knew. Bened, the smith of Gwytherin, a little rounder in the belly and a little greyer in the hair, had found the time ripe for realising an old ambition, and was on his way in a pilgrim's gown to the shrine of Our Lady of Walsingham.

"If I'd put it off much longer," he confided, when they were private together with a bottle of wine in a corner of the herb-garden, "I should have grown too old to relish the journey. And what was there to keep me now, with a good lad ready and able to take over the smithy while I'm gone? He took to it like a duck to water. Oh, yes, they've been man and wife eighteen months now, and as happy as larks. Annest always knew her own mind, and this time I will say she's made no mistake."

"And have they a child yet?" asked Brother Cadfael, imagining a bold, sturdy boy-baby with a bush of red hair, rubbed away by his pillow in an infant tonsure.

"Not yet, but there's one on the way. By the time I get back he'll be with us."

"And Annest is well?"

"Blossoming like a rose."

"And Sioned and Engelard? They had no troubles after we were gone?"

"None, bless you! Griffith ap Rhys let it be known that all was well, and should be let well alone. They're married, and snug, and I'm to bring you their warmest greetings, and to tell you they have a fine son—three months old, I reckon he'd be now—dark and Welsh like his mother. And they've named him Cadfael."

"Well, well!" said Brother Cadfael, absurdly gratified. "The best way to get the sweet out of children and escape the bitter is to have them by proxy. But I hope they'll never find anything but

---

◆127◆

sweet in their youngster. There'll be a Bened yet, in one household or the other."

Bened the pilgrim shook his head, but without any deep regret, and reached for the bottle. "There was a time when I'd hoped.... But it would never have done. I was an old fool ever to think of it, and it's better this way. And Cai's well, and sends you remembrances, and says drink down one cup for him."

They drank many more than one before it was time for Vespers. "And you'll see me again at chapter tomorrow," said Bened, as they walked back to the great court, "for I'm charged with greetings from Father Huw to Prior Robert and Abbot Heribert, and I'll need you to be my interpreter."

"Father Huw must be the one person in Gwytherin, I suppose, who doesn't know the truth by this time," said Cadfael, with some compunction. "But it wouldn't have been fair to lay such a load on his conscience. Better to let him keep his innocence."

"His innocence is safe enough," said Bened, "for he's never said word to bring it in question, but for all that I wouldn't be too sure that he doesn't know. There's a lot of merit in silence."

The next morning at chapter he delivered his messages of goodwill and commendation to the monastery in general, and the members of Prior Robert's mission in particular, from the parish of Saint Winifred's ministry to the altar of her glorification. Abbot Heribert questioned him amiably about the chapel and the graveyard which he himself had never seen, and to which, as he said, the abbey owed its most distinguished patroness and most precious relics.

"And we trust," he said gently, "that in our great gain you have not suffered equally great deprivation, for that was never our intent."

"No, Father Abbot," Bened reassured him heartily, "you need have no regrets upon that score. For I must tell you that at the place of Saint Winifred's grave wonderful things are happening. More people come there for help than ever before. There have been marvellous cures."

Prior Robert stiffened in his place, and his austere face turned bluish-white and pinched with incredulous resentment.

"Even now, when the saint is here on our altar, and all the devout come to pray to her here? Ah, but small things—the residue of grace...."

"No, Father Prior, great things! Women in mortal labour with cross-births have been brought there and laid on the grave from which she was taken, where we buried Rhisiart, and their children have been soothed into the world whole and perfect, with no harm to the mothers. A man blind for years came and bathes his eyes in a distillation of her mayblossoms, and threw away his stick and went home seeing. A young man whose leg-bone had been broken and knitted awry came in pain, and set his teeth and danced before her, and as he danced the pain left him, and his bones straightened. I cannot tell you half the wonders we have seen in Gwytherin these last two years."

Prior Robert's livid countenance was taking on a shade of green, and under his careful eyelids his eyes sparkled emerald jealousy. How dare that obscure village, bereft of its saint, outdo the small prodigies of rain that held off from falling, and superficial wounds that healed with commendable but hardly miraculous speed, and even the slightly suspicious numbers of lame who brought their crutches and left them before the altar, and walked away unsupported?

"There was a child of three who went into a fit," pursued Bened with gusto, "stiff as a board in his mother's arms, and stopped breathing, and she ran with him all the way from the far fields, fording the river, and carried him to Winifred's grave, and laid him down in the grass there dead. And when he touched the chill of the earth, he breathed and cried out, and she picked him up living, and took him home joyfully, and he is live and well to this day."

"What, even the dead raised?" croaked Prior Robert, almost speechless with envy.

"Father Prior," said Brother Cadfael soothingly, "surely this is but another proof, the strongest possible, of the surpassing merit and potency of Saint Winifred. Even the soil that once held her bones works wonders, and every wonder must redound to the credit and glory of that place which houses the very body that blessed the earth still blesses others."

And Abbot Heribert, oblivious of the chagrin that was consuming his prior, benignly agreed that it was so, and that universal grace, whether it manifested itself in Wales, or England, or the Holy Land, or wheresoever, was to be hailed with universal gratitude.

"Was that innocence or mischief?" demanded Cadfael, when he saw Bened off from the gatehouse afterwards.

"Work it out for yourself! The great thing is, Cadfael, it was truth! These things happened, and are happening yet."

Brother Cadfael stood looking after him as he took the road towards Lilleshall, until the stocky figure with its long, easy strides dwindled to child-size, and vanished at the curve of the wall. Then he turned back towards his garden, where a new young novice, barely sixteen and homesick, was waiting earnestly for his orders, having finished planting out lettuces to follow in succession. A silent lad as yet. Maybe once he had taken Brother Cadfael's measure his tongue would begin to wag, and then there'd be no stopping it. He knew nothing, but was quick to learn, and though he was still near enough to childhood to attract any available moist soil to his own person, things grew for him. On the whole, Cadfael was well content.

I don't see, he thought, reviewing the whole business again from this peaceful distance, how I could have done much better. The little Welsh saint's back where she always wanted to be, bless her, and showing her pleasure by taking good care of her own, it seems. And we've got what belonged to us in the first place, all we have a right to, and probably all we deserve, too, and by and large it seems to be thought satisfactory. Evidently the body of a calculating murderer does almost as well as the real thing, given faith enough. Almost, but never quite! Knowing what they all know by now, those good people up there in Gwytherin may well look forward to great things. And if a little of their thanks and gratitude rubs off on Rhisiart, well, why not? He earned it, and it's a sign she's made him welcome. She may even be glad of his company. He's no threat to her virginity now, and if he is trespassing, that's no fault of his. His bed-fellow won't grudge him a leaf or two from her garland!

CADFAEL COUNTRY

CADFAEL COUNTRY

Shropshire and the Welsh Borders

ROB TALBOT AND
ROBIN WHITEMAN

Shrewsbury Abbey from the south

Brother Cadfael

The heat of the sun rebounded from honed facets of pale, baked rock, scorching his face, as the floating arid dust burned his throat. From where he crouched with his fellows in cover he could see the long crest of the wall, and the steel-capped heads of the guards on the turrets glittering in the fierce light. A landscape carved out of reddish stone and fire, all deep gullies and sheer cliffs, with never a cool green leaf to temper it, and before him the object of all his journeyings, the holy city of Jerusalem, crowned with towers and domes within white walls. The dust of battle hung in the air, dimming the clarity of battlement and gate, and the hoarse shouting and clashing of armour filled his ears. He was waiting for the trumpet to sound the final assault, and keeping well in cover while he waited, for he had learned to respect the range of the short, curly Saracen bow. He saw the banners surge forward out of hiding, streaming on the burning wind. He saw the flash of the raised trumpet, and braced himself for the blare.

The sound that brought him leaping wide-awake out of his dream was loud enough and stirring enough, but not the brazen blast of a trumpet, nor was he launched from his stillness towards the triumphant storming of Jerusalem. He was back in his stall in the dark corner of the chapter-house.

It was Brother Cadfael's habit to doze during the dull, routine businesses of the house, confident, since 'he held no troublesome parchment office', that it was unlikely he would be called upon to speak. One of his conscious decisions, shortly after entering the Rule of Saint Benedict in the Abbey of Saint Peter and Saint Paul, at Shrewsbury, was to select a seat in the chapter-house, 'well to the rear and poorly lit, half-concealed behind one of the stone pillars'. During his crusading and seafaring past, Cadfael had acquired the knack of sleeping 'without quite sleeping', which he had put to good use since he took the cowl.

Sitting 'bolt upright and undetected in his shadowy corner' of the chapter-house, he had a 'sixth sense which alerted him at need, and brought him awake instantly and plausibly. He had even been known to answer a question pat, when it was certain he had been asleep when it was put to him.'

Cadfael ap Meilyr ap Dafydd 'sprang to life suddenly and unexpectedly when he was approaching sixty, mature, experienced, fully armed and seventeen years tonsured', wrote his creator, Ellis Peters, in the introduction to *A Rare Bene-dictine*. 'His name,' she confides, 'was chosen as being so rare that I can find it only once in Welsh history, and even in that instance it disappears almost as soon as it is bestowed in baptism. Saint Cadog, contemporary and rival of Saint David, a powerful saint in Glamorgan, was actually christened Cadfael, but ever after seems to have been "familiarly known", as Sir John Lloyd says, as Cadog. A name of which the saint had no further need, and which appears, as far as I know, nowhere else, seemed just the thing for my man.' However, she warns wryly: 'No implication of saintliness was intended.'

Ellis Peters' medieval protagonist was 'launched on the world' as a 'squat, barrel-chested, bandy-legged veteran of fifty-seven', with a 'rolling, seaman's gait' and 'two broad feet' that had always been firmly planted on the ground. 'Solid and practical', 'without personal ambitions', Cadfael had been a Bene-dictine monk of Shrewsbury for nearly seventeen years, 'with a world of experience stored away inside him, and still as tough as a badger'. Although he was 'somewhat over the peak of a man's prime' and beginning to feel his years in small ways – the occasional rheumatic creak in his joints and twinge in his back – Cadfael had 'a nose sharp as fox or hound', 'the hearing of a wild creature' and eyesight that was excellent for his age. Short, sturdy, 'below middle height', with a 'broad, weathered face', he had a 'blunt, battered and brown nose', 'bushy eyebrows' and a thick hedge of bushy, greying hair ringing his nut-brown tonsure. His complexion was of 'a rosy russet colouring, confirmed by long years of outdoor living in both east and west, so engrained now that winters merely tarnished it a little, and summers regularly renewed the gloss'.

'Cadfael's warrior blood, long since abjured, had a way of coming to the boil when he heard steel in the offing. His chief uneasiness was that he could not be truly penitent about it. His king was not of this world, but in this world he could not help having a preference.' And that preference was for King Stephen, probably because he had briefly met 'and liked the man, even at his ill-advised worst, when he had slaughtered the garrison of Shrewsbury Castle'.

If Cadfael had to confess to a prevalent sin, it was to being 'endlessly curious' – a sin which, he admitted, was 'well worth a penance'. 'As long as man is curious about his fellow man,' he said, 'that appetite alone will keep him alive.' But, of all his vows, it was the vow of obedience that he always found the hardest to keep.

The north porch,
Shrewsbury Abbey

Choir and parish altar,
Shrewsbury Abbey

'*All the shapes within the vast stone ship showed dimly by the small altar lamps. Cadfael never passed through without stepping for a moment into the choir, to cast a glance and a thought towards Saint Winifred's altar, in affectionate remembrance of their first encounter, and gratitude for her forbearance.*'

An Excellent Mystery

To enable Cadfael to be in a position to solve the complex murders and mysteries that occur inside and outside the walls of Shrewsbury Abbey, it was essential for him to be able to have a reason to escape from the confines of the cloister; not just once, but regularly. Ellis Peters' inspired solution was to make him a herbalist who, in order to be able to doctor the sick, 'had, within reason, authority to come and go as he thought fit, even to absent himself from services if his aid was required elsewhere'. Through the continual process of going in and out of 'a workshop saturated with years of harvesting herbs', Cadfael could not help but 'carry the scent of them about his garments'.

In the *Eighth Chronicle of Brother Cadfael* (*The Devil's Novice*), when asked what he did in the monastery, Cadfael replied: 'I grow herbs, and dry them, and make remedies for all the ills that visit us. I physic a great many souls besides those of us within.' Pressed further, on whether his chosen vocation satisfied him, he said: 'To heal men, after years of injuring them? What could be more fitting? A man does what he must do, whether the duty he has taken on himself is to fight, or to salvage poor souls from the fighting, to kill, to die or to heal.' Cadfael had learned much of his craft in the Holy Land from both Saracen and Syrian physicians and, without any formal training, had acquired his medical skills 'by experience, by trial and study, accumulating knowledge over the years, until some preferred his ministrations to those of the acknowledged physicians'.

'The vegetable gardens of the Gaye unfolded green and neat along the riverside, the uncut grass of the bank making a thick emerald barrier between water and tillage. Beyond were the orchards, and then two fields of grain and the disused mill, and after that trees and bushes leaning over the swift, silent currents, crowding an overhanging bank, indented here and there by little coves, where the water lay deceptively innocent and still, lipping sandy shallows. Cadfael wanted comfrey and marsh mallow, both the leaves and the roots, and knew exactly where they grew profusely.'

The Heretic's Apprentice

ABOVE: *Marsh mallow (marsh marigold)*; BELOW: *Lovage*

Plants and herbs have been used since ancient times for a whole range of purposes, including cooking, dyeing and making medicine, perfumes and insecticides. The Anglo-Saxon herb garden at Lucy Cavendish College, Cambridge, was established in 1987 to show the range of plants known to have been used in Anglo-Saxon England. Evidence that the herbs now grown in the garden were used over a thousand years ago has been painstakingly gathered from two main areas of investigation: the physical remains of plants, mainly seeds, discovered during archaeological excavations; and literary references, especially medical books from monastic libraries, successive copies of which were sometimes beautifully illustrated.

Cadfael made his debut in *A Morbid Taste for Bones*, first published in 1977, a chronicle based on Prior Robert Pennant's historical expedition into Wales in 1137 to bring back the bones of Saint Winifred for Shrewsbury Abbey. This fictional monk, herbalist and medieval detective, 'coming, as he did, of antique Welsh stock without superhuman pretensions', was born fourteen years after the Norman Conquest in the year 1080 in the vale of Conway, 'near by Trefriw' (Gwynedd). 'Cadfael's numerous kinsfolk, first and second cousins and shared forbears' ranged across North Wales 'over much of Clywd and part of Gwynedd'.

'Bred up on the borders with a foot on either side', Cadfael came to Shrewsbury with the household of an English wool-merchant. As he recalled:

> Fourteen, I was then – in Wales fourteen is manhood, and as I was a good lad with the short bow, and took kindly to the sword, I suppose I was worth my keep. The best of my following years were spent in Shrewsbury; I know it like my own palm, abbey and all. My master sent me there a year and more, to get my letters. But I quit that service when he died. I'd pledged nothing to his son, and he was a poor shadow of his father.

Shortly after, in a fit of youthful enthusiasm, he took up the Cross and left England for the Holy Land, leaving behind him a young girl of seventeen, Richildis, to whom he had been 'affianced, though nobody knew it but themselves, and probably her family would have made short work of the agreement if they had known of it'.

Having vowed to return to Shrewsbury to 'claim' her, Cadfael had 'forgotten everything in the fever and glamour and peril of a life divided impartially between soldier and sailor, and delayed his coming far too long; and she, for all her pledges to wait for him, had tired at last and succumbed to her parent's urgings, and married a more stable character'.

For fifteen years Cadfael roved as far afield as Venice, Cyprus and the Holy Land, fighting in one campaign after another, first as a soldier and later as a sailor. In 1098, he was in the First Crusade 'with Godfrey de Bouillon at Antioch, when the Saracens surrendered it'. The following year he was at the seige and storming of Jerusalem, in which, it is estimated, 70,000 Muslims were massacred. In August of the same year he was 'at the fight at Ascalon', when he came up against 'the Fatamids of Egypt'. And 'when the king of Jerusalem ruled all the coast of the Holy Land', he took to the seas and 'spent ten years as a sea captain about the coasts of the Holy Land, where fighting hardly ceased'.

There were women also 'with whom he had enjoyed encounters pleasurable to both parties, and no harm to either': 'Arianna, the Greek boat-girl'; Bianca, whom he met in Venice; and Mariam, 'the Saracen widow who sold spices and fruits in Antioch, and found him man enough to replace for a while the man she had lost'.

Welsh Mountains from Carreg-y-Ffordd, Conwy Valley, Gwynedd

It was at Antioch that Cadfael 'began and ended his long career as a crusader, and his love affair with Palestine, that lovely inhospitable, cruel land of gold and sand and drought'. He had first met Mariam there, selling her 'fruit and vegetables in the Street of the Sailmakers, her young, fine-boned face honed into gold and silver by the fierce sunlight, her black, oiled hair gleaming beneath her veil. She had graced his arrival in the east, a mere boy of eighteen, and his departure, a seasoned soldier and seafarer of thirty-three. A widow, young, passionate and lonely, a woman of the people, not to everyone's taste, too spare, too strong, too scornful. The void left by her dead man had ached unbearably, and she had drawn in the young stranger heart and soul into her life, to fill the gap. For a whole year he had known her, before the forces of the Cross had moved on to invest Jerusalem.'

In his fifty-ninth year, having been a Benedictine monk of Shrewsbury for nearly twenty years, Cadfael had good cause to remember Mariam again. In the *Sixth Chronicle (The Virgin in the Ice)*, he discovered, to his surprise and joy, that in 1113 – when he had left Antioch for the last time – Mariam was pregnant and, in due course of time, she had borne him a son.

River Conwy near Gwydir Castle, Gwynedd

Rising in the Cambrian Mountains at Llyn Conwy, a lake over 1,600 feet above sea level and five miles west of the mining town of Blaenau Ffestiniog, the River Conwy flows south to Pont a Conwy, plunges over a waterfall and heads north-east towards the village of Pentrefoelas. One mile before reaching the village, the Conwy veers sharply north-west and heads for the popular tourist centre of Betws-y-Coed, where there is a celebrated collection of bridges. Upstream from Betws-y-Coed, near the spectacular Conwy Falls, the river is joined by the River Machno; within a mile of their confluence, the waters of the Conwy are swelled further by the River Lledr and, beyond Betws-y-Coed, by the River Llugwy. At the small market town of Llanrwst, just outside the eastern border of Snowdonia National Park, the Conwy passes Gwydir Castle, a Tudor mansion set in attractive grounds. The three-arched bridge (Pont Fawr) over the river, built in 1636, is reputed to have been designed by Inigo Jones.

From Llanrwst the river flows north past Trefriw and, after a journey of about ten miles, enters the sea at Conwy, a fortified town with a castle built by Edward I in 1283–87.

It appears that in about 1114 Cadfael returned briefly to England to discover that Richildis had tired of waiting for him and married 'an honest craftsman of Shrewsbury'. Shortly after he enlisted in the 'muddled mêlée of a war' in which the English under Henry I fought to consolidate their earlier conquest of Normandy. Although Henry's brother, Robert of Normandy, was defeated and imprisoned for life in 1106, fighting continued sporadically for another thirteen or so years, until the King had 'got everything he wanted, married his son to Anjou and Maine, and made an end of fighting'.

The account of Cadfael's decision to abandon arms for the cowl is told in *A Light on the Road to Woodstock (A Rare Benedictine)*. He is not a convert, however, 'for this is not a conversion', as Ellis Peters emphasises in her introduction.

In an age of relatively uncomplicated faith, not yet obsessed and tormented by cantankerous schisms, sects and politicians, Cadfael has always been an unquestioning believer. What happens to him on the road to Woodstock is simply the acceptance of a revelation from within that the life he has lived to date, active, mobile and often violent, has reached its natural end, and he is confronted by a new need and a different challenge.

Vale of Conwy from Llanrwst, Gwynedd

Cadfael sailed into Southampton from Normandy in mid-November 1120, in the employ of Roger Mauduit, a Northampton knight who owned a manor at Sutton Mauduit. He had agreed to remain in his service, as man-at-arms, until 'a certain lawsuit' Roger had against the Abbey of Shrewsbury was resolved. King Henry had intended to preside over the case himself at Woodstock, near Oxford, on 23 November. But, after the tragic news that the *Blanche Nef* (White Ship) had sunk crossing the Channel, drowning his son and heir, Prince William, Henry 'willed that his justice should still prevail' and delegated the judgement to his officers.

Prior Heribert (later to become Abbot) was kidnapped by Roger Mauduit's men to prevent him from bringing the abbey's case before the King's court. Due to Cadfael's intervention, however, the prior escaped and, free to attend and present his evidence, received judgement in the abbey's favour. With the conclusion of Roger's suit, Cadfael was released from his service.

Still carrying his weapons, he immediately went to Vespers in the parish church at Woodstock, 'for no better reason – or so he thought then – than that the dimness within the open doorway beckoned him as he turned his back on a duty completed, inviting him to quietness and thought, and the bell was just sounding. The little prior was there, ardent in thanksgiving, one more creature who had fumbled his way to the completion of a task, and the turning of a leaf in the book of his life.'

> Cadfael watched out the office, and stood mute and still for some time after priest and worshippers had departed. The silence after their going was deeper than the ocean and more secure than the earth. Cadfael breathed and consumed it like new bread. It was the light touch of a small hand on the hilt of his sword that startled him out of that profound isolation. He looked down to see a little acolyte, no higher than his elbow, regarding him gravely from great round eyes of blinding blue, intent and challenging, as solemn as ever was angelic messenger.
>
> 'Sir,' said the child in stern treble reproof, tapping the hilt with an infant finger, 'should not all weapons of war be laid aside here?'
>
> 'Sir,' said Cadfael hardly less gravely, though he was smiling, 'you may very well be right.' And slowly he unbuckled the sword from his belt, and went and laid it down, flatlings, on the lowest step under the altar. It looked strangely appropriate and at peace there. The hilt, after all, was a cross.

Later that same day, Cadfael went to seek an audience with Prior Heribert, who was returning to Shrewsbury the next morning. 'The little man came out graciously to welcome a stranger, and knew him for an acquaintance at least, and now at a breath certainly a friend.

'"Father," Cadfael said simply, "here am I at the turning of my life, free of one man's service, and finished with arms. Take me with you!"'

*Church of St Mary
Magdalene, Woodstock,
Oxfordshire*

Norman south door, Church
of St Mary Magdalene,
Woodstock, Oxfordshire

*Founded in the reign of Henry II (1153–1189) as a chapel-of-ease to the Parish
Church of St Martin at the nearby village of Bladon, the Church of St Mary
Magdalene was often used by the King when he was in residence at his royal manor
of Woodstock. The only surviving feature of the original church is the Norman
south door decorated with a zig-zag pattern which, dispensing with the usual
capitals, goes round the arch and down both sides to the ground. Over the centuries
the church was altered and enlarged and in 1878 it was extensively restored.
Preserved inside the church, on the south arcade, are over twenty beautifully carved
stone heads thought to be portraits of people living in the thirteenth century,
including a man wearing a coronet said to be King Henry III (1216–1272).*

Having lived most of his life 'in the thick of battles', Cadfael returned with the
Benedictine brothers of the Abbey of Saint Peter and Saint Paul at Shrewsbury
in November 1120 to become a monk. Despite the fact that he had come late to
monastic life, 'like a battered ship settling at last for a quiet harbour', he never
had any regrets. Gradually, over the years, he worked hard to create one of the
finest Benedictine herb gardens in the whole of England, stocked with 'many
exotic plants of his own careful raising', collected in his travels throughout
Europe and the Holy Land. It was 'his own small kingdom' and within it 'he
ruled unchallenged'. In a sheltered corner of the walled herbarium he had a
wooden work-shed, 'his own particular pride', where he prepared his medicines,
dried his herbs and brewed his mysteries. It was 'a home within a home'; a
refuge within which he could withdraw from the outside world, 'always a
convenient excuse for not being where according to the horarium he should
have been'; and a place where he 'spent so much of his time, and did his best
thinking'.

He was well aware that in the first years of his vows the novices and lay servants had
been wont to point out to one another with awed whisperings,
'See that brother working in the garden there? The thickset fellow who rolls from
one leg to the other like a sailor? You wouldn't think to look at him, would you, that
he went on crusade when he was young? ... Hard to believe it now, eh?'
Brother Cadfael himself found nothing strange in his wide-ranging career, and had
forgotten nothing and regretted nothing. He saw no contradiction in the delight he
had taken in battle and adventure, and the keen pleasure he now found in quietude.
Spiced, to be truthful, with more than a little mischief when he could get it, as he
liked his victuals well flavoured, but quietude all the same, a ship becalmed and
enjoying it.

Whenever his friend Hugh Beringar, the Sheriff of Shropshire, came to the
abbey to confer with the Abbot on 'shire affairs' he always sought Cadfael out

afterwards and, more often than not, found him working in his herb garden or busy in his workshop. Together they spent many pleasurable hours 'sitting easy', sharing a jug of wine and chatting beneath the 'rustling bunches of dried herbs hung from the roof-beams'.

And sometimes, when he was alone and had nothing more to do than put his feet up on the wooden bench, Cadfael 'remembered and acknowledged with gratitude and joy the years of his sojourning in the world, the lusty childhood and venturous youth, the taking of the Cross and the passion of the Crusade, the women he had known and loved, the years of his sea-faring off the coast of the Holy Kingdom of Jerusalem, all that pilgrimage that had led him here at last to his chosen retreat. None of it wasted, however foolish and amiss, nothing lost, nothing vain, all of it somehow fitting him to the narrow niche where he now served and rested.'

Yes, indeed, Brother Cadfael 'had no need to regret anything'. And what he 'did not regret, he found grave difficulty in remembering to confess'.

Shrewsbury Castle

King Stephen and the Empress Maud

In the year 1100 – on the death of his brother, William Rufus – Henry, the youngest son of William the Conqueror, seized the crown of England. Rufus was killed by an arrow while hunting in the New Forest and, despite later speculation that Henry might have 'arranged' his brother's death, it was widely held to have been an accident. Robert of Normandy, the eldest of the Conqueror's three sons and rightful heir to the English throne, was in Jerusalem at the time. The *Chronicles of Brother Cadfael* state that Cadfael had been a part of Robert's 'mongrel' company during the First Crusade and, when Jerusalem 'was settled and Baldwin crowned', had taken to the sea and become a sailor.

Although Robert returned to Normandy in September 1100, it was not until the following year that he attempted an invasion. When he landed with a considerable force at Portsmouth in July 1101, many of the great Norman barons in England rallied to his side, including the powerful Earl Robert de Bellême, the son of Earl Roger de Montgomery, founder of Shrewsbury Abbey (see Shrewsbury Abbey, p. 69).

The two armies met at Alton, near Winchester. But instead of resolving their dispute on the field of battle, both sides withdrew to explore the possibility of a peaceful settlement. In the event, a treaty was successfully negotiated, allowing Henry to keep the crown of England in return for paying his brother, Robert of Normandy, a pension of 2,000 pounds a year. Henry also agreed to renounce any claims to lands in Normandy, excepting the fortress of Domfront.

*Henry I with his brother
William Rufus*

Once the danger was over, however, and Robert had returned to Normandy, Henry set about strengthening his realm by removing any further threat of either rebellion or invasion. One by one he confiscated the lands of the prominent Normans who had opposed him, including the powerful Robert de Bellême, who was banished from the kingdom, having forfeited his earldom and had his strongholds in the Welsh Marches seized.

But Henry was not content just to assert his royal authority; he was also set on taking Normandy from his brother. In 1106, at the battle of Tinchebrai, Robert was captured and imprisoned for the remaining twenty-eight years of his life. With the incarceration of his brother, Henry had removed the main threat to his authority and power, yet the wars in Normandy dragged on intermittently for years.

In November 1120 Cadfael, 'experienced and accomplished in arms', sailed from Normandy to England in the service of Roger Mauduit, a Northampton knight. Although he was unaware of it at the time, the Welsh man-at-arms was at the turning of his life, for before the year was out he was to exchange the discipline of a soldier for that of a monk.

Henry I was in Normandy when Cadfael crossed the Channel for the last time. *A Light on the Road to Woodstock (A Rare Benedictine)* sets the scene:

> The King's court was in no hurry to return to England, that late autumn of 1120, even though the fighting, somewhat desultory in these last stages, was long over, and the enforced peace sealed by a royal marriage. King Henry had brought to a successful conclusion his sixteen years of patient, cunning, relentless plotting, fighting and manipulating, and could now sit back in high content, master not only of England but of Normandy, too. What the Conqueror had misguidedly dealt out in two separate parcels to his elder sons, his youngest son had now put together again and clamped into one. Not without a hand in removing from the light of day, some said, both of his brothers, one of whom had been shovelled into a hasty grave under the tower at Winchester, while the other was now a prisoner in Devizes, and unlikely ever to be seen again by the outer world.
>
> The court could well afford to linger to enjoy victory, while Henry trimmed into neatness the last loose edges still to be made secure. But his fleet was already preparing at Barfleur for the voyage back to England, and he would be home before the month ended.

In that autumn of 1120, having finally triumphed over French and Angevin opposition to become master of England and Normandy, Henry suffered a dreadful tragedy that upset everything he had planned. On the night of 25 November, the *Blanche Nef* (White Ship), in which his only legitimate son and heir, Prince William, 'with all his companions and many other noble souls were embarked, put to sea late, and was caught in gales before ever clearing Barfleur.

The ship was lost, split upon a rock, foundered with all hands', and 'half the young chivalry of England' was 'wiped out in one blow'.

> So that was the end of one man's year of triumph, an empty achievement, a ruinous victory, Normandy won, his enemies routed, and now everything swept aside, broken apart upon an obstinate rock, washed away in a malicious sea. His only lawful son, recently married in splendour, now denied even a coffin and a grave, for if ever they found those royal bodies it would be by the relenting grace of God, for the sea seldom put its winnings ashore by Barfleur. Even some of his unlawful sons, of whom there were many, gone down with their royal brother, no one left but the one legal daughter to inherit a barren empire.

Henry's 'one legal daughter' was Matilda, or Maud, who was 'married in childhood to the Holy Roman Emperor Henry V' of Germany. When the Emperor died in 1125, Henry recalled the Empress Maud to England and made his barons acknowledge her as his heir. Three years later, in order to form an alliance with Fulk V of Anjou, Henry forced her to marry the count's fourteen-year-old son and heir, Geoffrey Plantagenet, or Geoffrey of Anjou.

'Countess of Anjou', according to the *Twelfth Chronicle (The Raven in the Foregate)*, was a title she 'detested, as belittling both her birth and her rank by her first marriage, a king's daughter and the widow of an emperor, now reduced to a title borrowed from her none-too-loved and none-too-loving second husband, Geoffrey of Anjou, her inferior in every particular but talent, common sense and efficiency'. In fact, it was said, all he ever did for Maud was give her three sons, one of whom she eventually saw crowned as Henry II.

When Henry I died on 1 December 1135, the Empress Maud and Geoffrey of Anjou, to whom he had promised the succession of his Anglo-Norman realm, were 'far away in Normandy, thinking no evil'. His favourite nephew, Count Stephen of Blois, however, who was little more than a day away in Boulogne, rushed to England and, with the help of his brother, Henry of Blois, Bishop of Winchester, seized the throne and had himself crowned King at Westminster within the month. Many of the barons who had sworn fealty to the Empress retracted their oaths and declared themselves for him. Stephen's action was to herald the start of a long civil war for the crown of England, a struggle, fought between cousins and rival claimants to the throne, that was to last for nearly nineteen years. It is during this troubled period – with fortune swinging like a pendulum many times between the warring factions – that the *Chronicles* are set.

The *Second Chronicle (One Corpse too Many)* is based on King Stephen's siege of Shrewsbury Castle in the summer of 1138, the year after Prior Robert Pennant's expedition into Wales to bring back the bones of Saint Winifred (see Saint Winifred, p. 85). The Sheriff, William FitzAlan, owed his office to Stephen, yet he held the castle for the Empress Maud.

King Stephen, nephew of Henry I

The west front of Winchester Cathedral, Hampshire

The first cathedral at Winchester, known as the Old Minster, was built by the Saxon King Cenwalh in about 645 and dedicated to St Peter. Its foundations lie just to the north of the present cathedral. The first Norman Bishop of Winchester was William Walkelin and he began the construction of the present cathedral in 1079. It was consecrated in 1093 and, shortly after, the Old Minster was demolished. Winchester Cathedral, 556 feet from east to west, is the longest in Europe. The Perpendicular arches and vaulting of the nave are the work of the fourteenth-century Bishop, William of Wykeham, who continued the transformation from Norman to Gothic started by his predecessor William of Edington. Inside the cathedral there are a number of monuments to Saxon kings and queens, the tomb of the Norman King, William Rufus, who reigned from 1087–1100, and also the graves of Jane Austen (1775–1817) and Izaak Walton (1593–1683).

In his siege camp, deployed across the entire land approach to the Castle Foregate, between broad coils of the River Severn, King Stephen fretted, fumed and feasted, celebrating the few loyal Salopians – loyal to him, that is! – who came to offer him aid, and planning his revenge upon the many disloyal who absented themselves.

He was a big, noisy, handsome, simple-minded man, very fair in colouring, very comely in countenance, and at this stage in his fortunes totally bewildered by the contention between his natural good nature and his smarting sense of injury. He was said to be slow-witted, but when his Uncle Henry had died and left no heir but a daughter, and she handicapped by an Angevin husband and far away in France, no matter how slavishly her father's vassals had bowed to his will and accepted her as queen, Stephen for once in his life had moved with admirable speed and precision, and surprised his potential subjects into accepting him at his own valuation before they even had time to consider their own interests, much less remember reluctant vows. So why had such a successful coup abruptly turned sour? He would never understand. Why had half of his more influential subjects, apparently stunned into immobility for a time, revived into revolt now? Conscience? Dislike of the King imposed upon them? Superstitious dread of King Henry and his influence with God?

Forced to take the opposition seriously and resort to arms, Stephen had opened in the way that came naturally to him, striking hard where he must, but holding the door cheerfully open for penitents to come in. And what had been the result? He had spared, and they had taken advantage and despised him for it. He had invited submission without penalty, as he moved north against rebel holds, and the local baronage had held off from him with contempt. Well, tomorrow's dawn should settle the fate of the Shrewsbury garrison, and make an example once for all. If these midlanders would not come peacefully and loyally at his invitation, they should come scurrying like rats to save their own skins.

The following day, after a siege that had lasted four weeks, Stephen's army took Shrewsbury Castle:

> Long before noon it was all over, the gates fired with brushwood and battered down, the baileys cleared one by one, the last defiant bowman hunted down from the wall and towers, smoke heavy and thick like a pall over fortress and town. In the streets not a human creature or even a dog stirred. At the first assault every man had gone to earth with wife and family and beasts behind locked and barred doors and crouched listening with stretched ears to the thunder and clash and yelling of battle. It lasted only a short while. The garrison had reached exhaustion, ill-supplied, thinned by desertions as long as there was any possibility of escape. Everyone had been certain the next determined attack must carry the town. The merchants of Shrewsbury waited with held breath for the inevitable looting, and heaved sighs of relief when it was called to heel peremptorily by the King himself – not because he grudged his Flemings their booty but because he wanted them close about his person. Even a king is vulnerable, and this had been an enemy town, and was still unpacified. Moreover, his urgent business was with the garrison of the castle, and in particular with FitzAlan and Adeney, and Arnulf of Hesdin.

Although William FitzAlan and Fulke Adeney, loyal supporters of the Empress Maud, managed to escape, Arnulf of Hesdin was captured and, along with ninety-three others, was hanged from the walls of the castle. Stephen's chief aide, Gilbert Prestcote, 'a lean, middle-aged knight browed and nosed like a falcon, his black, forked beard veined with grey', was made Sheriff of Shropshire in place of FitzAlan. Prestcote's right-hand man, Adam Courcelle, was made his deputy. According to the *Second Chronicle*, however, Courcelle was killed shortly after during a 'trial by combat' and his victorious opponent, Hugh Beringar, was appointed deputy in his stead.

When Prestcote was murdered in 1141, Beringar became Sheriff, and throughout the rest of the *Chronicles* – despite pendulum-like swings of fortune between the two rival claimants to the throne – he doggedly remained 'King Stephen's man, and held the shire for him loyally enough, but with even greater goodwill he held it for the folk who lived in it'. Beringar 'was only too glad to be guardian of a shire which had changed hands but once', and, from the outset, was determined to 'keep King Stephen's title unchallenged and the tide of unrest at bay from its borders, whether the threat came from the Empress's forces, the unpredictable cantrips of the Welsh of Powys to the west, or the calculating ambition of the Earl of Chester in the north'. Hugh managed to balance his 'relationships with all these perilous neighbours' for many years 'with fair success'.

Hugh Beringar was 'a man whose energy did not flag as Stephen's did, who did not abandon one enterprise to go off after another, as Stephen did'. Small and slender, with a tanned, clean-shaven face and cropped black hair, his 'modest stature and light weight had deceived many a man to his undoing'. He owned a manor at Maesbury, near Oswestry, in the north-west corner of the shire, and also a house in Shrewsbury, which he shared with his wife, Aline, and their son, Giles, to whom Cadfael was godfather.

In a country debilitated by 'years of desultory civil war it behoved state and church to work closely together, and where sheriff and abbot were of like mind they could secure for their people a comparatively calm and orderly existence, and fend off the worst excesses of the times'. Hugh and Abbot Radulfus grew to know and trust each other over the years, and were 'accustomed to sharing with complete confidence, for the sake of order and England, whatever they gathered of events and tendencies, without ever questioning whether they shared the same opinions. Their disciplines were separate and very different, but their acceptance of service was one, and mutually recognised.'

Although Cadfael's first encounters with Hugh had 'been a puzzle to him', proof upon proof since then 'had sealed him friend, the closest and dearest'. Despite the difference in their ages – a gap of over thirty years – Cadfael and Hugh were 'closer than father and son, having not only that easy and tolerant relationship of two generations, but shared experiences that made of them contemporaries. They sharpened minds, one upon the other, for the better protection of values and institutions that needed defence with every passing day in a land so shaken and disrupted.'

After the siege and fall of Shrewsbury Castle, the 'tide of civil war between King Stephen and the partisans of the Empress Maud ... receded into the south-western borders, leaving Shrewsbury to recover cautiously from having backed the weaker side and paid a bloody price for it'. On 30 September 1139 the Empress Maud and her half-brother Robert of Gloucester landed near Arundel, on the south coast, and seemed to be within Stephen's grasp, but 'through the misplaced generosity of the King, or the dishonest advice of some of his false friends, had been allowed to reach Bristol, where her cause was impregnably installed already'. With both rival factions now in England the nation was in a state of anarchy.

In November 1139 the city of Worcester was taken by the forces of the Empress, and 'all those of its inhabitants who could get away in time' fled north into Shropshire. On the southern border, the castellan of Ludlow Castle, Josce de Dinan was, according to the *Sixth Chronicle (The Virgin in the Ice)*, 'contemplating defection'. It is said, though not confirmed by modern historians, that the castle was besieged in 1139 by King Stephen, who is reputed to have rescued his ally, Prince Henry of Scotland, from the hook of a grappling iron thrown down from the walls by one of the defenders.

*Ludlow Castle,
domestic buildings*

December of the following year brought news of treason in the north-east. The *Eighth Chronicle (The Devil's Novice)* relates that two days after Stephen had left Lincoln, having received pledges of loyalty from Ranulf of Chester and William of Roumare, they reneged on their oaths, 'made their way into the King's castle by a subterfuge' and took it by force. In February 1141 Stephen mustered a 'creditable force' to try and oust the Earls of Chester and Lincoln, 'ambitious half-brothers', from their hill-top fortress at Lincoln. In the battle which followed, Stephen, who bravely fought on when he might have escaped, was captured and taken to Bristol, where he was held prisoner in the castle.

The Observatory Tower at Lincoln Castle

The Empress Maud was up in the clouds, and Stephen, crowned and anointed though he might be, was down in the midden, close-bound and close-guarded, and his brother Henry of Blois, bishop of Winchester and papal legate, far the most influential of the magnates and hitherto his brother's supporter, had found himself in a dilemma. He could either be a hero, and adhere loudly and firmly to his allegiance, thus incurring the formidable animosity of a lady who was in the ascendant and could be dangerous, or trim his sails and accommodate himself to the reverses of fortune by coming over to her side.

He chose the latter. 'Discreetly, of course, and with well-prepared arguments to render his about face respectable.' And in the summer of 1141 the Empress was allowed to enter London and make preparations for her coronation. But 'the fool woman, with the table spread for her at Westminster and the crown all but touching her hair, had seen fit to conduct herself in so arrogant and overbearing

The ancient hill city of Lincoln was a settlement long before the Romans invaded England in the first century AD and built a military fortress on the limestone ridge overlooking the flat Lincolnshire plain. Strategically sited to command the meeting of two great highways, the Fosse Way and Ermine Street, Lincoln became a fortified town. By the beginning of the second century it was a colony for retired soldiers, known in its Latin form as Lindum Colonia, from which the name of Lincoln is derived.

In about 1072 the first Norman Bishop, Remigius, began building a great cathedral opposite the castle, on a site which dominated the town and skyline for miles around. Consecrated in 1092, it was damaged by fire in 1141 and by an earthquake in 1185. Work on rebuilding and enlarging the cathedral was started by Bishop Hugh of Avalon in 1192 and continued after his death in 1200. The spire on the central tower, rising 525 feet from the ground, collapsed in 1549 during a violent storm and the smaller spires on the two western towers were removed in 1807.

Lincoln Cathedral, Lincolnshire

a manner towards the citizens of London that they had risen in fury to drive her out in ignominious flight, and let King Stephen's valiant queen into the city in her place'.

A few months later, in September 1141, the Empress Maud, until then besieged in her castle at Winchester, managed to escape into the safety of her western stronghold. Robert of Gloucester, the Empress's half-brother and leader of her party, however, was captured trying to ford the River Test at Stockbridge. Maud was left with no other alternative but to exchange Stephen for Robert, 'without whom she could not hope to achieve anything. And here was England back to the beginning, with all to do again. For if she could not win, neither could she give up.'

Robert died in October 1147, and early in the following year the Empress left England disheartened, never to return. When Stephen's son and heir, Eustace, died in August 1153, a settlement was negotiated and in December, with the signing of a treaty at Westminster, it was agreed that Stephen should remain King for life and that, after his death, the Empress's son, Henry would succeed to the throne. Stephen, however, found himself King of a peaceful, undivided realm for less than a year, for on 25 October 1154 he died. He was buried beside his wife and eldest son in the small Cluniac monastery they had founded at Faversham. For the first time in over a hundred years, the next heir to the English throne was undisputed: Maud's son by Geoffrey of Anjou, with no rival contenders, was crowned King Henry II.

Wolvesey Castle,
Winchester

To the south of Winchester Cathedral are the remains of Wolvesey Castle, a great fortified palace built in 1138 by Bishop Henry de Blois, brother of King Stephen, on the site of an earlier Anglo-Saxon bishop's palace. Bishop Henry's structure also incorporated the stone residence, now known as the West Hall, built by the Norman Bishop, William Giffard, in about 1107. In the summer of 1141, during the fratricidal war between Stephen and Maud, the Empress and her forces besieged Bishop Henry in his castle. He retaliated by setting fire to the city, and was only relieved when Maud's army, weakened by disease and starvation, decided to retreat. Wolvesey Castle was virtually abandoned in the seventeenth century and in the early 1680s Bishop George Morley decided to build a new palace in its place. The house was again neglected in the following century and in 1786 the building was demolished except for the west wing. It was used for a number of purposes until 1928, when it became once again the residence of the bishops of Winchester. The remains of the medieval palace are now in the care of English Heritage.

*Wolvesey Castle,
Winchester*

The north side of Shrewsbury Abbey showing the remains of the demolished outer walls of the north transept

The Benedictines

aint Benedict, the father of Western monasticism, was born in the Italian town of Nursia (present-day Norcia, some forty miles south-east of Perugia), in about AD 480. All that is known of his life, apart from what can be deduced from his Rule, is contained in the *Dialogues* of Saint Gregory the Great, who was Pope Gregory I from 590 to 604. Born into a middle-class family, Benedict was sent by his parents to Rome to be educated, but he was disgusted by the decadent culture he found there and decided to abandon his studies and devote himself to God. After staying a while in a small religious community at Enfide (modern Affile), about forty miles east of Rome, he left to become a hermit, spending several years in the solitude of the nearby mountains round Subiaco. His fame as a holy man grew and in time he was persuaded to become the Abbot of a neighbouring monastery. It is said, however, that the monks rebelled against the severity of his discipline and, after an unsuccessful attempt to poison him, he willingly returned to his solitude.

Nevertheless, his reputation for holiness was such that within a short period of time he had attracted a large number of disciples – so many, in fact, that he was able to found twelve monasteries, each containing twelve monks, with himself in overall control. Among the best known of his followers were Maurus and Placidius, both sons of Roman noblemen, who were later to travel through Gaul (roughly the territory of modern-day France, Luxembourg and Belgium) and Sicily respectively to spread the Benedictine message.

In about 529, after being at Subiaco for some thirty years, Benedict left the area, according to Saint Gregory, because of the nuisance caused by Florentius, a jealous local priest. He and a few of his disciples went to Monte Cassino, half-

Saint Benedict, father of Western monasticism

way between Rome and Naples, where they built a monastery on the summit of a hill overlooking Cassino. It is said that the inhabitants of the district, still mostly pagan, were converted to Christianity by his preaching. His sister, Saint Scholastica, founded a nunnery in a place called Pinmarola nearby.

In 542 Benedict was visited by Totila, King of the Goths. Rebuking Totila for his evil deeds, the Saint prophesied that he would enter Rome to rule for nine years but would die in the tenth. The prophecy was fulfilled. Saint Gregory relates many accounts of Benedict's miracle-making and prophetic abilities, including the prediction that Monte Cassino would be destroyed by 'Barbarians'. Indeed, the Lombards, one of the Germanic conquerors of Italy, sacked the monastery in 583 and it was left deserted until about 720, when it was refounded.

According to legend, Saint Benedict died on 21 March 543 at Monte Cassino, not long after the death of Saint Scholastica, and was buried there with her in the oratory of Saint John the Baptist. Although there has been a great deal of controversy about subsequent events, it seems that the remains of the two saints were removed from Italy to France in about 660, Benedict's relics ending up in the Monastery of Fleury-sur-Loire.

More than half a century after Benedict's death, Saint Augustine, the prior of Pope Gregory I's Monastery of Saint Andrew in Rome, was sent on a mission to England with some forty monks to preach the gospel. He was favourably received by Ethelbert, King of Kent, in 597 and founded a number of religious houses, including the Monastery of Saint Peter and Saint Paul outside the walls of Canterbury. In spite of some early spectacular successes, the conversion of the Anglo-Saxons was slow, with frequent relapses into paganism. Nevertheless, towards the close of the sixth century, Augustine had introduced not only Roman Christianity but also the Benedictine Order to England. From that moment onwards, the Benedictine monasteries stood unrivalled until the collective reforms of the Carthusians, Cistercians and Cluniacs, which occurred roughly in Cadfael's lifetime. The earliest order of regular canons following a monastic rule were the Augustinians, who were introduced to England in 1095. Haughmond Abbey, a house of Augustinian canons (who were also known as Black or Austin canons) was founded in about 1135 by William FitzAlan, a loyal supporter of the Empress Maud. The abbey is situated a few miles north-east of Shrewsbury and is mentioned in the *Sixteenth Chronicle of Brother Cadfael (The Heretic's Apprentice)* and the *Seventeenth Chronicle (The Potter's Field)*.

It was while he was at Monte Cassino that Saint Benedict, making extensive use of existing writings, composed the Rule for which he is famous. The document consists of a prologue and seventy-three chapters, and, according to Saint Gregory, is 'remarkable for its discretion and for the clearness of its language'. The Rule, which demanded from the monks a life-long vow of poverty, chastity, obedience and stability, was adopted not only by the Benedictines but also, with modifications, by later orders. For Brother Cadfael, the 'vow of stability, however gravely undertaken, sometimes proved as hard to keep as the vow of obedience', which he 'had always found his chief stumbling block'.

Although Saint Benedict had been a hermit, he considered that the solitary life was fraught with spiritual dangers for the young and inexperienced. His Rule, therefore, is concerned with a life spent entirely within a monastic community, with the emphasis on moderation. 'We propose', says the prologue, 'to establish a school of the Lord's service and in setting it up we hope to order nothing that is harsh or hard to bear.' The waking day was divided into three roughly equal portions to provide a balance between prayer, work and study. 'Idleness is the enemy of the soul', warns the Rule, 'and for this reason the brethren should be occupied, at fixed periods, in manual labour, and at other times in spiritual reading .

The monastic horarium differed in summer and winter because of the varying hours of daylight. The day began at midnight with Matins, the first and longest service, 'the celebration of God made flesh, virgin-born and wonderful'. This was followed, almost immediately, by Lauds, a short office which ended between one and two in the morning, after which the monks retired to their beds in the *dortoir*.

> Cadfael always rose from Matins and Lauds not sleepy and unwilling, but a degree more awake than at any other time, as though his senses quickened to the sense of separateness of the community gathered here, to a degree impossible by daylight. The dimness of the light, the solidity of the enclosing shadows, the muted voices, the absence of lay worshippers, all contributed to the sense of being enfolded in a sealed haven, where all those who shared in it were his own flesh and blood and spirit, responsible for him as he for them, even some for whom, in the active and arduous day, he could feel no love, and pretended none. The burden of his vows became also his privilege, and the night's first worship was the next day's energy.

In order to check on his workshop or to collect plants, Cadfael 'was often up well before Prime', the first office of the monastic day, which was held at dawn. Terce occurred at about nine; Sext at about noon; None at about three; Vespers in the late afternoon; and Compline, the last office before the community retired for the night, at about eight-thirty in summer and about seven-thirty in winter. The *Twelfth Chronicle (The Raven in the Foregate)* says that Cadfael went to his bed in the *dortoir*, 'mindful of the rule that the words of Compline, the completion, the perfecting of the day's worship, should be the last words uttered before sleep, that the mind should not be distracted from the "Opus Dei"'.

Immediately after Prime, at about eight-thirty in the morning, was the Morning Mass, or the Lady Mass, held for the servants and manual workers. High Mass, the principal mass of the day, was held at about ten in the morning and lasted about an hour.

Chapter, usually following the office of Prime, was held in the chapter-house, and it was here that Cadfael often dozed behind his pillar while the dull routine business of the community was being discussed. After supper in the refectory, the monks went to Collations in the chapter-house; 'the formal reading from the lives of the saints was a part of the day that Cadfael often missed if he had vulnerable preparations brewing in his workshop.' It was the tending of these culinary and medicinal preparations that always provided him with 'a convenient excuse for not being where according to the horarium he should have been'. In between these daylight offices the monks would, besides taking regular meals in the refectory, pursue the round of their duties with study and work.

The Benedictines, also known as Black monks because of the colour of their habits, not only provided for their own needs – running a self-contained and self-sufficient community – but also looked after the needs of others: teaching students; caring for the sick and the elderly; distributing alms to the poor; and housing travellers, whether penniless pilgrims or wealthy kings.

The Officers of Shrewsbury Abbey in 1140

Saint Benedict called the abbot the father of all the monks and said, in chapter two of his Rule, that 'in the monastery he is considered to represent the person of Christ, since he is called by His name'.

In 1140 Abbot Radulfus was the head of the Abbey of Saint Peter and Saint Paul at Shrewsbury, having been 'sent from London to trim an easy-going provincial house into more zealous shape.' Like many abbots, he 'was an aristocrat and the equal of a baron', and, in addition to his monastic responsibilities, his rank meant that he was also involved in feudal and secular duties. Although Radulfus owed his office to the King and the papal legate, it was usual for the abbot to be elected by the monks and, thereafter, hold office for life. 'Though a man of few words himself', Radulfus 'was disposed, as a rule, to allow plenty of scope to those who were rambling and loquacious about their requests and suggestions'. In his fifties, he 'was more than commonly tall, erect as a lance, and sinewy, with a lean hawkface and a calmly measuring eye'. Abbot Radulfus 'had long had qualms of conscience about accepting infants committed by their fathers to the cloister, and had resolved to admit no more boys until they were of an age to make the choice for themselves'.

The choir and nave looking towards the west window of the fourteenth-century tower, Shrewsbury Abbey

'In the dim space of the choir, partially shut off from the nave of the church by the parish altar, the brothers in their stalls showed like carven copies, in this twilight without age or youth, comeliness or homeliness, so many matched shadows. The height of the vault, the solid stone of the pillars and walls, took up the sound of Brother Anselm's voice, and made of it a disembodied magic, high in air.'

The Sanctuary Sparrow

The south side,
Shrewsbury Abbey

Before the Dissolution, when
the abbey was a Benedictine
monastery, the south side of the
church adjoined the north wall
of the cloister and contained no
windows. The present windows
of the south wall replaced
earlier ones and were inserted
in the early nineteenth century

Second in command to the abbot was the prior, who had particular responsibility for maintaining order in the enclave, both spiritually and physically. In the absence of the abbot he took charge of the affairs of the monastery. Chapter sixty-five of the Rule warns that 'serious scandals often occur in monasteries because of the appointment of a prior; for there are those who, swelling up with evil pride, consider themselves to be second abbots and act like tyrants, thereby nourishing scandals and quarrels in the community'. Prior Robert Pennant, 'of mixed Welsh and English blood, was more than six feet tall, attenuated and graceful, silver-grey of hair at fifty, blanched and beautiful of visage, with long aristocratic features and lofty marble brow. There was no man in the midland shires would look more splendid in a mitre, superhuman in height and authority, and there was no man in England better aware of it, or more determined to prove it at the earliest opportunity.' Whatever 'virtues might be found in Prior Robert, humility was not one, nor magnanimity. He was invariably sure of his own rightness, and where it was challenged he was not a forgiving man.'

The prior's clerk, according to the *Chronicles*, was Brother Jerome, 'reflecting Robert's pleasure or displeasure like a small, warped mirror'. Jerome, Robert's 'ear and shadow', was about twenty years younger than Cadfael. 'They were old enemies, in so far as Brother Cadfael entertained enmities. He abhorred a sickly-pale tonsure.' 'A meagre man in the flesh was Brother Jerome, but he made up for it in zeal, though there were those who found that zeal too narrowly channelled, and somewhat dehydrated of the milk of human tolerance.'

Brother Richard, the sub-prior, was Robert's assistant and as such shared the responsibility for order and the observance of discipline in the monastery. Between them, as Radulfus says in the *Eighth Chronicle (The Devil's Novice)*, they bore 'the daily weight of the household and family'. The sub-prior, however, was the antithesis of Prior Robert, 'large, ungainly, amiable and benevolent, of good mind, but mentally lazy'; a 'good man at managing day-to-day affairs, but indolent at attempting decisions'.

Brother Matthew, the cellarer, was in charge of the abbey's stores, and as such was responsible for the purchase of everything concerning food, drink, fuel and other basic requirements. He also looked after the mills, brewhouse, bakery and many other buildings and estates belonging to the monastery. Chapter thirty-one of the Rule says that he is to 'have charge of all affairs, but he is not to act without the abbot's approval, and must carry out his orders'.

Brother Ambrose, the cellarer's clerk, always collected the yearly rents 'within the town and suburbs of Shrewsbury in person. No one knew the abbey rolls as Brother Ambrose did.' In 1140 he had been Matthew's clerk for about four years 'during which time fresh grants to the abbey had been flooding in richly, a new mill on the Tern, pastures, assarts, messuages in the town, glebes in the countryside, a fishery up-river, even a church or two, and there was no one who could match him at putting a finger on the slippery tenant or the field-lawyer, or the householder who had always three good stories to account for his inability to pay'.

Brother Anselm, the precentor, 'scholar and historian', made all the arrangements for the church services and was responsible not only for the music and the readings but also for training the monks to sing, ordering processions and looking after the service books. Anselm 'had his workshop in a corner carrel of the north walk of the cloister, where he kept the manuscripts of his music in neat and loving store'.

> [The] precentor, who also presided over the library, was ten years younger than Cadfael, a vague, unworldly man except where his personal enthusiasms were concerned, but alert and subtle enough in anything that concerned books, music or the instruments that make music, best of all the most perfect, the human voice. The blue eyes that peered out beneath his bushy brown eyebrows and shock of shaggy brown hair might be short-sighted, but they missed very little that went on, and had a tolerant twinkle for fallible human creatures and their failings, especially among the young.

The monk responsible for the welfare of all the abbey's guests was Brother Denis, the hospitaller, 'whose duties kept him most of the time around the court, and within sight of the gate'. Denis, with his 'round, rosy, tonsured head' and sharp brown eyes, 'had a retentive memory and an appetite for news and rumours that usually kept him the best-informed person in the enclave. The fuller his halls, the more pleasure he took in knowing everything that went on there, and the name and vocations of every guest. He also kept meticulous books to record the visitations.'

A 'child of the cloister from his fourth year' and only eight years younger than Cadfael, Brother Edmund, the infirmarer, was responsible for the care of the sick and 'old, retired brothers in the infirmary'. 'Meticulous in observation', Edmund was 'a grave, handsome, thoughtful creature who might have looked equally well on horseback and in arms, or farming a manor and keeping a patron's eye on his tenants'. Brother Cadfael, who regularly replenished the medicine-cupboard with his 'medicines, salves and febrifuges', was Edmund's 'closest friend and associate among the sick'. Standing at 'opposite poles of *oblatus* and *conversus*', herbalist and infirmarer 'understood each other so well that few words ever needed to pass between them'.

Brother Benedict, the sacristan, was essentially 'responsible for the upkeep of the church and enclave', including the contents of the church, its furniture, fittings and supplies. Sometimes, during the sacristan's 'long-winded legal haverings', Cadfael would quietly doze behind his pillar in the chapter-house.

Gaye Orchard,
Shrewsbury Abbey

The lush level land known as the Gaye lay outside the loop of the River Severn, stretching from the English bridge to almost opposite Shrewsbury Castle. Today much of the land is occupied by the Gaye Meadow, the home ground of Shrewsbury Town Football Club. To the north and east lie the sprawling railway lines and sidings of Shrewsbury station. At the southern corner is a small park called the Abbey Gardens, sandwiched between the football ground, the Wakeman School and the abbey side of the English bridge.

Brother Ambrose (not the cellarer's clerk of the same name) held the office of almoner, which 'brought him into contact with the poorest of the poor throughout the Foregate'. Every religious house was obliged to look after the needy and it was Ambrose's responsibility to distribute alms to those who queued up each day outside the abbey gates for food, clothing and sometimes money and medicine.

Brother Paul was not only the master of the novices and the boys, 'but the chief of their confessors, too'. He had 'never engendered, christened, nursed, tended young of his own, and yet there had been some quality in him that the old Abbot Heribert, no subtle nor very wise man, had rightly detected, and confided to him the boys and the novices in a trust he had never betrayed'. Although Paul was a good teacher, it

> had always been Brother Jerome's contention, frequently and vociferously expressed, that Brother Paul exercised far too slack an authority over his young charges, both the novices and the children. It was Paul's way to make his supervision of their days as unobtrusive as possible except when actually teaching, though he was prompt to appear if any of them needed or wanted him. But such routine matters as their ablutions, their orderly behaviour at meals, and their retiring at night and rising in the morning were left to their good consciences and to the sound habits of cleanliness and punctuality they had been taught. Brother Jerome was convinced that no boy under sixteen could be trusted to keep any rule, and that even those who had reached the mature age still had more of the devil in them than of the angels. He would have watched and hounded and corrected their every movement, had he been master of the boys, and made a great deal more use of punishments than ever Paul could be brought to contemplate.

Brother Eluric, custodian of Saint Mary's altar in the Lady Chapel, was, like Brother Edmund the infirmarer, 'a child of the cloister'. Aged about twenty in 1140, Eluric was 'the most learned and devout of his contemporaries, a tall, well-made young man, black-haired and black-eyed. He had been in the cloister since he was three years old, and knew nothing outside it. Unacquainted with sin, he was all the more haunted by it, as by some unknown monster, and assiduous in confession, he picked to pieces his own infinitesimal failings, with the mortal penitence due to deadly sins.'

Brother Petrus, a man who 'could not relax his hold on perfection', had been Abbot Heribert's cook long before he served Radulfus. Cadfael 'was one of a dozen or so people' within the abbey walls 'who were not afraid of Brother Petrus. Fanatics are always frightening, and Brother Petrus was a fanatic, not for his religion or his vocation, those he took for granted, but for his art. His dedicated fire tinted black hair and black eyes, scorching both with a fiery red. His northern blood boiled like his own cauldron. His temper, barbarian from the borders, was as hot as his own oven.'

Although seldom, if ever, mentioned in the *Chronicles*, there were a number of other obedientiaries who had specific responsibilities within the monastery: the succentor was the precentor's assistant; the sub-sacristan was responsible for ringing the bell for each of the services throughout the day and was the sacristan's chief helper; the chamberlain, an official not mentioned in Benedict's original Rule, was in charge of the care of clothes and linen (among his numerous other responsibilities was the duty to provide hot water and soap for washing and shaving); the kitchener was in charge of the cooking of food in the kitchens; and the fraterer looked after the refectory, its equipment, service and meals.

Brother Cadfael was an 'elderly and ordinary monk', and 'held no troublesome parchment office'; 'within the Benedictine Rule, and in genial companionship with it, he had perfected a daily discipline of his own, that suited his needs admirably'. As Ellis Peters says in her introduction to *A Rare Benedictine*, although Cadfael may on occasions break the rules for what he feels to be good reasons, 'he will never transgress against the Rule, and never abandon it'.

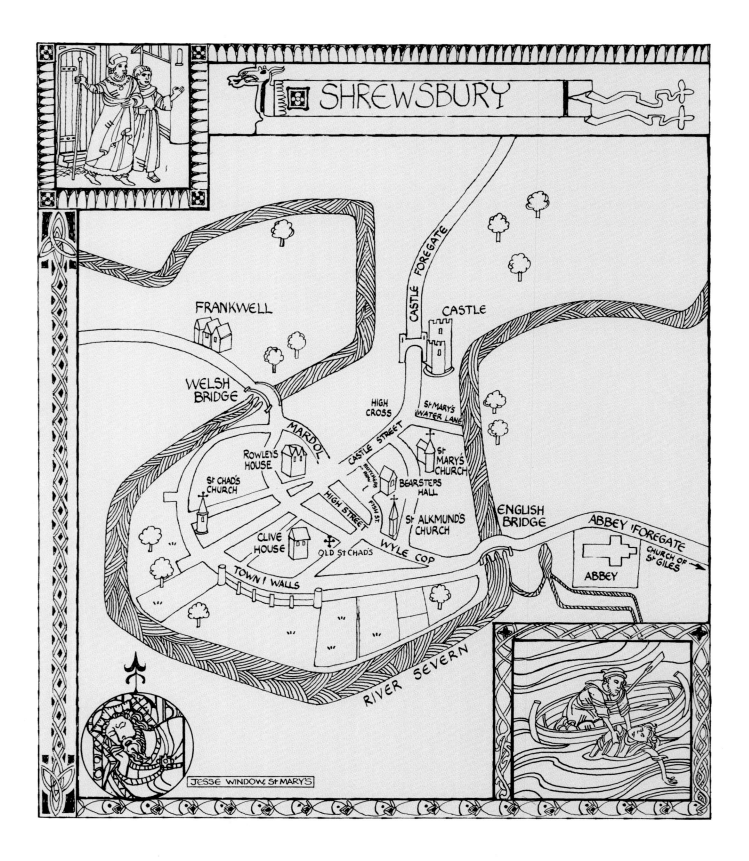

SHREWSBURY

FRANKWELL

CASTLE FOREGATE

CASTLE

WELSH BRIDGE

MARDOL

HIGH CROSS

St MARY'S WATER LANE

ROWLEYS HOUSE

CASTLE STREET

St MARY'S CHURCH

St CHAD'S CHURCH

BUTCHER ROW

BEARSTEPS HALL

HIGH STREET

FISH ST.

CLIVE HOUSE

OLD St CHAD'S

St ALKMUND'S CHURCH

ENGLISH BRIDGE

ABBEY FOREGATE

CHURCH OF St GILES

ABBEY

WYLE COP

TOWN WALLS

RIVER SEVERN

JESSE WINDOW, St MARY'S

Shrewsbury

The longest river in Britain, the Severn, rises on Plynlimon in the mountains of central Wales to flow, in a huge semi-circular curve, to the Bristol Channel and the Atlantic Ocean. Beginning as a mountain stream and ending as a tidal estuary, its approximate 200-mile journey takes it north-eastward, through Powys to Welshpool and across the Welsh border into Shropshire. The first English town on the river is Shrewsbury, situated in 'a close loop of the Severn', and the place where most of the *Chronicles of Brother Cadfael* are set. From Shrewsbury the river winds south across the Shropshire plain, past the Wrekin, through the Ironbridge Gorge to Bridgnorth and on through the counties of Hereford and Worcester and Gloucester to the sea.

During the nineteenth century barges, travelling from as far away as Bristol, could reach Welshpool. But today the recommended upper limit for navigation is Stourport-on-Severn, about seventeen miles down river from Bridgnorth. In the *Fourth Chronicle (Saint Peter's Fair)*, set in the summer of 1139, boats came to Shrewsbury from Gloucester, Buildwas, Brigge (Bridgnorth) and even Wales. One 'fellow, by the name of Rhodri ap Huw, from Mold', in Clwyd, brought his wool-clip, including honey, mead and hides, to Saint Peter's fair by boat; 'a great load', which he shipped up the River Dee and then had transported, at considerable expense, overland to the River Vrnwy (Vyrnwy), a tributary of the Severn. Thomas of Bristol, too, brought his wares by river to the annual Shrewsbury fair. He was 'a man of consequence in the city of Bristol', in 'very good odour with Robert of Gloucester' (the half-brother of the Empress Maud), and was 'one of the biggest importers of wine into the port there'.

Although Shrewsbury lies only five miles north-west of the Roman city of

River Severn at Shrewsbury

Viroconium (Wroxeter), no evidence of Roman occupation has been found in the town. Its origins, however, date back at least to Saxon times. In his writings, Llywarc Hen, a sixth-century poet, refers to Shrewsbury by its Welsh name of Pengwern, meaning 'the hill of alders'. It is reputed that Brocwael, King of Powys, had a palace on the hill where the old Church of Saint Chad now stands. By the ninth century, however, the settlement was part of the kingdom of Mercia, and known by the Anglo-Saxon name of Scrobbesbyrig, probably meaning the 'town on the shrub-covered hill'. Some historians, however, have suggested that Scrobbes is a personal name.

Towards the end of the ninth century, King Alfred the Great granted Mercia to his son-in-law, Ethelred, and on this nobleman's death in about 910 his widow, Ethelfleda, Alfred's eldest daughter, ruled as the 'Lady of the Mercians'. By this time Shrewsbury was an important administrative centre in the Severn valley, and was guarded by a timber fortification at the narrow neck of land where the castle now stands. Ethelfleda, who died in 918, spent the rest of her reign trying to defend her kingdom from Welsh border hostilities and Danish incursions, building numerous fortifications, including castles at Quatford (near Bridgnorth) and Chirbury (near Montgomery). According to tradition, she frequently visited Shrewsbury, where she founded the church dedicated to Saint Alkmund, a prince of the royal house of Northumbria, from which she herself was descended.

In 924 Aethelstan, the eldest son of Edward the Elder, succeeded his father as King of Wessex and Mercia, and in the following year he passed a law to unify the coinage throughout his empire, by specifying the number of moneyers allowed in certain towns or cities. Henceforth, in addition to the previous practice of including the name of the moneyer on the coin, the place where it was struck was also to be included. Shrewsbury was one of the places allowed to mint coins and examples of these still exist. In 1936 a hoard of coins of Edward the Elder, from the early tenth century, was discovered during excavations near the castle.

In the *Seventh Chronicle (The Sanctuary Sparrow)* Brother Cadfael discovers in Shrewsbury a silver penny struck in the reign of the Confessor, 'the sainted Edward, King before the Normans came, a beautiful piece minted in this town. The moneyer was one Godesbrond, there are a few of his pieces to be found, but few indeed in the town where they were struck.'

The Domesday Survey of 1086 shows that, in the reign of Edward the Confessor, Shrewsbury had 252 houses, each inhabited by a burgess, and a population of nearly a thousand (including Godesbrond and two other moneyers). In pre-Norman times the town was probably surrounded by defensive earthworks, while most of the dwellings were of timber construction. There were five principal churches: four built of stone – Saint Chad's, Saint Alkmund's,

Old Saint Chad's, Shrewsbury

The first Church of Saint Chad is reputed to have been founded at the end of the eighth century by Offa, King of Mercia. It was recorded in the Norman survey of 1086 as holding, in addition to other lands and tithes in Shropshire, one and a half hides of land (about 180 acres) in Shrewsbury. The collegiate church was not dissolved until the reign of Edward VI. It continued to be used as a parish church until 9 July 1788 when the tower and the north side of the building collapsed. Although large sections of the church remained standing, the building was demolished in 1789, except for the Lady Chapel, now known as Old Saint Chad's.

Saint Mary's and Saint Julian's – and one built of wood (St Peter's), which stood outside the loop of the river on the site where the abbey now stands (see Shrewsbury Abbey, p. 69).

After the Norman invasion of 1066, William the Conqueror allowed Earl Edwin of Mercia, grandson of Leofric and Lady Godiva, to retain his Midland kingdom, which included Shrewsbury. A few years later, however, the Earl joined an unsuccessful Anglo-Welsh rebellion against the Normans, led by Edric Syvaticus, or Edric the Wild. According to Ordericus Vitalis, himself a native of Shrewsbury, Earl Edwin, attempting to avenge his brother's imprisonment by the Normans, was 'slain on the banks of a river, from which he could not escape, on account of a high tide'.

Shortly after the death of Edwin, William the Conqueror conferred the earldom of Shrewsbury upon his kinsman Roger de Montgomery, the founder of the Abbey of Saint Peter and Saint Paul. In about 1070 Earl Roger began to enlarge and strengthen the wooden fortifications at Shrewsbury, and in the process of clearing the ground to provide more space, over a hundred houses were demolished. It is from this stronghold that Earl Roger led campaigns into the Welsh borderlands. From here, too, in 1088, rebelling against William Rufus, Earl Roger led an 'ill-assorted army' (according to Owen and Blakeway's *A History of Shrewsbury*) in an unsuccessful attempt to capture Worcester.

Earl Roger died in 1094, having made peace with Rufus, and his possessions were divided between his two sons: Hugh de Montgomery inherited his Shropshire lands and became the Second Earl of Shrewsbury, while Robert de Bellême inherited his estates in Normandy. Earl Hugh also inherited a land torn by warfare, for, in 1094, according to Owen and Blakeway, 'Shropshire was laid waste by the Welsh incursions under the command of Griffith ap Cynan, King of North Wales, and Cadwgaun, Prince of Powis; and in the following year they destroyed the castle of Montgomery'. When Earl Hugh was killed in a battle against Danish invaders in 1098, Robert de Belleme, having paid William Rufus a large sum of money for the privilege, became the Third Earl of Shrewsbury.

Earl Robert strengthened not only his castle at Shrewsbury but also those at Montgomery and Ludlow, and in addition built a new castle at Bridgnorth. When Robert of Normandy, brother of King Henry I, invaded England in 1101, Robert de Bellême rallied to his side. Bloodshed, however, was avoided by a peaceful settlement and, in the following year, Henry marched north into Mercia to rid himself of the rebellious Earl and his followers. He captured the castle at Bridgnorth and forced Earl Robert to surrender at Shrewsbury. Robert de Bellême, who confessed to treason, was banished from the country and his castles, lands and properties were forfeited to the Crown (see King Stephen and the Empress Maud, p. 25).

*The great hall,
Shrewsbury Castle*

*Window on south side of the
great hall, Shrewsbury Castle*

*Apart from the Norman gateway, very little survives of the original Norman
castle of Shrewsbury, founded by Earl Roger de Montgomery in about 1070, as
Edward I, rebuilding and strengthening the castle in about 1300, demolished much
of the Norman building and added an outer bailey. It was never used as a fortress
after this date and, over the centuries, was allowed to fall into disrepair. Queen
Elizabeth I gave the castle to the bailiffs and burgesses of Shrewsbury in 1586 and
little was done to the building until the Civil War, when further alterations were
made. The interior of the great hall was partitioned and extra floors were
constructed, including an upper floor lit by a row of square mullioned windows on
the south side. The doors in the main gateway date from this time. It was captured
by the Parliamentarians in 1645 and it was not until 1660, when Charles II was
restored to the throne, that it was surrendered to the Crown. The King granted the
castle to Sir Francis Newport of High Ercall, Shropshire, in 1663 and it remained
in private hands until 1924, when it was acquired by the Corporation of
Shrewsbury. It was restored as much as possible to its Edwardian condition and
opened to the public in 1926.*

*Laura's Tower,
Shrewsbury Castle*

*Doorway to the great hall,
Shrewsbury Castle*

By 1100, the year when Henry seized the crown of England to become King, Shrewsbury already had two bridges over the Severn: the Welsh Bridge and the English Bridge, which was probably built by the monks of the nearby Benedictine abbey. The first record of the town being enclosed by stone walls was in the thirteenth century, during the reign of Henry III. It is thought, however, that the town had walled defences long before this. Owen and Blakeway state that it 'must have been at least surrounded with a rampart of earth, when Aethelstan gave it the privilege of a minter, and when Edgar or Ethelred honoured it with their residence; and that rampart, in all probability, pursued nearly the same circuit which was afterwards adopted by the masons of Henry III'.

In the *Fourth Chronicle (Saint Peter's Fair)*, set a year after the damage caused to the town by Stephen's storming of the castle in 1138, a delegation from the Guild Merchants of Shrewsbury appealed to the abbey 'to set aside a proportion of the fair tolls on goods, whether by horse-load or cart or boat, to be handed over to the town, and spent on restoring the walls'.

Under Henry I Shrewsbury was granted its first charter, but the terms have been lost. The King visited the town in about 1115 and in 1126 he gave it to his second wife, Adeliza, who appointed William FitzAlan as Sheriff to look after her interests in the shire. During the 'civil war for the crown of England' which followed Henry's death in 1135, FitzAlan held Shrewsbury Castle for the Empress Maud. The *Second Chronicle (One Corpse Too Many)* is based on King Stephen's siege and conquest of this Midland stronghold. FitzAlan managed to escape to Normandy, but in 1154, when Stephen died and the Empress's son became King Henry II, he returned to England and was 're-instated in all his vast possessions, both in Shropshire and elsewhere' (Owen and Blakeway).

The *Chronicles* begin in 1137 (one year before the siege and capture of Shrewsbury by King Stephen) and proceed 'steadily season by season, year by year', describing life not only in the Benedictine monastery but also in the medieval town.

At Shrewsbury the river 'made a great moat about the walls, turning the town almost into an island, but for the neck of land covered and protected by the castle'. There were 'only two bridges, one towards the abbey and London' and 'one towards Wales, with a fan of roads branching out westwards'. The eastern bridge, known as the English Bridge because it was on the English side of the town, was stone-built with a drawbridge that 'could cut off approach to the town at need'. Under the first arch of the bridge there used to be moored a boat-mill, the mooring chain of which, during the period of the *Chronicles*, was still in evidence, bolted to a ring in the stone. From this chain FitzAlan's treasury was hidden beneath the waters of the Severn, until it was removed and returned to its rightful owner in the *Second Chronicle (One Corpse Too Many)*.

Meole Brook in the frost

*Norman gateway,
Shrewsbury Castle*

'Where the causeway swept up from the street to the gate of the castle, the beggars who followed the king's camp had taken up new stations, hopeful and expectant, for the king's justiciar, Bishop Robert of Salisbury, had arrived to join his master, and brought a train of wealthy and important clerics with him. In the lee of the gate-house wall Lame Osbern's little trolley was drawn up, where he could beg comfortably without having to move. The worn wooden pattens he used for his callused knuckles lay tidily beside him on the trolley, on top of the folded black cloak he would not need until night fell. It was so folded that the bronze clasp at the neck showed up proudly against the black, the dragon of eternity with his tail in his mouth.'

One Corpse Too Many

'Meantime, Cadfael went up to Saint Mary's churchyard, and sought out the venerable beggar who sat beside the west door, in his privileged and honoured place. Rhodri the Less – for his father had been Rhodri, too, and a respected beggar like his son – knew the footstep, and turned up a wrinkled and pock-marked face, brown as the soil, smiling.

"Brother Cadfael, well met, and what's the news with you?"

'Cadfael sat down beside him, and chatted with the blind old man for a while about Master William Rede, Brother Matthew's chief steward, who was attacked the previous night while collecting the abbey rents in the passage between Saint Mary's and the water-gate.

'Rhodri leaned to rattle his begging-bowl at the pious lady who had been putting up prayers in the church. Business was business, and the pitch he held was the envy of the beggars of Shrewsbury. He blessed the giver, and reached a delaying hand to halt Cadfael, who was rising to depart.'

A Rare Benedictine: Eye Witness

The south side of Saint Mary's Church, Shrewsbury

Brother Cadfael's 'friend and fellow Welshman, Madog of the Dead Boat, who knew everything there was to be known about water and its properties', was a familiar sight on the Severn. He 'had got his name as a result of the cargo he most often had to carry, by reason of his knowledge of all the places where missing persons, thought to have been taken by the river whether in flood or felony, were likely to fetch up'. Madog received 'a fee for every Christian body' he brought out of the water; 'he had indeed a right to it. The duty had edged its way in on him long ago, almost unaware, but other men's dying was the better part of his living now. And an honest, useful, decent art, for which many a family had been thankful.'

Madog of the Dead Boat, who could 'outswim most fish', had a 'hut tucked under the lee of the western bridge that opened the road into his native Wales, and there he made coracles, or timber boats if required, fished in season, ferried fares on request, carried goods for a fee, anything to do with transport by water'.

The suburb of Frankwell lay at the end of the western bridge, outside the town walls and over the river. Beyond Frankwell, Walter Aurifaber, a wealthy Shrewsbury goldsmith, owned 'a pasture and a stable', and it is there that his daughter, Susanna, was killed by an arrow loosed by one of the Sheriff's marksmen in the *Seventh Chronicle*. According to the *Sixteenth Chronicle (The Heretic's Apprentice)*:

> The workshop where Jevan of Lythwood treated his sheepskins lay well beyond the last houses of the suburb of Frankwell, solitary by the right bank of the river, at the foot of a steep meadow backed by a ridge of trees and bushes higher up the slope. Here the land rose, and the water, even at its summer level, ran deep, and with a rapid and forceful current, ideal for Jevan's occupation. The making of vellum demanded an unfailing supply of water, for the first several days of the process running water, and this spot where the Severn ran rapidly provided perfect anchorage for the open wooden frames covered with netting, in which the raw skins were fastened, so that the water could flow freely down the whole length of them, day and night, until they were ready to go into a solution of lime and water in which they would spend a fortnight, before being scraped clean of all remaining hair, and another fortnight afterwards to complete the long bleaching.

From the abbey – sited outside the town walls on the eastern bank of the Severn – Brother Cadfael made regular journeys into the town to attend his patients or visit his friend Hugh Beringar, who was initially Deputy Sheriff of Shropshire and later Sheriff. In 1141 he found himself making one such journey:

> There was no real need for Cadfael to deliver the herbs and medicines in person, but he took advantage of the opportunity as much to satisfy his curiosity as to enjoy the walk and the fresh air on a fine, if blustery, March day. Along the Foregate, over the bridge spanning the Severn, muddied and turgid from the thaw in the mountains, in

through the town gate, up the long, steep curve of the Wyle, and gently downhill from the High Cross to the castle gatehouse, he went with eyes and ears alert, stopping many times to exchange greetings and pass the time of day.

The town gate 'on the eastern side was a part of the castle defences', and was 'closed and guarded during the night hours'. Since King Stephen's siege,

> Shrewsbury had been safe enough from any threat on the eastern approach, only the occasional brief Welsh raid from the west had troubled the peace of the shire, but Hugh Beringar maintained the routine watchfulness without a break. But the most easterly wicket, giving access to the river under the very towers of the fortress, was there to be used freely. Only in times of possible danger were all the wickets closed and barred, and sentries set on the walls. Horsemen, carts, market wagons, all must wait for the gates to be opened at dawn, but a solitary man might pass through at any hour.

High Cross, Shrewsbury

Outside the northern gate of Shrewsbury 'the Castle Foregate housed a tight little suburb of houses and shops, but it ended very soon, and gave place to meadows on either side the road.' Here the 'river twined serpentine coils on both sides, beyond the fields', and 'in the first level meadow on the left' Hugh Beringar fought a duel to the death with Adam Courcelle, Deputy Sheriff of Shropshire in the *Second Chronicle*.

Lame Osbern, one of the town beggars, had his pitch outside the castle gates. He 'had been born with both legs withered, and scuttled around at unbelievable speed on hands provided with wooded pattens, dragging his shrivelled knees behind him on a little wheeled trolley'. In the *Second Chronicle* Cadfael presented him with a thick, warm cloak.

Up until his death in March 1141, Gilbert Prestcote, Sheriff of Shropshire, had made his family apartments high in the corner tower of the castle. His successor, Hugh Beringar, however, had preferred to maintain a residence in the town. He lived with his wife, Aline, and their son, Giles, in a house by Saint Mary's Church, 'only up the curve of the Wyle and the level street beyond'.

Several old streets in Shrewsbury were named after the traders who lived or carried out their business in them: Butcher Row, Milk Street, Fish Street, all survive today. Other names, however, have disappeared: Corviser's or Shoe-maker's Row is now known as Pride Hill, while Baker's or Baxter's Row has been swallowed by the High Street. Nevertheless, all of the street names mentioned in the *Chronicles* still exist (their layout, too, has hardly changed): the Wyle (its summit known as the Wyle Cop) is a long, steep, winding road that climbs uphill from the eastern gate towards the High Cross (it was in this street that Martin Bellecote, master carpenter, lived with his wife and family); High Street runs between the Wyle and Maerdol-head; Butcher Row lies midway between the High Street and Saint Mary's Church and is where Edric Flesher,

St Mary's Church from the altar to the west door, Shrewsbury

The Norman south door of St Mary's Church, Shrewsbury

In about 970, after King Edgar had made it a royal chapel, with a dean, seven prebends and a parish priest, St Mary's Church was rebuilt on the site of probably two earlier Saxon churches. It remained a collegiate church, with the King as its patron, until the Dissolution when in 1547–48 it became a parish church. It continued, however, to be a royal chapel until 1846. The Saxon church was demolished during the reign of Henry II (1153–1189), and in its place a cruciform Norman church without aisles was constructed of red sandstone. The Trinity Chapel was added in about 1360, and the central tower removed in about 1471 and a clerestory built from the east end of the church to the west. The octagonal stone spire, reaching a height of over 138 feet, partly collapsed in 1894 and was rebuilt. The church was extensively restored in Victorian times. St Mary's is the largest church in Shrewsbury, measuring 185 feet in length.

'chief of the butchers of Shrewsbury', had his shop; the burgage of Walter Aurifaber, the goldsmith, was 'situated on the street leading to the gateway of the castle' (Castle Street); while the Vestiers, 'the biggest and best-known clothiers in Shrewsbury', had a house and shop at Mardol-head (Maerdol). According to the *Thirteenth Chronicle (The Rose Rent)*:

> The burgage of the Vestier family occupied a prominent place at the head of the street called Maerdol, which led downhill to the western bridge. A right-angled house, with wide shop-front on the street, and the long stem of the hall and chambers running well back behind, with a spacious yard and stables. There was room enough in all that elongated building, besides the living rooms of the family, to house ample stores in a good dry undercroft, and provide space for all the girls who carded and combed the newly dyed wool, besides three horizontal looms set up in their own outbuilding, and plenty of room in the long hall for half a dozen spinsters at once. Others worked in their own homes, and so did five other weavers about the town.

A wool merchant's town property is described in the *Sixteenth Chronicle*:

> The house of Girard of Lythwood, like so many of the merchant burgages of Shrewsbury, was in the shape of an L, the short base directly on the street, and pierced by an arched entry leading through to the yard and garden behind. The base of the L was of only one storey, and provided the shop where Jevan, the younger brother, stored and sold his finished leaves and gatherings of vellum and the cured skins from which they were folded and cut to order. The upright of the L showed its gable end to the street, and consisted of a low undercroft and the living floor above, with a loft in the steep roof that provided extra sleeping quarters. The entire burgage was not large, space being valuable within so enclosed a town, in its tight noose of river. Outside the loop, in the suburbs of Frankwell on one side and the Foregate on the other, there was room to expand, but within the wall every inch of ground had to be used to the best advantage.

Ralph Giffard, 'the Lord of two or three country manors', owned a town house near Saint Chad's Church, where he preferred to spend his winters in comfort. According to the *Twelfth Chronicle (The Raven in the Foregate)*:

> He had lost one manor through loyalty to the cause of his overlord FitzAlan and his sovereign, the Empress Maud, and it had taken him a good deal of cautious treading and quiet submission to achieve the successful retention of what remained. He had but one cause that mattered to him now, and that was to preserve his own situation and leave his remaining estate intact to his son. His life had never been threatened, he had not been so deeply involved as to invite death. But possessions are possessions, and he was an ageing man, by no means minded to abandon his lands and flee either abroad, to Normandy or Anjou, where he had no status, or to Gloucester, to take up arms for the liege lady who had already cost him dear. No, better far to sit still, shun every tempter, and forget old allegiance. Only so he could ensure that young Ralph [his son], . . . playing the lord of the manor at home, should survive this long conflict for the crown without loss, no matter which of the two claimants finally triumphed.

By the middle of the twelfth century, the period of the *Chronicles*, Shrewsbury was a charter borough, where, in Cadfael's words, 'the unfree may work their way to freedom in a year and a day. And sensible boroughs encourage the coming of good craftsmen, and will go far to hide and protect them.' Among those to take advantage of the chance to earn their freedom were the villein Harald, who was taken on by 'a farrier on the town side of the western bridge'; and Alard the silversmith, who had escaped from his brutal master, Hamo FitzHamon of Lidyate, and been hidden by the merchants of the town until he was a free man.

Between the main streets in Shrewsbury, in medieval times, there existed a warren of shuts and passages, and despite the enormous changes that have taken place in the town throughout the intervening centuries, a considerable number have survived. The word 'shut', according to J.B. Blakeway (Salop MSS 1817), is 'not, as might be imagined, a cul-de-sac or alley shut at one end, but, on the contrary, one open at both extremes, enabling the pedestrian, for it is previous only to such, to shoot or move rapidly from one street into another'. Others, however, have suggested that the word may be derived from 'Schutte', the name of a family who once owned a house in Drayton's Passage. Although the origins of some of the names of these shuts and passages are obscure, among those that have survived there are a few worthy of note: Bear Steps, Plough Shut, Compasses Passage, Golden Cross Passage, Barracks Passage, Saint Mary's Shut, and, two with particularly graphic names, Gullet Passage and Grope Lane.

The *Chronicles* suggest that there were a number of alehouses in the town, and mention two in particular: one in Mardol and another in 'a narrow, secluded close off the upper end of the steep, descending Wyle'. It was sited about midway between 'Saint Alkmund's church and the town gate, and the lanes leading to it were shut between high walls'. Outside the town walls, in the extensive parish of Holy Cross to the east of Shrewsbury, there was an inn owned by Walter Renold, better known as Wat's tavern. It 'lay at the far corner of the horse-fair, not on the London highroad, but on the quieter road that bore away north-eastwards' and 'was handy for the country people who brought goods to market'.

A number of alehouses were situated in the Abbey Foregate itself, and alongside them were the houses and shops of the local tradesmen. Among these were the premises of Erwald the wheelwright, who was provost of the Foregate; the bakery of Jordan Achard, who 'bakes good bread, and never cheats on the weight'; the forge of Thomas the farrier; and the workshop and house of Niall the bronzesmith, rented to the abbey by Judith Perle, née Vestier, for an annual payment of one white rose.

St Alkmund's Church from the west door to the altar, Shrewsbury

St Alkmund's Church, Shrewsbury

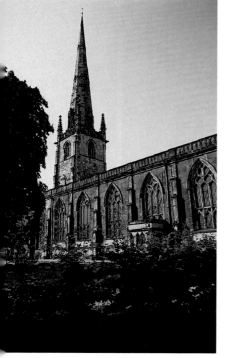

The Church of St Alkmund dates from Saxon times and is thought to have been founded by Ethelfleda, the 'Lady of the Mercians'. It became a collegiate church during the reign of King Edgar (957–975). At the time of the Norman Conquest, its parish was one of four in Shrewsbury: the others being St Chad's, St Julian's and St Mary's. The church was granted to Richard de Belmeis and, when he and his brother Philip founded Lilleshall Abbey in about 1148, much of the wealth of St Alkmund's went towards the building and maintenance of the abbey. After the collapse of Old St Chad's in 1788, it was decided to pull down and rebuild the medieval church of St Alkmund, except for the 184 foot high spire dating from the fifteenth century. The new building was designed by Carline and Tilley and was completed in 1795.

There were few inhabitants of the parish of Holy Cross that Brother Cadfael did not know:

> He had treated many of them, or their children, at some time in these his cloistered years; even, sometimes, their beasts, for he who learns about sickness of men cannot but pick up, here and there, some knowledge of the sicknesses of their animals, creatures with as great a capacity for suffering as their masters, and much less means of complaining, together with far less inclination to complain. Cadfael often wished that men would use their beasts better, and tried to show them that it would be good husbandry. The horses of war had been part of that curious, slow process within him that had turned him at length from trade in arms into the cloister (see Brother Cadfael, p. 19).

In addition to knowing many of the parishioners of Holy Cross, there was also very little about the abbey precinct and the town of Shrewsbury that Cadfael did not know. As Hugh Beringar good-humouredly remarked to him one day before Mass: 'How many eyes and ears have you in every street in Shrewsbury? I wish my own intelligencers knew half as much of what goes on'.

To Cadfael, people were endlessly mysterious and, as he himself admitted, 'I am endlessly curious. A sin to be confessed, no doubt, and well worth a penance. As long as man is curious about his fellowman, that appetite alone will keep him alive.' And, as the *Chronicles* reveal, there was always plenty going on in the town of Shrewsbury to 'satisfy his curiosity', particularly when it came to solving crimes.

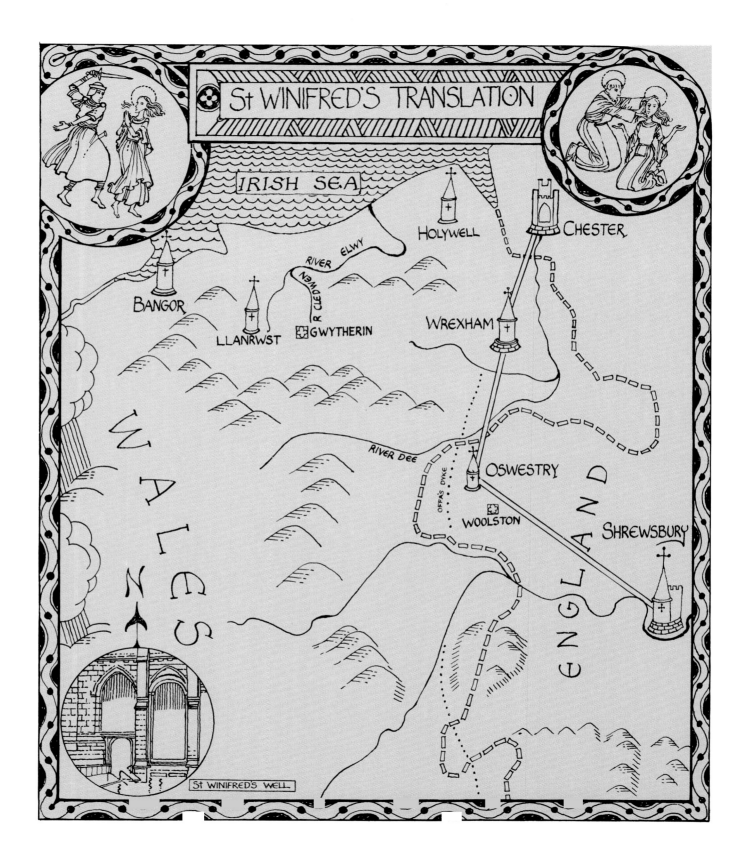

St WINIFRED'S TRANSLATION

IRISH SEA

HOLYWELL

CHESTER

BANGOR

RIVER ELWY

R CLEDWEN

WREXHAM

LLANRWST

GWYTHERIN

WALES

RIVER DEE

OFFA'S DYKE

OSWESTRY

WOOLSTON

ENGLAND

SHREWSBURY

St WINIFRED'S WELL

Saint Winifred

n a remote Welsh mountain valley, almost five miles directly east of Llanrwst (Gwynedd), lies the village of Gwytherin in the county of Clwyd, the burial place of Saint Winifred and the objective of an expedition taken by the Benedictine monks of Shrewsbury in 1137* to acquire her sacred bones for their monastery. Although the *First Chronicle of Brother Cadfael (A Morbid Taste for Bones)* is based on this historical journey, the events and monastic characters depicted in it – except Prior Robert Pennant and Abbot Heribert – are entirely fictional.

When the expedition returned to the Abbey of Saint Peter and Saint Paul at Shrewsbury, according to the *Chronicle*, all but Brother Cadfael were confident that they had triumphed in their mission. He, however, knew otherwise, having gone to great pains to conceal from Prior Robert and his fellow brothers the 'truth' about certain happenings at Gwytherin. He felt strongly that he had no alternative, for had the 'truth' been revealed, it would have brought a 'fearful scandal … to smirch the abbey of Shrewsbury, and all the force of the Benedictine Order'. How could he reveal that it was not Saint Winifred they had brought back from Wales in their 'resplendent coffin' but the body of Brother Columbanus, who in ignorance they thought had been miraculously 'taken up living out of this world'?

Saint Winifred, says the *Chronicle*,

was the only child of a knight named Tevyth, who lived in those parts when the princes were yet heathens. But this knight and all his household were converted by Saint Beuno, and made him a church there, and gave him house-room. The girl was devoted even above her parents, and pledged herself to a virgin life, hearing Mass

---

*Some histories give the year of Saint Winifred's translation as 1138, not 1137. Prior Robert Pennant's book states that the expedition took place 'in the second regnal year of King Stephen'. As Stephen was anointed King on 22 December 1135, his second year begins on 22 December 1136, making the May journey definitely 1137.

every day. But one Sunday it happened that she was sick, and stayed at home when all the rest of the household went to church. And there came to the door the prince of those parts, Cradoc, son of the king, who had fallen in love with her at a distance. For this girl was very beautiful.

Pleading 'that he was hot and parched from hunting', he 'asked for a drink of water, and the girl let him in and gave him to drink'. Once inside, he 'pressed his suit upon her, and grappled her in his arms'. The 'faithful virgin put him off with soft words, and escaping into another room, climbed from a window and fled towards the church. But finding that she had eluded him, Prince Cradoc took horse and rode after, and overtaking her just within sight of the church, and dreading that she would reveal his infamy, struck off her head with his sword.' At that moment,

> Saint Beuno and the congregation were coming out of the church, and saw what had passed. The saint drew a terrible curse upon the murderer, who at once sank to the ground, and began to melt like wax in a fire, until all his body had sunk away into the grass. Then Saint Beuno fitted the head of the virgin onto her neck, and the flesh grew together, and she stood up alive, and the holy fountain sprang up on the spot where she arose.

The place where this miraculous fountain of water sprang up became known as Treffynnon in Welsh and Holywell in English.

Later, Saint Winifred went on a pilgrimage to Rome, 'and she attended at a great synod of saints, and was appointed to be prioress over a community of virgin sisters at Gwytherin, by Llanrwst. And there she lived many years, and did many miracles in her lifetime.'

St Winifred (also spelled Winefride and known as Gwenfrewi in Welsh) lived in the seventh century, almost certainly at Holywell (Treffynnon) in North Wales. One legend says that, after Prince Caradoc had cut off her head with his sword, it rolled down the hillside and where it came to rest a fountain of pure water gushed out of the ground. Holywell became a great centre of pilgrimage and the water from the well was famed for its miraculous healing properties. The present chapel which encloses the well was built at the end of the fifteenth century. It was drastically altered from the eighteenth century onwards and only recently restored. The water was cut off in 1917 when mining operations at Halkyn diverted the underground stream and although the supply of water was connected to another source, the flow is now much reduced.

*St Winefride's Well,
Holywell, Clwyd*

The Church of St Winifred, Gwytherin, Clwyd

She was buried in the churchyard at Gwytherin, overlooking the valley of the Afon Cledwen, a tributary of the Elwy which joins the Clwyd near Llanelwy (St Asaph). Her bones remained undisturbed at Gwytherin for almost five hundred years, until Prior Robert, envious of the Cluniac priory of Wenlock, 'a few miles distant, with its own miracle-working saint', decided to find 'a spare saint' for the Benedictine abbey of Shrewsbury and – seemingly through divine guidance – was directed to Winifred.

The events, as described in the *First Chronicle*, are as follows. One May morning in the year 1137 Brother Columbanus, a young Benedictine monk of Shrewsbury, 'barely a year tonsured' and coming from a 'formidable, aristocratic Norman family, a younger son despatched to make his way in the monastic ranks as next-best to inheriting land', fell to the floor of the chapter-house, overcome by some kind of fit. Many of the brothers 'hovered in helpless shock' as the young man 'lay on his face, threshing and jerking like a landed fish, beating his forehead and his palms against the flagstones, kicking and flailing with long, pale legs bared to the knee by his contortions, and barking out of him those extraordinary sounds of shattering physical excitement'. Eventually Columbanus was overpowered and, after being securely bound and gagged to prevent him from hurting himself, he was carried to the infirmary, where he was subdued by a draught of Brother Cadfael's 'poppy-juice'. Prior Robert instructed his 'faithful hound', 'toady and shadow', Brother Jerome, to sit constantly by the young man's bedside day and night to watch over him, in case the fit should come again.

Brother Jerome appeared at chapter next morning with an exalted countenance, and the air of one bursting with momentous news. At Abbot Heribert's mild reproof for leaving his patient without permission, he folded his hands meekly and bowed his head, but lost none of his rapt assurance.

'Father, I am sent here by another duty, that seemed to me even more urgent. I have left Brother Columbanus sleeping, though not peacefully, for even his sleep is tormented. But two lay-brothers are watching by him. If I have done wrong, I will abide it humbly.'

'Our brother is no better?' asked the abbot anxiously.

'He is still deeply troubled, and when he wakes he raves. But Father, this is my errand! There is a sure hope for him! In the night I have been miraculously visited. I have come to tell you what divine mercy has instructed me. Father, in the small hours I fell into a doze beside Brother Columbanus' bed, and had a marvellous sweet dream.'

'Father,' Jerome continued, 'it seemed to me that the wall of the room opened, and a great light shone in, and through the light and radiating the light there came in a most beautiful young virgin, and stood beside our brother's bed, and spoke to me. She told me that her name was Winifred, and that in Wales there is a holy spring, that rose to the light where she suffered martyrdom. And she said that if Brother

Columbanus bathed in the water of that well, he would surely be healed, and restored at once to his senses. Then she uttered a blessing upon our house, and vanished in a great light, and I awoke.'

Through the murmur of excitement that went round the chapter-house, Prior Robert's voice rose in reverent triumph: 'Father Abbot, we are being guided! Our quest for a saint has drawn to us this sign of favour, in token that we should persevere.'

And persevere they did. With the blessing and prayers of the Abbot, Brother Columbanus was escorted to Holywell, a village located across the border in Clwyd, North Wales, two days distant, where he was immersed in the sacred waters of Saint Winifred's spring and instantly healed. Jerome, who witnessed the 'miracle', brought back encouraging news, confirming the whereabouts of the virgin's bones:

'And, Father,' he duly reported to the abbot, 'the people there told us that the saint is indeed buried at Gwytherin, where she died after her ministry, and that the place where her body is laid has done many miracles. But they say that her tomb, after so long, is neglected and little thought of, and it may well be that she longs for a better recognition, and to be installed in some place where pilgrims may come, where she may be revered as is her due, and have room to enlarge her grace and blessing to reach more people in need.'

'You are inspired, having been present at this miracle,' said Prior Robert, tall and splendid with faith rewarded, 'and you speak out what I have felt in listening to you. Surely Saint Winifred is calling us to her rescue as she came to the rescue of Brother Columbanus. Many have need of her goodness as he had, and know nothing of her. In our hands she would be exalted as she deserves, and those who need her grace would know where to come and seek it. I pray that we may mount that expedition of faith to which she summons us. Father Abbot, give me your leave to petition the church, and bring this blessed lady home to rest here among us, and be our proudest boast. For I believe it is her will and her command.'

'In the name of God,' said Abbot Heribert devoutly, 'I approve that project, and pray the blessing of heaven upon it!'

Later that same May day, Cadfael and his 'cheerful, blunt, extrovert' assistant, Brother John, were working in the herb garden. Prior Robert

'had it all planned beforehand,' said Brother John over the bed of mint, between envy and scorn. 'That was all a show, all that wonder and amazement, and asking who Saint Winifred was, and where to find her. He knew it all along. He'd already picked her out from those he's discovered neglected in Wales, and decided she was the one most likely to be available, as well as the one to shed most lustre on him. But it had to come out into the open by miraculous means. There'll be another prodigy whenever he needs his way smoothed for him, until he gets the girl here safely installed in the church, to his glory. It's a great enterprise, he means to climb high on the strength of

The statue of St Winefride, depicting the saint as an abbess carrying a crook, was placed in the niche above the well in 1888. The palm leaf signifies her martyrdom and the thin line around her neck shows where her head was severed from her body before being miraculously restored

it. So he starts out with a vision, and a prodigious healing, and divine grace leading his footsteps. It's as plain as the nose on your face.'

'And are you saying,' asked Brother Cadfael mildly, 'that Brother Columbanus is in the plot as well as Brother Jerome, and that falling fit of his was a fake, too? I should be very sure of my reward in heaven before I volunteered to break the paving with my forehead, even to provide Prior Robert with a miracle.'

Brother John considered seriously, frowning. 'No, that I don't say. We all know our meek white lamb is liable to the horrors over a penance scamped, and ecstasies over a vigil or a fast, and pouring ice-cold water over him at Holywell would be the very treatment to jolt him back into his right wits. We could just as well have tossed him in the fish-pond here! But of course he'd believe what they told him, and credit it all to the saint. Catch him missing such a chance! No, I wouldn't say he was a party to it – not knowingly. But he gave them the opportunity for a splendid demonstration of grace. You notice it was Jerome who was set to take care of him overnight! It takes only one man to be favoured with a vision, but it has to be the right man.' He rolled a sprig of the young green leaves sadly between his palms, and the fragrance distilled richly on the early morning air. 'And it will be the right men who'll accompany Prior Robert into Wales,' he said with sour certainty. 'You'll see!'

No doubt about it, this young man was hankering after a glimpse of the world again, and a breath of air from outside the walls, Brother Cadfael pondered, not only with sympathy for his young assistant, but also with some pleasurable stirrings of his own. So momentous an event in the otherwise even course of monastic life ought not to be missed. Besides the undoubted possibilities of mischief!

'True!' he said thoughtfully. 'Perhaps we ought to take some steps to leaven the lump. Wales should not be left with the notion that Jerome is the best Shrewsbury can muster, that's very true.'

'You have about as much chance of being invited as I,' said Brother John with his customary bluntness. 'Jerome is sure of his place, Prior Robert must have his right hand with him. And Columbanus, fool innocent, was the instrument of grace, and could be made to serve the same turn again. Brother Sub-Prior they have to take along, for form's sake. Surely we could think up some way of getting a foot in the door? They can't move for a few days yet, the carpenters and carvers are working hard on this splendid reliquary coffin they're going to take with them for the lady, but it will take them a while to finish it. Get your wits to work, brother! There isn't anything you couldn't do, if you've a mind! Prior or no prior!'

'Well, well, did I say you had not faith?' wondered Brother Cadfael, charmed and disarmed. 'I might worm my way in, there could be ways, but how am I to recommend a graceless rogue like you? What are you good at, to be taken along on such an errand?'

'I'm a good hand with mules,' said Brother John hopefully, 'and you don't think Prior Robert intends to go on foot, I suppose? Or to do the grooming and feeding and watering himself? Or the mucking-out? They'll need somebody to do the hard work, and wait on them. Why not me?'

Chapel of St Winefride,
Holywell, Clwyd

St Winefride's Well, together with the parish church at Holywell, belonged to the Cistercian monks of Basingwerk Abbey from 1240 until the Dissolution. The Church of St James, on the opposite side of the road to the well, stands on the same site as the seventh-century chapel, built of wood by St Beuno. The Countess Adeliza of Chester gave the church, probably then built of stone, to the Benedictine Abbey of St Werburgh at Chester in 1093. By the end of the fifteenth century the parish church was rebuilt, except for the west tower, and the present chapel enclosing the well was constructed in Perpendicular style. The Chapel of St Winefride was probably built under the patronage of Lady Margaret, Countess of Richmond, mother of Henry VII. It was a major centre of pilgrimage until the Reformation, when measures were taken to inhibit people from visiting the sacred waters. Today, the well is still a place of pilgrimage and is called the Lourdes of Wales.

Why not indeed? After dinner Brother Cadfael sought out Abbot Heribert in his study.

'Father Abbot, it is on my mind that we are undertaking this pilgrimage to Gwytherin without full consideration. First we must send to the bishop of Bangor, in whose see Gwytherin lies, for without his approval the matter cannot proceed. Now it is not essential to have a speaker fluent in Welsh there, since the bishop is obviously conversant with Latin. But not every parish priest in Wales has that tongue, and it is vital to be able to speak freely with the priest at Gwytherin, should the bishop sanction our quest. But most of all, the see of Bangor is wholly within the sovereignty of the king of Gwynedd, and surely his goodwill and permission are essential as those of the church. The princes of Gwynedd speak only in Welsh, though they have learned clerks. Father Prior, certainly, has a smattering of Welsh, but . . .'

'That is very true,' said Abbot Heribert, easily dismayed. 'It is but a smattering. And the king's agreement is all-important. Brother Cadfael, Welsh is your first, best language, and has no mysteries for you. Could *you* . . .? The garden, I am aware . . . But with your aid there would be no problem.'

'In the garden,' said Brother Cadfael, 'everything is well forward, and can manage without me ten days or more, and take no hurt. I should be glad indeed to be the interpreter, and lend my skills also in Gwytherin.'

'Then so be it!' sighed the abbot in heartfelt relief. 'Go with Prior Robert, and be our voice to the Welsh people. I shall sanction your errand myself, and you will have my authority.'

He was old and human and gentle, full of experience, short on ambition, self-righteousness and resolution. There could have been two ways of approaching him concerning Brother John. Cadfael took the more honest and simple way.

'Father, there is a young brother concerning whose vocation I have doubts, but concerning whose goodness I have none. He is close to me, and I would that he might find his true way, for if he finds it he will not forsake it. But it may not be with us. I beg that I may take him with me, as our hewer of wood and drawer of water in this enterprise, to allow him time to consider.'

The Abbot, although 'faintly dismayed and apprehensive', proved to be sympathetic to Cadfael's request and permission was granted. The inclusion of Cadfael and Brother John in the expedition swelled the number to six, the other four being Prior Robert, Sub-Prior Richard, Brother Jerome and Brother Columbanus.

They set out from Shrewsbury as soon as 'the fine reliquary for the saint's bones was ready, polished oak ornamented with silver, to serve as a proof what honours awaited Winifred in her new shrine', and arrived in Bangor in the third week of May. Bishop David and Prince Owain, 'who was the regent of Gwynedd', both readily agreed to the proposed translation and, 'episcopally and royally blessed', Prior Robert's party set off for Gwytherin, confident of a 'triumphant end'.

They turned aside from the Conway valley at Llanrwst, climbing away from the river into forested country. Beyond the watershed they crossed the Elwy where it is young and small, and moved steadily south-eastwards through thick woods, over another ridge of high land, to descend once again into the upland valley of a little river, that provided some marshy water-meadows along its banks, and a narrow band of tilled fields, sloping and sturdy but protected by the forests above these lush pastures. The wooded ridge on either hand ran in oblique folds, richly green, hiding the scattered house-steads. The fields were already planted, and here and there orchards flowered. Below them, there was a small stone church, whitewashed and shimmering, and a little wooden house beside it.

'You see the goal of your pilgrimage,' said the chaplain Urien [who had been sent by Prince Owain to be their guide]. He was a compact, neat, well-shaven personage, handsomely dressed and mounted, more of an ambassador than a clerk.

'That is Gwytherin?' asked Prior Robert.

'It is the church and priest's house of Gwytherin. The parish stretches for several miles along the river valley, and a mile or more from the Cledwen on either bank. We do not congregate in villages as you English do. Land good for hunting is plentiful, but good for tillage meagre. Every man lives where best suits him for working his fields and conserving his game.'

'It is a very fair place,' said the sub-prior, and meant it, for the fold on fold of well-treed hills beyond the river made a pattern of spring beauty in a hundred different greens, and the water-meadows were strung like a necklace of emeralds along the fringes of a necklace of silver and lapis-lazuli.

Across the river, some way below them and a great way off, the snaky curve of the furrows already patterned the slope between cultivated fields and leaning trees, a dark brown writing upon the hillside, and on the higher furrow, as yet uncompleted, the oxen leaned into their yokes and heaved, and the ploughman behind them clung and dragged at the heavy share. Before the leading pair a man walked backwards, arms gently waving and beckoning, his goad only a wand, flourished for magic, not for its sting, his high, pure calls carried aloft on the air, cajoling and praising. Towards him the beasts leaned willingly, following his cries with all their might. The new-turned soil, greyish-brown and sluggish, heaved moist and fresh to light after the share.

'A harsh country,' said Urien, as one assessing, not complaining, and set his horse moving downhill towards the church. 'Come, I'll hand you over to Father Huw, and see you well-received.'

Father Huw, the parish priest, welcomed the Benedictine delegation from Shrewsbury but, although they came with the blessing of the Welsh Prince and also the Bishop, he warned them that the people of Gwytherin were not going to like their saint being 'dug up out of her grave and taken away into England'.

After severe opposition from the local Welsh inhabitants, Prior Robert eventually 'succeeded' in his mission and returned to the Abbey of Saint Peter and Saint Paul with what everyone – except Cadfael – thought were the bones of Saint Winifred.

Woods near Gwytherin, Clwyd

Hills above Gwytherin

It was not until four years later, in the *Tenth Chronicle (The Pilgrim of Hate)*, that Cadfael finally confided to his close friend, Hugh Beringar of Maesbury, Sheriff of Shropshire, the truth about what had happened in Gwytherin – a secret that both friends took for granted would be safely kept between them.

'There was one Welsh lord of Gwytherin,' said Cadfael, 'who would not suffer the girl to be disturbed, and would not be persuaded or bribed or threatened into letting her go. And he died, Hugh – murdered. By one of us, a brother who came from high rank, and had his eyes already set on a mitre. And when we came near to accusing him, it was his life or a better. There were certain young people of that place put in peril by him, the dead lord's daughter and her lover. The boy lashed out in anger, with good reason, seeing his girl wounded and bleeding. He was stronger than he knew. The murderer's neck was broken.'

'How many knew of this?' asked Hugh, his eyes narrowed thoughtfully upon the glossy-leaved rose-bushes.

'When it befell, only the lovers, the dead man and I. And Saint Winifred, who had been raised from her grave and laid in that casket of which you and all men know. She knew. She was there. From the moment I raised her,' said Cadfael, 'and by God, it was I who took her from the soil, and I who restored her – and still that makes me glad – from the moment I uncovered those slender bones, I felt in mine they wished only to be left in peace. It was so little and so wild and quiet a graveyard there, with the small church long out of use, meadow flowers growing over all, and the mounds so modest and green. And Welsh soil! The girl was Welsh, like me, her church was of the old persuasion, what did she know of this alien English shire? And I had those young things to keep. Who would have taken their word or mine against all the force of the church? They would have closed their ranks to bury the scandal, and bury the boy with it, and he guilty of nothing but defending his dear. So I took measures.'

Hugh's mobile lips twitched. 'Now indeed you amaze me! And what measures were those? With a dead brother to account for, and Prior Robert to keep sweet ...'

'Ah, well, Robert is a simpler soul than he supposes, and then I had a good deal of help from the dead brother himself. He'd been busy building himself such a reputation for sanctity, delivering messages from the saint herself – it was he told us she was offering the grave she'd left to the murdered man – and going into trance-sleeps, and praying to leave this world and be taken into bliss living ... So we did him that small favour. He'd been keeping a solitary night-watch in the old church, and in the morning when it ended, there were his habit and sandals fallen together at his prayer-stool, and the body of him lifted clean out of them, in sweet odours and a shower of may-blossom. That was how he claimed the saint had already visited him, why should not Robert recall it and believe? Certainly he was gone. Why look for him? Would a modest brother of our house be running through the Welsh woods mother-naked?'

'Are you telling me,' asked Hugh cautiously, 'that what you have there in the reliquary is *not* ... Then the casket had not yet been sealed?' His eyebrows were tangling with his black forelock, but his voice was soft and unsurprised.

'Well ...' Cadfael twitched his blunt brown nose bashfully between finger and thumb. 'Sealed it was, but there are ways of dealing with seals that leave them unblemished. It's one of the more dubious of my remembered skills, but for all that I was glad of it then.'

'And you put the lady back in the place that was hers, along with her champion?'

'He was a decent, good man, and had spoken up for her nobly. She would not grudge him house-room. I have always thought,' confided Cadfael, 'that she was not displeased with us. She has shown her power in Gwytherin since that time, by many miracles, so I cannot believe she is angry. But what a little troubles me is that she has not so far chosen to favour us with any great mark of her patronage here, to keep Robert happy, and set my mind at rest.'

St Winifred's Well, Woolston

Thirteen miles north-west of Shrewsbury and four miles south-east of Oswestry is the hamlet of Woolston, once a place of pilgrimage. It is reputed that, while the relics of St Winifred were being carried from North Wales to Shrewsbury in 1137, a spring miraculously appeared at Woolston on the spot where the saint's reliquary was put down to rest. Today the spring, which still flows, is housed beneath the projecting gabled porch of a timber-framed cottage, built about 400 years ago as a courthouse. The water in the well is reputed to heal wounds, bruises and fractured bones, while the small spring below is alleged to relieve sore eyes

Yet, despite his misgivings, Cadfael, even then, did not see what else he could have done.

'It was an ending that satisfied everyone,' he confessed, 'both here and there. The children were free to marry and be happy, the village still had its saint, and she had her own people around her. Robert had what he had gone to find – or thought he had, which is the same thing. And Shrewsbury abbey has its festival, with every hope of a full guest-hall, and glory and gain in good measure ...'

'And you've never said word of this to anyone?'

'Never a word. But the whole village of Gwytherin knows it,' admitted Cadfael with a remembering grin. 'No one told, no one had to tell, but they knew. There wasn't a man missing when we took up the reliquary and set out for home. They helped to carry it, whipped together a little chariot to bear it. Robert thought he had them nicely tamed, even those who'd been most reluctant from the first. It was a great joy to him. A simple soul at bottom! It would be great pity to undo him now, when he's busy writing his book about the saint's life, and how he brought her to Shrewsbury.'

The historical facts are that Prior Robert Pennant really did write a book about the life of Saint Winifred, completing it with an account of the translation of her bones from Gwytherin to England. As most of the events in the *First Chronicle* are fictitious, there is, of course, no mention in his record of Brother Columbanus's body, or indeed any other, being substituted for the saint's bones; nor for that matter is there any mention of a brother named Cadfael. That omission, however, Cadfael himself had confidently predicted!

The relics of Saint Winifred remained in the abbey at Shrewsbury for a further four hundred years, until the dissolution of the monastery in 1540, when her shrine was demolished and her bones disappeared. Parts of her shrine were discovered in 1933 in a Shrewsbury garden and were returned to the abbey. Today Saint Winifred has a small shrine in the nave, where there is an ancient stone bearing three carved figures: Saint Winifred in the centre, flanked by Saint Beuno, her uncle, on the right and Saint John the Baptist on the left. One of her finger-bones found its way to Rome and was returned to England in 1852, where it was divided in two, 'one half being sent to Holywell and the other to Shrewsbury where presumably it still exists'.

As a place of pilgrimage, Shrewsbury ranked second only to the shrine of Saint Thomas at Canterbury. In 1487 Abbot Thomas Mynde, by payment of 'a great sum of money to the royal coffers' (Forrest), obtained a licence from Henry VII to found the 'Guild of Saint Winefride'. Five centuries later, in 1987, the Guild was revived by the Friends of the Abbey; according to the notes adjacent to her shrine, Saint Winifred's cult is the only one in England to have persisted to the present day.

St Winifred flanked by St Beuno and St John the Baptist, St Winifred's Shrine, Shrewsbury Abbey

'*After dinner, in the half-hour or so allowed for rest, Cadfael went into the church, into the grateful stony coolness, and stood for some minutes silent before St Winifred's altar. Of late, if he felt the need to speak to her in actual words at all, he found himself addressing her in Welsh, but usually he relied on her to know all the preoccupations of his mind without words. Doubtful, in any case, if the young and beautiful Welsh girl of her first brief life had known any English or Latin, or even been able to read and write her own language, though the stately prioress of her second life, pilgrim to Rome and head of a community of holy women, must have had time to learn and study to her heart's content. But it was as the girl that Cadfael always imagined her. A girl whose beauty was legendary, and caused her to be coveted by princes.*'

The Heretic's Apprentice

ONE CORPSE TOO MANY

ONE CORPSE TOO MANY

Chapter One

rother Cadfael was working in the small kitchen garden by the abbot's fish-ponds when the boy was first brought to him. It was hot August noon, and if he had had his proper quota of helpers they would all have been snoring in the shade at this hour, instead of sweating in the sun; but one of his regular assistants, not yet out of his novitiate, had thought better of the monastic vocation and taken himself off to join his elder brother in arms on King Stephen's side, in the civil war for the crown of England, and the other had taken fright at the approach of the royal army because his family were of the Empress Maud's faction, and their manor in Cheshire seemed a far safer place to be than Shrewsbury under siege. Cadfael was left to do everything alone, but he had in his time laboured under far hotter suns than this, and was doggedly determined not to let his domain run wild, whether the outside world fell into chaos or no.

In this early summer of 1138 the fratricidal strife, hitherto somewhat desultory, was already two years old, but never before had it approached Shrewsbury so closely. Now its threat hung over castle and town like the shadow of death. But for all that, Brother Cadfael's mind was firmly upon life and growth, rather than destruction and war, and certainly he had no suspicion that another manner of killing, simple murder, furtive and unlicensed even in these anarchic times, was soon to disrupt the calm of his chosen life.

August should not, in normal circumstances, have been one of his busiest times in the gardens, but there was more than enough for one man to do properly, and the only relief they had to offer him was Brother Athanasius, who was deaf, half-senile, and not to be relied upon to know a useful herb from a weed, and the offer had been firmly declined. Better by far manage alone. There was a bed to be prepared for planting out late cabbages for succession, and fresh seed to be sown for the kind that can weather the winter, as well as pease to be gathered, and the dead, dried haulms of the early crop to be cleared away for fodder and litter. And in his wooden work-shed in the herbarium, his own particular pride, he had half a dozen preparations working in glass vessels and mortars on the shelves, all of them needing attention at least once a day, besides the herb wines that bubbled busily on their own at this stage. It was high harvest time among the herbs, and all the medicines for the winter demanding his care.

However, he was not the man to let any part of his kingdom slip out of his control, however wastefully the royal cousins Stephen and Maud contended for the throne of England outside the abbey walls. If he lifted his head from digging compost into the cabbage bed he could see the sluggish plumes of smoke hanging over the abbey roofs and the town and castle beyond, and smell the acrid residue of yesterday's fires. That shadow and stink had hung like a pall over Shrewsbury for almost a month, while King Stephen stamped and raged in his camp beyond the Castle Foregate, the one dry-foot way into the town unless he could get possession of the bridges, and William FitzAlan within the fortress held on grimly, keeping an anxious eye on his dwindling supplies, and left the thundering of defiance to his incorrigible uncle, Arnulf of Hesdin, who had never learned to temper valour with discretion. The townspeople kept their heads low, locked their doors, shuttered their shops, or, if they could, made off westwards into Wales, to old, friendly enemies less to be feared than Stephen. It suited the Welsh very well that Englishmen should fear Englishmen—if either Maud or Stephen could be regarded as English!—and let Wales alone, and they would not grudge a helping hand to the fleeing casualties, provided the war went on merrily.

Cadfael straightened his back and mopped the sweat from a tonsured scalp burned to the colour of a ripe hazel-nut; and there was Brother Oswald the almoner bustling along the path towards him, with skirts flapping, and propelling before him by the shoulder a boy of about sixteen, in the coarse brown cotte and short summer hose of the countryside, barelegged but very decently shod in leather, and altogether looking carefully scrubbed and neat for a special occasion. The boy went where he was directed, and kept his eyes lowered with nervous meekness. Another family taking care to put its children out of reach of being pressed for either side, thought Cadfael, and small blame to them.

"Brother Cadfael, I think you have need of a helper, and here is a youngster who says he's not afraid of hard work. A good woman of the town has brought him in to the porter, and asked that he be taken and taught as a lay servant. Her nephew from Hencot, she says, and his parents dead. There's a year's endowment with him. Prior Robert has given leave to take him, and there's room in the boys' dortoir. He'll attend school with the novices, but he'll not take vows unless he himself comes to wish it. What do you say, will you have him?"

Cadfael looked the boy over with interest, but said yes without hesitation, glad enough to be offered someone young, able-bodied and willing. The lad was slenderly built, but vigorous and firm on his feet, and moved with a spring. He looked up warily from under a cropped tangle of brown curls, and his eyes were long-lashed and darkly blue, very shrewd and bright. He was behaving himself meekly and decorously, but he did not look intimidated.

"Very heartily I'll have you," said Cadfael,

"if you'll take to this outdoor work with me. And what's your name, boy?"

"Godric, sir," said the young thing, in a small, gruff voice, appraising Cadfael just as earnestly as he was being appraised.

"Good, then, Godric, you and I will get on well enough. And first, if you will, walk around the gardens here with me and see what we have in hand, and get used to being within these walls. Strange enough I daresay you'll find it, but safer than in the town yonder, which I make no doubt is why your good aunt brought you here."

The blue, bright eyes flashed him one glance and were veiled again.

"See you come to Vespers with Brother Cadfael," the almoner instructed, "and Brother Paul, the master of the novices, will show you your bed, and tell you your duties after supper. Pay attention to what Brother Cadfael tells you, and be obedient to him as you should."

"Yes, sir," said the boy virtuously. Under the meek accents a small bubble of laughter seemed to be trying, though vainly, to burst. When Brother Oswald hurried away, the blue eyes watched him out of sight, and then turned their intent gaze upon Cadfael. A demure, oval face, with a wide, firm mouth shaped properly for laughter, but quick to revert to a very sombre gravity. Even for those meant to be light-hearted, these were grave times.

"Come, see what manner of labour you're taking on yourself," said Cadfael cheerfully, and downed his spade to take his new boy round the enclosed garden, showing him the vegetables, the herbs that made the noon air heady and drunken with fragrance, the fish ponds and the beds of pease that ran down almost to the brook. The early field was already dried and flaxen in the sun, all its harvest gathered, even the later-sown hung heavy and full in pod.

"These we should gather today and tomorrow. In this heat they'll pass their best in a day. And these spent ones have to be cleared. You can begin that for me. Don't pull them up, take the sickle and cut them off low to the ground, and the roots we plough in, they're good food for the soil." He was talking in an easy, good-humoured flow, to pass off peacefully whatever residue of regret and strangeness there might be in this abrupt change. "How old are you, Godric?"

"Seventeen," said the husky voice beside him. He was on the small side for seventeen; let him try his hand at digging later on, the ground Cadfael was working was heavy to till. "I can work hard," said the boy, almost as though he had guessed at the thought, and resented it. "I don't know much, but I can do whatever you tell me."

"So you shall, then, and you can begin with the pease. Stack the dry stuff aside here, and it goes to provide stable litter. And the roots go back to the ground."

"Like humankind," said Godric unexpectedly.

"Yes, like humankind." Too many were going back to the earth prematurely now in this fratricidal war. He saw the boy turn his head, almost involuntarily, and look across the abbey grounds and roofs to where the battered towers of the castle loomed in their pall of smoke. "Have you kin within there, child?" asked Cadfael gently.

"No!" said the boy, too quickly. "But I can't but think of them. They're saying in the town it can't last long—that it may fall tomorrow. And surely they've done only rightly! Before

King Henry died he made his barons acknowledge the Empress Maud as his heir, and they all swore fealty. She was his only living child, she *should* be queen. And yet when her cousin, Count Stephen, seized the throne and had himself crowned, all too many of them took it meekly and forgot their oaths. That can't be right. And it can't be wrong to stand by the empress faithfully. How can they excuse changing sides? How can they justify Count Stephen's claim?"

"Justify may not be the apt word, but there are those among the lords, more by far than take the opposite view, who would say, better a man for overlord than a woman. And if a man, why, Stephen was as near as any to the throne. He is King William's grandchild, just as Maud is."

"But not son to the last king. And in any case, through his mother, who was a woman like Maud, so where's the difference?" The young voice had emerged from its guarded undertone, and rang clear and vehement. "But the real difference was that Count Stephen rushed here and took what he wanted, while the empress was far away in Normandy, thinking no evil. And now that half the barons have recollected their oaths and declared for her, after all, it's late, and what's to come of it but bloodshed and deaths? It begins here, in Shrewsbury, and this won't be the end."

"Child," said Cadfael mildly, "are you not trusting me to extremes?"

The boy, who had picked up the sickle and was swinging it in a capable, testing hand, turned and looked at him with blue eyes suddenly wide open and unguarded. "Well, so I do," he said.

"And so you may, for that matter. But keep your lips locked among others. We are in the battlefield here, as sure as in the town, our gates never being closed to any. All manner of men rub shoulders here, and in rough times some may try to buy favour with carrying tales. Some may even be collectors of such tales for their living. Your thoughts are safe in your head, best keep them there."

The boy drew back a little, and hung his head. Possibly he felt himself reproved. Possibly not! "I'll pay you trust for trust," said Cadfael. "In my measure there's little to choose between two such monarchs, but much to be said for keeping a man's fealty and word. And now let me see you hard at work, and when I've finished my cabbage patch I'll come and help you."

He watched the boy set to work, which he did with immense vigour. The coarse tunic was cut very full, turning a lissome body into a bundle of cloth tied at the waist; possibly he had got it from some older and larger relative after the best of the wear was out of it. My friend, thought Cadfael, in this heat you won't keep up that pace very long, and then we shall see!

By the time he joined his assistant in the rustling field of bleached pea-stems, the boy was red in the face and sweating, and puffing audibly with the strokes of the sickle, but had not relaxed his efforts. Cadfael swept an armful of cut haulms to the edge of the field, and said earnestly: "No need to make a penance of it, lad. Strip off to the waist and be comfortable." And he slid his own frock, already kilted to the knee, down from powerful brown shoulders, and let the folds hang at his middle.

The effect was complex, but by no means decisive. The boy checked momentarily in his stroke, said: "I'm well enough as I am!" with admirable composure, but several tones above the gruff, young-mannish level of his earlier utterances, and went on resolutely with his labours, at the same time as a distinct wave of red arose from his collar to engulf his slender neck and the curve of his cheek. Did that necessarily mean what it seemed to mean? He might have lied about his age, his voice might be but newly broken and still unstable. And perhaps he wore no shirt beneath the cotte, and was ashamed to reveal his lacks to a new acquaintance. Ah, well, there were other tests. Better make sure at once. If what Cadfael suspected was true, the matter was going to require very serious thought.

"There's that heron that robs our hatcheries, again!" he cried suddenly, pointing across the Meole brook, where the unsuspecting bird waded, just folding immense wings. "Toss a stone across at him, boy, you're nearer than I!" The heron was an innocent stranger, but if Cadfael was right he was unlikely to come to any harm.

Godric stared, clawed up a sizeable stone, and heaved it heartily. His arm swung far back, swung forward with his slight weight willingly behind it, and hurled the stone underarm across the brook and into the shallows, with a splash that sent the heron soaring, certainly, but several feet from where he had been standing.

"Well, well!" said Cadfael silently, and settled down to do some hard thinking.

In his siege camp, deployed across the entire land approach to the Castle Foregate, between broad coils of the river Severn, King Stephen fretted, fumed and feasted, celebrating the few loyal Salopians—loyal to him, that is!—who came to offer him aid, and planning his revenge upon the many disloyal who absented themselves.

He was a big, noisy, handsome, simple-minded man, very fair in colouring, very comely in countenance, and at this stage in his fortunes totally bewildered by the contention between his natural good nature and his smarting sense of injury. He was said to be slow-witted, but when his Uncle Henry had died and left no heir but a daughter, and she handicapped by an Angevin husband and far away in France, no matter how slavishly her father's vassals had bowed to his will and accepted her as queen, Stephen for once in his life had moved with admirable speed and precision, and surprised his potential subjects into accepting him at his own valuation before they even had time to consider their own interests, much less remember reluctant vows. So why had such a successful coup abruptly turned sour? He would never understand. Why had half of his more influential subjects, apparently stunned into immobility for a time, revived into revolt now? Conscience? Dislike of the king imposed upon them? Superstitious dread of King Henry and his influence with God?

Forced to take the opposition seriously and resort to arms, Stephen had opened in the way that came naturally to him, striking hard where he must, but holding the door cheerfully open for penitents to come in. And what had been the result? He had spared, and they had taken advantage and despised him for it. He had invited submission without penalty, as he moved north against the rebel holds, and the local baronage had held off from him with contempt. Well, tomorrow's dawn attack should settle the fate of the Shrewsbury garrison, and make an example once for all. If these midlanders would not come peacefully and loyally at his invitation, they should come scurrying like rats to save their own skins. As for Arnulf of Hesdin...The obscenities and defiances he had hurled from the towers of Shrewsbury should be regretted bitterly, if briefly.

The king was conferring in his tent in the meads in the late afternoon, with Gilbert Prestcote, his chief aide and sheriff-designate of Salop, and Willem Ten Heyt, the captain of his Flemish mercenaries. It was about the time that Brother Cadfael and the boy Godric were washing their hands and tidying their clothing to go to Vespers. The failure of the local gentry to bring in their own levies to his support had caused Stephen to lean heavily upon his Flemings, who inconsequence were very well hated, both as aliens and as impervious professionals, who would as soon burn down a village as get drunk, and were not at all averse to doing both together. Ten Heyt was a huge, well-favoured man with reddish-fair hair and long moustaches, barely thirty years old but a veteran in warfare. Prestcote was a quiet, laconic knight past fifty, experienced and formidable in battle, cautious in counsel, not a man to go to extremes, but even he was arguing for severity.

"Your Grace has tried generosity, and it has been shamelessly exploited to your loss. It's time to strike terror."

"First," said Stephen drily, "to take castle and town."

"That your Grace may consider as done. What we have mounted for the morning will get you into Shrewsbury. Then, if they survive the assault, your Grace may do what you will with FitzAlan, and Adeney, and Hesdin, and the commons of the garrison are no great

matter, but even there you may be well advised to consider an example."

The king would have been content enough then with his revenge on those three who led the resistance here. William FitzAlan owed his office as sheriff of Salop to Stephen, and yet had declared and held the castle for his rival. Fulke Adeney, the greatest of FitzAlan's vassal lords, had connived at the treason and supported his overlord wholeheartedly. And Hesdin had condemned himself over and over out of his own arrogant mouth. The rest were pawns, expendable but of no importance.

"They are noising it abroad in the town, as I've heard," said Prestcote, "that FitzAlan had already sent his wife and children away before we closed the way north out of the town. But Adeney also has a child, a daughter. She's said to be still within the walls. They got the women out of the castle early." Prestcote was a man of the shire himself, and knew the local baronage at least by name and repute. "Adeney's girl was betrothed from a child to Robert Beringar's son, of Maesbury, by Oswestry. They had lands neighbouring in those parts. I mention it because this is the man who is asking audience of you now, Hugh Beringar of Maesbury. Use him as you find, your Grace, but until today I would have said he was FitzAlan's man, and your enemy. Have him in and judge for yourself. If he's changed his coat, well and good, he has men enough at his command to be useful, but I would not let him in too easily."

The officer of the guard had entered the pavilion, and stood waiting to be invited to speak; Adam Courcelle was one of Prestcote's chief tenants and his right-hand man, a tested soldier at thirty years old.

"Your Grace has another visitor," he said,

when the king turned to acknowledge his presence. "A lady. Will you see her first? She has no lodging here as yet, and in view of the hour . . . She gives her name as Aline Siward, and says that her father, whom she has only recently buried, was always your man."

"Time presses," said the king. "Let them both come, and the lady shall have first word."

Courcelle led her by the hand into the royal presence, with every mark of deference and admiration, and she was indeed well worth any man's attention. She was slender and shy, and surely no older than eighteen, and the austerity of her mourning, the white cap and wimple from which a few strands of gold hair crept out to frame her cheeks, only served to make her look younger still, and more touching. She had a child's proud, shy dignity. Great eyes the colour of dark irises widened wonderingly upon the king's large comeliness as she made her reverence.

"Madam," said Stephen, reaching a hand to her, "I am sorry indeed for your loss, of which I have this minute heard. If my protection can in any way serve you, command me."

"Your Grace is very kind," said the girl in a soft, awed voice. "I am now an orphan, and the only one of my house left to bring you the duty and fealty we owe. I am doing what my father would have wished, and but for his illness and death he would have come himself, or I would have come earlier. Until your Grace came to Shrewsbury we had no opportunity to render you the keys of the two castles we hold. As I do now!"

Her maid, a self-possessed young woman a good ten years older than her mistress, had followed into the tent and stood withdrawn. She came forward now to hand the keys to Aline, who laid them formally in the king's hands.

"We can raise for your Grace five knights, and more than forty men-at-arms, but at this time I have left all to supply the garrisons at home, since they may be of more use to your Grace so." She named her properties and her castellans. It was like hearing a child recite a lesson learned by heart, but her dignity and gravity were those of a general in the field. "There is one more thing I should say plainly, and to my much sorrow. I have a brother, who should have been the one to perform this duty and service." Her voice shook slightly, and gallantly recovered. "When your Grace assumed the crown, my brother Giles took the part of the Empress Maud, and after an open quarrel with my father, left home to join her party. I do not know where he is now, though we have heard rumours that he made his way to her in France. I could not leave your Grace in ignorance of the dissension that grieves me as it must you. I hope you will not therefore refuse what I can bring, but use it freely, as my father would have wished, and as I wish."

She heaved a great sigh, as if she had thrown off a weight. The king was enchanted. He drew her by the hand and kissed her heartily on the cheek. To judge by the look on his face, Courcelle was envying him the opportunity.

"God forbid, child," said the king, "that I should add any morsel to your sorrows, or fail to lift what I may of them. With all my heart I take your fealty, as dear to me as that of earl or baron, and thank you for your pains taken to help me. And now show me what I can do to serve you, for there can be no fit lodging for you here in a military camp, and I hear you have made no provision as yet for yourself. It will soon be evening."

"I had thought," she said timidly, "that I might lodge in the abbey guest house, if we can get a boat to put us across the river."

"Certainly you shall have safe escort over the river, and our request to the abbot to give you one of the grace houses belonging to the abbey, where you may be private but protected, until we can spare a safe escort to see you to your home." He looked about him for a ready messenger, and could not well miss Adam Courcelle's glowing eagerness. The young man had bright chestnut hair, and eyes of the same burning brown, and knew that he stood well with his king. "Adam, will you conduct Mistress Siward, and see her safely installed?"

"With all my heart, your Grace," said Courcelle fervently, and offered an ardent hand to the lady.

Hugh Beringar watched the girl pass by, her hand submissive in the broad brown hand that clasped it, her eyes cast down, her small, gentle face with its disproportionately large and noble brow tired and sad now that she had done her errand faithfully. From outside the royal tent he had heard every word. She looked now as if she might melt into tears at any moment, like a little girl after a formal ordeal, a child-bride dressed up to advertise her riches or her lineage, and then as briskly dismissed to the nursery when the transaction was assured. The king's officer walked delicately beside her, like a conqueror conquered, and no wonder.

"Come, the lord king waits," said the guttural voice of Willem Ten Heyt in his ear, and he turned and ducked his head beneath the awning of the tent. The comparative dimness

within veiled the large, fair presence of the king.

"I am here, my liege," said Hugh Beringar, and made his obeisance. "Hugh Beringar of Maesbury, at your Grace's service with all that I hold. My muster is not great, six knights and some fifty men-at-arms, but half of them bowmen, and skilled. And all are yours."

"Your name, Master Beringar, is known to us," said the king drily. "Your establishment also. That it was devoted to our cause was not so well known. As I have heard of you, you have been an associate of FitzAlan and Adeney, our traitors, until very recently. And even this change of heart comes rather belatedly. I have been some four weeks in these parts, without word from you."

"Your Grace," said Beringar, without haste to excuse himself or apparent discomfort at his cool reception, "I grew up from a child regarding these men whom you understandably name your traitors, as my peers and friends, and in friendship have never found them wanting. Your Grace is too fairminded a man not to admit that for one like me, who has not so far sworn fealty to any, the choice of a path at this moment may require a deal of thought, if it is to be made once for all. That King Henry's daughter has a reasonable claim is surely beyond question, I cannot call a man traitor for choosing that cause, though I may blame him for breaking his oath to you. As for me, I came into my lands only some months ago, and I have so far sworn fealty to none. I have taken my time in choosing where I will serve. I am here. Those who flock to you without thought may fall away from you just as lightly."

"And you will not?" said the king sceptically. He was studying this bold and possibly over-fluent young man with critical attention. A lightweight, not above the middle height and slenderly built, but of balanced and assured movement; he might well make up in speed and agility what he lacked in bulk and reach. Perhaps two or three years past twenty, black-avised, with thin, alert features and thick, quirky dark brows. An unchancy fellow, because there was no guessing from his face what went on behind the deep-set eyes. His forthright speech might be honest, or it might be calculated. He looked quite subtle enough to have weighed up his sovereign and reasoned that boldness might not be displeasing.

"And I will not," he said firmly. "But that need not pass on my word. It can be put to the proof hereafter. I am on your Grace's probation."

"You have not brought your force with you?"

"Three men only are with me. It would have been folly to leave a good castle unmanned or half-manned, and small service to you to ask that you feed fifty more without due provision for the increase. Your Grace has only to tell me where you would have me serve, and it shall be done."

"Not so fast," said Stephen. "Others may also have need of time and thought before they embrace you, young man. You were close and in confidence with FitzAlan, some time ago."

"I was. I still have nothing against him but that he has chosen one way, and I the other."

"And as I hear, you are betrothed to Fulke Adeney's daughter."

"I hardly know whether to say to that: I am! or: I was! The times have altered a great many plans previously made, for others as well as for me. As at this time, I do not know

where the girl is, or whether the bargain still holds."

"There are said to be no women now in the castle," said the king, eyeing him closely. "FitzAlan's family may well be clean away, perhaps out of the country by now. But Adeney's daughter is thought to be in hiding in the town. It would not be displeasing to me," he said with soft emphasis, "to have so valuable a lady in safe-keeping—in case even my plans should need to be altered. You were of her father's party, you must know the places likely to be sheltering her now. When the way is clear, you, of all people, should be able to find her."

The young man gazed back at him with an inscrutable face, in which shrewd black eyes signalled understanding, but nothing more, neither consent nor resistance, no admission at all that he knew he was being set a task on which acceptance and favour might well depend. His face was bland and his voice guileless as he said: "That is my intent, your Grace. I came from Maesbury with that also in mind."

"Well," said Stephen, warily content, "you may remain in attendance against the town's fall, but we have no immediate work for you here. Should I have occasion to call you, where will you be found?"

"If they have room," said Beringar, "at the abbey guest house."

The boy Godric stood through Vespers among the pupils and the novices, far back among the small fry of the house, and close to the laity, such as lived here outside the walls on the hither bank of the river, and could still reach this refuge. He looked, as Brother Cadfael reflected when he turned his head to look for the child, very small and rather forlorn, and his face, bright and impudent enough in the herbarium, had grown very solemn indeed here in church. Night was looming, his first night in this abode. Ah well, his affairs were being taken in hand more consolingly than he supposed, and the ordeal he was bracing himself to master need not confront him at all, if things went right, and at all events not tonight. Brother Paul, the master of the novices, had several other youngsters to look after, and was glad to have one taken firmly off his hands.

Cadfael reclaimed his protégé after supper, at which meal he was glad to see that Godric ate heartily. Evidently the boy was of a mettle to fight back against whatever fears and qualms possessed him, and had the good sense to fortify himself with the things of the flesh for the struggles of the spirit. Even more reassuringly, he looked up with relief and recognition when Cadfael laid a hand on his shoulder as they left the refectory.

"Come, we're free until Compline, and it's cool out in the gardens. No need to stay inside here, unless you wish."

The boy Godric did not wish, he was happy to escape into the summer evening. They went down at leisure towards the fish ponds and the herbarium, and the boy skipped at Cadfael's side, and burst into a gay whistling, abruptly broken off.

"He said the master of the novices would want me, after supper. Is it really proper for me to come with you, like this?"

"All approved and blessed, child, don't be afraid. I've spoken with Brother Paul, we have his good word. You are my boy, and I am responsible for you." They had entered the walled garden, and were suddenly engulfed

and drowned in all those sun-drenched fragrances, rosemary, thyme, fennel, dill, sage, lavender, a whole world of secret sweetness. The heat of the sun lingered, heady with scent, even into the cool of the evening. Over their heads swifts wheeled and screamed in ecstasy.

They had arrived at the wooden shed, its oiled timbers radiated warmth towards them. Cadfael opened the door. "This is your sleeping-place, Godric."

There was a low bench-bed neatly arrayed at the end of the room. The boy stared, and quaked under Cadfael's hand.

"I have all these medicines brewing here, and some of them need tending regularly, some very early, they'd spoil if no one minded them. I'll show you all you have to do, it's not so heavy a task. And here you have your bed, and here a grid you may open for fresh air." The boy had stopped shaking, the dark blue eyes were large and measuring, and fixed implacably upon Cadfael. There seemed to be a smile pending, but there was also a certain aura of offended pride. Cadfael turned to the door, and showed the heavy bar that guarded it within, and the impossibility of opening it from without, once that was dropped into its socket. "You may shut out the world and me until you're ready to come out to us."

The boy Godric, who was not a boy at all, was staring now in direct accusation, half-offended, half-radiant, wholly relieved.

"How did you know?" she demanded, jutting a belligerent chin.

"How were you going to manage in the dortoir?" responded Brother Cadfael mildly.

"I would have managed. Boys are not so clever, I could have cozened them. Under a wall like this," she said, hoisting handfuls of her ample tunic, "all bodies look the same, and men are blind and stupid." She laughed then, viewing Cadfael's placid competence, and suddenly she was all woman, and startlingly pretty in her gaiety and relief. "Oh, not *you*! How *did* you know? I tried so hard, I thought I could pass all trials. Where did I go wrong?"

"You did very well," said Cadfael soothingly. "But, child, I was forty years about the world, and from end to end of it, before I took the cowl and came to my green, sweet ending here. Where did you go wrong? Don't take it amiss, take it as sound advice from an ally, if I answer you. When you came to argument, and meant it with all your heart, you let your voice soar. And never a crack in it, mind you, to cover the change. That can be learned, I'll show you when we have leisure. And then, when I bade you strip and be easy—ah, never blush, child, I was all but certain then!—of course you put me off. And last, when I got you to toss a stone across the brook, you did it like a girl, under-arm, with a round swing. When did you ever see a boy throw like that? Don't let anyone else trick you into such another throw, not until you master the art. It betrays you at once."

He stood patiently silent then, for she had dropped on to the bed, and sat with her head in her hands, and first she began to laugh, and then to cry, and then both together; and all the while he let her alone, for she was no more out of control than a man tossed between gain and loss, and manfully balancing his books. Now he could believe she was seventeen, a budding woman, and a fine one, too.

When she was ready, she wiped her eyes on the back of her hand, and looked up alertly, smiling like sunlight through a rainbow. "And did you mean it?" she said. "That you're responsible for me? I *said* I trusted you to extremes!"

"Daughter dear," said Cadfael patiently, "what should I do with you now but serve you as best I can, and see you safe out of here to wherever you would be?"

"And you don't even know who I am," she said, marvelling. "Who is trusting too far now?"

"What difference should it make to me, child, what your name may be? A lass left forlorn here to weather out this storm and be restored to her own people—is not that enough? What you want to tell, you'll tell, and I need no more."

"I think I want to tell you everything," said the girl simply, looking up at him with eyes wide and candid as the sky. "My father is either in Shrewsbury castle this minute with his death hanging over him, or out of it and running for his life with William FitzAlan for the empress's lands in Normandy, with a hue and cry ready to be loosed after him any moment. I'm a burden to anyone who befriends me now, and likely to be a hunted hostage as soon as I'm missed from where I should be. Even to you, Brother Cadfael, I could be dangerous. I'm daughter to FitzAlan's chief ally and friend. My name is Godith Adeney."

Lame Osbern, who had been born with both legs withered, and scuttled around at unbelievable speed on hands provided with wooden pattens, dragging his shrivelled knees behind him on a little wheeled trolley, was the humblest of the king's campfollowers. Normally he had his pitch by the castle gates in the town, but he had forsaken in time a spot now so dangerous, and transferred his hopeful allegiance to the edge of the siege camp, as near as he was allowed to get to the main guard, where the great went in and out. The king was notoriously open-handed, except towards his enemies-at-arms, and the pickings were good. The chief military officers, perhaps, were too preoccupied to waste thought or alms on a beggar, but some of those who came belatedly seeking favour, having decided which way fortune was tending, were apt to give to the poor as a kind of sop to God for luck, and the common bowmen and even the Flemings, when off-duty and merry, tossed Osbern a few coppers, or the scraps from their mess.

He had his little wagon backed well into the lee of a clump of half-grown trees, close to the guard-post, where he might come in for a crust of bread or a drink, and could enjoy the glow of the field-fire at night. Even summer nights can strike chill after the heat of the August day, when you have only a few rags to cover you, and the fire was doubly welcome. They kept it partially turfed, to subdue the glow, but left themselves light enough to scrutinise any who came late.

It was close to midnight when Osbern stirred out of an uneasy sleep, and straining his ears for the reason, caught the rustling of the bushes behind and to his left, towards the Castle Foregate but well aside from the open road. Someone was approaching from the direction of the town, and certainly not from the main gates, but roundabout in cover from along the riverside. Osbern knew the town like his own callused palm. Either this was a scout returning from reconnaissance—but why keep up this stealth right into the camp?—or else someone had crept out of town or castle by the only other way through the wall on this side, the water-port that led down to the river.

A dark figure, visible rather as movement than matter in a moonless night, slid out from the bushes and made at a crouching, silent scurry for the guard-post. At the sentry's challenge he halted immediately, and stood frozen but eager, and Osbern saw the faint outline of a slight, willowy body, wrapped closely in a black cloak, so that only a gleam of pale face showed. The voice that answered the challenge was young, high-pitched, tormentedly afraid and desperately urgent.

"I beg audience—I am not armed! Take me to your officer. I have something to tell—to the king's advantage...."

They hauled him in and went over him roughly to ensure he bore no weapons; and whatever was said between them did not reach Osbern's ears, but the upshot of it was that he had his will. They led him within the camp, and there he vanished from view.

Osbern did not doze again, the cold of the small hours was gnawing through his rags. Such a cloak as that, he thought, shivering, I wish the good God would send me! Yet even the owner of so fine a garment had been shaking, the quavering voice had betrayed his fear, but also his avid hope. A curious incident, but of no profit to a poor beggar. Not, that is, until he saw the same figure emerge from the shadowy alleys of the camp and halt once more at the gate. His step was lighter and longer now, his bearing less furtive and fearful. He bore some token from the authorities that was enough to let him out again as he had entered, unharmed and unmolested. Osbern heard a few words pass: "I am to go back, there must be no suspicion . . . I have my orders!"

Ah, now, in pure thankfulness for some alleviating mercy, he might be disposed to give. Osbern wheeled himself forward hurriedly into the man's path, and extended a pleading hand.

"For God's love, master! If he has been gracious to you, be gracious to the poor!"

He caught a glimpse of a pale face much eased, heard long breaths of relief and hope. A flicker of firelight caught the elaborate shape of a metal clasp that fastened the cloak at the throat. Out of the muffling folds a hand emerged, and dropped a coin into the extended palm. "Say some prayers for me tomorrow," said a low, breathless whisper, and the stranger flitted away as he had come, and vanished into the trees before Osbern had done blessing him for his alms.

Before dawn Osbern was roused again from fitful sleep, to withdraw himself hastily into the bushes out of all men's way. For it was still only the promise of a clear dawn, but the royal camp was astir, so quietly and in such practical order that he felt rather than heard the mustering of men, the ordering of ranks, the checking of weapons. The air of the morning seemed to shake to the tramping of regiments, while barely a sound could be heard. From curve to curve of Severn, across the neck of land that afforded the only dry approach to the town, the steady murmur of activity rippled, awesome and exhilarating, as King Stephen's army turned out and formed its divisions for the final assault of Shrewsbury castle.

Chapter
Two

ong before noon it was all over, the gates fired with brushwood and battered down, the baileys cleared one by one, the last defiant bowman hunted down from the walls and towers, smoke heavy and thick like a pall over fortress and town. In the streets not a human creature or even a dog stirred. At the first assault every man had gone to earth with wife and family and beasts behind locked and barred doors, and crouched listening with stretched ears to the thunder and clash and yelling of battle. It lasted only a short while. The garrison had reached exhaustion, ill-supplied, thinned by desertions as long as there was any possibility of escape. Everyone had been certain the next determined attack must carry the town. The merchants of Shrewsbury waited with held breath for the inevitable looting, and heaved sighs of relief when it was called to heel peremptorily by the king himself—not because he grudged his Flemings their booty, but because he wanted them close about his person. Even a king is vulnerable, and this had been an enemy town, and was still unpacified. Moreover, his urgent business was with the garrison of the castle, and in particular with FitzAlan, and Adeney, and Arnulf of Hesdin.

Stephen stalked through the smoky, bloody, steel-littered bailey into the hall, and despatched Courcelle and Ten Heyt and their men with express orders to isolate the ring leaders and bring them before him. Prestcote he kept at his side; the keys were in the new lieutenant's hands, and provisions for the royal garrison were already in consideration.

"In the end," said Prestcote critically, "it has cost your Grace fairly low. In losses, certainly. In money—the delay was costly, but the castle is intact. Some repairs to the walls—new gates... This is a stronghold you need never lose again, I count it worth the time it took to win it."

"We shall see," said Stephen grimly, thinking of Arnulf of Hesdin bellowing his lordly insults from the towers. As though he courted death!

Courcelle came in, his helmet off and his chestnut hair blazing. A promising officer, alert, immensely strong in personal combat, commanding with his men: Stephen approved him. "Well,

Adam. Are they run to earth? Surely FitzAlan is not hiding somewhere among the barns, like a craven servant?"

"No, your Grace, by no means!" said Courcelle ruefully. "We have combed this fortress from roof to dungeons, I promise you we have missed nothing. But FitzAlan is clean gone! Give us time, and we'll find for you the day, the hour, the route they took, their plans..."

"*They?*" blazed Stephen, catching at the plural.

"Adeney is away with him. Not a doubt of it, they're loose. Sorry I am to bring your Grace such news, but truth is truth." And give him his due, he had the guts to utter such truths. "Hesdin," he said, "we have. He is here without. Wounded, but not gravely, nothing but scratched. I put him in irons for safety, but I think he is hardly in such heart as when he lorded it within here, and your Grace was well outside."

"Bring him in," ordered the king, enraged afresh to find he had let two of his chief enemies slip through his fingers.

Arnulf of Hesdin came in limping heavily, and dragging chains at wrist and ankle; a big, florid man nearing sixty, soiled with dust, smoke and blood. Two of the Flemings thrust him to his knees before the king. His face was fixed and fearful, but defiant still.

"What, are you tamed?" exulted the king. "Where's your insolence now? You had plenty to say for yourself only a day or two ago, are you silenced? Or have you the wit to talk another language now?"

"Your Grace," said Hesdin, grating out words evidently hateful to him, "you are the victor, and I am at your mercy, and at your feet, and I have fought you fair, and I look to be treated honourably now. I am a nobleman of England and of France. You have need of money, and I am worth an earl's ransom, and I can pay it."

"Too late to speak me fair, you who were loud-mouthed and foul-mouthed when there were walls between us. I swore to have your life then, and have it I will. An earl's ransom cannot buy it back. Shall I quote you my price? Where is FitzAlan? Where is Adeney? Tell me in short order where I may lay hands on those two, and better pray that I succeed, and I may—*may!*—consider letting you keep your miserable life."

Hesdin reared his head and stared the king in the eyes. "I find your price too high," he said. "Only one thing I'll tell you concerning my comrades, they did not run from you until all was already lost. And live or die, that's all you'll get from me. Go hunt your own noble game!"

"We shall see!" flared the king, infuriated. "We shall see whether we get no more from you! Have him away, Adam, give him to Ten Heyt, and see what can be done with him. Hesdin, you have until two of the clock to tell us everything you know concerning their flight, or else I hang you from the battlements. Take him away!"

They dragged him out still on his knees. Stephen sat fuming and gnawing at his knuckles. "Is it true, you think, Prestcote, the one thing he did say? That they fled only when the fight was already lost? Then they may well be still in the town. How could they break through? Not by the Foregate, clean through our ranks. And the first companies within were sped straight for the two bridges. Somewhere in this island of a town they must be hiding. Find them!"

THE BENEDICTION OF BROTHER CADFAEL

"They could not have reached the bridges," said Prestcote positively. "There's only one other way out, and that's by the water-gate to the river. I doubt if they could have swum Severn there without being seen, I am sure they had no boat. Most likely they are in hiding somewhere in the town."

"Scour it! Find them! No looting until I have them safe in hold. Search everywhere, but find them."

While Ten Heyt and his Flemings rounded up the prisoners taken in arms, and disposed the new garrison under Prestcote's orders, Courcelle and others with their companies pressed on through the town, confirmed the security of the two bridges, and set about searching every house and shop within the walls. The king, his conquest assured, returned to his camp with his own bodyguard, and waited grimly for news of his two fugitives. It was past two o'clock when Courcelle reported back to him.

"Your Grace," he said bluntly, "there is no better word than failure to bring you. We have searched every street, every officer and merchant of the town has been questioned, all premises ransacked. It is not such a great town, and unless by some miracle I do not see how they can well have got outside the walls unseen. But we have not found them, neither FitzAlan nor Adeney, nor trace nor word of them. In case they've swum the river and got clear beyond the Abbey Foregate, I've sent out a fast patrol that way, but I doubt if we shall hear of them now. And Hesdin is obdurate still. Not a word to be got from him, and Ten Heyt has done his best, short of killing too soon. We shall get nothing from him. He knows the penalty. Threats will do nothing."

"He shall have what he was promised," said Stephen grimly. "And the rest? How many were taken of the garrison?"

"Apart from Hesdin, ninety-three in arms." Courcelle watched the handsome, frowning face; bitterly angry and frustrated as the king was, he was unlikely to keep his grudges hot too long. They had been telling him for weeks that it was a fault in him to forgive too readily. "Your Grace, clemency now would be taken for weakness," said Courcelle emphatically.

"Hang them!" said Stephen, jerking out sentence harshly before he wavered.

"All?"

"All! And at once. Have them all out of the world before tomorrow."

They gave the grisly work to the Flemings to do. It was what mercenaries were for, and it kept them busy all that day, and out of the houses of the town, which otherwise would have been pillaged of everything of value. The interlude, dreadful as it was, gave the guilds and the reeve and the bailiffs time to muster a hasty delegation of loyalty to the king, and obtain at least a grim and sceptical motion of grace. He might not believe in their sudden devotion, but he could appreciate its urgency.

Prestcote deployed his new garrison and made all orderly in the castle below, while Ten Heyt and his companies despatched the old garrison wholesale from the battlements. Arnulf of Hesdin was the first to die. The second was a young squire who had had a minor command under him; he was in a state of frenzied dread, and was hauled to his death yelling and protesting that he had been promised his life. The Flemings who handled him spoke little English, and were highly diverted by his pleadings, until the noose cut them off short.

Adam Courcelle confessed himself only too glad to get away from the slaughter, and pursue his searches to the very edges of the town, and across the bridges into the suburbs. But he found no trace of William FitzAlan or Fulke Adeney.

From the morning's early alarm to the night's continuing slaughter, a chill hush of horror hung over the abbey of St Peter and St Paul. Rumours flew thick as bees in swarm, no one knew what was really happening, but everyone knew that it would be terrible. The brothers doggedly pursued their chosen régime, service after service, chapter and Mass and the hours of work, because life could only be sustained by refusing to let it be disrupted, by war, catastrophe or death. To the Mass after chapter came Aline Siward with her maid Constance, pale and anxious and heroically composed; and perhaps as a result, Hugh Beringar also attended, for he had observed the lady passing from the house she had been given in the Foregate, close to the abbey's main mill. During the service he paid rather more attention to the troubled, childish profile beneath the white mourning wimple than to the words of the celebrant.

Her small hands were devoutly folded, her resolute, vulnerable lips moved silently, praying piteously for all those dying and being hurt while she knelt here. The girl Constance watched her closely and jealously, a protective presence, but could not drive the war away from her.

Beringar followed at a distance until she re-entered her house. He did not seek to overtake her, nor attempt as yet to speak to her. When she had vanished, he left his henchmen behind, and went out along the Foregate to the end of the bridge. The section that drew up was still lifted, sealing in the town, but the clamour and shrieking of battle was already subsiding to his right, where the castle loomed in its smoky halo beyond the river. He would still have to wait before he could carry out his promised search for his affianced bride. Within the hour, if he had read the signs aright, the bridge should be down, and open. Meantime, he went at leisure to take his midday meal. There was no hurry.

Rumours flew in the guest house, as everywhere else. Those who had business of unimpeachable honesty elsewhere were all seeking to pack their bags and leave. The consensus of opinion was that the castle had certainly fallen, and the cost would run very high. King Stephen's writ had better be respected henceforth, for he was here, and victorious, and the Empress Maud, however legitimate her claim, was far away in Normandy, and unlikely to provide any adequate protection. There were whispers, also, that FitzAlan and Adeney, at the last moment, had broken out of the trap and were away. For which many breathed thanks, though silently.

When Beringar went out again, the bridge was down, the way open, and King Stephen's sentries manning the passage. They were strict in scrutinising his credentials, but passed him within respectfully when they were satisfied. Stephen must have given orders concerning him. He crossed, and entered at the guarded but open gate in the wall. The street rose steeply, the island town sat high. Beringar knew it well, and knew where he was bound. At the summit of the hill the row of the butchers' stalls and houses levelled out, silent and deserted.

Edric Flesher's shop was the finest of the row, but it was shuttered and still like all the rest. Hardly a head looked out, and even then only briefly and fearfully, and was withdrawn as abruptly behind barred doors. By the look of the street, they had not so far been ravaged. Beringar thudded at the shut door, and when he heard furtive stirrings within, lifted his voice: "Open to me, Hugh Beringar! Edric—Petronilla—Let me in, I'm alone!"

He had half expected that the door would remain sealed like a tomb, and those within silent, and he would not have blamed them; but, instead, the door was flung wide, and there was Petronilla beaming and opening her arms to him as if to a saviour. She was getting old, but still plump, succulent and kindly, the most wholesome thing he had seen in this siege town so far. Her grey hair was tight and neat under its white cap, and her twinkling grey eyes bright and intelligent as ever, welcoming him in.

"Master Hugh—to see a known and trusted face here now!" Beringar was instantly sure that she did not quite trust him! "Come in, and welcome! Edric, here's Hugh—Hugh Beringar!" And there was her husband, prompt to her call, large and rubicund and competent, the master of his craft in this town, and a councillor.

They drew him within, and closed the door firmly, as he noted and approved. Beringar said what a lover should say, without preamble: "Where is Godith? I came to look for her, to provide for her. Where has he hidden her?"

It seemed they were too intent on making sure the shutters were fast, and listening for hostile footsteps outside, to pay immediate attention to what he was saying. And too

ready with questions of their own to answer his questions.

"Are you hunted?" asked Edric anxiously. "Do you need a place to hide?"

And: "Were you in the garrison?" demanded Petronilla, and patted him concernedly in search of wounds. As though she had been his nurse once, instead of Godith's, and seen him every day of his life instead of twice or thrice since the childhood betrothal. A little too much solicitude! And a neat, brief breathing-space while they considered how much or how little to tell him!

"They've been hunting here already," said Edric. "I doubt if they'll come again, they had the place to pieces after the sheriff and the Lord Fulke. You're welcome to a shelter here if you need it. Are they close on your heels?"

He was sure by that time that they knew he had never been inside the castle, nor committed in any way to FitzAlan's stand. This clever, trusted old servant and her husband had been deep in Adeney's confidence, they knew very well who had held with him, and who had held aloof.

"No, it's not that. I'm in no danger and no need. I came only to look for Godith. They're saying he left it too late to send her away with FitzAlan's family. Where can I find her?"

"Did someone send you here to look for her?" asked Edric.

"No, no, none . . . But where else would he place her? Who is there to be trusted like her nurse? Of course I came first to you! Never tell me she was not here!"

"She was here," said Petronilla. "Until a week ago we had her. But she's gone, Hugh, you're too late. He sent two knights to fetch her away, and not even we were told where she was bound. What we don't know we can't be made to tell, he said. But it's my belief they got her away out of the town in good time, and she's far off by now, and safe, pray God!" No doubt about the fervency of that prayer, she would fight and die for her nurseling. And lie for her, too, if need be!

"But for God's sake, friends, can you not help me to her at all? I'm her intended husband. I'm responsible for her if her father is dead, as by now, for all I know, he may well be...."

That got him something for his trouble, at any rate, if it was no more than the flicker of a glance passing between them, before they exclaimed their "God forbid!" in unison. They knew very well, by the frenzied search, that FitzAlan and Adeney had been neither killed nor taken. They could not yet be sure that they were clean away and safe, but they were staking their lives and loyalty on it. So now he knew he would get nothing more from them, he, the renegade. Not, at any rate, by this direct means.

"Sorry I am, lad," said Edric Flesher weightily, "to have no better comfort for you, but so it is. Take heart that at least no enemy has laid hand on her, and we pray none ever will." Which could well be taken, reflected Beringar whimsically, as a thrust at me.

"Then I must away, and try what I can discover elsewhere," he said dejectedly. "I'll not put you in further peril. Open, Petronilla, and look if the street's empty for me." Which she did, nothing loth, and reported it as empty as a beggar's palm. Beringar clasped Edric's hand, and leaned and kissed Edric's wife, and was rewarded and avenged by a vivid, guilty blush.

"Pray for her," he said, asking one thing at least they would not grudge him, and slipped

through the half-open door, and heard it closed firmly behind him. Not too loudly, since he was supposed to be affecting stealth, but still audibly, he tramped with hasty steps along the street as far as the corner of the house. Then, whirling, he skipped back silently on his toes to lay an ear to the shutter.

"Hunting for his bride!" Petronilla was saying scornfully. "Yes, and a fair price he'd pay for her, too, and she a certain decoy for her father's return, if not for FitzAlan's! He has his way to make with Stephen now, and my girl's his best weapon."

"Maybe we're too hard on him," responded Edric mildly. "Who's to say he doesn't truly want to see the girl safe? But I grant you we dared take no chances. Let him do his own hunting."

"Thank God," she said fiercely, "he can't well know I've hid my lamb away in the one place where no sane man will look for her!" And she chuckled at the word "man." "There'll be a time to get her out of there later, when all the hue and cry's forgotten. Now I pray her father's miles from here and riding hard. And that those two lads in Frankwell will have a lucky run westward with the sheriff's treasury tonight. May they all come safe to Normandy, and be serviceable to the empress, bless her!"

"Hush, love!" said Edric chidingly. "Even behind locked doors..."

They had moved away into an inner room; a door closed between. Hugh Beringar abandoned his listening-post and walked demurely away down the long, curving hill to the town gate and the bridge, whistling softly and contentedly as he went.

He had got more even than he had bargained for. So they were hoping to smuggle out

FitzAlan's treasury, as well as his person, and this very night, westward into Wales! And had had the forethought to stow it away meantime, against this desperate contingency, outside the walls of the town, somewhere in the suburb of Frankwell. No gates to pass, no bridges to cross. As for Godith—he had a shrewd idea now where to look for her. With the girl *and* the money, he reflected, a man could buy the favour of far less corruptible men than King Stephen!

Godith was in the herbarium workshop, obstinately stirring, diluting and mixing as she had been shown, an hour before Vespers, with her heart in anguished suspense, and her mind in a twilight between hope and despair. Her face was grubby from smearing away tears with a hand still soiled from the garden, and her eyes were rimmed with the washed hollows and grimed uplands of her grief and tension. Two tears escaped from her angry efforts at damming them, while both hands were occupied, and fell into a brew which should not have been weakened. Godith swore, an oath she had learned in the mews, long ago, when the falconers were suffering from a careless and impudent apprentice who had been her close friend.

"Rather say a blessing with them," said Brother Cadfael's voice behind her shoulder, gently and easily. "That's likely to be the finest tisane for the eyes I ever brewed. Never doubt God was watching." She had turned her dirty, dogged, appealing face to him in silence, finding encouragement in the very tone of his voice. "I've been to the gate house, and the mill, and the bridge. Such ill news as there is, is ill indeed, and presently we'll go pray for the souls of those quitting this world. But all of us quit it at last, by whatever way, that's not the worst of evils. And there is some news not all evil. From all I can hear this side Severn, and at the bridge itself—there's an archer among the guard there was with me in the Holy Land—your father and FitzAlan are neither dead, wounded nor captive, and all search of the town has failed to find them. They're clear away, Godric, my lad. I doubt if Stephen for all his hunting will lay hand on them now. And now you may tend to that wine you're watering, and practise your young manhood until we can get you safely out of here after your sire."

Just for a moment she rained tears like the spring thaw, and then she glinted radiance like the spring sun. There was so much to grieve over, and so much to celebrate, she did not know which to do first, and essayed both together, like April. But her age was April, and the hopeful sunshine won.

"Brother Cadfael," she said when she was calm, "I wish my father could have known you. And yet you are not of his persuasion, are you?"

"Child, dear," said Cadfael comfortably, "my monarch is neither Stephen nor Maud, and in all my life and all my fighting I've fought for only one king. But I value devotion and fidelity, and doubt if it matters whether the object falls short. What you do and what you are is what matters. Your loyalty is as sacred as mine. Now wash your face and bathe your eyes, and you can sleep for half an hour before Vespers—but no, you're too young to have the gift!"

She had not the gift that comes with age, but she had the exhaustion that comes of youthful stress, and she fell asleep on her bench-bed within seconds, drugged with the syrup of relief. He awoke her in time to cross the close for Vespers. She walked beside him discreetly, her shock of clipped curls combed forward on her brow to hide her still reddened eyes.

Driven to piety by shock and terror, all the inhabitants of the guest house were also converging on the church, among them Hugh Beringar; not, perhaps, a victim of fear, but drawn by the delicate bait of Aline Siward, who came hastening from her house by the mill with lowered eyes and heavy heart. Beringar had, none the less, a quick eye for whatever else of interest might be going on round about him. He saw the two oddly contrasted figures coming in from the gardens, the squat, solid, powerful middle-aged monk with the outdoor tan and the rolling, seaman's gait, with his hand protectively upon the shoulder of a slip of a boy in a cotte surely inherited from an older and larger kinsman, a bare-legged, striding youth squinting warily through a bush of brown hair. Beringar looked, and considered; he smiled, but so inwardly that on his long, mobile mouth the smile hardly showed.

Godith controlled both her face and her pace, and gave no sign of recognition. In the church she strolled away to join her fellow-pupils, and even exchange a few nudges and grins with them. If he was still watching, let him wonder, doubt, change his mind. He had not seen her for more than five years. Whatever his speculations, he could not be sure. Nor was he watching this part of the church, she noted; his eyes were on the unknown lady in mourning most of the time. Godith began to breathe more easily, and even allowed herself to examine her affianced bridegroom almost as attentively as he was observing Aline Siward. When last seen, he had been a coltish boy of eighteen, all elbows and knees, not yet in full command of his body. Now he had a cat's assured and contemptuous grace, and a cool, aloof way with him. A presentable enough fellow, she owned critically, but no longer of interest to her, or possessed of any rights in her. Circumstances alter fortunes. She was relieved to see that he did not look in her direction again.

All the same, she told Brother Cadfael about it, as soon as they were alone together in the garden after supper, and her evening lesson with the boys was over. Cadfael took it gravely.

"So that's the fellow you were to marry! He came here straight from the king's camp, and has certainly joined the king's party, though according to Brother Dennis, who collects all the gossip that's going among his guests, he's on sufferance as yet, and has to prove himself before he'll get a command." He scrubbed thoughtfully at his blunt, brown nose, and pondered. "Did it seem to you that he recognised you? Or even looked over-hard at you, as if you reminded him of someone known?"

"I thought at first he did give me a hard glance, as though he might be wondering. But then he never looked my way again, or showed any interest. No, I think I was mistaken. He doesn't know me. I've changed in five years, and in this guise...In another year," said Godith, astonished and almost alarmed at the thought, "we should have been married."

"I don't like it!" said Cadfael, brooding. "We shall have to keep you well out of his sight. If he wins his way in with the king, maybe he'll leave here with him in a week or so. Until then, keep far from the guest house or the stables, or the gate house, or anywhere he may be. Never let him set eyes on you if you can avoid."

"I know!" said Godith, shaken and grave. "If he does find me he may turn me to account for his own advancement. I do know! Even if my father had reached shipboard, he would come back and surrender himself, if I were threatened. And then he would die, as all those poor souls over there have died...." She could not bear to turn her head to look towards the towers of the castle, hideously ornamented. They were dying there still, though she did not know it; the work went on well into the hours of darkness. "I will avoid him, like the plague," she said fervently, "and pray that he'll leave soon."

Abbot Heribert was an old, tired and peace-loving man, and disillusionment with the ugly tendencies of the time, combined with the vigour and ambition of his prior, Robert, had disposed him to withdraw from the world ever deeper into his own private consolations of the spirit. Moreover, he knew he was in disfavour with the king, like all those who had been slow to rally to him with vociferous support. But confronted with an unmistakable duty, however monstrous, the abbot could still muster courage enough to rise to the occasion. There were ninety-four dead or dying men being disposed of like animals, and every

one had a soul, and a right to proper burial, whatever his crimes and errors. The Benedictines of the abbey were the natural protectors of those rights, and Heribert did not intend King Stephen's felons to be shovelled haphazard and nameless into an unmarked grave. All the same, he shrank from the horror of the task, and looked about him for someone more accomplished in these hard matters of warfare and bloodshed than himself, to lend support. And the obvious person was Brother Cadfael, who had crossed the world in the first Crusade, and afterwards spent ten years as a sea captain about the coasts of the Holy Land, where fighting hardly ever ceased.

After Compline, Abbot Heribert sent for Cadfael to his private parlour.

"Brother, I am going—now, this night—to ask King Stephen for his leave and authority to give Christian burial to all those slaughtered prisoners. If he consents, tomorrow we must take up their poor bodies, and prepare them decently for the grave. There will be some who can be claimed by their own families, the rest we shall bury honourably with the rites due to them. Brother, you have yourself been a soldier. Will you—if I speed with the king—will you take charge of this work?"

"Not gladly, but with all my heart, for all that," said Brother Cadfael, "yes, Father, I will."

Chapter
Three

es, I will," said Godith, "if that's how I can best be useful to you. Yes, I will go to my morning lesson and my evening lesson, eat my dinner without a word or a look to anyone, and then make myself scarce and shut myself up here among the potions. Yes, and drop the bar on the door, if need be, and wait until I hear your voice before I open again. Of course I'll do as you bid. But for all that, I wish I could go with you. These are my father's people and my people, I wish I could have some small part in doing them these last services."

"Even if it were safe for you to venture there," said Cadfael firmly, "and it is not, I would not let you go. The ugliness that man can do to man might cast a shadow between you and the certainty of the justice and mercy God can do to him hereafter. It takes half a lifetime to reach the spot where eternity is always visible, and the crude injustice of the hour shrivels out of sight. You'll come to it when the time's right. No, you stay here and keep well out of Hugh Beringar's way."

He had even thought of recruiting that young man into his working-party of able-bodied and devoutly inclined helpers, to make sure that he spent the day away from anywhere Godith might be. Whether in a bid to acquire merit for their own souls, out of secret partisan sympathy with the dead men's cause, or to search anxiously for friends or kin, three of the travellers in the guest house had volunteered their aid, and it might have been possible, with such an example, to inveigle others, even Beringar, into feeling obliged to follow suit. But it seemed that the young man was already out and away on horseback, perhaps dancing hopeful attendance on the king; a newcomer seeking office can't afford to let his face be forgotten. He had also ridden out the previous evening as soon as Vespers was over, so said the lay brothers in the stables. His three men-at-arms were here, idling their day away with nothing to do once the horses were groomed, fed and exercised, but they saw no reason why they should involve themselves in an activity certainly unpleasant, and possibly displeasing to the king. Cadfael could not blame them. He had a muster of twenty, brothers, lay brothers and the three benevolent travellers, when they set out across the bridge and through the streets of the town to the castle.

Probably King Stephen had been glad enough to have a service offered voluntarily which he might otherwise have had to impose by order. Someone had to bury the dead, or the new garrison would be the first to suffer, and in an enclosed fortress in a tightly walled town disease can fester and multiply fearfully. All the same, the king would perhaps never forgive Abbot Heribert for the implied reproach, and the reminder of his Christian duty. Howbeit, the old man had brought back the needful authority; Cadfael's party was passed through the gates without question, and Cadfael himself admitted to Prestcote's presence.

"Your lordship will have had orders about us," he said briskly. "We are here to take charge of the dead, and I require clean and adequate space where they may be decently laid until we take them away for burial. If we may draw water from the well, that's all besides that we need ask. Linen we have brought with us."

"The inner ward has been left empty," said Prestcote indifferently. "There is room there, and there are boards you may use if you need them."

"The king has also granted that such of these unfortunates as were men of this town, and have families or neighbours here, can be claimed and taken away for private burial. Will you have that cried through the town, when I am satisfied that all is ready? And give them free passage in and out?"

"If there are any bold enough to come," said Prestcote drily, "they may have their kin and welcome. The sooner all this carrion is removed, the better shall I be pleased."

"Very well! Then what have you done with them?" For the walls and towers had been denuded before dawn of their sudden crop of sorry fruit. The Flemings must have worked half the night to put the evidence out of sight, which was surely not their idea, but might well be Prestcote's. He had approved these deaths, he did not therefore have to take pleasure in them, and he was an old soldier of strict and orderly habits, who liked a clean garrison.

"We cut them down, when they were well dead, and dropped them over the parapet into the green ditch under the wall. Go out by the Foregate, and between the towers and the road you'll find them."

Cadfael inspected the small ward offered him, and it was at least clean and private, and had room for all. He led his party out through the gate in the town wall, and down into the deep, dry ditch beneath the towers. Long, fruiting grasses and low bushes partially hid what on closer approach looked like a battlefield. The dead lay piled deep at one spot close under the wall, and were sprawled and scattered like broken toys for yards on either side. Cadfael and his helpers tucked up their gowns and went to work in pairs, without word spoken, disentangling the knotted skein of bodies, carrying away first the most accessible, lifting apart those shattered into boneless embraces by their fall from above. The sun climbed high, and the heat was reflected upon them from the stone of the walls. The three pious travellers shed their cottes. In the deep hollow the air grew heavy and stifling, and they sweated and laboured for breath, but never flagged.

"Pay close attention always," said Cadfael warningly, "in case some poor soul still breathes. They were in haste, they may have cut someone down early. And in this depth of cushioning below, a man could survive even the fall."

But the Flemings, for all their hurry, had been thorough. There was no live man salvaged out of that massacre.

They had started work early, but it was approaching noon by the time they had all the dead laid out in the ward, and were beginning the work of washing and composing the bodies as becomingly as possible, straightening broken limbs, closing and weighting eyelids, even brushing tangled hair into order, and binding fallen jaws, so that the dead face might be no horror to some unfortunate parent or wife who had loved it in life. Before he would go to Prestcote and ask for the promised proclamation to be made, Cadfael walked the range of his salvaged children, and checked that they were as presentable as they could well be made. And as he paced, he counted. At the end he frowned, and stood to consider, then went back and counted again. And that done, he began a much closer scrutiny of all those he had not himself handled, drawing down the linen wrappings that covered the worst ravages. When he rose from the last of them, his face was grim, and he marched away in search of Prestcote without a word to any.

"How many," demanded Cadfael, "did you say you despatched at the king's order?"

"Ninety-four," said Prestcote, puzzled and impatient.

"Either you did not count," said Cadfael, "or you miscounted. There are ninety-five here."

"Ninety-four or ninety-five," said Prestcote, exasperated, "one more or less, what does it matter? Traitors all, and condemned, am I to tear my hair because the number does not tally?"

"Not you, perhaps," said Cadfael simply, "but God will require an accounting. Ninety-four, including Arnulf of Hesdin, you had orders to slay. Justified or not, that at least was ordered, you had your sanction, the thing is registered and understood. Any accounting for those comes later and in another court. But the ninety-fifth is not in the reckoning, no king authorised his removal out of this world, no castellan had orders to kill him, never was he accused or convicted of rebellion, treason or any other crime, and the man who destroyed him is guilty of murder."

"God's wounds!" exploded Prestcote violently. "An officer in the heat of fighting miscounts by one, and you would make a *coram rege* case out of it! He was omitted in the count delivered, but he was taken in arms and hanged like the rest, and no more than his deserts. He rebelled like the rest, he is hanged like the rest, and that's an end of it. In God's name, man, what do you want me to do?"

"It would be well," said Cadfael flatly, "if you would come and look at him, to begin with. For he is *not* like the rest. He was not hanged like the rest, his hands were not bound like the rest—he is in no way comparable, though someone took it for granted we would all see and think as you, and omit to count. I am telling you, my lord Prestcote, there is a murdered man among your executed men, a leaf hidden in your forest. And if you regret that my eyes found him, do you think God had not seen him long before? And supposing you could silence me, do you think God will keep silence?"

Prestcote had stopped pacing by that time,

and stood staring very intently. "You are in good earnest," he said, shaken. "How could there be a man there dead in some other way? Are you sure of what you say?"

"I am sure. Come and see! He is there because some felon put him there, to pass for one among the many, and arouse no curiosity, and start no questions."

"Then he would need to know that the many would be there."

"Most of this town and all this garrison would know that, by nightfall. This was a deed of night. Come and see!"

And Prestcote went with him, and showed every sign of consternation and concern. But so would a guilty man, and who was better placed to know all a guilty man needed to know, to protect himself? Still, he kneeled with Cadfael beside the body that was different, there in the confines of the ward, between high walls, with the odour of death just spreading its first insidious pall over them.

A young man, this. No armour on him, but naturally the rest had been stripped of theirs, nail and plate being valuable. But his dress was such as to suggest that he had worn neither mail nor leather, he was clad in lightweight, dark cloth, but booted, the manner of dress a man would wear for a journey in summer weather, to ride light, be warm enough by night, and shed the short cotte to be cool enough by day. He looked about twenty-five years old, no more, reddish brown in colouring and round and comely of face, if the eye could make allowance for the congestion of strangulation, now partially smoothed out by Cadfael's experienced fingers. The bulge and stare of the eyes was covered, but the lids stood large.

"He died strangled," said Prestcote, relieved to see the signs.

"He did, but not by a rope. And not with hands bound, like these others. Look!" Cadfael drew down the folds of the capuchon from the round young throat, and showed the sharp, cruel line that seemed to sever head from body. "You see the thinness of this cord that took his life? No man ever dangled from such a noose. It runs level round his neck, and is fine as fishing line. It may well have been fishing line. You see the edges of this furrow in his flesh, discoloured, and shiny? The cord that killed him was waxed, to bite smooth and deep. And you see this pit here behind?" He raised the lifeless head gently on his arm, and showed, close to the knotted cord of the spine, a single, deep, bruised hollow, with a speck of black blood at its heart. "The mark of one end of a wooden peg, a hand-hold to twist when the cord was round the victim's throat. Stranglers use such waxed cords, with two hand-holds at the ends—killers by stealth, highway birds of prey. Given strength of hand and wrist, it is a very easy way of seeing your enemies out of this world. And do you see, my lord, how his neck, where the thong bites, is lacerated and beaded with dried blood? Now see here, both hands—Look at his nails, black at the tips with his own blood. He clawed at the cord that was killing him. His hands were free. Did you hang any whose hands were not tied?"

"No!" Prestcote was so fascinated by the details he could not deny that the answer escaped him involuntarily. It would have been futile to snatch it back. He looked up at Brother Cadfael across the unknown young man's body, and his face sharpened and hardened into hostility. "There is nothing to be gained," he said deliberately, "by making public so wild a tale. Bury your dead and be content. Let the rest be!"

"You have not considered," said Cadfael mildly, "that as yet there is no one who can put a name or a badge to this boy. He may as well be an envoy of the king as an enemy. Better treat him fairly, and keep your peace with both God and man. Also," he said, in a tone even more cloistrally innocent, "you may raise doubts of your own integrity if you meddle with truth. If I were you, I would report this faithfully, and send out that proclamation to the townsfolk at once, for we are ready. Then, if any can claim this young man, you have delivered your soul. And if not, then clearly you have done all man can do to right a wrong. And your duty ends there."

Prestcote eyed him darkly for some moments, and then rose abruptly from his knees. "I will send out the word," he said, and stalked away into the hall.

The news was cried through the town, and word sent formally to the abbey, so that the same announcement might be made at the guest house there. Hugh Beringar, riding in from the east on his return from the king's camp, having forded the river at an island downstream, heard the proclamation at the gate house of the abbey, and saw among those anxiously listening the slight figure of Aline Siward, who had come out from her house to hear the news. For the first time he saw her with head uncovered. Her hair was the light, bright gold he had imagined it would be, and shed a few curling strands on either side her oval face. The long lashes shadowing her eyes were many shades darker, a rich bronze. She stood listening intently, gnawed a doubtful lip, and knotted her small hands together. She looked hesitant, and burdened, and very young.

Beringar dismounted only a few paces from her, as if he had by mere chance chosen that spot in order to be still and hear to the end what Prior Robert was saying.

"—and his Grace the king gives free warranty to any who may wish, to come and claim their kin, if there be any such among the executed, and give them burial in their own place and at their own charge. Also, since there is one in particular whose identity is not know, he desires that all who come may view him, and if they can, name him. All which may be done without fear of penalty or disfavour."

Not everyone would take that at its face value, but she did. What was troubling her was not fear of any consequences to herself, but a desperate feeling that she ought to make this dolorous pilgrimage, while equally earnestly she shrank from the horrors she might have to see. She had, Beringar remembered, a brother who had defied his father and run off to join the empress's adherents; and though she had heard rumours that he might have reached France, she had no means of knowing if they were true. Now she was struggling to escape the conviction that wherever there were garrisons of her brother's faction fallen victims of this civil war, she ought to go and assure herself that he was not among them. She had the most innocent and eloquent of faces, her every thought shone through.

"Madam," said Beringar, very softly and respectfully, "if there is any way I can be of service to you, I beg you command me."

She turned to look at him, and smiled, for she had seen him in church, and knew him to be a guest here like herself, and stress had turned Shrewsbury into a town where people behaved to one another either as loyal neighbours or potential informers, and of the latter attitude she was incapable. Nevertheless, he saw fit to establish his credentials. "You will remember I came to offer the king my troth when you did. My name is Hugh Beringar of Maesbury. It would give me pleasure to serve you. And it seemed to me that you were finding cause for perplexity and distress in what we have just heard. If there is any errand I can do for you, I will, gladly."

"I do remember you," said Aline, "and I take your offer very kindly, but this is something only I can do, if it must be done. No one else here would know my brother's face. To tell the truth, I was hesitating . . . But there will be women from the town, I know, going there with certain knowledge to find their sons. If they can do it, so can I."

"But you have no good reason," he said, "to suppose that your brother may be among these unfortunates."

"None, except that I don't know *where* he is, and I do know he embraced the empress's cause. It would be better, wouldn't it, to be sure? Not to miss any possibility? As often as I do not find him dead, I may hope to see him again alive."

"Was he very dear to you?" asked Beringar gently.

She hesitated to answer that, taking it very gravely. "No, I never knew him as sister should know brother. Giles was always for his own friends and his own way, and five years my elder. By the time I was eleven or twelve he was for ever away from home, and came back only to quarrel with my father. But he is

the only brother I have, and *I* have not disinherited him. And they're saying there's one there more than they counted, and unknown."

"It will not be Giles," he said firmly.

"But if it were? Then he needs his name, and his sister to do what's right." She had made up her mind. "I must go."

"I think you should not. But I am sure you should not go alone." He thought ruefully that her answer to that would be that she had her maid to accompany her, but instead she said at once: "I will not take Constance into such a scene! She has no kin there, and why should she have to suffer it as well as I?"

"Then, if you will have me, I will go with you."

He doubted if she had any artifice in her; certainly at this pass she showed none. Her anxious face brightened joyfully, she looked at him with the most ingenuous astonishment, hope and gratitude. But she still hesitated. "That is kind indeed, but I can't let you do it. Why should you be subjected to such pain, just because I have a duty?"

"Oh, come now!" he said indulgently, sure of himself and of her. "I shall not have a moment's peace if you refuse me and go alone. But if you tell me I shall only be adding to your distress by insisting, then I'll be silent and obey you. On no other condition."

It was more than she could do. Her lips quivered. "No—it would be a lie. I am not very brave!" she said sadly. "I shall be grateful indeed."

He had what he had wanted; he made the most of it. Why ride, when the walk through the town could be made to last so much longer, and provide so much more opportunity to get to know her better? Hugh Beringar sent his horse to the stables, and set out with Aline along the highway and over the bridge into Shrewsbury.

Brother Cadfael was standing guard over his murdered man in a corner of the inner ward, beside the archway, where every citizen who came in search of child or kinsman must pass close, and could be questioned. But all he got so far was mute shaking of heads and glances half-pitying, half-relieved. No one knew the young man. And how could he expect great concern from these poor souls who came looking, every one, for some known face, and barely saw the rest?

Prestcote had made good his word, there was no tally kept of those who came, and no hindrance placed in their way, or question asked of them. He wanted his castle rid of its grim reminders as quickly as possible. The guard, under Adam Courcelle, had orders to remain unobtrusive, even to help if that would get the unwelcome guests off the premises by nightfall.

Cadfael had persuaded every man of the guard to view his unknown, but none of them could identify him. Courcelle had frowned down at the body long and sombrely, and shaken his head.

"I never saw him before, to my knowledge. What can there possibly have been about a mere young squire like this, to make someone hate him enough to kill?"

"There can be murders without hate," said Cadfael grimly. "Footpads and forest robbers take their victims as they come, without any feeling of liking or disliking."

"Why, what can such a youth have had to make him worth killing for gain?"

"Friend," said Cadfael, "there are those in the world would kill for the few coins a beggar has begged during the day. When they see kings cut down more than ninety in one sweep, whose fault was only to be in arms on the other side, is it much wonder rogues take that for justification? Or at least for licence!" He saw the colour burn high in Courcelle's face, and a momentary spark of anger in his eye, but the young man made no protest. "Oh, I know you had your orders, and no choice but to obey them. I have been a soldier in my time, and borne the same discipline and done things I would be glad now to think I had not done. That's one reason I've accepted, in the end, another discipline."

"I doubt," said Courcelle drily, "if I shall ever come to that."

"So would I have doubted it, then. But here I am, and would not change again to your calling. Well, we do the best we can with our lives!" And the worst, he thought, viewing the long lines of motionless forms laid out along the ward, with other men's lives, if we have power.

There were some gaps in the silent ranks by then. Some dozen or so had been claimed by parents and wives. Soon there would be piteous little hand-carts pushed up the slope to the gate, and brothers and neighbours lifting limp bodies to carry them away. More of the townspeople were still coming timidly in through the archway, women with shawls drawn close over their heads and faces half-hidden, gaunt old men trudging resignedly to look for their sons. No wonder Courcelle, whose duties could hardly have encompassed this sort of guard before, looked almost as unhappy as the mourners.

He was frowning down at the ground in morose thought when Aline came into view in the archway, her hand drawn protectively through Hugh Beringar's arm. Her face was white and taut, her eyes very wide and her lips stiffly set, and her fingers clutched at her escort's sleeve as drowning men clutch at floating twigs, but she kept her head up and her step steady and firm. Beringar matched his pace attentively to hers, made no effort to divert her eyes from the sorry spectacle in the ward, and cast only few and brief, but very intent, side-glances at her pale countenance. It would certainly have been a tactical error, Cadfael thought critically, to attempt the kind of protective ardour that claims possession; young and ingenuous and tender as she might be, this was a proud patrician girl of old blood, not to be trifled with if once that blood was up. If she had come here on her own family business, like these poor, prowling citizens, she would not thank any man to try and take it out of her hands. She might, none the less, be deeply thankful for his considerate and reticent presence.

Courcelle looked up, almost as though he had felt a breath of unease moving before them, and saw the pair emerge into the sunlight in the ward, cruel afternoon sunlight that spared no detail. His head jerked up and caught the light, his bright hair burning up like a furze fire. "Christ God!" he said in a hissing undertone, and went plunging to intercept them on the threshold.

"Aline!—Madam, should you be here? This is no place for you, so desolate a spectacle. I marvel," he said furiously to Beringar, "that you should bring her here, to face a scene so harrowing."

"He did not bring me," said Aline quickly. "It was I insisted on coming. Since he could not prevent me, he has been kind enough to come with me."

"Then, dear lady, you were foolish to impose such a penance on yourself," said Courcelle fiercely. "Why, how can you have business here? Surely there's none here belonging to you."

"I pray you may be right," she said. Her eyes, huge in the white face, ranged in fearful fascination over the shrouded ranks at her feet, and visibly the first horror and revulsion changed gradually into appalled human pity. "But I must know! Like all these others! I have only one way of being certain, and it's no worse for me than for them. You know I have a brother— you were there when I told the king...."

"But he cannot be here. You said he was fled to Normandy."

"I said it was rumoured so—but how can I be sure? He *may* have won to France, he may have joined some company of the empress's men nearer home, how can I tell? I must see for myself whether he chose Shrewsbury or not."

"But surely the garrison here were known. Your name is very unlikely to have been among them."

"The sheriff's proclamation," said Beringar mildly, speaking up for the first time in this encounter, "mentioned that there was one here, at least, who was not known. One more, apparently, than the expected tally."

"You must let me see for myself," said Aline, gently and firmly, "or how can I have any peace?"

Courcelle had no right to prevent, however it grieved and enraged him. And at least this particular corpse was close at hand, and could bring her nothing but reassurance. "He lies here," he said, and turned her towards the corner where Brother Cadfael stood. She gazed, and was surprised into the faint brightness of a smile, a genuine smile though it faded soon.

"I think I should know you. I've seen you about the abbey, you are Brother Cadfael, the herbalist."

"That is my name," said Cadfael. "Though why you should have learned it I hardly know."

"I was asking the porter about you," she owned, flushing. "I saw you at Vespers and Compline, and—Forgive me, brother, if I have trespassed, but you had such an air—as though you had lived adventures before you came to the cloister. He told me you were in the Crusade—with Godfrey of Bouillon at the siege of Jerusalem! I have only dreamed of such service … Oh!" She had lowered her eyes from his face, half abashed by her own ardour, and seen the young, dead face exposed at his feet. She gazed and gazed, in controlled silence. The face was not offensive, rather its congestion had subsided; the unknown lay youthful and almost comely.

"This a most Christian service you are doing now," said Aline, low-voiced, "for all these here. This is the unexpected one? The one more than was counted?"

"This is he." Cadfael stooped and drew down the linen to show the good but simple clothing, the absence of anything warlike about the young man. "But for the dagger, which every man wears when he travels, he was unarmed."

She looked up sharply. Over her shoulder Beringar was gazing down with frowning concentration at the rounded face that must have been cheerful and merry in life. "Are you saying," asked Aline, "that he was not in the fight here? Not captured with the garrison?"

"So it seems to me. You don't know him?"

"No." She looked down with pure, impersonal compassion. "So young! It's great pity! I wish I could tell you his name, but I never saw him before."

"Master Beringar?"

"No. A stranger to me." Beringar was still staring down very sombrely at the dead. They were almost of an age, surely no more than a year between them. Every man burying his twin sees his own burial.

Courcelle, hovering solicitously, laid a hand on the girl's arm, and said persuasively: "Come now, you've done your errand, you should quit this sad place at once, it is not for you. You see your fears were groundless, your brother is not here."

"No," said Aline, "this is not he, but for all that he *may*—How can I be sure unless I see them all?" She put off the urging touch, but very gently. "I've ventured this far, and how is it worse for me than for any of these others?" She looked round appealingly. "Brother Cadfael, this is your charge now. You know I must ease my mind. Will you come with me?"

"Very willingly," said Cadfael, and led the way without more words, for words were not going to dissuade her, and he thought her right not to be dissuaded. The two young men followed side by side, neither willing to give the other precedence. Aline looked down at every exposed face, wrung but resolute.

"He was twenty-four years old—not very

like me, his hair was darker . . . Oh, here are all too many no older than he!"

They had traversed more than half of the dolorous passage when suddenly she caught at Cadfael's arm, and froze where she stood. She made no outcry, she had breath only for a soft moan, audible as a word only to Cadfael, who was nearest. "Giles!" she said again more strongly, and what colour she had drained from her face and left her almost translucent, staring down at a face once imperious, wilful and handsome. She sank to her knees, stooping to study the dead face close, and then she uttered the only cry she ever made over her brother, and that very brief and private, and swooped breast to breast with him, gathering the body into her arms. The mass of her hair slipped out of its coils and spilled gold over them both.

Brother Cadfael, who was experienced enough to let her alone until she seemed to need comfort for her grief instead of decent reticence, would have waited quietly, but he was hurriedly thrust aside, and Adam Courcelle fell on his knees beside her, and took her beneath the arms to lift her against his shoulder. The shock of discovery seemed to have shaken him fully as deeply as it had Aline, his face was stricken and dismayed, his voice an appalled stammer.

"Madam!—Aline—Dear God, is this indeed your brother? If I'd known . . . if I'd known, I'd have saved him for you. . . . Whatever the cost, I would have delivered him . . . God forgive me!"

She lifted a tearless face from the curtain of her yellow hair, and looked at him with wonder and compunction, seeing him so shattered. "Oh, hush! How can this be any fault of yours? You could not know. You did only

what you were ordered to do. And how could you have saved one, and let the rest die?"

"Then truly this *is* your brother?"

"Yes," she said, gazing down at the dead youth with a face now drained even of shock and grief. "This is Giles." Now she knew the worst, and now she had only to do what was needful, what fell to her for want of father and brothers. She crouched motionless in Courcelle's arm, earnestly regarding the dead face. Cadfael, watching, was glad he had managed to mould some form back into features once handsome, but in death fallen into a total collapse of terror. At least she was not viewing that hardly human disintegration.

Presently she heaved a short, sharp sigh, and made to rise, and Hugh Beringar, who had shown admirably judicious restraint throughout, reached a hand to her on the other side, and lifted her to her feet. She was mistress of herself as perhaps she had never been before, never having had to meet such a test until now. What was required of her she could and would do.

"Brother Cadfael, I do thank you for all you have done, not only for Giles and me, but for all these. Now, if you permit, I will take my brother's burial into my charge, as is only fitting."

Close and anxious at her shoulder, still deeply shaken, Courcelle asked: "Where would you have him conveyed? My men shall carry him there for you, and be at your orders as long as you need them. I wish I might attend you myself, but I must not leave my guard."

"You are very kind," she said, quite composed now. "My mother's family has a tomb at St. Alkmund's church, here in the town. Father Elias knows me. I shall be grateful for help in taking my brother there, but I need not keep your men from their duties longer. All the rest I will do." Her face had grown intent and practical, she had work to do, all manner of things to take into account, the need for speed, the summer heat, the provision of all the materials proper to decent preparation for the grave. She made her dispositions with authority.

"Messire Beringar, you have been kind, and I do value it, but now I must stay to see to my family's rites. There is no need to sadden all the rest of your day, I shall be safe enough."

"I came with you," said Hugh Beringar, "and I shall not return without you." The very way to talk to her now, without argument, without outward show of sympathy. She accepted his resolve simply, and turned to her duty. Two of the guards brought a narrow litter, and lifted Giles Siward's body into it, and she herself steadied and straightened the lolling head.

At the last moment Courcelle, frowning down distressfully at the corpse, said abruptly: "Wait! I have remembered—I believe there is something here that must have belonged to him."

He went hastily through the archway and across the outer ward to the guard-towers, and in a few moments came back carrying over his arm a black cloak. "This was among the gear they left behind in the guardroom at the end. I think it must have been his—this clasp at the neck has the same design, see, as the buckle of his belt."

It was true enough, there was the same dragon of eternity, tail in mouth, lavishly worked in bronze. "I noticed it only now. That cannot be by chance. Let me at least restore him this." He spread out the cloak and

draped it gently over the litter, covering the dead face. When he looked up, it was into Aline's eyes, and for the first time they regarded him through a sheen of tears.

"That was very kindly done," she said in a low voice, and gave him her hand. "I shall not forget it."

Cadfael went back to his vigil by the unknown, and continued his questioning, but it brought no useful response. In the coming night all these dead remaining must be taken on carts down the Wyle and out to the abbey; this hot summer would not permit further delay. At dawn Abbot Heribert would consecrate a new piece of ground at the edge of the abbey enclosure, for a mass grave. But this unknown, never condemned, never charged with any crime, whose dead body cried aloud for justice, should not be buried among the executed, nor should there be any rest until he could go to his grave under his own rightful name, and with all the individual honours due to him.

In the house of Father Elias, priest of St Alkmund's church, Giles Siward was reverently stripped, washed, composed and shrouded, all by his sister's hands, the good father assisting. Hugh Beringar stood by to fetch and carry for them, but did not enter the room where they worked. She wanted no one else, she was quite sufficient to the task laid on her, and if she was robbed of any part of it now she would feel deprivation and resentment, not gratitude. But when all was done, and her brother laid ready for rest before the altar of the church, she was suddenly weary to death, and glad enough of Beringar's almost silent company and ready arm back to her house by the mill.

On the following morning Giles Siward was interred with all due ceremony in the tomb of his maternal grandfather in the church of St Alkmund, and the monks of the abbey of St Peter and St Paul buried with due rites all the sixty-six soldiers of the defeated garrison still remaining in their charge.

Chapter Four

line brought back with her the cotte and hose her brother had worn, and the cloak that had covered him, and herself carefully brushed and folded them. The shirt no one should ever wear again, she would burn it and forget; but these stout garments of good cloth must not go to waste, in a world where so many went half-naked and cold. She took the neat bundle, and went in at the abbey gate house, and finding the whole courtyard deserted, cross to the ponds and the gardens in search of Brother Cadfael. She did not find him. The digging out of a grave large enough to hold sixty-six victims, and the sheer repetitive labour of laying them in it, takes longer than the opening of a stone tomb to make room for one more kinsman. The brothers were hard at work until past two o'clock, even with every man assisting.

But if Cadfael was not there, his garden-boy was, industriously clipping off flower-heads dead in the heat, and cutting leaves and stems of blossoming savory to hang up in bunches for drying. All the end of the hut, under the eaves, was festooned with drying herbs. The diligent boy worked barefoot and dusty from the powdery soil, and a smear of green coloured one cheek. At the sound of approaching footsteps he looked round, and came out in haste from among his plants, in a great wave of fragrance, which clung about him and distilled from the folds of his coarse tunic like the miraculous sweetness conferred upon some otherwise unimpressive-looking saint. The hurried swipe of a hand over his tangle of hair only served to smear the other cheek and half his forehead.

"I was looking," said Aline, almost apologetically, "for Brother Cadfael. You must be the boy called Godric, who works for him."

"Yes, my lady," said Godith gruffly. "Brother Cadfael is still busy, they are not finished yet." She had wanted to attend, but he would not let her; the less she was seen in full daylight, the better.

"Oh!" said Aline, abashed. "Of course, I should have known. Then may I leave my message with you? It is only—I've brought these, my brother's clothes. He no longer needs them, and they are still good, someone could be glad of them. Will you ask Brother Cadfael to dispose of them somewhere they can do good? However he thinks best."

Godith had scrubbed grubby hands down the skirts of her cotte before extending them to take the bundle. She stood suddenly very still, eyeing the other girl and clutching the dead man's clothes, so startled and shaken that she forgot for a moment to keep her voice low. "No longer needs... You had a brother in there, in the castle? Oh, I am sorry! Very sorry!"

Aline looked down at her own hands, empty and rather lost now that even this last small duty was done. "Yes. One of many," she said. "He made his choice. I was taught to think it the wrong one, but at least he stood by it to the end. My father might have been angry with him, but he would not have had to be ashamed."

"I am sorry!" Godith hugged the folded garments to her breast and could find no better words. "I'll deliver your message to Brother Cadfael as soon as he comes. And he would want me to give you his thanks for your most feeling charity, until he can do it for himself."

"And give him this purse, too. It is for Masses for them all. But especially a Mass for the one who should not have been there—the one nobody knows."

Godith stared in bewilderment and wonder. "Is there one like that? One who did not belong? I didn't know!" She had seen Cadfael for only a few hurried moments when he came home late and weary, and he had had no time to tell her anything. All she knew was that the remaining dead had been brought to the abbey for burial; this mysterious mention of one who had no place in the common tragedy was new to her.

"So he said. There were ninety-five where there should have been only ninety-four, and one did not seem to have been in arms. Brother Cadfael was asking all who came, to look and see if they knew him, but I think no one has yet put a name to him."

"And where, then is he now?" asked Godith, marvelling.

"That I don't know. Though they must have brought him here to the abbey. Somehow I don't think Brother Cadfael will let him be put into the earth with all the rest, and he nameless and unaccounted for. You must know his ways better than I. Have you worked with him long?"

"No, a very short time," said Godith, "but I do begin to know him." She was growing a little uneasy, thus innocently studied at close quarters by those clear iris eyes. A woman might be more dangerous to her secret than a man. She cast a glance back towards the beds of herbs where she had been working.

"Yes," said Aline, taking the allusion, "I must not keep you from your proper work."

Godith watched her withdraw, almost regretting that she dared not prolong this encounter with another girl in this sanctuary of men. She laid the bundle of clothing on her bed in the hut, and went back to work, waiting in some disquiet for Cadfael to come; and even when he did appear he was tired, and still burdened with business.

"I'm sent for to the king's camp. It seems his sheriff has thought best to let him know what sort of unexpected hare I've started, and he wants an accounting from me. But I'm forgetting," he said, passing a hard palm over cheeks stiff with weariness, "I've had no time to talk to you at all, you've heard nothing of all that—"

"Ah, but I have," said Godith. "Aline Siward was here looking for you. She brought these, see, for you to give as alms, wherever you think best. They were her brother's. She told me. And this money is for Masses—she said especially a Mass for this one man more than was looked for. Now tell me, what is this mystery?"

It was pleasant to sit quietly for a while and let things slide, and therefore he relaxed and sat down with her, and told her. She listened intently, and when he was done she asked at once: "And where is he now, this stranger nobody knows?"

"He is in the church, on a bier before the altar. I want all who come to services to pass by him, in the hope that someone must know him, and give him a name. We can't keep him beyond tomorrow," he said fretfully, "the season is too hot. But if we must bury him unknown, I intend it to be where he can as easily be taken up again, and to keep his clothes and a drawing of his face, until we discover the poor lad."

"And you truly believe," she questioned, awed, "that he was murdered? And then cast in among the king's victims, to hide the crime away for ever?"

"Child, I've told you! He was taken from behind, with a strangler's cord ready prepared for the deed. And it was done in the same night that the others died and were flung over into the ditch. What better opportunity could a murderer have? Among so many, who was to count, and separate, and demand answers? He had been dead much the same time as some of those others. It should have been a certain cover."

"But it was not!" she said, vengefully glowing. "Because *you* came. Who else would have cared to be so particular among ninety-five dead men? Who else would have stood out alone for the rights of a man not condemned—killed without vestige of law? Oh, Brother Cadfael, you have made me as irreconcilable as you are on this. Here am I, and have not seen this man. Let the king wait a little while! Let me go and see! Or go with me, if you must, but let me look at him."

Cadfael considered and got to his feet, groaning a little at the effort. He was not so young as he once had been, and he had had a hard day and night. "Come, then, have your will, who am I to shut you out where I invite others in? It should be quiet enough there now, but keep close to me. Oh, girl, dear, I must also be about getting you safe out of here as soon as I may."

"Are you so eager to get rid of me?" she said, offended. "And just when I'm getting to know sage from marjoram! What would you do without me?"

"Why, train some novice I can expect to keep longer than a few weeks. And speaking of herbs," said Cadfael, drawing out a little leather bag from the breast of his habit, and shaking out a six-inch sprig of sun-dried herbage, a thin, square stem studded at intervals with pairs of spreading leaves, with tiny brown balls set in the joints of them, "do you know what this one is?"

She peered at it curiously, having learned much in a few days. "No. We don't grow it here. But I might know it if I saw it growing fresh."

"It's goose-grass—cleavers it's also called. A queer, creeping thing that grows little hooks to hold fast, even on these tiny seeds you see here. And you see it's broken in the middle of this straight stem?"

She saw, and was curiously subdued. There was something here beyond her vision; the thing was a wisp of brown, bleached and dry, but indeed folded sharply in the midst by a thin fracture. "What is it? Where did you find it?"

"Caught into the furrow in this poor lad's throat," he said, so gently that she could take it in without shock, "broken here by the ligament that strangled him. And it's last year's crop, not new. The stuff is growing richly at this season, seeding wild everywhere, this was in fodder, or litter, grass cut last autumn and dried out. Never turn against the herb, it's sovereign for healing green wounds that are stubborn to knit. All the things of the wild have their proper uses, only misuse makes them evil." He put the small slip of dryness away carefully in his bosom, and laid an arm about her shoulders. "Come, then, let's go and look at this youngster, you and I together."

It was mid-afternoon, the time of work for the brothers, play for the boys and the novices, once their limited tasks were done. They came down to the church without meeting any but a few half-grown boys at play, and entered the cool dimness within.

The mysterious young man from the castle ditch lay austerely shrouded on his bier in the choir end of the nave, his head and face uncovered. Dim but pure light fell upon him; it needed only a few minutes to get accustomed to the soft interior glow in this summer afternoon, and he shone clear to view. Godith stood beside him and gazed in silence. They were alone there, but for him, and they could speak, in low voices. But when Cadfael asked softly: "Do you know him?" he was already sure of the answer.

A fine thread of a whisper beside him said: "Yes."

"Come!" He led her out as softly as they had come. In the sunlight he heard her draw breath very deep and long. She made no other comment until they were secure together in the herbarium, in the drowning summer sweetness, sitting in the shade of the hut.

"Well, who is he, this young fellow who troubles both you and me?"

"His name," she said, very low and wonderingly, "is Nicholas Faintree. I've known him, by fits and starts, since I was twelve years old. He is a squire of FitzAlan's, from one of his northern manors, he's ridden courier for his lord several times in the last few years. He would not be much known in Shrewsbury, no. If he was waylaid and murdered here, he must have been on his lord's business. But FitzAlan's business was almost finished in these parts." She hugged her head between her hands, and thought passionately. "There are some in Shrewsbury could have named him for you, you know, if they had reason to come looking for men of their own. I know of some who may be able to tell you what he was doing here that day and that night. If you can be sure no ill will come to them?"

"Never by me," said Cadfael, "that I promise."

"There's my nurse, the one who brought me here and called me her nephew. Petronilla served my family all her grown life, until she married late, too late for children of her own, and she married a good friend to FitzAlan's house and ours, Edric Flesher, the chief of the butchers' guild in town. The two of them were close in all the plans when FitzAlan declared for the empress Maud. If you go to them from me," she said confidently, "they'll tell you anything they know. You'll know the shop, it has the sign of the boar's head, in the butchers' row."

Cadfael scrubbed thoughtfully at his nose. "If I borrow the abbot's mule, I can make better speed, and spare my legs, too. There'll be no keeping the king waiting, but on the way back I can halt at the shop. Give me some token, to show you trust me, and they can do as much without fear."

"Petronilla can read, and knows my hand. I'll write you a line to her, if you'll lend me a little leaf of vellum, a mere corner will do." She was alight with ardour, as intent as he. "He was a merry person, Nicholas, he never did harm to anyone, that I know, and he was never out of temper. He laughed a great deal. . . . But if you tell the king he was of the opposite party, he won't care to pursue the murderer, will he? He'll call it a just fate, and bid you leave well alone."

"I shall tell the king," said Cadfael, "that we have a man plainly murdered, and the method and time we know, but not the place or the reason. I will also tell him that we have a name for him—it's a modest name enough, it can mean nothing to Stephen. As at this moment there's no more to tell, for I know no more. And even if the king should shrug it off and bid me let things lie, I shall not do it. By my means or God's means, or the both of us together, Nicholas Faintree shall have justice before I let this matter rest."

Having the loan of the abbot's own mule, Brother Cadfael took with him in this errand the good cloth garments Aline had entrusted to him. It was his way to carry out at once whatever tasks fell him, rather than put them off until the morrow, and there were beggars enough on his way through the town. The hose he gave to an elderly man with eyes whitened over with thick cauls, who sat with stick beside him and palm extended in the shade of the town gate. He looked of a suitable figure, and was in much-patched and threadbare nethers that would certainly fall apart very soon. The good brown cotte went to a frail creature no more than twenty years old who begged at the high cross, a poor feeble-wit with hanging lip and a palsied shake, who had a tiny old woman holding him by the hand and caring for him jealously. Her shrill blessings followed Cadfael down towards the castle gate. The cloak he still had folded before him when he came to the guard-post of the king's camp, and saw Lame Osbern's little wooden trolley tucked into the bole of a tree close by, and marked the useless, withered legs, and the hands callused and muscular from dragging all that dead weight about by force. His wooden pattens lay beside him in the grass. Seeing a frocked monk approaching on a good riding mule, Osbern seized them and propelled himself forward into Cadfael's path. And it was wonderful how fast he could move, over short distances and with intervals for rest, but all the same so immobilised a creature, half his body inert, must suffer cold in even the milder nights, and in the winter terribly.

"Good brother," coaxed Osbern, "spare an alms for a poor cripple, and God will reward you!"

"So I will, friend," said Cadfael, "and better than a small coin, too. And you may say a prayer for a gentle lady who sends it to you by my hand." And he unfolded from the saddle before him, and dropped into the startled, malformed hands, Giles Siward's cloak.

*　*　*

"You did right to report truly what you found," said the king consideringly. "Small wonder that my castellan did not make the same discovery, he had his hands full. You say this man was taken from behind by stealth, with a strangler's cord? It's a footpad's way, and foul. And above all, to cast his victim in among my executed enemies to cover the crime—that I will not bear! How dared he make me and my officers his accomplices! That I count an affront to the crown, and for that alone I would wish the felon taken and judged. And the young man's name—Faintree, you said?"

"Nicholas Faintree. So I was told by one who came and saw him, where we had laid him in the church. He comes from a family in the north of the county. But that is all I know of him."

"It is possible," reflected the king hopefully, "that he had ridden to Shrewsbury to seek service with us. Several such young men from north of the county have joined us here."

"It is possible," agreed Cadfael gravely; for all things are possible, and men do turn their coats.

"And to be cut off by some forest thief for what he carried—it happens! I wish I could say our roads are safe, but in this new anarchy, God knows, I dare not claim it. Well, you may pursue such enquiries as can be made into this matter, if that's your wish, and call upon my sheriff to do justice if the murderer can be found. He knows my will. I do not like being made use of to shield so mean a crime."

And that was truth, and the heart of the matter for him, and perhaps it would not have changed his attitude, thought Cadfael, even if he had known that Faintree was FitzAlan's squire and courier, even if it were proved, as so far it certainly was not, that he was on FitzAlan's rebellious business when he died. By all the signs, there would be plenty of killing in Stephen's realm in the near future, and he would not lose his sleep over most of it, but to have a killer-by-stealth creeping for cover into his shadow, that he would take as a deadly insult to himself, and avenge accordingly. Energy and lethargy, generosity and spite, shrewd action and incomprehensible inaction, would always alternate and startle in King Stephen. But somewhere within that tall, comely, simple-minded person there was a grain of nobility hidden.

"I accept and value your Grace's support," said Brother Cadfael truthfully, "and I will do my best to see justice done. A man cannot lay down and abandon the duty God has placed in his hands. Of this young man I know only his name, and the appearance of his person, which is open and innocent, and that he was accused of no crime, and no man has complained of wrong by him, and he is dead unjustly. I think this as unpleasing to your Grace as ever it can be to me. If I can right it, so I will."

At the sign of the boar's head in the butcher's row he was received with the common wary civility any citizen would show to a monk of the abbey. Petronilla, rounded and comfortable and grey, bade him in and would have offered all the small attentions that provide a wall between suspicious people, if he had not at once given her the worn and much-used leaf of vellum on which Godith had, somewhat cautiously and laboriously, inscribed her trust in the messenger, and her name. Petronilla peered and flushed with pleasure, and looked up at this elderly, solid, homely brown monk through blissful tears.

"The lamb, she's managing well, then, my girl? And you taking good care of her! Here she says it, I know that scrawl, I learned to write with her. I had her almost from birth, the darling, and she the only one, more's the pity, she should have had brothers and sisters. It was why I wanted to do everything with her, even the letters, to be by her whatever she needed. Sit down, brother, sit down and tell me of her, if she's well, if she needs anything I can send her by you. Oh, and, brother, how are we to get her safely away? Can she stay with you, if it runs to weeks?"

When Cadfael could wedge a word or two into the flow he told her how her nurseling was faring, and how he would see to it that she continued to fare. It had not occurred to him until then what a way the girl had of taking hold of hearts, without at all designing it. By the time Edric Flesher came in from a cautious skirmish through the town, to see how the land lay, Cadfael was firmly established in Petronilla's favour, and vouched for as a friend to be trusted.

Edric settled his solid bulk into a broad chair, and said with a gusty breath of cautious relief: "Tomorrow I'll open the shop. We're fortunate! Ask me, he rues the vengeance he took for those he failed to capture. He's called off all pillage here, and for once he's enforcing it. If only his claims were just, and he had more spine in his body, I think I'd be for him. And to look like a hero, and be none, that's hard on a man." He gathered his great legs under him, and looked at his wife, and then, longer, at Cadfael. "She says you have the girl's good word, and that's enough. Name your need, and if we have it, it's yours."

"For the girl," said Cadfael briskly, "I will keep her safe as long as need be, and when the right chance offers, I'll get her away to where she should be. For my need, yes, there you may help me. We have in the abbey church, and we shall bury there tomorrow, a young man you may know, murdered on the night after the castle fell, the night the prisoners were hanged and thrown into the ditch. But he was killed elsewhere, and thrown among the rest to have him away into the ground unquestioned. I can tell you how he died, and when. I cannot tell you where, or why, or who did this thing. But Godith tells me that his name is Nicholas Faintree, and he was a squire of FitzAlan."

All this he let fall between them in so many words, and heard and felt their silence. Certainly there were things they knew, and equally certainly this death they had not known, and it struck at them like a mortal blow.

"One more thing I may tell you," he said. "I intend to have the truth out into the open concerning this thing, and see him avenged. And more, I have the king's word to pursue the murderer. He likes the deed no more than I like it."

After a long moment Edric asked: "There was only one, dead after this fashion? No second?"

"Should there have been? Is not one enough?"

"There were two," said Edric harshly. "Two who set out together upon the same errand. How did this death come to light? It seems you are the only man who knows."

Brother Cadfael sat back and told them all, without haste. If he had missed Vespers, so be it. He valued and respected his duties, but if they clashed, he knew which way he must go.

Godith would not stir from her safe solitude without him, not until her evening schooling.

"Now," he said, "you had better tell me. I have Godith to protect, and Faintree to avenge, and I mean to do both as best I can."

The two of them exchanged glances, and understood each other. It was the man who took up the tale.

"A week before the castle and the town fell, with FitzAlan's family already away, and our plans made to place the girl with your abbey in hiding, FitzAlan also took thought for the end, if he died. He never ran until they broke in at the gates, you know that? By the skin of his teeth he got away, swam the river with Adeney at his shoulder, and got clear. God be thanked! But the day before the end he made provision for whether he lived or died. His whole treasury had been left with us here, he wanted it to reach the empress if he were slain. That day we moved it out into Frankwell, to a garden I hold there, so that there need be no bridge to pass if we had to convey it away at short notice. And we fixed a signal. If any of his party came with a certain token—a trifle it was, a drawing, but private to us who knew—they should be shown where the treasury was, provided with horses, all they might need, and put over there to pick up the valuables and make their break by night."

"And so it was done?" said Cadfael.

"On the morning of the fall. It came so early, and in such force, we'd left it all but too late. Two of them came. We sent them over the bridge to wait for night. What could they have done by daylight?"

"Tell me more. What time did these two come to you that morning, what had they to say, how did they get their orders? How many may have known what was toward? How many would have known the way they would take? When did you last see them both alive?"

"They came just at dawn. We could hear the din by then, the assault had begun. They had the parchment leaf that was the signal, the head of a saint drawn in ink. They said there had been a council the night before, and FitzAlan had said then he would have them go the following day, whatever happened and whether he lived or no, get the treasury away safe to the empress, for her use in defending her right."

"Then all who were at that council would know those two would be on the road the following night, as soon as it was dark enough. Would they also know the road? Did they know where the treasury was hidden?"

"No, where we had put it, beyond that it was in Frankwell, no one had been told. Only FitzAlan and I knew that. Those two squires had to come to me."

"Then any who had ill designs on the treasury, even if they knew the time of its removal, could not go and get it for themselves, they could only waylay it on the road. If all those officers close to FitzAlan knew that it was to be taken westward into Wales from Frankwell, there'd be no doubt about the road. For the first mile and more there is but one, by reason of the coils of the river on either side."

"You are thinking that one of those who knew thought to get the gold for himself, by murder?" said Edric. "One of FitzAlan's own men? I cannot believe it! And surely all, or most, stayed to the end, and died. Two men riding by night could well be waylaid by pure chance, by men living wild in the forest..."

"Within a mile of the town walls? Don't forget, whoever killed this lad did so close enough to Shrewsbury castle to have ample time and means to take his body and toss it among all those others in the ditch, long before the night was over. Knowing very well that all those others would be there. Well, so they came, they showed their credentials, they told you the plan had been made the previous evening, come what might. But what came, came earlier and more fiercely than anyone had expected, and all done in haste. Then what? You went with them over to Frankwell?"

"I did. I have a garden and a barn there, where they and their horses lay in hiding until dark. The valuables were packed into two pairs of saddle-bags—one horse with his rider and that load would have been overdone—in a cavity in a dry well on my land there. I saw them safe under cover, and left them there about nine in the morning."

"And at what time would they venture to start?"

"Not until full dark. And do you truly tell me Faintree was murdered, soon after they set out?"

"Past doubt he was. Had it been done miles away, he would have been disposed of some other way. This was planned, and ingenious. But not ingenious enough. You knew Faintree well—or so Godith gave me to think. Who was the other? Did you also know him?"

Heavily and slowly, Edric said, "No! It seemed to me that Nicholas knew him well enough, they were familiar together like good comrades, but Nicholas was one open to any new friend. I had never seen this lad before. He was from another of FitzAlan's northern manors. He gave his name as Torold Blund."

They had told him all they knew, and something more than had been said in words. Edric's brooding frown spoke for him. The young man they knew and trusted was dead, the one they did not know vanished, and with him FitzAlan's valuables, plate and coin and jewellery, intended for the empress's coffers. Enough to tempt any man. The murderer clearly knew all he needed to know in order to get possession of that hoard; and who could have known half so well as the second courier himself? Another might certainly way-lay the prize on the road. Torold Blund need not even have waited for that. Those two had been in hiding together all that day in Edric's barn. It was possible that Nicholas Faintree had never left it until he was dead, draped over a horse for the short ride back to the castle ditch, before two horses with one rider set out westward into Wales.

"There was one more thing happened that day," said Petronilla, as Cadfael rose to take his leave. "About two of the clock, after the king's men had manned both bridges and dropped the draw-bridge, *he* came—Hugh Beringar, he that was betrothed to my girl from years back—making pretence to be all concern for her, and asking where he could find her. Tell him? No, what do you take me for? I told him she'd been taken away a good week before the town fell, and we were not told where, but I thought she was far away by now, and safe out of Stephen's country. Right well we knew he must have come to us with Stephen's authority, or he would never have been let through so soon. He'd been to the king's camp before ever he came hunting for my Godith, and it's not for love he's searching for her. She's worth a fat commission, as bait for her father, if not for FitzAlan himself. Don't let my lamb get within his sight, for I hear he's living in the abbey now."

"And he was here that very afternoon?" pressed Cadfael, concerned. "Yes, yes, I'll take good care to keep her away from him, I've seen that danger. But there could not have been any mention when he came here, could there, of Faintree's mission? Nothing to make him prick his ears? He's very quick, and very private! No—no, I ask your pardon, I know you'd never let out word. Ah, well, my thanks for your help, and you shall know if I make progress."

He was at the door when Petronilla said grievingly at his shoulder: "And he seemed such a fine young lad, this Torold Blund! How can a body tell what lies behind the decent, ordinary face?"

"Torold Blund!" said Godith, testing the name slow syllable by syllable. "That's a Saxon name. There are plenty of them up there in the northern manors, good blood and old. But I don't know him. I think I can never have seen him. And Nicholas was on good, close terms with him? Nicholas was easy, but not stupid, and they sound much of an age, he must have known him well. And yet..."

"Yes," said Cadfael, "I know! And yet! Girl dear, I am too tired to think any more. I'm going to Compline, and then to my bed, and so should you. And tomorrow..."

"Tomorrow," she said, rising to the touch of his hand, "we shall bury Nicholas. *We!* He was in some measure my friend, and I shall be there."

"So you shall, my heart," said Cadfael, yawning, and led her away in his arm to celebrate, with gratitude and grief and hope, the ending of the day.

Chapter
Five

icholas Faintree was laid, with due honours, under a stone in the transept of the abbey church, an exceptional privilege. He was but one, after so many, and his singleness was matter for celebration, besides the fact that there was room within rather than without, and the labour involved was less. Abbot Heribert was increasingly disillusioned and depressed with all the affairs of this world, and welcomed a solitary guest who was not a symbol of civil war, but the victim of personal malice and ferocity. Against all the probabilities, in due course Nicholas might find himself a saint. He was mysterious, feloniously slain, young, to all appearances clean of heart and life, innocent of evil, the stuff of which martyrs are made.

Aline Seward was present at the funeral service, and had brought with her, intentionally or otherwise, Hugh Beringar. That young man made Cadfael increasingly uneasy. True, he was making no inimical move, nor showing any great diligence in his search for his affianced bride, if, indeed, he was in search of her at all. But there was something daunting in the very ease and impudence of his carriage, the small, sardonic turn of his lip, and the guileless clarity of the black eyes when they happened to encounter Cadfael's. No doubt about it, thought Cadfael, I shall be happier when I've got the girl safely away from here, but in the meantime at least I can move her away from anywhere he's likely to be.

The main orchards and vegetable gardens of the abbey were not within the precinct, but across the main road, stretched along the rich level beside the river, called the Gaye; and at the far end of this fertile reach there was a slightly higher field of corn. It lay almost opposite the castle, and no great distance from the king's siege camp, and had suffered some damage during the siege; and though what remained had been ripe for cutting for almost a week, it had been too dangerous to attempt to get it in. Now that all was quiet, they were in haste to salvage a crop that could not be spared, and all hands possible were mustered to do the work in one day. The second of the abbey's mills was at the end of the field, and because of the same dangers had been abandoned for the season, just when it was beginning to be needed, and had suffered damage which would keep it out of use until repairs could be undertaken.

"You go with the reapers," said Cadfael to Godith. "My thumbs prick, and rightly or wrongly, I'd rather have you out of the enclave, if only for a day."

"Without you?" said Godith, surprised.

"I must stay here and keep an eye on things. If anything threatens, I'll be with you as fast as legs can go. But you'll be well enough, no one is going to have leisure to look hard at you until that corn is in the barns. But stay by Brother Athanasius, he's as blind as a mole, he wouldn't know a stag from a hind. And take care how you swing a sickle, and don't come back short of a foot!"

She went off quite happily among the crowd of reapers in the end, glad of an outing and a change of scene. She was not afraid. Not afraid enough, Cadfael considered censoriously, but then, she had an old fool here to do the fearing for her, just as she'd once had an old nurse, protective as a hen with one chick. He watched them out of the gate house and over the road towards the Gaye, and went back with a relieved sigh to his own labours in the inner gardens. He had not been long on his knees, weeding, when a cool, light voice behind him, almost as quiet as the steps he had not heard in the grass, said: "So this is where you spend your more peaceful hours. A far cry and a pleasant change from harvesting dead men."

Brother Cadfael finished the last corner of the bed of mint before he turned to acknowledge the presence of Hugh Beringar. "A pleasant change, right enough. Let's hope we've finished with that kind of crop, here in Shrewsbury."

"And you found a name for your stranger in the end. How was that? No one in the town seemed to know him."

"All questions get their answers," said Brother Cadfael sententiously, "if you wait long enough."

"And all searchers are bound to find? But of course," said Beringar, smiling, "you did not say how long is long enough. If a man found at eighty what he was searching for at twenty, he might prove a shade ungrateful."

"He might well have stopped wanting it long before that," said Brother Cadfael drily, "which is in itself an answer to any want. Is there anything you are looking for here in the herbarium, that I can help you to, or are you curious to learn about these simples of mine?"

"No," owned Beringar, his smile deepening, "I would hardly say it was any simplicity I came to study." He pinched off a sprig of mint, crushed it between his fingers, and set it first to his nose and then closed fine white teeth upon its savour. "And what should such as I be looking for here? I may have *caused* a few ills in my time, I'm no hand at healing them. They tell me, Brother Cadfael, you have had a wide-ranging career before you came into the cloister. Don't you find it unbearably dull here, after such battles, with no enemy left to fight?"

"I am not finding it at all dull, these days," said Cadfael, plucking out willowherb from among the thyme. "And as for enemies, the devil makes his way in everywhere, even into cloister, and church, and herbarium."

Beringar threw his head back and laughed aloud, until the short black hair danced on his forehead. "Vainly, if he comes looking for mischief where you are! But he'd hardly expect to blunt his horns against an old crusader here! I take the hint!"

But all the time, though he scarcely seemed to turn his head or pay much attention to anything round him, his black eyes were missing nothing, and his ears were at stretch while he laughed and jested. By this time he knew that the well-spoken and well-favoured boy of whom Aline had innocently spoken was not going to make his appearance, and more, that Brother Cadfael did not care if he poked his nose into every corner of the garden, sniffed at every drying herb and peered at every potion in the hut, for they would tell him nothing. The benchbed was stripped of its blanket, and laden with a large mortar and a gently bubbling jar of wine. There was no trace of Godith anywhere to be found. The boy was simply a boy like the rest, and no doubt slept in the dortoir with the rest.

"Well, I'll leave you to your cleansing labours," said Beringar, "and stop hampering your meditations with my prattle. Or have you work for me to do?"

"The king has none?" said Cadfael solicitously.

Another ungrudging laugh acknowledged the thrust. "Not yet, not yet, but that will come. Such talent he cannot afford to hold off suspiciously for ever. Though to be sure, he did lay one testing task upon me, and I seem to be making very little progress in that." He plucked another tip of mint, and bruised and bit it with pleasure. "Brother Cadfael, it seems to me that you are the most practical man of hand and brain here. Supposing I should have need of your help, you would not refuse it without due thought—would you?"

Brother Cadfael straightened up, with some creaking of back muscles, to give him a long,

considering look. "I hope," he said cautiously, "I never do anything without due thought— even if the thought sometimes has to shift its feet pretty briskly to keep up with the deed."

"So I supposed," said Beringar, sweet-voiced and smiling. "I'll bear that in mind as a promise." And he made a small, graceful obeisance, and walked away at leisure to the courtyard.

The reapers came back in time for Vespers, sun-reddened, weary and sweat-stained, but with the corn all cut and stacked for carrying. After supper Godith slipped out of the refectory in haste, and came to pluck at Cadfael's sleeve.

"Brother Cadfael, you must come! Something vital!" He felt the quivering excitement of her hand, and the quiet intensity of her whispering voice. "There's time before Compline— come back to the field with me."

"What is it?" he asked as softly, for they were within earshot of a dozen people if they had spoken aloud, and she was not the woman to fuss over nothing. "What has happened to you? What have you left down there that's so urgent?"

"A man! A wounded man! He's been in the river, he was hunted into it upstream and came down with the current. I dared not stay to question, but I knew he's in need. And hungry! He's been there a night and a day...."

"How did you find him? You alone? No one else knows?"

"No one else." She gripped Cadfael's sleeve more tightly, and her whisper grew gruff with shyness. "It was a long day...I went aside, and had to go far aside, into the bushes near the mill. Nobody saw..."

"Surely, child! I know!" Please God all the

boys, her contemporaries, were kept hard at it, and never noticed such daintiness. Brother Athanasius would not have noticed a thunderclap right behind him. "He was there in the bushes? And is still?"

"Yes. I gave him the bread and meat I had with me, and told him I'd come back when I could. His clothes have dried on him—there's blood on his sleeve . . . But I think he'll do well, if *you* take care of him. We could hide him in the mill—no one goes there yet." She had thought of all the essentials, she was towing him towards his hut in the herb garden, not directly towards the gate house. Medicines, linen, food, they would need all these.

"Of what age," asked Cadfael, more easily now they were well away from listeners, "is this wounded man of yours?"

"A boy," she said on a soft breath. "Hardly older than I am. And hunted! He thinks *I* am a boy, of course. I gave him the water from my bottle, and he called me Ganymede. . . ."

Well, well, thought Cadfael, bustling before her into the hut, a young man of some learning, it seems! "Then, Ganymede," he said, bundling a roll of linen, a blanket and a pot of salve into her arms, "stow these about you, while I fill this little vial and put some vittles together. Wait here a few minutes for me, and we'll be off. And on the way you can tell me everything about this young fellow you've discovered, for once across the road no one is going to hear us."

And on the way she did indeed pour out in her relief and eagerness what she could not have said so freely by daylight. It was not yet dark, but a fine neutral twilight in which they saw each other clear but without colours.

"The bushes there are thick. I heard him

stir and groan, and I went to look. He looks like a young gentleman of family, someone's squire. Yes, he talked to me, but—but told me nothing, it was like talking to a wilful child. So weak, and blood on his shoulder and arm, and making little jests . . . But he trusted me enough to know I wouldn't betray him." She skipped beside Cadfael through the tall stubble into which the abbey sheep would soon be turned to graze, and to fertilise the field with their droppings. "I gave him what I had, and told him to lie still, and I would bring help as soon as it grew dusk."

"Now we're near, do you lead the way. You he'll know."

There was already starlight before the sun was gone, a lovely August light that would still last them, their eyes being accustomed, an hour or more, while veiling them from other eyes. Godith withdrew from Cadfael's clasp the hand that had clung like a child's through the stubble, and waded forward into the low, loose thicket of bushes. On their left hand, within a few yards of them, the river ran, dark and still, only the thrusting sound of its current like a low throb shaking the silence, and an occasional gleam of silver showing where its eddies swirled.

"Hush! It's me—Ganymede! And a friend to us both!"

In the sheltered dimness a darker form stirred, and raised into sight a pale oval of face and a tangled head of hair almost as pale. A hand was braced into the grass to thrust the half-seen stranger up from the ground. No broken bones there, thought Cadfael with satisfaction. The hard-drawn breath signalled stiffness and pain, but nothing mortal. A young, muted voice said: "Good lad! Friends I surely need . . ."

Cadfael kneeled beside him and lent him a shoulder to lean against. "First, before we move you, where's the damage? Nothing out of joint—by the look of you, where's the damage? Nothing out of joint—by the look of you, nothing broken." His hands were busy about the young man's body and limbs, he grunted cautious content.

"Nothing but gashes," muttered the boy laboriously, and gasped at a shrewd touch. "I lost enough blood to betray me, but into the river...And half-drowned...they must think wholly..." He relaxed with a great sigh, feeling how confidently he was handled.

"Food and wine will put the blood back into you, in time. Can you rise and go?"

"Yes," said his patient grimly, and all but brought his careful supporters down with him, proving it.

"No, let be, we can do better for you than that. Hold fast by me, and turn behind me. Now, your arms round my neck...."

He was long, but a light weight. Cadfael stooped forward, hooked his thick arms round slim, muscular thighs, and shrugged the weight securely into balance on his solid back. The dank scent of the river water still hung about the young man's clothing. "I'm too great a load," he fretted feebly. "I could have walked..."

"You'll do as you're bid, and no argument. Godric, go before, and see there's no one in sight."

It was only a short way to the shadow of the mill. Its bulk loomed dark against the still lambent sky, the great round of the undershot wheel showing gaps here and there like breaks in a set of teeth. Godith heaved open the leaning door, and felt her way before them into gloom. Through narrow cracks in the floorboards on the left side she caught fleet-ing, spun gleams of the river water hurrying beneath. Even in this hot, dry season, lower than it had been for some years, the Severn flowed fast and still.

"There'll be dry sacks in plenty piled somewhere by the landward wall," puffed Cadfael at her back. "Feel your way along and find them." There was also a dusty, rustling layer of last harvest's chaff under their feet, sending up fine powder to tickle their noses. Godith groped her way to the corner, and spread sacks there in a thick, comfortable mattress, with two folded close for a pillow. "Now take this long-legged heron of yours under the armpits, and help me ease him down....There, as good a bed as mine in the dortoir! Now close the door, before I make a light to see him by."

He had brought a good end of candle with him, and a handful of the dry chaff spread on a millstone made excellent tinder for the spark he struck. When his candle was burning steadily he ground it into place on the flickering chaff, quenching the fire that might have blown and spread, and anchoring his light on a safe candlestick, as the wax first softened and then congealed again. "Now let's look at you!"

The young man lay back gratefully and heaved a huge sigh, meekly abandoning the responsibility for himself. Out of a soiled and weary face, eyes irrepressibly lively gazed up at them, of some light, bright colour not then identifiable. He had a large, generous mouth, drawn with exhaustion but wryly smiling, and the tangle of hair matted and stained from the river would be as fair as corn-stalks when it was clean. "One of them ripped your shoulder for you, I see," said Cadfael, hands busy unfastening and drawing off the dark cotte encrusted down one sleeve with dried blood.

"Now the shirt—you'll be needing new clothes, my friend, before you leave this hostelry."

"I'll have trouble paying my shot," said the boy, valiantly grinning, and ended the grin with a sharp indrawn breath as the sleeve was detached painfully from his wound.

"Our charges are low. For a straight story you can buy such hospitality as we're offering. Godric, lad, I need water, and river water's better than none. See if you can find anything in this place to carry it in."

She found the sound half of a large pitcher among the debris under the wheel, left by some customer after its handle and lip had got broken, scrubbed it out industriously with the skirt of her cotte, and went obediently to bring water, he hoped safely. The flow of the river here would be fresher than the leat, and occupy her longer on the journey, while Cadfael undid the boy's belt, and stripped off his shoes and hose, shaking out the blanket to spread over his nakedness. There was a long but not deep gash, he judged from a sword-cut, down the right thigh, a variety of bruises showing bluish on his fair skin, and most strangely, a thin, broken graze on the left side of his neck, and another curiously like it on the outer side of his right wrist. More healed, dark lines, these, older by a day or two than his wounds. "No question," mused Cadfael aloud, "but you've been living an interesting life lately."

"Lucky to keep it," murmured the boy, half-asleep in his new ease.

"Who was hunting you?"

"The king's men—who else?"

"And still will be?"

"Surely. But in a few days I'll be fit to relieve you of the burden of me..."

"Never mind that now. Turn a little to me— so! Let's get this thigh bound up, it's clean enough, it's knitting already. This will sting." It did, the youth stiffened and gasped a little, but made no complaint. Cadfael had the wound bound and under the blanket by the time Godith came with the pitcher of water. For want of a handle she had to use two hands to carry it.

"Now we'll see to this shoulder. This is where you lost so much blood. An arrow did this!" It was an oblique cut sliced through the outer part of his left arm just below the shoulder, bone-deep, leaving an ugly flap of flesh gaping. Cadfael began to sponge away the encrustations of blood from it, and press it firmly together beneath a pad of linen soaked in one of his herbal salves. "This will need help to knit clean," he said, busy rolling his bandage tightly round the arm. "There, now you should eat, but not too much, you're over-weary to make the best use of it. Here's meat and cheese and bread, and keep some by you for morning, you may well be ravenous when you wake."

"If there's water left," besought the young man meekly, "I should like to wash my hands and face. I'm foul!"

Godith kneeled beside him, moistened a piece of linen in the pitcher, and instead of putting it into his hand, very earnestly and thoroughly did it for him, putting back the matted hair from his forehead, which was wide and candid, even teasing out some of the knots with solicitous fingers. After the first surprise he lay quietly and submissively under her ministering touch, but his eyes, cleansed of the soiled shadows, watched her face as she bent over him, and grew larger and larger in respectful wonder. And all this while she had hardly said a word.

The young man was almost too worn out to eat at all, and flagged very soon. He lay for a few moments with lids drooping, peering at his rescuers in silent thought. Then he said, his tongue stumbling sleepily: "I owe you a name, after all you've done for me...."

"Tomorrow," said Cadfael firmly. "You're in the best case to sleep sound, and here I believe you may. Now drink this down—it helps keep wounds from festering, and eases the heart." It was a strong cordial of his own brewing, he tucked away the empty vial in his gown. "And here's a little flask of wine to bear you company if you wake. In the morning I'll be with you early."

"We!" said Godith, low but firmly.

"Wait, one more thing!" Cadfael had remembered it at the last moment. "You've no weapon on you—yet I think you did wear a sword."

"I shed it," mumbled the boy drowsily, "in the river. I had too much weight to keep afloat—and they were shooting. It was in the water I got this clout...I had the wit to go down, I hope they believe I stayed down...God knows it was touch and go!"

"Yes, well, tomorrow will do. And we must find you a weapon. Now, good night!"

He was asleep before ever they put out the candle, and drew the door closed. They walked wordlessly through the rustling stubble for some minutes, the sky over them an arch of dark and vivid blue paling at the edges into a fringe of sea-green. Godith asked abruptly: "Brother Cadfael, who was Ganymede?"

"A beautiful youth who was cup-bearer to Jove, and much loved by him."

"Oh!" said Godith, uncertain whether to be delighted or rueful, this success being wholly due to her boyishness.

"But some say that it's also another name for Hebe," said Cadfael.

"Oh! And who is Hebe?"

"Cup-bearer to Jove, and much loved by him—but a beautiful maiden."

"Ah!" said Godith profoundly. And as they reached the road and crossed towards the abbey, she said seriously: "You know who he must be, don't you?"

"Jove? The most god-like of all the pagan gods..."

"*He!*" she said severely, and caught and shook Brother Cadfael's arm in her solemnity. "A Saxon name, and Saxon hair, and on the run from the king's men....He's Torold Blund, who set out with Nicholas to save FitzAlan's treasury for the empress. And of course he had nothing to do with poor Nicholas's death. I don't believe he ever did a shabby thing in his whole life!"

"That," said Cadfael, "I hesitate to say of any man, least of all myself. But I give you my word, child, this one most shabby thing he certainly did not do. You may sleep in peace!"

It was nothing out of the ordinary for Brother Cadfael, that devoted gardener and apothecary, to rise long before it was necessary for Prime, and have an hour's work done before he joined his brothers at the first service; so no one thought anything of it when he dressed and went out early on that particular morning, and no one even knew that he also roused his boy, as he had promised. They went out with more medicaments and food, and a cotte and hose that Brother Cadfael had filched from the charity offerings that came in to the almoner. Godith had taken away with her the young man's bloodstained shirt, which was of fine linen and not to be wasted, had washed it before she slept, and mended it on rising, where the arrow-head had sliced the threads asunder. On such a warm August night, spread out carefully on the bushes in the garden, it had dried well.

Their patient was sitting up in his bed of sacks, munching bread with appetite, and seemed to have total trust in them, for he made no move to seek cover when the door began to open. He had draped his torn and stained cotte round his shoulders, but for the rest was naked under his blanket, and the bared, smooth chest and narrow flanks were elegantly formed. Body and eyes still showed blue bruises, but he was certainly much restored after one long night of rest.

"Now," said Cadfael with satisfaction, "you may talk as much as you like, my friend, while I dress this wound of yours. The leg will do very well until we have more time, but this shoulder is a tricky thing. Godric, see to him on the other side while I uncover it, it may well stick. You steady bandage and arm while I unbind. Now, sir . . ." And he added, for fair exchange: "They call me Brother Cadfael, I'm as Welsh as Dewi Sant, and I've been about the world, as you may have guessed. And this boy of mine is Godric, as you've heard, and brought me to you. Trust us both, or neither."

"I trust both," said the boy. He had more colour this morning, or it was the flush of dawn reflected, his eyes were bright and hazel, more green than brown. "I owe you more than trust can pay, but shew me more I can do, and I'll do it. My name is Torold Blund, I come from a hamlet by Oswestry, and I'm FitzAlan's man from head to foot." The bandage stuck then, and Godith felt him flinch, and locked the fold until she could ease it

free, by delicate touches. "If that puts you in peril," said Torold, suppressing the pain, "I do believe I'm fit to go, and go I will. I would not for the world shrug off my danger upon you."

"You'll go when you're let," said Godith, and for revenge snatched off the last fold of bandage, but very circumspectly, and holding the anointed pad in place. "And it won't be today."

"Hush, let him talk, time's short," said Cadfael. "Go to it, lad. We're not in the business of selling Maud's men to Stephen, or Stephen's men to Maud. How did you come here in this pass?"

Torold took a deep breath, and talked to some purpose. "I came to the castle here with Nicholas Faintree, who was also FitzAlan's man, from the next manor to my father's, we joined the garrison only a week before it fell. The evening before the assault there was a council—we were not there, we were small fry—and they resolved to get the FitzAlan treasury away the very next day for the use of the empress, not knowing then it would be the last day. Nicholas and I were told off to be the messengers because we were new to Shrewsbury, and not known, and might get through well enough where others senior to us might be known and cut down at sight. The goods—they were not too bulky, thank God, not much plate, more coin, and most of all in jewellery—were hidden somewhere no one knew but our lord and his agent who had them in guard. We had to ride to him when the word was given, take them from where he would show us, and get clear by night for Wales. FitzAlan had an accord with Owain Gwynedd—not that he's for either party here, he's for Wales, but civil war here suits him well, and he and FitzAlan are friends. Before it was well dawn they attacked, and it was plain we could not hold. So we were sent off on our errand—it was to a shop in the town…" He wavered, uneasy at giving any clue.

"I know," said Cadfael, wiping away the exudation of the night from the shoulder wound, and anointing a new pad. "It was Edric Flesher, who himself has told me his part in it. You were taken out to his barn in Frankwell, and the treasury laid up with you to wait for the cover of night. Go on!"

The young man, watching the dressing of his own hurts without emotion, went on obediently: "We rode as soon as it was dark. From there clear of the suburb and into trees is only a short way. There's a herdsman's hut there in the piece where the track is in woodland, though only along the edge, the fields still close. We were on this stretch when Nick's horse fell lame. I lit down to see, for he went very badly, and he had picked up a caltrop, and was cut to the bone."

"Caltrops?" said Brother Cadfael, startled. "On such a forest path, away from any field of battle?" For those unobtrusive martial cruelties, made in such a shape as to be scattered under the hooves of cavalry, and leaving always one crippling spike upturned, surely had no part to play on a narrow forest ride.

"Caltrops," said Torold positively. "I don't speak simply from the wound, the thing was there embedded, I know, I wrenched it out. But the poor beast was foundered, he could go, but not far, and not loaded. There's a farm I know of very close there, I thought I could get a fresh horse in exchange for Nick's, a poor exchange but what could we do? We did not even unload, but Nick lighted down, to ease the poor creature of his weight, and

said he would wait there in the hut for me. And I went, and I got a mount from the farm—it's off to the right, heading west as we were, the man's name is Ulf, he's distant kin to me on my mother's side—and rode back, with Nick's half the load on this new nag.

"I came up towards the hut," he said, stiffening at the recollection, "and I thought he would be looking out for me, ready to mount, and he was not. I don't know why that made me so uneasy. Not a breath stirring, and for all I was cautious, I knew I could be heard by any man truly listening. And he never showed face or called out word. So I never went too near. I drew off, and reined forward a little way, and made a single tether of the horses, to be off as fast as might be. One knot to undo, and with a single pluck. And then I went to the hut."

"It was full dark then?" asked Cadfael, rolling bandage.

"Full dark, but I could see, having been out in it. Inside it was black as pitch. The door stood half open to the wall. I went inside stretching my ears, and not a murmur. But in the middle of the hut I fell over him. Over Nick! If I hadn't I might not be here to tell as much," said Torold grimly, and cast a sudden uneasy glance at his Ganymede, so plainly some years his junior, and attending him with such sedulous devotion. "This is not good hearing." His eyes appealed eloquently to Cadfael over Godith's shoulder.

"You'd best go on freely," said Cadfael with sympathy. "He's deeper in this than you think, and will have your blood and mine if we dare try to banish him. No part of this matter of Shrewsbury has been good hearing, but something may be saved. Tell your part, we'll tell ours."

Godith, all eyes, ears and serviceable hands, wisely said nothing at all.

"He was dead," said Torold starkly. "I fell on him, mouth to mouth, there was no breath in him. I held him, reaching forward to save myself as I fell, I had him in my arms and he was like an armful of rags. And then I heard the dry fodder rustle behind me, and started round, because there was no wind to stir it, and I was frightened..."

"Small blame!" said Cadfael, smoothing a fresh pad soaked in his herbal salve against the moist wound. "You had good reason. Trouble no more for your friend, he is with God surely. We buried him yesterday within the abbey. He has a prince's tomb. You, I think, escaped the like very narrowly, when his murderer lunged from behind the door."

"So I think, too," said the boy, and drew in hissing breath at the bite of Cadfael's dressing. "There he must have been. The grass warned me when he made his assay. I don't know how it is, every man throws up his right arm to ward off blows from his head, and so did I. His cord went round my wrist as well as my throat. I was not clever or a hero, I lashed out in fright and jerked it out of his hands. It brought him down on top of me in the dark. I know only too well," he said, defensively, "that you may not believe me."

"There are things that go to confirm you. Spare to be so wary of your friends. So you were man to man, at least, better odds than before. How did you escape him?"

"More by luck than valour," said Torold ruefully. "We were rolling about in the hay, wrestling and trying for each other's throat, everything by feel and nothing by sight, and neither of us could get space or time to draw, for I don't know how long, but I suppose it was no more than minutes. What ended it was that there must have been an old manger there against the wall, half fallen to pieces, and I banged my head against one of the boards lying loose in the hay. I hit him with it, two-handed, and he dropped. I doubt I did him any lasting damage, but it knocked him witless long enough for me to run, and run I did, and loosed both the horses, and made off westward like a hunted hare. I still had work to do, and there was no one but me left to do it, or I might have stayed to try and even the account for Nick. Or I might not," owned Torold with scowling honesty. "I doubt I was even thinking about FitzAlan's errand then, though I'm thinking of it now, and have been ever since. I ran for my life. I was afraid he might have had others lying in ambush to come to his aid. All I wanted was out of there as fast as my legs would go."

"No need to make a penance of it," said Cadfael mildly, securing his bandage. "Sound sense is something to be glad of, not ashamed. But, my friend, it's taken you two full days, by your own account, to get to much the same spot you started from. I take it, by that, the king has allies pretty thick between here and Wales, at least by the roads."

"Thick as bees in swarm! I got well forward by the more northerly road, and all but ran my head into a patrol where there was no passing. They were stopping everything that moved, what chance had I with two horses and a load of valuables? I had to draw off into the woods, and by that time it was getting light, there was nothing to be done but lie up until dark again and try the southerly road. And that was no better, they had loose companies ranging the countryside by then. I thought I might make my way through by keeping off the roads and close to the curve of the river, but it was another night lost. I lay up in a copse on the hill all day Thursday, and tried again by night, and that was when they winded me, four or five of them, and I had to run for it, with only one way to run, down towards the river. They had me penned, I couldn't get out of the trap. I took the saddle-bags from both horses, and turned the beasts loose, and started them off at a panic gallop, hoping they'd crash through and lead the pursuit away from me, but there was one of the fellows too near, he saw the trick, and made for me instead. He gave me this slash in the thigh, and his yell brought the others running. There was only one thing to do. I took to the water, saddle-bags and all. I'm a strong swimmer, but with that weight it was hard work to stay afloat, and let the current bring me downstream. That's when they started shooting. Dark as it was, they'd been out in it long enough to have fair vision, and there's always light from the water when there's something moving in it. So I got this shoulder wound, and had the sense to go under and stay under as long as I had breath. Severn's fast, even in summer water it carried me down well. They followed along the bank for a while, and loosed one or two more arrows, but then I think they were sure I was under for good. I worked my way towards the bank as soon as it seemed safe, to get a foot to ground and draw breath here and there, but I stayed in the water. I knew the bridge would be manned, I dared not drag myself ashore until I was well past. It was high time by then. I remember crawling into the bushes, but not much else, except rousing just enough to be afraid to stir when your people came

reaping. And then Godric here found me. And that's the truth of it," he ended firmly, and looked Cadfael unblinkingly in the eye.

"But not the whole truth," said Cadfael, placidly enough. "Godric found no saddle-bags along with you." He eyed the young face that fronted him steadily, lips firmly closed, and smiled. "No, never fret, we won't question you. You are the sole custodian of FitzAlan's treasury, and what you've done with it, and how, God knows, you ever managed to do anything sensible with it in your condition, that's your affair. You haven't the air of a courier who has failed in his mission, I'll say that for you. And for your better peace, all the talk in the town is that FitzAlan and Adeney were not taken, but broke out of the ring and are got clean away. Now we have to leave you alone here until afternoon, we have duties, too. But one of us, or both, will come and see how you're faring then. And here's food and drink, and clothes I hope will fit you well enough to pass. But lie quiet for today, you're not your own man yet however wholeheartedly you may be FitzAlan's."

Godith laid the washed and mended shirt on top of the folded garments, and was following Cadfael to the door when the look on Torold's face halted her, half uneasy, half triumphant. His eyes grew round with amazement as he stared at the crisp, clean linen, and the fine stitches of the long mend where the blood-stained gash had been. A soft whistle of admiration saluted the wonder.

"Holy Mary! Who did this? Do you keep an expert seamstress within the abbey walls? Or did you pray for a miracle?"

"That? That's Godric's work," said Cadfael, not altogether innocently, and walked out into the early sunshine, leaving Godith flushed to the ears. "We learn more skills in the cloister than merely cutting wheat and brewing cordials," she said loftily, and fled after Cadfael.

But she was grave enough on the way back, going over in her mind Torold's story, and reflecting how easily he might have died before ever she met him; not merely once, in the murderer's cord, nor the second time from King Stephen's roaming companies, but in the river, or from his wounds in the bushes. It seemed to her that divine grace was taking care of him, and had provided her as the instrument. There remained lingering anxieties.

"Brother Cadfael, you do believe him?"

"I believe him. What he could not tell truth about, he would not lie about, either. Why, what's on your mind still?"

"Only that the night before I saw him I said—I was afraid the companion who rode with Nicholas was far the most likely to be tempted to kill him. How simple it would have been! But you said yesterday, you *did* say, he did not do it. Are you quite sure? How do you know?"

"Nothing simpler, girl dear! The mark of the strangler's cord is on his neck and on his wrist. Did you not understand those thin scars? He was meant to go after his friend out of this world. No, you need have no fear on that score, what he told us is truth. But there may be things he could not tell us, things we ought to discover, for Nicholas Faintree's sake. Godith, this afternoon, when you've seen to the lotions and wines, you may leave the garden and go and keep him company if you please, and I'll come there as soon as I can. There are things I must look into, over there on the Frankwell side of Shrewsbury."

Chapter Six

rom the Frankwell end of the western bridge, the suburb outside the walls and over the river, the road set off due west, climbing steadily, leaving behind the gardens that fringed the settlement. At first it was but a single road mounting the hill that rose high above Severn, then shortly it branched into two, of which the more southerly soon branched again, three spread fingers pointing into Wales. But Cadfael took the road Nicholas and Torold had taken on the night after the castle fell, the most northerly of the three.

He had thought of calling on Edric Flesher in the town, and giving him the news that one, at least, of the two young couriers had survived and preserved his charge, but then he had decided against it. As yet Torold was by no means safe, and until he was well away, the fewer people who knew of his whereabouts the better, the less likely was word of him to slip out in the wrong place, where his enemies might overhear. There would be time later to share any good news with Edric and Petronilla.

The road entered the thick woodland of which Torold had spoken, and narrowed into a grassy track, within the trees but keeping close to the edge, where cultivated fields showed between the trunks. And there, withdrawn a little deeper into the woods, lay the hut, low and roughly timbered. From this place it would be a simple matter to carry a dead body on horseback as far as the castle ditch. The river, as everywhere here, meandered in intricate coils, and would have to be crossed in order to reach the place where the dead had been flung, but there was a place opposite the castle on this side where a central island made the stream fordable even on foot in such a dry season, once the castle itself was taken. The distance was small, the night had been long enough. Then somewhere off to the right lay Ulf's holding, where Torold had got his exchange of horses. Cadfael turned off in that direction, and found the croft not a quarter of a mile from the track.

Ulf was busy gleaning after carrying his corn, and not at first disposed to be talkative to an unknown monk, but the mention of Torold's name, and the clear intimation that here was someone Torold had trusted, loosened his tongue.

"Yes, he did come with a lamed horse, and I did let him have the best of mine in exchange. I was the gainer, though, even so, for the beast he left with me came from FitzAlan's stables. He's still lame, but healing. Would you see him? His fine gear is well hidden, it would mark him out for stolen or worse if it was seen."

Even without his noble harness the horse, a tall roan, showed suspiciously fine for a working farmer to possess, and undoubtedly he was still lame of one fore-foot. Ulf showed him the wound.

"Torold said a caltrop did this," mused Cadfael. "Strange place to find such."

"Yet a caltrop it was, for I have it, and several more like it that I went and combed out of the grass there next day. My beasts cross there, I wanted no more of them lamed. Someone seeded a dozen yards of the path at its narrowest there. To halt them by the hut, what else?"

"Someone who knew in advance what they were about and the road they'd take, and gave himself plenty of time to lay his trap, and wait in ambush for them to spring it."

"The king had got wind of the matter somehow," Ulf opined darkly, "and sent some of his men secretly to get hold of whatever they were carrying. He's desperate for money—as bad as the other side."

Nevertheless, thought Cadfael, as he walked back to the hut in the woods, for all that I can see, this was no party sent out by the king, but one man's enterprise for his own private gain. If he had indeed been the king's emissary he would have had a company with him. It was not King Stephen's coffers that were to have profited, if all had gone according to plan.

To sum up, then, it was proven there had indeed been a third here that night. Over and over Torold was cleared of blame. The caltrops were real, a trail of them had been laid to ensure laming one or other of the horses, and so far the stratagem had succeeded, perhaps even better than expected, since it had severed the two companions, leaving the murderer free to deal with one first, and then lie in wait for the other.

Cadfael did not at once go into the hut; the surroundings equally interested him. Somewhere here, well clear of the hut itself, Torold had regarded the pricking of his thumbs, and tethered the horses forward on the road, ready for flight. And somewhere here, too, probably withdrawn deeper into cover, the third man had also had a horse in waiting. It should still be possible to find their traces. It had not rained since that night, nor was it likely that many men had roamed these woods since. All the inhabitants of Shrewsbury were still keeping close under their own roof-trees unless forced to go abroad, and the king's patrols rode in the open, where they could ride fast.

It took him a little while, but he found both places. The solitary horse had been hobbled and left to graze, and by the signs he had been a fine creature, for the hoof-marks he had left in a patch of softer ground, a hollow of dried mud where water habitually lay after rain, and had left a smooth silt, showed large and well shod. The spot where two had waited together was well to westward of the hut, and in thick cover. A low branch showed the peeled scar where the tether had been pulled clear in haste, and two distinguishable sets of prints could be discerned where the grass thinned to bare ground.

Cadfael went into the hut. He had broad daylight to aid him, and with the door set wide there was ample light even within. The murderer had waited here for his victim, he must have left his traces.

The remains of the winter fodder, mown along the sunlit fringes of the woods, had been left here against the return of autumn, originally in a neat stack against the rear wall, but now a stormy sea of grass was spread and tossed over the entire earthen floor, as though a gale had played havoc within there. The decrepit manger from which Torold had plucked his loose plank was there, drunkenly leaning. The dry grass was well laced with small herbs now rustling and dead but still fragrant, and there was a liberal admixture of hooky, clinging goose-grass in it. That reminded him not only of the shred of stem dragged deep into Nick Faintree's throat by the ligature that killed him, but also of Torold's ugly shoulder wound. He needed goose-grass to make a dressing for it, he would look along the fringe of the fields, it must be plentiful here. God's even-handed justice, that called attention to one friend's murder with a dry stem of last year's crop, might well, by the same token, design to soothe and heal the other friend's injuries by the gift of this year's.

Meantime, the hut yielded little, except the evident chaos of a hand-to-hand struggle waged within it. But in the rough timbers behind the door there were a few roving threads of deep blue woollen cloth, rather pile than thread. Someone had certainly lain in hiding there, the door drawn close to his body. There was also one clot of dried clover that bore a smaller clot of blood. But Cadfael raked and combed in vain among the rustling fodder in search of the strangler's weapon. Either the murderer had found it again and taken it away with him, or else it lay deeply entangled in some corner, evading search. Cadfael worked his way backwards on hands and knees from the manger to the doorway, and was about to give up, and prise himself up from his knees, when the hand on which he supported his weight bore down on something hard and sharp, and winced from the contact in surprise. Something was driven half into the earth floor under the thinning layers of hay, like another caltrop planted here for inquisitive monks to encounter to their grief and injury. He sat back on his heels, and carefully brushed aside the rustling grasses, until he could get a hand to the hidden thing and prise it loose. It came away into his hand readily, filling his palm, hard, encrusted and chill. He lifted it to the invading sunlight in the doorway behind him, and it glittered with pinpoints of yellow, a miniature sun.

Brother Cadfael rose from his knees and took it into the full daylight of afternoon to see what he had found. It was a large, rough-cut gem stone, as big as a crab-apple, a deep-yellow topaz still gripped and half-enclosed by an eagle's talon of silver-gilt. The claw was complete, finely shaped, but broken off at the stem, below the stone it clutched. This was the tip of some excellent setting in silver, perhaps the end of a brooch-pin—no, too large for that. The apex of a dagger-hilt? If so, a noble dagger, no common working knife. Beneath that jagged tip would have been the rounded hand-grip, and on the cross-piece, perhaps, some smaller topaz stones to match this master-stone. Broken off thus, it lay in his hand a sullen, faceted ball of gold.

One man had threshed and clawed here in his death-throes, two others had rolled and flailed in mortal combat; any one of the three, with a thrusting hip and the weight of a convulsed body, could have bored this hilt into the hardpacked earth of the floor, and snapped off the crown-stone thus at its most fragile point, and never realised the loss.

Brother Cadfael put it away carefully in the scrip at his girdle, and went to look for his goose-grass. In the thick herbage at the edge of the trees, where the sun reached in, he found sprawling, angular mats of it, filled his scrip, and set off for home with dozens of the little hooked seeds clinging in his skirts.

Godith slipped away as soon as all the brothers had dispersed to their afternoon work, and made her way by circumspect deviations to the mill at the end of the Gaye. She had taken with her some ripe plums from the orchard, the half of a small loaf of new bread, and a fresh flask of Cadfael's wine. The patient had rapidly developed a healthy appetite, and it was her pleasure to enjoy his enjoyment of food and drink, as though she had a proprietorial interest in him by reason of having found him in need.

He was sitting on his bed of sacks, fully dressed, his back against the warm timbers of the wall, his long legs stretched out comfortably before him with ankles crossed. The cotte and hose fitted reasonably well, perhaps a little short in the sleeves. He looked surprisingly lively, though still rather greyish in the face, and careful in his movements because of the lingering aches and pains from his wounds. She was not best pleased to see that he had struggled into the cotte, and said so.

"You should keep that shoulder easy, there was no need to force it into a sleeve yet. If you don't rest it, it won't heal."

"I've very well," he said abstractedly. "And I must bear whatever discomfort there may be, if I'm to get on my way soon. It will knit well enough, I dare say." His mind was not on his own ills, he was frowning thoughtfully over other matters. "Godric, I had no time to question, this morning, but—your Brother Cadfael said Nick's buried, and in the abbey. Is that truth?" He was not so much doubting their word as marvelling how it had come about. "How did they ever find him?"

"That was Brother Cadfael's own doing," said Godith. She sat down beside him and told him. "There was one more than there should have been, and Brother Cadfael would not rest until he had found the one who was different, and since then he has not let anyone else rest. The king knows there was murder done, and has said it should be avenged. If anyone can get justice for your friend, Brother Cadfael is the man."

"So whoever it was, there in the hut, it seems I did him little harm, only dimmed his wits for a matter of minutes. I was afraid of it. He was fit enough and cunning enough to get rid of his dead man before morning."

"But not clever enough to deceive Brother Cadfael. Every individual soul must be accounted for. Now at least Nicholas has had all the rites of the church in his own clean name, and has a noble tomb."

"I'm glad," said Torold, "to know he was not left there to rot unhonoured, or put into the ground nameless among all the rest, though they were our comrades, too, and not deserving of such a death. If we had stayed, we should have suffered the same fate. If they caught me, I might suffer it yet. And yet King

Stephen approves the hunt for the murderer who did his work for him! What a mad world!"

Godith thought so, too; but for all that, there was a difference, a sort of logic in it, that the king should accept the onus of the ninety-four whose deaths he had decreed, but utterly reject the guilt for the ninety-fifth, killed treacherously and without his sanction.

"He despised the manner of the killing, and he resented being made an accomplice in it. And no one is going to capture you," she said firmly, and hoisted the plums out of the breast of her cotte, and tumbled them between them on the blanket. "Here's a taste of something sweeter than bread. Try them!"

They sat companionably eating, and slipping the stones through a chink in the floorboards into the river below. "I still have a task laid on me," said Torold at length, soberly, "and now I'm alone to see it done. And heaven knows, Godric, what I should have done without you and Brother Cadfael, and sad I shall be to set off and leave you behind, with small chance of seeing you again. Never shall I forget what you've done for me. But go I must, as soon as I'm fit and can get clear. It will be better for you when I'm gone, you'll be safer so."

"Who is safe? Where?" said Godith, biting into another ripe purple plum. "There is no safe place."

"There are degrees in danger, at any rate. And I have work to do, and I'm fit to get on with it now."

She turned and gave him a long, roused look. Never until that moment had she looked far enough ahead to confront the idea of his departure. He was something she had only newly discovered, and here he was, unless she

was mistaking his meaning, threatening to take himself off, out of her hands and out of her life. Well, she had an ally in Brother Cadfael. With the authority of her master she said sternly: "If you're thinking you're going to set off anywhere until you're fully healed, then think again, and smartly, too. You'll stay here until you're given leave to go, and that won't be today, or tomorrow, you can make up your mind to that!"

Torold gaped at her in startled and delighted amusement, laid his head back against the rough timber of the wall, and laughed aloud. "You sound like my mother, the time I had a bad fall at the quintain. And dearly I love you, but so I did her, and I still went my own way. I'm fit and strong and able, Godric, and I'm under order that came before your orders. I must go. In my place, you'd have been out of here before now, as fierce as you are."

"I would not," she said furiously, "I have more sense. What use would you be, on the run from here, without even a weapon, without a horse—you turned your horses loose, remember, to baffle the pursuit, you told us so! How far would you get? And how grateful would FitzAlan be for your folly? Not that we need go into it," she said loftily, "seeing you're not fit even to walk out of here as far as the river. You'd be carried back on Brother Cadfael's shoulders, just as you came here the first time."

"Oh, would I so, Godric, my little cousin?" Torold's eyes were sparkling mischief. He had forgotten for the moment all his graver cares, amused and nettled by the impudence of this urchin, vehemently threatening him with humiliation and failure. "Do I look to you so feeble?"

"As a starving cat," she said, and plunged a

plum-stone between the boards with a vicious snap. "A ten-year-old could lay you on your back!"

"You think so, do you?" Torold rolled sideways and took her about the middle in his good arm. "I'll show you, Master Godric, whether I'm fit or no!" He was laughing for pure pleasure, feeling his muscles stretch and exult again in a sudden, sweet bout of horseplay with a trusted familiar, who needed taking down a little for everyone's good. He reached his wounded arm to pin the boy down by the shoulders. The arrogant imp had uttered only one muffled squeak as he was tipped on his back. "One hand of mine can more than deal with you, my lovely lad!" crowed Torold, withdrawing half his weight, and flattening his left palm firmly in the breast of the over-ample cotte, to demonstrate.

He recoiled, stricken and enlightened, just as Godith got breath enough to swear at him, and strike out furiously with her right hand, catching him a salutary box on the ear. They fell apart in a huge, ominous silence, and sat up among the rumpled sacks with a yard or more between them.

The silence and stillness lasted long. It was a full minute before they so much as tilted cautious heads and looked sidewise at each other. Her profile, warily emerging from anger into guilty sympathy, was delicate and pert and utterly feminine, he must have been weak and sick indeed, or he would surely have known. The soft, gruff voice was only an ambiguous charm, a natural deceit. Torold scrubbed thoughtfully at his stinging ear, and asked at last, very carefully: "Why didn't you tell me? I never meant to offend you, but how was I to know?"

"There was no need for you to know,"

snapped Godith, still ruffled, "if you'd had the sense to do as you're bid, or the courtesy to treat your friends gently."

"But you goaded me! Good God," protested Torold, "it was only the rough play I'd have used on a younger brother of my own, and you asked for it." He demanded suddenly: "Does Brother Cadfael know?"

"Of course he does! Brother Cadfael at least can tell a hart from a hind."

There fell a second and longer silence, full of resentment, curiosity and caution, while they continued to study each other through lowered lashes, she furtively eyeing the sleeve that covered his wound, in case a telltale smear of blood should break through, he surveying again the delicate curves of her face, the jut of lip and lowering of brows that warned him she was still offended.

Two small, wary voices uttered together, grudgingly: "Did I hurt you?"

They began to laugh at the same instant, suddenly aware of their own absurdity. The illusion of estrangement vanished utterly; they fell into each other's arms helpless with laughter, and nothing was left to complicate their relationship but the slightly exaggerated gentleness with which they touched each other.

"But you shouldn't have used that arm so," she reproached at last, as they disentangled themselves and sat back, eased and content. "You could have started it open again, it's a bad gash."

"Oh, no, there's no damage. But you—I wouldn't for the world have vexed you." And he asked, quite simply, and certain of his right to be told: "Who are you? And how did you ever come into such a coil as this?"

She turned her head and looked at him long and earnestly; there would never again be anything with which she would hesitate to trust him.

"They left it too late," she said, "to send me away out of Shrewsbury before the town fell. This was a desperate throw, turning me into an abbey servant, but I was sure I could carry it off. And I did, with everyone but Brother Cadfael. *You* were taken in, weren't you? I'm a fugitive of your party, Torold, we're two of a kind. I'm Godith Adeney."

"Truly?" He beamed at her, round-eyed with wonder and delight. "You're Fulke Adeney's daughter? Praise God! We were anxious for you! Nick especially, for he knew you...I never saw you till now, but I, too..." He stooped his fair head and lightly kissed the small, none too clean hand that had just picked up the last of the plums. "Mistress Godith, I am your servant to command! This is splendid! If I'd known, I'd have told you better than half a tale."

"Tell me now," said Godith, and generously split the plum in half, and sent the stone whirling down into the Severn. The riper half she presented to his open mouth, effectively closing it for a moment. "And then," she said, "I'll tell you my side of it, and we shall have a useful whole."

Brother Cadfael did not go straight to the mill on his return, but halted to check that his workshop was in order, and to pound up his goose-grass in a mortar, and prepare a smooth green salve from it. Then he went to join his young charges, careful to circle into the shadow of the mill from the opposite direction, and to keep an eye open for any observer. Time was marching all too swiftly, within an hour he and Godith would have to go back for Vespers.

They had both known his step; when he entered they were sitting side by side with backs propped against the wall, watching the doorway with rapt, expectant smiles. They had a certain serene, aloof air about them, as though they inhabited a world immune from common contacts or common cares, but generously accessible to him. He had only to look at them, and he knew they had no more secrets; they were so rashly and candidly man and woman together that there was no need even to ask anything. Though they were both waiting expectantly to tell him!

"Brother Cadfael..." Godith began, distantly radiant.

"First things first," said Cadfael briskly. "Help him out of cotte and shirt, and start unwinding the bandage until it sticks—as it will, my friend, you're not out of the wood yet. Then wait, and I'll ease it off."

There was no disconcerting or chastening them. The girl was up in a moment, easing the seam of the cotte away from Torold's wound, loosening the ties of his shirt to slip it down from his shoulder, gently freeing the end of the linen bandage and beginning to roll it up. The boy inclined this way and that to help, and never took his eyes from Godith's face, as she seldom took hers from his absorbed countenance, and only to concentrate upon his needs.

"Well, well!" thought Cadfael philosophically. "It seems Hugh Beringar will seek his promised bride to little purpose—if, indeed, he really is seeking her?"

"Well, youngster," he said aloud, "you're a credit to me and to yourself, as clean-healing flesh as ever I saw. This slice of you that somebody tried to sever will stay with you lifelong, after all, and the arm will even serve you to hold a bow in a month or so. But you'll have the scar as long as you live. Now hold steady, this may burn, but trust me, it's the best salve you could have for green wounds. Torn muscles hurt as they knit, but knit they will."

"It doesn't hurt," said Torold in a dream. "Brother Cadfael..."

"Hold your tongue until we have you all bound up trim. Then you can talk your hearts out, the both of you."

And talk they did, as soon as Torold was helped back into his shirt, and the cotte draped over his shoulders. Each of them took up the thread from the other, as though handed it in a fixed and formal ceremony, like a favour in a dance. Even their voices had grown somehow alike, as if they matched tones without understanding that they did it. They had not the least idea, as yet, that they were in love. The innocents believed they were involved in a partisan comradeship, which was but the lesser half of what had happened to them in his absence.

"So I have told Torold all about myself," said Godith, "and he has told me the only thing he did not tell us before. And now he wants to tell you."

Torold picked up the tendered thread willingly. "I have FitzAlan's treasury safely hidden," he said simply. "I had it in two pairs of linked saddle-bags, and I kept it afloat, too, all down the river, though I had to shed sword and swordbelt and dagger and all to lighten the load. I fetched up under the first arch of the stone bridge. You'll know it as well as I. That first pier spreads, there used to be a boat-mill moored under it, some time ago, and the mooring chain is still there, bolted to a ring in the stone. A man can hold on there and get his breath, and so I did. And

I hauled up the chain and hooked my saddle-bags on to it, and let them down under the water, out of sight. Then I left them there, and drifted on down here just about alive, to where Godith found me." He found no difficulty in speaking of her as Godith; the name had a jubilant sound in his mouth. "And there all that gold is dangling in the Severn still, I hope and believe, until I can reclaim it and get it away to its rightful owner. Thank God he's alive to benefit by it." A last qualm shook him suddenly and severely. "There's been no word of anyone finding it?" he questioned anxiously. "We should know if they had?"

"We should know, never doubt it! No, no one's hooked any such fish. Why should anyone look for it there? But getting it out again undetected may not be so easy. We three must put our wits together," said Cadfael, "and see what we can do between us. And while you two have been swearing your alliance, let me tell you what I've been doing."

He made it brief enough. "I found all as you told it. The traces of your horses are there, and of your enemy's, too. One horse only. This was a thief bent on his own enrichment, no zealot trying to fill the king's coffers. He had seeded the path for you liberally with caltrops, your kinsman collected several of them next day, for the sake of his own cattle. The signs of your struggle within the hut are plain enough. And pressed into the earth floor I found this." He produced it from his scrip, a lump of deep yellow roughly faceted, and clenched in the broken silver-gilt claw. Torold took it from him and examined it curiously, but without apparent recognition.

"Broken off from a hilt, would you think?"

"Not from yours, then?"

"Mine?" Torold laughed. "Where would a

poor squire with his way to make get hold of so fine a weapon as this must have been? No, mine was a plain old sword my grandsire wore before me, and a dagger to match, in a heavy hide sheath. If it had been light as this, I'd have tried to keep it. No, this is none of mine."

"Nor Faintree's, either?"

Torold shook his head decidedly. "If he had any such, I should have known. Nick and I are of the same condition, and friends three years and more." He looked up intently into Brother Cadfael's face. "Now I remember a very small thing that may have meaning, after all. When I broke free and left the other fellow dazed, I trod on something under the hay where we'd been struggling, a small, hard thing that almost threw me. I think it could well have been this. It was *his*? Yes, it must have been his! Snapped off against the ground as we rolled."

"His, almost certainly, and the only thing we have to lead us to him," said Cadfael, taking back the stone and hiding it again from view in his pouch. "No man would willingly discard so fine a thing because one stone was broken from it. Whoever owned it still has it, and will get it repaired when he dare. If we can find the dagger, we shall have found the murderer."

"I wish," said Torold fiercely, "I could both go and stay! I should be glad to be the one to avenge Nick, he was a good friend to me. But my part is to obey my orders, and get FitzAlan's goods safely over to him in France. And," he said, regarding Cadfael steadily, "to take with me also Fulke Adeney's daughter, and deliver her safe to her father. If you will trust her to me."

"And help us," added Godith with immense confidence.

"Trust her to you—I might," said Cadfael mildly. "And help you both I surely will, as best I can. A very simple matter! All I have to do—and mark you, she has the assurance to demand it of me!—is to conjure you two good horses out of the empty air, where even poor hacks are gold, retrieve your hidden treasure for you, and see you well clear of the town, westward into Wales. Just a trifle! Harder things are done daily by the saints..."

He had reached this point when he stiffened suddenly, and spread a warning hand to enjoin silence. Listening with ears stretched, he caught for a second time the soft sound of a foot moving warily in the edge of the rustling stubble, close to the open door.

"What is it?" asked Godith in a soundless whisper, her eyes immense in alarm.

"Nothing!" said Cadfael as softly. "My ears playing tricks." And aloud he said: "Well, you and I must be getting back for Vespers. Come! It wouldn't do to be late."

Torold accepted his silent orders, and let them go without a word from him. If someone had indeed been listening...But he had heard nothing, and it seemed to him that even Cadfael was not sure. Why alarm Godith? Brother Cadfael was her best protector here, and once within the abbey walls she would again be in sanctuary. As for Torold, he was his own responsibility, though he would have been happier if he had had a sword!

Brother Cadfael reached down into the capacious waist of his habit, and drew out a long poniard in a rubbed and worn leather scabbard. Silently he put it into Torold's hands. The young man took it, marvelling, staring as reverently as at a first small miracle, so apt was the answer to his thought. He had it by the sheath, the cross of the hilt before his face, and was still gazing in wonder as they went out from him into the evening, and drew the door closed after them. Cadfael took the memory of that look with him into the fresh, saffron air of sunset. He himself must once have worn the same rapt expression, contemplating the same uplifted hilt. When he had taken the Cross, long ago, his vow had been made on that hilt, and the dagger had gone with him to Jerusalem, and roved the eastern seas with him for ten years. Even when he gave up his sword along with the things of this world, and surrendered all pride of possessions, he had kept the poniard. Just as well to part with it at last, to someone who had need of it and would not disgrace it.

He looked about him very cautiously as they rounded the corner of the mill and crossed the race. His hearing was sharp as a wild creature's, and he had heard no whisper or rustle from outside until the last few moments of their talk together, nor could he now be certain that what he had heard was a human foot, it might well have been a small animal slipping through the stubble. All the same, he must take thought for what might happen if they really had been spied upon. Surely, at the worst, only the last few exchanges could have been overheard, though those were revealing enough. Had the treasure been mentioned? Yes, he himself had said that all that was required of him was to obtain two horses, retrieve the treasure, and see them safely headed for Wales. Had anything been said then of *where* the treasure was hidden? No, that had been much earlier. But the listener, if listener there had been, could well have learned that a hunted fugitive of

FitzAlan's party was in hiding there, and worse, that Adeney's daughter was being sheltered in the abbey.

This was getting too warm for comfort. Best get them away as soon as the boy was fit to ride. But if this evening passed, and the night, and no move was made to betray them, he would suspect he had been fretting over nothing. There was no one in sight here but a solitary boy fishing, absorbed and distant on the river bank.

"What was it?" asked Godith, meek and attentive beside him. "Something made you uneasy, I know."

"Nothing to worry your head about," said Cadfael. "I was mistaken. Everything is as it should be."

From the corner of his eye, at that moment, he caught the sudden movement down towards the river, beyond the clump of bushes where she had found Torold. Out of the meagre cover a slight, agile body unfolded and stood erect, stretching lazily, and drifted at an oblique angle towards the path on which they walked, his course converging with theirs. Hugh Beringar, his stride nicely calculated to look accidental and yet bring him athwart their path at the right moment, showed them a placid and amiable face, recognising Cadfael with pleasure, accepting his attendant boy with benevolence.

"A very fair evening, brother! You're bound for Vespers? So am I. We may walk together?"

"Very gladly," said Cadfael heartily. He tapped Godith on the shoulder, and handed her the small sacking bundle that held his herbs and dressings. "Run ahead, Godric, and put these away for me, and come down to Vespers with the rest of the boys. You'll save my legs, and have time to give a stir to that lotion I have been brewing. Go on, child, run!"

And Godith clasped the bundle and ran, taking good care to run like an athletic boy, rattling one hand along the tall stubble, and whistling as she went, glad enough to put herself out of that young man's sight. Her own eyes and mind were full of another young man.

"A most biddable lad you have," said Hugh Beringar benignly, watching her race ahead.

"A good boy," said Cadfael placidly, matching him step for step across the field blanched to the colour of cream. "He has a year's endowment with us, but I doubt if he'll take the cowl. But he'll have learned his letters, and figuring, and a good deal about herbs and medicines, it will stand him in good stead. You're at leisure today, my lord?"

"Not so much at leisure," said Hugh Beringar with equal serenity, "as in need of your skills and knowledge. I tried your garden first, and not finding you there, thought you might have business today over here in the main gardens and orchard. But for want of a sight of you anywhere, I sat down to enjoy the evening sunshine, here by the river. I knew you'd come to Vespers, but never realised you had fields beyond here. Is all the corn brought in now?"

"All that we have here. The sheep will be grazing the stubble very shortly. What was it you wanted of me, my lord? If I may serve you in accord with my duty, be sure I will."

"Yesterday morning, Brother Cadfael, I asked you if you would give any request of mine fair consideration, and you told me you give fair consideration to all that you do. And I believe it. I had in mind what was then no more than a rumoured threat, now it's a real

one. I have reason to know that King Stephen is already making plans to move on, and means to make sure of his supplies and his mounts. The siege of Shrewsbury has cost him plenty, and he now has more mouths to feed and more men to mount. It's not generally known, or too many would be taking thought to evade it, as I am," owned Beringar blithely, "but he's about to issue orders to have every homestead in the town searched, and a tithe of all fodder and provisions in store commandeered for the army's use. And all—mark that, *all*—the good horses to be found, no matter who owns them, that are not already in army or garrison service. The abbey stables will not be exempt."

This Cadfael did not like at all. It came far too pat, a shrewd thrust at his own need of horses, and most ominous indication that Hugh Beringar, who had this information in advance of the general citizens, might also be as well informed of what went on in other quarters. Nothing this young man said or did would ever be quite what it seemed, but whatever game he played would always be his own game. The less said in reply, at this stage, the better. Two could play their own games, and both, possibly, benefit. Let him first say out what he wanted, even if what he said would have to be scrutinised from all angles, and subjected to every known test.

"That will be bad news to Brother Prior," said Cadfael mildly.

"It's bad news to me," said Beringar ruefully. "For I have four horses in those same abbey stables, and while I might have a claim to retain them all for myself and my men, once the king has given me his commission, I can't make any such claim at this moment with security. It might be allowed, it might not.

And to be open with you, I have no intention of letting my two best horses be drafted for the king's army. I want them out of here and in some private place, where they can escape Prestcote's foraging parties, until this flurry is over."

"Only two?" said Cadfael innocently. "Why not all?"

"Oh, come, I know you have more cunning than that. Would I be here without horses at all? If they found none of mine, they'd be hunting for all, and small chance I'd have left for royal favour. But let them take the two nags, and they won't question further. Two I can afford. Brother Cadfael, it takes no more than a few days in this place to know that you are the man to take any enterprise in hand, however rough and however risky." His voice was brisk and bland, even hearty, he seemed to intend no double meanings. "The lord abbot turns to you when he's faced with an ordeal beyond his powers. I turn to you for practical help. You know all this countryside. Is there a place of safety where my horses can lie up for a few days, until this round-up is over?"

So improbable a proposal Cadfael had not looked for, but it came as manna from heaven. Nor did he hesitate long over taking advantage of it for his own ends. Even if lives had not depended on the provision of those two horses, he was well aware that Beringar was making use of him without scruple, and he need have no scruples about doing as much in return. It went a little beyond that, even, for he had a shrewd suspicion that at this moment Beringar knew far too much of what was going on in his, Cadfael's mind, and had no objection whatever to any guesses Cadfael might be making as to what was

going on in his, Beringar's. Each of us, he thought, has a hold of sorts upon the other, and each of us has a reasonable insight into the other's methods, if not motives. It will be a fair fight. And yet this debonair being might very well be the murderer of Nicholas Faintree. That would be a very different duel, with no quarter asked or offered. In the meantime, make the most of what might or might not be quite accidental circumstances.

"Yes," said Cadfael, "I do know of such a place."

Beringar did not even ask him where, or question his judgment as to whether it would be remote enough and secret enough to be secure. "Show me the way tonight," he said outright, and smiled into Cadfael's face. "It's tonight or never, the order will be made public tomorrow. If you and I can make the return journey on foot before morning, ride with me. Rather you than any!"

Cadfael considered ways and means; there was no need to consider what his answer would be.

"Better get your horses out after Vespers, then, out to St Giles. I'll join you there when Compline is over, it will be getting dark then. It wouldn't do for me to be seen riding out with you, but you may exercise your own horses in the evening as the fit takes you."

"Good!" said Beringar with satisfaction. "Where is this place? Have we to cross the river anywhere?"

"No, nor even the brook. It's an old grange the abbey used to maintain in the Long Forest, out beyond Pulley. Since the times grew so unchancy we've withdrawn all our sheep and cattle from there, but keep two lay brothers still in the house. No one will look for horses there, they know it's all but abandoned. And the lay brothers will credit what I say."

"And St Giles is on our way?" It was a chapel of the abbey, away at the eastern end of the Foregate.

"It is. We'll go south to Sutton, and then bear west and into the forest. You'll have three miles or more to walk back by the shorter way. Without horses we may save a mile or so."

"I think my legs will hold me up for that distance," said Beringar demurely. "After Compline, then, at St Giles." And without any further word or question he left Cadfael's side, lengthening his easy stride to gain ground; for Aline Siward was just emerging from the doorway of her house and turning towards the abbey gateway on her way to church. Before she had gone many yards Beringar was at her elbow; she raised her head and smiled confidingly into his face. A creature quite without guile, but by no means without proper pride or shrewd sense, and she opened like a flower at sight of this young man devious as a serpent, whatever else of good or ill might be said of him. That, thought Cadfael, watching them walk before him in animated conversation, ought to signify something in his favour? Or was it only proof of her childlike trustfulness? Blameless young women have before now been taken in by black-hearted villains, even murderers; and black-hearted villains and murderers have been deeply devoted to blameless young women, contradicting their own nature in this one perverse tenderness.

Cadfael was consoled and cheered by the sight of Godith in church, nobody's fool, nudging and whispering among the boys, and flicking him one rapid, questioning blue glance, which he answered with a reassuring nod and smile. None too well-founded reassurance, but somehow he would make it good. Admirable as Aline was, Godith was the girl for him. She reminded him of Arianna, the Greek boat-girl, long ago, skirts kilted above the knee, short hair a cloud of curls, leaning on her long oar and calling across the water to him . . .

Ah, well! The age he had been then, young Torold had not even reached yet. These things are for the young. Meantime, tonight after Compline, at St Giles!

Chapter
Seven

he ride out through Sutton into the Long Forest, dense and primitive through all but the heathy summits of its fifteen square miles, was like a sudden return visit to aspects of his past, night raids and desperate ambushes once so familiar to him as to be almost tedious, but now, in this shadowy, elderly form, as near excitement as he wished to come. The horse under him was lofty and mettle-some and of high pedigree, he had not been astride such a creature for nearly twenty years, and the flattery and temptation reminded him of days past, when exalted and venturesome companions made all labours and privations pleasurable.

Hugh Beringar, once away from the used roads and into the trees and the night shadows, seemed to have no cares in the world, certainly no fear of any treachery on his companion's part. He chattered, even, to pass the time along the way, curious about Brother Cadfael's uncloistral past, and about the countries he had known as well as he knew this forest.

"So you lived in the world all those years, and saw so much of it, and never thought to marry? And half the world women, they say?" The light voice, seemingly idle and faintly mocking, nevertheless genuinely questioned and required an answer.

"I had thought to marry, once," said Cadfael honestly, "before I took the Cross, and she was a very fair woman, too, but to say truth, I forgot her in the east, and in the west she forgot me. I was away too long, she gave up waiting and married another man, small blame to her."

"Have you ever seen her again?" asked Hugh.

"No, never. She has grandchildren by now, may they be good to her. She was a fine woman, Richildis."

"But the east was also made up of men and women, and you a young crusader. I cannot but wonder," said Beringar dreamily.

"So, wonder! I also wonder about you," said Cadfael mildly. "Do you know any human creatures who are not strangers, one to another?"

A faint gleam of light showed among the trees. The lay brothers sat up late with a reed dip, Cadfael suspected playing at dice. Why not? The tedium here must be extreme. They were bringing these decent brothers a little diversion, undoubtedly welcome.

That they were alive and alert to the slightest sound of an unexpected approach was soon proved, as both emerged ware and ready in the doorway. Brother Anselm loomed huge and muscular, like an oak of his own fifty-five years, and swung a long staff in one hand. Brother Louis, French by descent but born in England, was small and wiry and agile, and in this solitude kept a dagger by him, and knew how to use it. Both of them came forth prepared for anything, placid of face and watchful of eye; but at sight of Brother Cadfael they fell to an easy grinning.

"What, is it you, old comrade? A pleasure to see a known face, but we hardly looked for you in the middle of the night. Are you biding over until tomorrow? Where's your errand?" They looked at Beringar with measuring interest, but he left it to Cadfael to do the dealing for him here, where the abbey's writ ran with more force than the king's.

"Our errand's here, to you," said Cadfael, lighting down. "My lord here asks that you'll give stabling and shelter for a few days to these two beasts, and keep them out of the public eye." No need to hide the reason from these two, who would have sympathised heartily with the owner of such horseflesh in his desire to keep it. "They're commandeering baggage horses for the army, and that's no fit life for these fellows, they'll be held back to serve in a better fashion."

Brother Anselm ran an appreciative eye over Beringar's mount, and an affectionate hand over the arched neck. "A long while since the stable here had such a beauty in it! Long enough since it had any at all, barring Prior Robert's mule when he visited, and he does that very rarely now. We expect to be recalled, to tell truth, this place is too isolated and unprofitable to be kept much longer. Yes, we'll give you house-room, my fine lad, gladly, and your mate, too. All the more gladly, my lord, if you'll let me get my leg across him now and again by way of exercise."

"I think he may carry even you without trouble," acknowledged Beringar amiably. "And surrender them to no one but myself or Brother Cadfael."

"That's understood. No one will set eyes on them here." They led the horses into the deserted stable, very content with the break in their tedious existence, and with Beringar's openhanded largesse for their services. "Though we'd have taken them in for the pleasure of it," said Brother Louis truthfully. "I was groom once in Earl Robert of Gloucester's household, I love a fine horse, one with a gloss and a gait to do me credit."

Cadfael and Hugh Beringar turned homeward together on foot. "An hour's walking, hardly more," said Cadfael, "by the way I'll take you. The path's too overgrown in parts for the horses, but I know it well, it cuts off the Foregate. We have to cross the brook, well upstream from the mill, and can enter the abbey grounds from the garden side, unnoticed, if you're willing to wade."

"I believe," said Beringar reflectively, but with complete placidity, "you are having a game with me. Do you mean to lose me in the woods, or drown me in the mill-race?"

"I doubt if I should succeed at either. No,

this will be a most amicable walk together, you'll see. And well worth it, I trust."

And curiously, for all each of them knew the other was making use of him, it was indeed a pleasant nocturnal journey they made, the elderly monk without personal ambitions, and the young man whose ambitions were limitless and daring. Probably Beringar was working hard at the puzzle of why Cadfael had so readily accommodated him, certainly Cadfael was just as busy trying to fathom why Beringar had ever invited him to conspire with him thus; it did not matter, it made the contest more interesting. And which of them was to win, and to get the most out of the tussle, was very much in the balance.

Keeping pace thus on the narrow forest path they were much of a height, though Cadfael was thickset and burly, and Beringar lean and lissome and light of foot. He followed Cadfael's steps attentively, and the darkness, only faintly alleviated by starlight between the branches, seemed to bother him not at all. And lightly and freely he talked.

"The king intends to move down into Gloucester's country again, in more strength, hence this drive for men and horses. In a few more days he'll surely be moving."

"And you go with him?" Since he was minded to be talkative, why not encourage him? Everything he said would be calculated, of course, but sooner or later even he might make a miscalculation.

"That depends on the king. Will you credit it, Brother Cadfael, the man distrusts me! Though in fact I'd liefer be put in charge of my own command here, where my lands lie. I've made myself as assiduous as I dare—to see the same face too constantly might have the worst effect, not to see it in attendance

at all would be fatal. A nice question of judgment."

"I feel," said Cadfael, "that a man might have considerable confidence in your judgment. Here we are at the brook, do you hear it?" There were stones there by which to cross dryshod, though the water was low and the bed narrowed, and Beringar, having rested his eyes a few moments to assay the distance and the ground, crossed in a nicely balanced leap that served to justify Cadfael's pronouncement.

"Do you indeed?" resumed the young man, falling in beside him again as they went on. "Have a high opinion of my judgment? Of risks and vantages only? Or, for instance, of men?—And women?"

"I can hardly question your judgment of men," said Cadfael drily, "since you've confided in me. If I doubted, I'd hardly be likely to own it."

"And of women?" They were moving more freely now through open fields.

"I think they might all be well advised to beware of you. And what else is gossiped about in the king's court, besides the next campaign? There's no fresh word of FitzAlan and Adeney being sighted?"

"None, nor will be now," said Beringar readily. "They had luck, and I'm not sorry. Where they are by now there's no knowing, but wherever it is, it's one stage on the way to France."

There was no reason to doubt him; whatever he was about he was making his dispositions by way of truth, not lies. So the news for Godith's peace of mind was still good, and every day better, as the distance between her father and Stephen's vengeance lengthened. And now there were two excellent horses well positioned on an escape road for Godith and Torold, in the care of two stalwart brothers who would release them at Cadfael's word. The first step was accomplished. Now to recover the saddle-bags from the river, and start them on their way. Not so simple a matter, but surely not impossible.

"I see now where we are," said Beringar, some twenty minutes later. They had cut straight across the mile of land enclosed by the brook's wanderings, and stood again on the bank; on the other side the stripped fields of pease whitened in the starlight, and beyond their smooth rise lay the gardens, and the great range of abbey buildings. "You have a nose for country, even in the dark. Lead the way, I'll trust you for an unpitted ford, too."

Cadfael had only to kilt his habit, having nothing but his sandals to get wet. He strode into the water at the point opposite the low roof of Godith's hut, which just showed above the trees and bushes and the containing wall of the herbarium. Beringar plunged in after him, boots and hose and all. The water was barely knee-deep, but clearly he cared not at all. And Cadfael noted how he moved, gently and steadily, hardly a ripple breaking from his steps. He had all the intuitive gifts of wild creatures, as alert by night as by day. On the abbey bank he set off instinctively round the edge of the low stubble of peasehaulms, to avoid any rustle among the dry roots soon to be dug in.

"A natural conspirator," said Cadfael, thinking aloud; and that he could do so was proof of a strong, if inimical, bond between them.

Beringar turned on him a face suddenly lit by a wild smile. "One knows another," he said. They had grown used to exchanging soundless whispers, and yet making them clear to be heard. "I've remembered one rumour that's making the rounds, that I forgot to tell you. A few days ago there was some fellow hunted into the river by night, said to be one of FitzAlan's squires. They say an archer got him behind the left shoulder, maybe through the heart. However it was, he went down, somewhere by Atcham his body may be cast up. But they caught a riderless horse, a good saddle-horse, the next day, sure to be his."

"Do you tell me?" said Cadfael, mildly marvelling. "You may speak here, there'll be no one prowling in my herb-garden by night, and they're used to me rising at odd times to tend my brews here."

"Does not your boy see to that?" asked Hugh Beringar innocently.

"A boy slipping out of the dortoir," said Brother Cadfael, "would soon have cause to rue it. We take better care of our children here, my lord, than you seem to think."

"I'm glad to hear it. It's well enough for seasoned old soldiers turned monk to risk the chills of the night, but the young things ought to be protected." His voice was sweet and smooth as honey. "I was telling you of this odd thing about the horses...A couple of days later, if you'll believe it, they rounded up another saddle-horse running loose, grazing up in the heathlands north of the town, still saddled. They're thinking there was a single bodyguard sent out from the castle, when the assault came, to pick up Adeney's daughter from wherever she was hidden, and escort her safely out of the ring round Shrewsbury. They think the attempt failed," he said softly, "when her attendant took to the river to save her. So she's still missing, and still thought to be somewhere here, close in hiding. And they'll be looking for her, Brother Cadfael—they'll be looking for her now more eagerly than ever."

They were up at the edge of the inner gardens by then. Hugh Beringar breathed an almost silent "Good night!" and was gone like a shadow towards the guest house.

Before he slept out the rest of the night, Brother Cadfael lay awake long enough to do some very hard thinking. And the longer he thought, the more convinced he became that someone had indeed approached the mill closely enough and silently enough to catch the last few sentences spoken within; and that the someone was Hugh Beringar, past all doubt. He had proved how softly he could move, how instinctively he adapted his movements to circumstances, he had provoked a shared expedition committing each of them to the other's discretion, and he had uttered a number of cryptic confidences calculated to arouse suspicion and alarm, and possibly precipitate unwise action—though Cadfael had no intention of giving him that last satisfaction. He did not believe the listener had been within earshot long. But the last thing Cadfael himself had said gave away plainly enough that he intended somehow to get hold of two horses, retrieve the hidden treasury, and see Torold on his way with "her." If Beringar had been at the door just a moment earlier, he must also have heard the girl named; but even without that he must surely have had his suspicions. Then just what game was he playing, with his own best horses, with the fugitives he could betray at any moment, yet had not so far betrayed, and with Brother Cadfael? A better

and larger prize offered than merely one young man's capture, and the exploitation of a girl against whom he had no real grudge. A man like Beringar might prefer to risk all and play for all, Torold, Godith and treasure in one swoop. For himself alone, as once before, though without success? Or for the king's gain and favour? He was indeed a young man of infinite possibilities.

Cadfael thought about him for a long time before he slept, and one thing, at least, was clear. If Beringar knew now that Cadfael had as good as undertaken to recover the treasury, then from this point on he would hardly let Cadfael out of his sight, for he needed him to lead him to the spot. A little light began to dawn, faint but promising, just before sleep came. It seemed no more than a moment before the bell was rousing him with the rest for Prime.

"Today," said Cadfael to Godith, in the garden after breakfast, "do all as usual, go to the Mass before chapter, and then to your schooling. After dinner you should work a little in the garden, and see to the medicines, but after that you can slip away to the old mill, discreetly, mind, until Vespers. Can you dress Torold's wound without me? I may not be seen there today."

"Surely I can," she said blithely. "I've seen it done, and I know the herbs now. But . . . If someone, if *he*, was spying on us yesterday, how if he comes today?" She had been told of the night's expedition, briefly, and the implications at once heartened and alarmed her.

"He will not," said Cadfael positively. "If all goes well, wherever *I* am today, there *he* will be. That's why I want you away from me, and why you may breathe more easily away from me. And there's something I may want you and Torold to do for me, late tonight, if things go as I expect. When we come to Vespers, then I'll tell you, yes or no. If it's yes, that's all I need say, and this is what you must do . . ."

She listened in glowing silence throughout, and nodded eager comprehension. "Yes, I saw the boat, leaning against the wall of the mill. Yes, I know the thicket of bushes at the beginning of the garden, close under the end of the bridge . . . Yes, of course we can do it, Torold and I together!"

"Wait long enough to be sure," cautioned Cadfael. "And now run off to the parish Mass, and your lessons, and look as like the other boys as you can, and don't be afraid. If there should be any cause for fear, I intend to hear of it early, and I'll be with you at once."

A part of Cadfael's thinking was rapidly proved right. He made it his business to be very active about the precincts that Sunday, attendant at every service, trotting on various errands from gate house to guest house, to the abbot's lodging, the infirmary, the gardens; and everywhere that he went, somewhere within view, unobtrusive but present, was Hugh Beringar. Never before had that young man been so constantly at church, in attendance even when Aline was not among the worshippers. Now let's see, thought Cadfael, with mild malice, whether I can lure him from the lists even when she does attend, and leave the field open for the other suitor. For Aline would certainly come to the Mass after chapter, and his last foray to the gate house had shown him Adam Courcelle, dressed for peace and piety, approaching the door of the small house where she and her maid were lodged.

It was unheard of for Cadfael to be absent from Mass, but for once he invented an errand which gave him fair excuse. His skills with medicines were known in the town, and people often asked for his help and advice. Abbot Heribert was indulgent to such requests, and lent his herbalist freely. There was a child along the Foregate towards St Giles who had been under his care from time to time for a skin infection, and though he was growing out of it gradually, and there was no great need for a visit this day, no one had the authority to contradict Cadfael when he pronounced it necessary to go.

In the gateway he met Aline Siward and Adam Courcelle entering, she slightly flushed, certainly not displeased with her escort, but perhaps a little embarrassed, the king's officer devoutly attentive and also warmly flushed, clearly in his case with pleasure. If Aline was expecting to be accosted by Beringar, as had become usual by this time, for once she was surprised. Whether relieved or disappointed there was no telling. Beringar was nowhere to be seen.

Proof positive, thought Cadfael, satisfied, and went on his physicianly visit serenely and without haste. Beringar was discretion itself in his surveillance, he contrived not to be seen at all until Cadfael, on his way home again, met him ambling out gently for exercise on one of his remaining horses, and whistling merrily as he rode.

He saluted Cadfael gaily, as though no encounter could have been more unexpected or more delightful. "Brother Cadfael, you astray on a Sunday morning?"

Very staidly Cadfael rehearsed his errand, and reported its satisfactory results.

"The range of your skills is admirable," said Beringar, twinkling. "I trust you had an undisturbed sleep after your long working day yesterday?"

"My mind was over-active for a while," said Cadfael, "but I slept well enough. And thus far you still have a horse to ride, I see."

"Ah, that! I was at fault, I should have realised that even if the order was issued on a Sunday, they would not move until the sabbath was over. Tomorrow you'll see for yourself." Unquestionably he was telling the truth, and certain of his information. "The hunt is likely to be very thorough," he said, and Cadfael knew he was not talking only of the horses and the provisions. "King Stephen is a little troubled about his relations with the church and its bishops. I ought to have known he would hold back on Sunday. Just as well, it gives us a day's credit and grace. Tonight we can stay blamelessly at home in all men's sight, as the innocent should. Eh, Cadfael?" And he laughed, and leaned to clap a hand on Brother Cadfael's shoulder, and rode on, kicking his heels into his horse's sides and rousing to a trot towards St Giles.

Nevertheless, when Cadfael emerged from the refectory after dinner, Beringar was visible just within the doorway of the guest-hall opposite, seemingly oblivious but well aware of everything within his field of vision. Cadfael led him harmlessly to the cloister, and sat down there in the sun, and dozed contentedly until he was sure that Godith would be well away and free from surveillance. Even when he awoke he sat for a while, to make quite sure, and to consider the implications.

No question but all his movements were being watched very narrowly, and by Beringar in person. He did not delegate such work to his men-at-arms, or to any other hired eyes, but did the duty himself, and probably took pleasure in it, too. If he was willing to surrender Aline to Courcelle, even for an hour, then maximum importance attached to what he was doing instead. I am elected, thought Cadfael, as the means to the end he desires, and that is FitzAlan's treasury. And his surveillance is going to be relentless. Very well! There's no way of evading it. The only thing to do is to make use of it.

Do not, therefore, tire out the witness too much, or alert him too soon of activities planned. He has you doing a deal of guessing, now keep him guessing.

So he betook himself to his herbarium, and worked conscientiously on all his preparations there, brewing and newly begun, all that afternoon until it was time to repair to church for Vespers. Where Beringar secreted himself he did not trouble to consider, he hoped the vigil was tedious in the extreme to a man so volatile and active.

Courcelle had either stayed—the opportunity being heaven-sent, and not to be wasted—or returned for the evening worship, he came with Aline demure and thoughtful on his arm. At sight of Brother Cadfael sallying forth from the gardens he halted, and greeted him warmly.

"A pleasure to see you in better circumstances than when last we met, brother. I hope you may have no more such duties. At least Aline and you, between you, lent some grace to what would otherwise have been a wholly ugly business. I wish I had some way of softening his Grace's mind towards your house, he still keeps a certain grudge that the lord abbot was in no hurry to come to his peace."

"A mistake a great many others also made," said Cadfael philosophically. "No doubt we shall weather it."

"I trust so. But as yet his Grace is in no mind to extend any privileges to the abbey above the other townsfolk. If I should be compelled to enforce, even within your walls, orders I'd rather see stop at the gates, I hope you'll understand that I do it reluctantly, and have no choice about it."

He is asking pardon in advance, thought Cadfael, enlightened, for tomorrow's invasion. So it's true enough, as I supposed, and he has been given the ill work to do, and is making it clear beforehand that he dislikes the business and would evade it if he could. He may even be making rather more than he need of his repugnance, for the lady's benefit.

"If that should happen," he said benignly, "I'm sure every man of my order will realise that you do only what you must, like any soldier under orders. You need not fear that any odium will attach to you."

"So I have assured Adam many times," said Aline warmly, and flushed vividly at hearing herself call him by his Christian name. Perhaps it was for the first time. "But he's hard to convince. No, Adam, it is true—you take to yourself blame which is not your due, as if you had killed Giles with your own hand, which you know is false. How could I even blame the Flemings? They were under orders, too. In such dreadful times as these no one can do more than choose his own road according to his conscience, and bear the consequences of his choice, whatever they may be."

"In no times, good or bad," said Cadfael sententiously, "can man do more or better

than that. Since I have this chance, lady, I should render you account of the alms you trusted to me, for all are bestowed, and they have benefited three poor, needy souls. For want of names, which I did not enquire, say some prayer for three worthy unfortunates who surely pray for you."

And so she would, he reflected as he watched her enter the church on Courcelle's arm. At this crisis season of her life, bereaved of kin, left mistress of a patrimony she had freely dedicated to the king's service, he judged she was perilously hesitant between the cloister and the world, and for all he had chosen the cloister in his maturity, he heartily wished her the world, if possible a more attractive world than surrounded her now, to employ and fulfil her youth.

Going in to take his place among his brothers, he met Godith making for her own corner. Her eyes questioned brightly, and he said softly: "Yes! Do all as I told you."

So now what mattered was to make certain that for the rest of the evening he led Beringar into pastures far apart from where Godith operated. What Cadfael did must be noted, what she did must go unseen and unsuspected. And that could not be secured by adhering faithfully to the evening routine. Supper was always a brief meal, Beringar would be sure to be somewhere within sight of the refectory when they emerged. Collations in the chapter house, the formal reading from the lives of the saints, was a part of the day that Cadfael had been known to miss on other occasions, and he did so now, leading his unobtrusive attendant first to the infirmary, where he paid a brief visit to Brother Reginald, who was old and deformed in the joints, and welcomed company, and then to the extreme end of the abbot's own garden, far away from the herbarium, and farther still from the gate house. By then Godith would be freed from her evening lesson with the novices, and might appear anywhere between the hut and the herbarium and the gates, so it was essential that Beringar should continue to concentrate on Cadfael, even if he was doing nothing more exciting than trimming the dead flowers from the abbot's roses and clove-pinks. By that stage Cadfael was checking only occasionally that the watch on his movements continued; he was quite certain that it would, and with exemplary patience. During the day it seemed almost casual, hardly expecting action, except that Cadfael was a tricky opponent, and might have decided to act precisely when it was unexpected of him. But it was after dark that things would begin to happen.

When Compline was over there was always, on fine evenings, a brief interlude of leisure in the cloister or the gardens, before the brothers went to their beds. By then it was almost fully dark, and Cadfael was satisfied that Godith was long since where she should be, and Torold beside her. But he thought it best to delay yet a while, and go to the dortoir with the rest. Whether he emerged thence by way of the night stairs into the church, or the outer staircase, someone keeping watch from across the great court, where the guest hall lay, would be able to pick up his traces without trouble.

He chose the night stairs and the open north door of the church, and slipped round the east end of the Lady Chapel and the chapter house to cross the court into the gardens. No need to look round or listen for his shadow, he knew it would be there, mov-

ing at leisure, hanging well back from him but keeping him in sight. The night was reasonably dark, but the eyes grew accustomed to it soon, and he knew how securely Beringar could move in darkness. He would expect the night-wanderer to leave by the ford, as they had returned together the previous night. Someone bound on secret business would not pass the porter on the gate, whatever his normal authority.

After he had waded the brook, Cadfael did pause to be sure Beringar was with him. The breaks in the rhythm of the water were very slight, but he caught them, and was content. Now to follow the course of the brook downstream on this side until nearing its junction with the river. There was a little footbridge there, and then it was only a step to the stone bridge that crossed into Shrewsbury. Over the road, and down the slope into the main abbey gardens, and he was already under the shadow of the first archway of the bridge, watching the faint flashes of light from the eddies where once a boat-mill had been moored. In this corner under the stone pier the bushes grew thick, such an awkward slope of ground was not worth clearing for what it would bear. Half-grown willows leaned, trailing leaves in the water, and the bushy growth under their branches would have hidden half a dozen well-screened witnesses.

The boat was there, afloat and tied up to one of the leaning branches, though it was of the light, withy-and-hide type that could be ported easily overland. This time there was good reason it should not, as it usually would, be drawn ashore and turned over in the turf. There was, Cadfael hoped, a solid bundle within it, securely tied up in one or two of the sacks from the mill. It would not have done for him to be seen to be carrying anything. Long before this, he trusted, he had been clearly seen to be empty-handed.

He stepped into the boat and loosed the mooring-rope. The sacking bundle was there, and convincingly heavy when he cautiously tested. A little above him on the slope, drawn into the edge of the bushes, he caught the slight movement of a deeper shadow as he pushed off with the long paddle into the flow under the first archway.

In the event it proved remarkably easy. No matter how keen Hugh Beringar's sight, he could not possibly discern everything that went on under the bridge, detail by detail. However sharp his hearing, it would bring him only a sound suggesting the rattling of a chain drawn up against stone, with some considerable weight on the end, the splash and trickle of water running out from something newly drawn up, and then the iron rattle of the chain descending; which was exactly what it was, except that Cadfael's hands slowed and muted the descent, to disguise the fact that the same weight was still attached, and only the bundle concealed in the boat had been sluiced in the Severn briefly, to provide the trickle of water on the stone ledge. The next part might be more risky, since he was by no means certain he had read Beringar's mind correctly. Brother Cadfael was staking his own life and those of others upon his judgment of men.

So far, however, it had gone perfectly. He paddled his light craft warily ashore, and above him a swift-moving shadow withdrew to higher ground, and, he surmised, went to earth close to the roadway, ready to fall in behind him whichever way he took. Though he would have wagered that the way was

already guessed at, and rightly. He tied up the boat again, hastily but securely; haste was a part of his disguise that night, like stealth. When he crept cautiously up to the highroad again, and loomed against the night sky for a moment in stillness, ostensibly waiting to be sure he could cross unnoticed, the watcher could hardly miss seeing that he had now a shape grossly humped by some large bundle he carried slung over his shoulder.

He crossed, rapidly and quietly, and returned by the way he had come, following the brook upstream from the river after passing the ford, and so into the fields and woods he had threaded with Beringar only one night past. The bundle he carried, mercifully, had not been loaded with the full weight it was supposed to represent, though either Torold or Godith had seen fit to give it a convincing bulk and heft. More than enough, Cadfael reflected ruefully, for an ageing monk to carry four miles or more. His nights were being relentlessly curtailed. Once these young folk were wafted away into relative safety he would sleep through Matins and Lauds, and possibly the next morning's Prime, as well, and do fitting penance for it.

Now everything was matter for guesswork. Would Beringar take it for granted where he was bound, and turn back too soon, and with some residue of suspicion, and ruin everything? No! Where Cadfael was concerned he would take nothing for granted, not until he was sure by his own observation where this load had been bestowed in safe-keeping, and satisfied that Cadfael had positively returned to his duty without it. But would he, by any chance, intercept it on the way? No, why should he? To do so would have been to burden himself with it, whereas now he had an old fool to carry it for him, to where he had his horses hidden to convey it with ease elsewhere.

Cadfael had the picture clear in his mind now, the reckoning at its worst. If Beringar had killed Nicholas Faintree in the attempt to possess himself of the treasury, then his aim now would be not only to accomplish what he had failed to do then, but also something beyond, a possibility which had been revealed to him only since that attempt. By letting Brother Cadfael stow away for him both horses and treasure at an advantageous place, he had ensured his primary objective; but in addition, if he waited for Cadfael to convey his fugitives secretly to the same spot, as he clearly intended to do, then Beringar could remove the only witness to his former murder, and capture his once affianced bride as hostage for her father. What an enormous boon to bestow on King Stephen! His own favoured place would be assured, his crime buried for ever.

So much, of course, for the worst. But the range of possibilities was wide. For Beringar might be quite innocent of Faintree's death, but very hot on the trail of FitzAlan's valuables, now he had detected their whereabouts; and an elderly monk might be no object to his plans for his own enrichment, or, if he preferred to serve his interests in another way, his means of ingratiating himself with the king. In which case Cadfael might not long survive his depositing this infernal nuisance he carried, on shoulders already aching, at the grange where the horses were stabled. Well, thought Cadfael, rather exhilarated than oppressed, we shall see!

Once into the woods beyond the coil of the brook, he halted, and dropped the load with a huge grunt from his shoulders, and sat down on it, ostensibly to rest, actually to listen for the soft sounds of another man halting, braced, not resting. Very soft they were, but he caught them, and was happy. The young man was there, tireless, serene, a born adventurer. He saw a dark, amused, saturnine face ready for laughter. He was reasonably sure, then, how the evening would end. With a little luck— better, with God's blessing, he reproved!—he would be back in time for Matins.

There was no perceptible light in the grange when he reached it, but it needed only the rustle and stir of footsteps, and Brother Louis was out with a little pine-flare in one hand and his dagger in the other, as wide awake as at midday, and more perilous.

"God bless you, brother," said Cadfael, easing the load gratefully from his back. He would have something to say to young Torold when next he talked to him! Someone or something other than his own shoulders could carry this the next time. "Let me within, and shut the door to."

"Gaily!" said Brother Louis, and haled him within and did as he was bid.

On the way back, not a quarter of an hour later, Brother Cadfael listened carefully as he went, but he heard nothing of anyone following or accompanying him, certainly of no menace. Hugh Beringar had watched him into the grange from cover, possibly even waited for him to emerge unburdened, and then melted away into the night to which he belonged, and made his own lightsome, satisfied way home to the abbey. Cadfael abandoned all precautions and did the same. He was certain, now, where he stood. By the time the bell rang for Matins he was ready to emerge with the rest of the dortoir, and proceed devoutly down the night-stairs to give due praise in the church.

Chapter Eight

efore dawn on that Monday morning in August the king's officers had deployed small parties to close every road out of Shrewsbury, while at every section within the town wall others stood ready to move methodically through the streets and search every house. There was more in the wind than the commandeering of horses and provisions, though that would certainly be done as they went, and done thoroughly.

"Everything shows that the girl must be in hiding somewhere near," Prestcote had insisted, reporting to the king after full enquiries. "The one horse we found turned loose is known to be from FitzAlan's stables, and this young man hunted into the Severn certainly had a companion who has not yet been run to earth. Left alone, she cannot have got far. All your advisers agree, your Grace cannot afford to let the chance of her capture slip. Adeney would certainly come back to redeem her, he has no other child. It's possible even FitzAlan could be forced to return, rather than face the shame of letting her die."

"Die?" echoed the king, bristling ominously. "Is it likely I'd take the girl's life? Who spoke of her dying?"

"Seen from here," said Prestcote drily, "it may be an absurdity to speak of any such matter, but to an anxious father waiting for better news it may seem all too possible. Of course you would do the girl no harm. No need even to harm her father if you get him into your hands, or even FitzAlan. But your Grace must consider that you should do everything possible to prevent their services from reaching the empress. It's no longer a matter of revenge for Shrewsbury, but simply of a sensible measure to conserve your own forces and cut down on your enemy's."

"That's true enough," admitted Stephen, without overmuch enthusiasm. His anger and hatred had simmered down into his more natural easiness of temperament, not to say laziness. "I am not sure that I like even making such use of the girl." He remembered that he had as good as ordered young Beringar to track down his affianced bride if he wanted to establish himself in royal favour, and the young man, though respectfully attendant since, if somewhat sporadically, had never yet produced any evidence of zeal in the search. Possibly, thought the king, he read my mind better than I did myself at the time.

"She need come by no injury, and your Grace would be saved having to contend with any forces attached to her father's standard, if not also his lord's. If you can cut off all those levies from the enemy, you will have saved yourself great labour, and a number of your men their lives. You cannot afford to neglect such a chance."

It was sound advice, and the king knew it. Weapons are where you find them, and Adeney could sit and kick his heels in an easy imprisonment enough, once he was safe in captivity.

"Very well!" he said. "Make your search and make it thoroughly."

The preparations were certainly thorough. Adam Courcelle descended upon the Abbey Foregate with his own command and a company of the Flemings. And while Willem Ten Heyt went ahead and established a guard-post at St Giles, to question every rider and search every cart attempting to leave the town, and his lieutenant posted sentries along every path and by every possible crossing-place along the riverside, Courcelle took possession, civilly but brusquely, of the abbey gate house, and ordered the gates closed to all attempting to enter or leave. It was then about twenty minutes before Prime, and already daylight. There had been very little noise made, but Prior Robert from the dortoir had caught the unusual stir and disquiet from the gate house, on which the window of his own chamber looked down, and he came out in haste to see what was afoot.

Courcelle made him a reverence that deceived nobody, and asked with respect for privileges everyone knew he was empowered to take; still, the veil of courtesy did something to placate the prior's indignation.

"Sir, I am ordered by his Grace King Stephen to require of your house free and orderly entry everywhere, a tithe of your stores for his Grace's necessary provision, and such serviceable horses as are not already in the use of people in his Grace's commission. I am also commanded to search and enquire everywhere for the girl Godith, daughter of his Grace's traitor Fulke Adeney, who is thought to be still in hiding here in Shrewsbury."

Prior Robert raised his thin, silver brows and looked down his long, aristocratic nose. "You would hardly expect to find such a person within our precincts? I assure you there is none such in the guest house, where alone she might becomingly be found."

"It is a formality here, I grant you," said Courcelle, "but I have my orders, and cannot treat one dwelling more favourably than another."

There were lay servants listening by then, standing apart silent and wary, and one or two of the boy pupils, sleepy-eyed and scared. The master of the novices came to herd his strays back into their quarters, and stayed, instead, to listen with them.

"This should be reported at once to the abbot," said the prior with admirable composure, and led the way at once to Abbot Heribert's lodging. Behind them, the Flemings were closing the gates and mounting a guard, before turning their practical attention to the barns and the stables.

Brother Cadfael, having for two nights running missed the first few hours of his rest,

slept profoundly through all the earliest manifestations of invasion, and awoke only when
the bell rang for Prime, far too late to do
anything but dress in haste and go down with
the rest of the brothers to the church. Only
when he heard the whispers passed from man
to man, and saw the closed gates, the loung-
ing Flemings, and the subdued and huge-eyed
boys, and heard the businesslike bustle and
clatter of hooves from the stable-yard, did he
realise that for once events had overtaken
him, and snatched the initiative from his hands.
For nowhere among the scared and anxious
youngsters in church could he see any sign of
Godith. As soon as Prime was over, and he
was free to go, he hurried away to the hut in
the herbarium. The door was unlatched and
open, the array of drying herbs and mortars
and bottles in shining order, the blankets had
been removed from the bench-bed, and a
basket of newly gathered lavender and one or
two bottles arranged innocently along it. Of
Godith there was no sign, in the hut, in the
gardens, in the peasefields along the brook,
where at one side the great stack of dried
haulms loomed pale as flax, waiting to be
carted away to join the hay in the barns. Nor
was there any trace of a large bundle wrapped
in sacking and probably damp from seeping
river-water, which had almost certainly spent
the night under that bleached pile, or the
small boat which should have been turned
down upon it and carefully covered over. The
boat, FitzAlan's treasury, and Godith had all
vanished into thin air. Godith had awakened
somewhat before Prime, uneasily aware of the
heavy responsibility that now lay upon her,
and gone out without undue alarm to find
out what was happening at the gate house.
Though all had been done briskly and quietly,

there was something about the stirring in the
air and the unusual voices, lacking the deco-
rous monastic calm of the brothers, that disturbed her mind. She was on the point of
emerging from the walled garden when she
saw the Flemings dismounting and closing
the gates, and Courcelle advancing to meet
the prior. She froze at the sound of her own
name thus coolly spoken. If they were bent
upon a thorough search, even here, they must
surely find her. Questioned like the other
boys, with all those enemy eyes upon her, she
could not possibly sustain the performance.
And if they found her, they might extend the
search and find what she had in her charge.
Besides, there was Brother Cadfael to protect,
and Torold. Torold had returned faithfully to
his mill once he had seen her safely home
with the treasure. Last night she had almost
wished he could have stayed with her, now
she was glad he had the whole length of the
Gaye between him and this dawn alarm, and
woods not far from his back, and quick senses
that would pick up the signs early, and give
him due warning to vanish.

Last night had been like a gay, adventurous
dream, for some reason inexpressibly sweet,
holding their breath together in cover until
Cadfael had led his shadow well away from
the bridge, loosing the little boat, hauling up
the dripping saddle-bags, swathing them in
dry sacks to make another bundle the image
of Cadfael's; their hands together on the chain,
holding it away from the stone, muting it so
that there should be no further sound, then
softly paddling the short way upstream to the
brook, and round to the peasefields. Hide the
boat, too, Cadfael had said, for we'll need it
tomorrow night, if the chance offers. Last
night's adventure had been the dream, this

morning was the awakening, and she needed the boat now, this moment.

There was no hope of reaching Brother Cadfael for orders, what she guarded must be got away from here at once, and it certainly could not go out through the gates. There was no one to tell her what to do, this fell upon her shoulders now. Blessedly, the Flemings were not likely to ransack the gardens until they had looted stables and barns and stores; she had a little time in hand.

She went back quickly to the hut, folded her blankets and hid them under the bench behind a row of jars and mortars, stripped the bed and turned it into a mere shelf for more such deceits, and set the door wide open to the innocent daylight. Then she slipped away to the stack of haulms, and dragged out the boat from its hiding-place, and the sacking bundle with it. A godsend that the gentle slope of the field was so glazed with the cropped stems, and the boat so light, that it slid down effortlessly into the brook. She left it beached, and returned to drag the treasury after it, and hoist it aboard. Until last night she had never been in such a boat, but Torold had shown her how to use the paddle, and the steady flow of the brook helped her.

She already knew what she would do. There was no hope at all of escaping notice if she went downstream to the Severn; with such a search in hand, there would be watchers on the main road, on the bridge, and probably along the banks. But only a short way from her launching-place a broad channel was drawn off to the right, to the pool of the main abbey mill, where the mill-race, drawn off upstream through the abbey pool and the fish ponds, turned the wheel and emptied itself again into the pond, to return to the main stream of the

brook and accompany it to the river. Just beyond the mill the three grace houses of the abbey were ranged, with little gardens down to the water, and three more like them protected the pond from open view on the other side. The house next to the mill was the one devoted to the use of Aline Siward. True, Courcelle had said he was to search for his fugitive everywhere; but if there was one place in this conventual enclosure that would receive no more than a formal visit from him, it was certainly the house where Aline was living.

What if we are on opposite sides, thought Godith, plying her paddle inexpertly but doggedly at the turn, and sailing into wider, smoother water, she can't throw me to the wolves, it isn't in her, with a face like hers! And are we on opposite sides? Are we on either side, by this time? She places everything she has at the king's disposal, and he hangs her brother! My father stakes life and lands for the empress, and I don't believe she cares what happens to him or any of his like, provided she gets her own way. I daresay Aline's brother was more to her than King Stephen will ever be, and I know I care more for my father and Torold than for the Empress Maud, and I wish the old king's son hadn't drowned when that awful ship went down, so that there'd have been no argument over who inherited, and Stephen and Maud alike could have stayed in their own manors, and left us alone!

The mill loomed on her right, but the wheel was still today, and the water of the race spilled over freely into the pond that opened beyond, with slow counter-currents flowing along the opposite bank to return to the brook. The bank here was sheer for a couple of feet, to level as much ground as possible for the narrow gardens; but if she could heave the bundle safely ashore, she thought she could drag up the boat. She caught at a naked root that jutted into the water from a leaning willow, and fastened her mooring-line to it, before she dared attempt to hoist her treasure up to the edge of the grass. It was heavy for her, but she rolled it on to the thwart, and thence manipulated it into her arms. She could just reach the level rim of turf without tilting the boat too far. The weight rested and remained stable, and Godith leaned her arms thankfully either side of it, and for the first time tears welled out of her eyes and ran down her face.

Why, she wondered rebelliously, why am I going to such trouble for this rubbish, when all I care about is Torold, and my father? And Brother Cadfael! I should be failing him if I tipped it down into the pond and left it there. He went to all sorts of pains to get it to this point, and now I have to go on with the work. And Torold cares greatly that he should carry out the task he was given. That's more than gold. It isn't this lump that matters!

She scrubbed an impatient and grubby hand over her cheeks and eyes, and set about climbing ashore, which proved tricky, for the boat tended to withdraw from under her foot to the length of its mooring; when at last she had scrambled to safety, swearing now instead of crying, she could not draw it up after her, she was afraid of holing it on the jagged roots. It would have to ride here. She lay on her stomach and shortened the mooring, and made sure the knot was fast. Then she towed her detested incubus up into the shadow of the house, and hammered at the door.

It was Constance who opened it. It was barely eight o'clock, Godith realized, and it

was Aline's habit to attend the mass at ten, she might not even be out of her bed yet. But the general disquiet in the abbey had reached these retired places also, it seemed, for Aline was up and dressed, and appeared at once behind her maid's shoulder.

"What is it, Constance?" She saw Godith, soiled and tousled and breathless, leaning over a great sacking bundle on the ground, and came forward in innocent concern. "Godric! What's the matter? Did Brother Cadfael send you? Is anything wrong?"

"You know the boy, do you, madam?" said Constance, surprised.

"I know him, he's Brother Cadfael's helper, we have talked together." She cast one luminous glance over Godith from head to foot, took in the smudged marks of tears and the heaving bosom, and put her maid quickly aside. She knew desperation when she saw it, even when it made no abject appeal. "Come within, come! Here, let me help you with this, whatever it may be. Now, Constance, close the door!" They were safe within, the wooden walls closed them round, the morning sun was warm and bright through an eastern window left open.

They stood looking at each other, Aline all woman in a blue gown, her golden hair loosed about her in a cloud, Godith brown and rumpled, and arrayed unbecomingly in an overlarge cotte and ill-fitting hose, short hair wild, and face strained and grubby from soil, grass and sweat.

"I came to ask you for shelter," said Godith simply. "The king's soldiers are hunting for me. I'm worth quite a lot to them if they find me. I'm not Godric, I'm Godith. Godith Adeney, Fulke Adeney's daughter."

Aline let her glance slide, startled and

touched, from the fine-featured oval face, down the drab-clad and slender limbs. She looked again into the challenging, determined face, and a spark started and glowed in her eyes.

"You'd better come through here," she said practically, with a glance at the open window, "into my own sleeping-chamber, away from the road. Nobody will trouble you there—we can talk freely. Yes, bring your belongings, I'll help you with them." FitzAlan's treasury was woman-handled between them into the inner room, where not even Courcelle, certainly not any other, would dare to go. Aline closed the door very softly. Godith sat down on a stool by the bed, and felt every sinew in her grown weak, and every stress relaxing. She leaned her head against the wall, and looked up at Aline.

"You do realise, lady, that I'm reckoned the king's enemy? I don't want to trick you into anything. You may think it your duty to give me up."

"You're very honest," said Aline, "and I'm not being tricked into anything. I'm not sure even the king would think the better of me if I gave you up to him, but I'm sure God would not, and I know I should not think the better of myself. You can rest safe here. Constance and I between us will see to it that no one comes near you."

Brother Cadfael preserved a tranquil face through Prime, and the first conventual Mass, and a greatly abbreviated chapter meeting, while mentally he was racking his brain and gnawing his knuckles over his own inexplicable complacence, which had let him sleep on while the opposing powers stole a march on him. The gates were fast shut, there was no way out there. He could not pass, and cer-

tainly by that route Godith had not passed. He had seen no soldiers on the other side of the brook, though they would certainly be watching the river bank. If Godith had taken the boat, where had she gone with it? Not upstream, for the brook was open to view for some way, and beyond that flowed through a bed too uneven and rocky to accommodate such craft. Every moment he was waiting for the outcry that would signal her capture, but every moment that passed without such an alarm was ease to him. She was no fool, and she seemed to have got away, though heaven knew where, with the treasure they were fighting to retain and speed on its way.

At chapter Abbot Heribert made a short, weary, disillusioned speech in explanation of the occupation that had descended upon them, instructed the brothers to obey whatever commands were given them by the king's officers with dignity and fortitude, and to adhere to the order of their day faithfully so far as they were permitted. To be deprived of the goods of this world should be no more than a welcome discipline to those who had aspired beyond the world. Brother Cadfael could at least feel some complacency concerning his own particular harvest; the king was not likely to demand tithes of his herbs and remedies, though he might welcome a cask or two of wine. Then the abbot dismissed them with the injunction to go quietly about their own work until High Mass at ten.

Brother Cadfael went back to the gardens and occupied himself distractedly with such small tasks as came to hand, his mind still busy elsewhere. Godith could safely have forded the brook by broad daylight, and taken to the nearest patch of woodland, but she could not have carried the unwieldy bundle of treasure with her, it was too heavy. She had chosen rather to remove all the evidence of irregular activities here, taking away with her both the treasure and the boat. He was sure she had not gone as far as the confluence with the river, or she would have been captured before this. Every moment without the evil news provided another morsel of reassurance. But wherever she was, she needed his help.

And there was Torold, away beyond the reaped fields, in the disused mill. Had he caught the meaning of these movements in good time, and taken to the woods? Devoutly Cadfael hoped so. In the meantime there was nothing he could do but wait, and give nothing away. But oh, if this inquisition passed before the end of the day, and he could retrieve his two strays after dark, this very night he must see them away to the west. This might well be the most favourable opportunity, with the premises already scoured, the searchers tired and glad to forget their vigilance, the community totally absorbed with their grievances and comparing notes on the army's deprivations, the brothers devoted wholly to fervent prayers of thanks for an ordeal ended.

Cadfael went out to the great court in good time for Mass. There were army carts being loaded with sacks from the barns, and a great bustle of Flemings about the stables. Dismayed guests, caught here in mid-journey with horses worth commandeering, came out in great agitation to argue and plead for their beasts, but it did them no good, unless the owners could prove they were in the king's service already. Only the poor hacks were spared. One of the abbey carts was also taken, with its team, and loaded with the abbey's wheat.

Something curious was happening at the gates, Cadfael saw. The great carriage doors were closed, and guarded, but someone had had the calm temerity to knock at the wicket and ask for entry. Since it could have been one of their own, a courier from the guard-post at St Giles, or from the royal camp, the wicket was opened, and in the narrow doorway appeared the demure figure of Aline Siward, prayer-book in hand, her gold hair covered decently by the white mourning cap and wimple.

"I have permission," she said sweetly, "to come in to church." And seeing that the guards who confronted her were not at home in English, she repeated it just as amiably in French. They were not disposed to admit her, and were on the point of closing the door in her face when one of their officers observed the encounter, and came in haste.

"I have permission," repeated Aline patiently, "from Messire Courcelle to come in to Mass. My name is Aline Siward. If you are in doubt, ask him, he will tell you."

It seemed that she had indeed secured her privilege, for after some hurried words the wicket was opened fully, and they stood back and let her pass. She walked through the turmoil of the great court as though nothing out of the ordinary were happening there, and made for the cloister and the south door of the church. But she slowed her pace on the way, for she was aware of Brother Cadfael weaving his way between the scurrying soldiers and the lamenting travellers to cross her path just at the porch. She gave him a demure public greeting, but in the moment when they were confidingly close she said privately and low:

"Be easy, Godric is safe in my house."

"Praise to God and you!" sighed Cadfael as

softly. "After dark I'll come for her." And though Aline had used the boyish name, he knew by her small, secret smile that the word he had used was no surprise to her. "The boat?" he questioned soundlessly.

"At the foot of my garden, ready."

She went on into the church, and Cadfael, with a heart suddenly light as thistledown, went decorously to take his place among the procession of his brothers.

Torold sat in the fork of a tree at the edge of the woods east of Shrewsbury castle, eating the remains of the bread he had brought away with him, and a couple of early apples stolen from a tree at the limit of the abbey property. Looking westward across the river he could see not only the great cliff of the castle walls and towers, but further to the right, just visible between the crests of trees, the tents of the royal camp. By the numbers busy about the abbey and the town, the camp itself must be almost empty at this moment.

Torold's body was coping well enough with this sudden crisis, to his satisfaction and, if he would have admitted it, surprise. His mind was suffering more. He had not yet walked very far, or exerted himself very much, apart from climbing into this comfortable and densely leafed tree, but he was delighted with the response of his damaged muscles, and the knit of the gash in his thigh, which hardly bothered him, and the worse one in his shoulder, which had neither broken nor greatly crippled his use of his arm. But all his mind fretted and ached for Godith, the little brother so suddenly transmuted into a creature half sister, half something more. He had confidence in Brother Cadfael, of course, but it was impossible to unload all the responsibility

for her on to one pair of cloistered shoulders, however wide and sustaining. Torold fumed and agonised, and yet went on eating his stolen apples. He was going to need all the sustenance he could muster.

There was a patrol moving methodically along the bank of the Severn, between him and the river, and he dared not move again until they had passed by and withdrawn from sight towards the abbey and the bridge. And how far round the outskirts of the town he would have to go, to outflank the royal cordon, was something he did not yet know.

He had awakened to the unmistakable sounds from the bridge, carried by the water, and insistent enough in their rhythm to break his sleep. Many, many men, mounted and foot, stamping out their presence and their passage upon a stone bow high above water, the combination sending echoes headlong down the river's course. The timber of the mill, the channels of water feeding it, carried the measure to his ears. He had started up and dressed instinctively, gathering everything that might betray his having been there, before he ventured out to look. He had seen the companies fan out at the end of the bridge, and waited to see no more, for this was a grimly thorough operation. He had wiped out all traces of his occupation of the mill, throwing into the river all those things he could not carry away with him, and then had slipped away across the limit of abbey land, away from the advancing patrol on the river bank, into the edge of the woodlands opposite the castle.

He did not know for whom or what this great hunt had been launched, but he knew all too well who was likely to be taken in it, and his one aim now was to get to Godith, wherever she might be, and stand between her and danger if he could. Better still, to take her away from here, into Normandy, where she would be safe.

Along the river bank the men of the patrol separated to beat a way through the bushes where Godith had first come to him. They had already searched the abandoned mill, but thank God they would find no traces there. Now they were almost out of sight, he felt safe in swinging down cautiously from his tree and withdrawing deeper into the belt of woodland. From the bridge to St Giles the king's highway, the road to London, was built up with shops and dwellings, he must keep well clear. Was it better to go on like this, eastward, and cross the highroad somewhere beyond St Giles, or to wait and go back the way he had come, after all the tumult was over? The trouble was that he did not know when that was likely to be, and his torment for Godith was something he did not want prolonged. He would have to go beyond St Giles, in all probability, before he dared cross the highroad, and though the brook, after that, need be no obstacle the approach to the spot opposite the abbey gardens would still be perilous. He could lie up in the nearest cover and watch, and slip over into the stack of pease-haulms when the opportunity offered, and thence, if all remained quiet, into the herbarium, where he had never yet been, and the hut where Godith had slept the last seven nights in sanctuary. Yes, better go forward and make that circle. Backward meant braving the end of the bridge, and there would be soldiers there until darkness fell, and probably through the night.

It proved a tedious business, when he was longing for swift action. The sudden assault had brought out all the inhabitants in frightened and indignant unrest, and Torold had to beware of any notice in such conditions, since he was a young fellow not known here, where neighbour knew neighbour like his own kin, and any stranger was liable to be accosted and challenged out of sheer alarm. Several times he had to draw off deeper into cover, and lie still until danger passed. Those who lived close to the highway, and had suffered the first shocks, tended to slip away into any available solitude. Those who were daily tending stock or cultivating land well away from the road heard the uproar, and gravitated close enough to satisfy their curiosity about what was going on. Caught between these two tides, Torold passed a miserable day of fretting and waiting; but it brought him at last well beyond Willem Ten Heyt's tight and brutal guard-post, which by then had amassed a great quantity of goods distrained from agitated travellers, and a dozen sound horses. Here the last houses of the town ended, and fields and hamlets stretched beyond. Traffic on the road, half a mile beyond the post, was thin and easily evaded. Torold crossed, and went to earth once more in a thicket above the brook, while he viewed the lie of the land.

The brook was dual here, the mill-race having been drawn off at a weir somewhat higher upstream. He could see both silver streaks in a sunlight now declining very slightly towards the west. It must be almost time for Vespers. Surely King Stephen had finished with the abbey by now, with all Shrewsbury to ransack?

The valley here was narrow and steep, and no one had built on it, the grass being given over to sheep. Torold slid down into the cleft, easily leaping the mill-race, and picking his way over the brook from stone to stone. He began to make his way downstream from one patch of cover to another, until about the time of Vespers he had reached the smoother meadows opposite Brother Cadfael's gleaned pease-fields. Here the ground was all too open, he had to withdraw further from the brook to find a copse to hide in while he viewed the way ahead. From here he could see the roofs of the convent buildings above the garden walls, and the loftier tower and roof of the church, but nothing of the activity within. The face that was presented to him looked placid enough, the pale slope stripped of its harvest, the stack of haulms where Godith and he had hidden boat and treasure barely nineteen hours ago, the russet wall of the enclosed garden beyond, the steep roof of a barn. He would have to wait some time for full daylight to pass, or else take a risk and run for it through the brook, and into the straw-stack beyond, when he saw his opportunity. And here there were people moving from time to time about their legitimate business, a shepherd urging his flock towards the home pasture, a woman coming home from the woods with mushrooms, two children driving geese. He might very well have strolled past all these with a greeting, and been taken for granted, but he could not be seen by any of them making a sudden dash for it through the ford and into the abbey gardens. That would have been enough to call their attention and raise an alarm, and there were sounds of unusual activity, shouts and orders and the creaking of carts and harness, still echoing distantly from beyond the gardens. Moreover, there was a man on horseback in sight on his side the brook, some distance away downstream but drawing gradually nearer, patrolling this stretch of meadows as though he had been posted here to secure the one unwalled

exit from the enclave. As probably he had, though he seemed to be taking the duty very easily, ambling his mount along the green at leisure. One man only, but one was enough. He had only to shout, or whistle shrilly on his fingers, and he could bring a dozen Flemings swarming.

Torold went to ground among the bushes, and watched him approach. A big, rawboned, powerful but unhandsome horse, dappled from cream to darkest grey, and the rider a young fellow black-haired and olive-complexioned, with a thin, assured, saturnine face and an arrogantly easy carriage in the saddle. It was this light, elegant seat of his, and the striking colouring of the horse, that caught Torold's closer attention. This was the very beast he had seen leading the patrol along the riverside at dawn, and this same man had surely lighted down from his mount and gone first into Torold's abandoned sanctuary at the mill. Then he had been attended by half a dozen footmen, and had emerged to loose them in after him, before they all mustered again and moved on. Torold was sure of this identification; he had had good reason to watch very closely, dreading that in spite of his precautions they might yet find some detail to arouse suspicion. This was the same horse, and the same man. Now he rode past upstream, apparently negligent and unobservant, but Torold knew better. There was nothing this man missed as he rode, those were lively, witty, formidable eyes that cast such seemingly languid looks about him.

But now his back was turned, and no one else moved at the moment in these evening fields. If he rode on far enough, Torold might attempt the crossing. Even if he misjudged in his haste and soaked himself, he could not possibly drown in this stream, and the night would be warm. Go he must, and find his way to Godith's bed, and somehow get some reassurance.

The king's officer rode on, oblivious, to the limit of the level ground, never turning his head. And no other creature stirred. Torold picked himself up and ran for it, across the open mead, into the brook, picking his footing by luck and instinct well enough, and out upon the pale, shaven fields on the other side. Like a mole burrowing into earth, he burrowed into the stack of haulms. In the turmoil of this day it was no surprise to find boat and bundle vanished, and he had no time to consider whether the omen was bad or good. He drew the disturbed stems about him, a stiff, creamy lace threaded by sunlight and warmth, and lay quivering, his face turned to peer through the network to where the enemy rode serenely.

And the enemy had also turned, sitting the dappled horse motionless, gazing downstream as though some pricking of his thumbs had warned him. For some minutes he remained still, as easy as before, and yet as alert; then he began the return journey, as softly as he had traced it upstream.

Torold held his breath and watched him come. He made no haste, but rode his beat in idle innocence, having nothing to do, and nothing but this repeated to and fro to pass the time here. But when he drew opposite the pease-fields he reined in, and sat gazing across the brook long and steadily, and his eyes homed in upon the loose stack of haulms, and lingered. Torold thought he saw the dark face melt into a secret smile; he even thought the raised bridle-hand made a small movement that could have been a salute. Though that was idiocy, he must have imagined it! For the horseman was moving on downstream on his patrol, gazing towards the outflow from the mill and the confluence with the river beyond. Never a glance behind.

Torold lay down under his weightless covering, burrowed his tired head into his arms, and his hips into the springy turf of the headland, and fell asleep in sheer, exhausted reaction. When he awoke it was more than half dark, and very quiet. He lay for a while listening intently, and then wormed his way out into a pallid solitude above a deserted valley, and crept furtively up the slope into the abbey gardens, moving alone among the myriad sun-warmed scents of Cadfael's herbs. He found the hut, its door hospitably open to the twilight, and peered almost fearfully into the warm silence and gloom within.

"Praise God!" said Brother Cadfael, rising from the bench to haul him briskly within. "I thought you'd aim for here, I've been keeping an eye open for you every half-hour or so, and at last I have you. Here, sit down and ease your heart, we've come through well enough!"

Urgent and low, Torold asked the one thing that mattered: *"Where is Godith?"*

Chapter Nine

odith, if he had but known it, was at that moment viewing her own reflection in Aline's glass, which Constance was holding well away from her to capture more of the total image. Washed and combed and arrayed in one of Aline's gowns, brocaded in brown and gold thread, with a thin gold bandeau of Aline's round her curls, she turned this way and that to admire herself with delight at being female again, and her face was no longer that of an urchin, but of an austere young gentlewoman aware of her advantages. The soft candlelight only made her more mysterious and strange in her own eyes.

"I wish he could see me like this," she said wistfully, forgetting that so far she had not mentioned any he except Brother Cadfael, and could not now, even to Aline, reveal anything concerning Torold's person and errand beyond his name. Concerning herself she had told almost everything, but that was the acknowledgement of a debt.

"There is a he?" asked Aline, sparking with sympathetic curiosity. "And he will escort you? Wherever you are going? No, I mustn't ask you anything, it would be unfair. But why shouldn't you wear the dress for him? Once away, you can as well travel as yourself as you can in boy's clothes."

"I doubt it," said Godith ruefully. "Not the way we shall be travelling."

"Then take it with you. You could put it in that great bundle of yours. I have plenty, and if you are going with nothing, then you'll need a gown for when you reach safety."

"Oh, if you knew how you tempt me! You are kind! But I couldn't take it. And we shall have weight enough to carry, the first miles. But I do thank you, and I shall never forget."

She had tried on, for pure pleasure, Constance assisting with relish, every dress Aline had with her, and in every one she had imagined herself confronting Torold, without warning, and studying his astonished and respectful face. And somehow, in spite of not knowing where he was or how he was faring, she had spent a blissful afternoon, unshaken by doubts. Certainly he would see her in her splendour, if not in this in other fine gowns, in jewels, with her hair, grown long again, plaited and coiled upon her head in a gold circlet like this one. Then she recalled how she had sat beside him, the two of them companionably eating plums and committing the stones to the Severn through the floorboards of the mill, and she laughed. What use would it ever be, putting on airs with Torold?

She was in the act of lifting the circlet from her head when they all heard the sudden but circumspect knocking on the outer door, and for a moment froze into wary stillness, looking at one another aghast.

"Do they mean to search here, after all?" wondered Godith in a shocked whisper. "Have I brought you into danger?"

"No! Adam assured me I should not be disturbed, this morning, when they came." Aline rose resolutely. "You stay here with Constance, and bolt the door. I'll go. Can it be Brother Cadfael come for you already?"

"No, surely not yet, they'll still be on the watch."

It had sounded the most deferential of knocks, but all the same, Godith sat very still behind the bolted door, and listened with strained attention to the snatches of voices that reached her from without. Aline had brought her visitor into the room. The voice that alternated with hers was a man's, low-pitched and ardently courteous.

"Adam Courcelle!" Constance mouthed silently, and smiled her knowing smile. "So deep in love, he can't keep away!"

"And she—Aline?" whispered Godith curiously.

"Who knows! Not *she*—not yet!"

Godith had heard the same voice that morn-ing, addressing the porter and the lay servants at the gate in a very different tone. But such duties can surely give no pleasure, and may well make even a decent man ill-humoured and overbearing. This devout and considerate soul enquiring tenderly after Aline's peace of mind might be his proper self.

"I hope you have not been too much put out by all this stir," he was saying. "There'll be no more disturbances, you may rest now."

"I haven't been molested at all," Aline assured him serenely. "I have no complaint, you have been considerate indeed. But I'm sorry for those who have had goods distrained. Is the same thing happening in the town?"

"It is," he said ruefully, "and will go on tomorrow, but the abbey may be at peace now. We have finished here."

"And you did not find her? The girl you had orders to search for?"

"No, we have not found her."

"What would you say," asked Aline deliberately, "if I said that I was glad?"

"I should say that I would expect nothing else from you, and I honour you for it. I know you could not wish danger or pain or captivity to any creature, much less a blameless girl. I've learned so much of you, Aline." The brief silence was charged, and when he resumed: "Aline—" his voice sank so low that Godith could not distinguish the words. She did not want to, the tone was too intimate and urgent. But in a few moments she heard Aline say gently:

"You must not ask me to be very receptive tonight, this has been a harrowing day for so many. I can't help but feel almost as weary as they must be. And as you! Leave me to sleep long tonight, there will be a better time for talking of these matters."

"True!" he said, resuming the soldier on duty as though he squared his shoulders to a load again. "Forgive me, this was not the time. Most of my men are out of the gates by now, I'll follow them, and let you rest. You may hear marching and the carts rolling for a quarter of an hour or so, after that it will be quiet."

The voices receded, towards the outer door. Godith heard it opened, and after a few exchanged and inaudible words, closed again. She heard the bolt shot, and in a few moments more Aline tapped at the bedroom door. "You can safely open, he's gone."

She stood in the doorway, flushed and frowning, rather in private perplexity than displeasure. "It seems," she said, and smiled in a way Adam Courcelle would have rejoiced to see, "that in sheltering you I've done him no wrong. I think he's relived at *not* finding you. They're all going. It's over. Now we have only to wait for Brother Cadfael and full darkness."

In the hut in the herbarium Brother Cadfael fed, reassured and doctored his patient. Torold, once the first question had been answered so satisfactorily, lay down submissively on Godith's bed, and let his shoulder be dressed again, and the gash in his thigh, already healed, nevertheless be well bandaged and padded. "For if you're to ride into Wales this night," said Cadfael, "we don't want any damage or delays, you could all too easily break that open again."

"Tonight?" said Torold eagerly. "Is it to be tonight? She and I together?"

"It is, it must, and high time, too. I don't think I could stand this sort of thing much longer," said Cadfael, though he sounded almost complacent about it. "Not that I've had too much of the pair of you, you understand, but all the same, I'll be relieved when you're well away towards Owain Gwynedd's country, and what's more, I'll give you a token from myself to the first Welsh you encounter. Though you already have Fitz-Alan's commendation to Owain, and Owain keeps his word."

"Once mounted and started," vowed Torold heartily, "I'll take good care of Godith."

"And so will she of you. I'll see she has a pot of this salve I've been using on you, and a few things she may need."

"And she took boat and load and all with her!" mused Torold, fond and proud. "How many girls could have kept their heads and done as well? And this other girl took her in! And brought you word of it, and so wisely! I tell you, Brother Cadfael, we breed fine women here in Salop." He was silent for a moment, and grew thoughtful. "Now how are we to get her out? They may have left a guard. And anyhow, I can hardly be seen to walk out at the gate house, seeing the porter will know I never walked in that way. And the boat is there, not here."

"Hush a while," said Cadfael, finishing off his bandage neatly, "while I think. What about your own day? You've done well, it seems to me, and come out of it none the worse. And you must have left all open and innocent, for there's been no whisper about the old mill. You caught the wind of them soon, it seems."

Torold told him about the whole long, dangerous and yet inexpressibly tedious day of starting and stopping, running and hiding, loitering and hurrying. "I saw the company that combed the river bank and the mill, six armed men on foot, and an officer riding. But I'd made sure there was no sign of me left there. The officer went in first, alone, and then turned his men into it. I saw the same fellow again," he recalled, suddenly alert to the coincidence, "this evening, when I crossed the ford and dived into the stack. He was riding the far bank up and down, between river and mill-race, alone. I knew him by his seat in the saddle, and the horse he was riding. I'd made the crossing behind his back, and when he rode back downstream he halted right opposite, and sat and gazed straight at where I was hiding. I could have sworn he'd seen me. He seemed to be staring directly at me. And smiling! I was sure I was found out. But then he rode on. He can't have seen me, after all."

Cadfael put away his medicines very thoughtfully. He asked mildly: "And you knew him by his horse again? What was so notable about it?"

"The size and colour. A great, gaunt, striding beast, not beautiful but strong, and dappled clean through from creamy belly to a back and quarters all but black."

Cadfael scrubbed at his blunt brown nose, and scratched his even browner tonsure. "And the man?"

A young fellow hardly older than I. Black-avised, and a light build to him. All I saw of him this morning was the clothes he wore and the way he rode, very easy on what I should guess might be a hard-mouthed brute. But I saw his face tonight. Not much flesh, and bold bones, and black eyes and brows. He whistles to himself," said Torold, surprised at remembering this. "Very sweetly!"

So he did! Cadfael also remembered. The horse, too, he recalled, left behind in the abbey stables when two better and less noticeable had been withdrawn. Two, their owner had said, he might be willing to sacrifice, but not all four, and not the pick of the four. Yet the cull had been made, and still he rode one of the remaining two, and doubtless the other, also, was still at his disposal. So he had lied. His position with the king was already assured, he had even been on duty in today's raiding. Very selective duty? And if so, who had selected it?

"And you thought he had seen you cross?"

"When I was safe hidden I looked, and he'd turned my way. I thought he'd seen me moving, from the corner of his eye."

That one, thought Cadfael, has eyes all round his head, and what he misses is not worth marking. But all he said to Torold was: "And he halted and stared across at you, and then rode on?"

"I even thought he lifted his bridle-hand a thought to me," owned Torold, grinning at his own credulity. "By that time I doubt I was seeing visions at every turn, I was so wild to get to Godith. But then he just turned and rode on, easy as ever. So he can't have seen me, after all."

Cadfael pondered the implications of all this in wonder and admiration. Light was dawning as dusk fell into night. Not complete darkness yet, simply the departure of the sun, afterglow and all, leaving a faint greenish radiance along the west; not complete dawn, but a promising confirmation of the first elusive beams.

"He can't have, can he?" demanded Torold, fearful that he might have drawn danger after him all too near to Godith.

"Never a fear of it," said Cadfael confidently. "All's well, child, don't fret, I see my way. And now it's time for me to go to Compline. You may drop the bolt after me, and lie down here on Godith's bed and get an hour or so of sleep, for by dawn you'll be needing it. I'll come back to you as soon as service is over."

He did, however, spare the few minutes necessary to amble through the stables, and was not surprised to note that neither the dapple-grey nor its companion, the broad-backed brown cob, was in its stall. An innocent visit to the guest hall after Compline further confirmed that Hugh Beringar was not there in the apartments for gentlefolk, nor were his three men-at-arms present among the commonalty. The porter recalled that the three retainers had gone forth soon after Beringar had ridden in from his day's duties at the end of the hunt, about the time that Vespers ended, and Beringar himself had followed, in no apparent haste, an hour or so later.

So that's how things stand, is it? thought Cadfael. He's staked his hand that's it's to be tonight, and is willing to stand or fall on his wager. Well, since he's so bold and so shrewd to read my mind, let's see how good I am at reading his, and I'll stake just as boldly.

Well, then: Beringar knew from the first that his service with the king was accepted and his horses safe enough, therefore he wanted them removed for some other purpose of his own. And made a fellow-conspirator of me! Why? He could have found a refuge for himself if he'd really needed one. No, he wanted me to know just where the horses were, avail-able and inviting. He knew I had two people to deliver out of this town and out of the king's hold, and would jump at his offer for my own ends. He offered me the bait of two horses so that I should transfer the treasury to the same place, ready for flight. And finally, he had no need to hunt for his fugitives, he had only to sit back and leave it to me to bring them to the grange as soon as I could, and then he had everything in one spot, ready to be gathered in.

It follows, therefore, that tonight he'll be waiting for us, and this time with his armed men at his back.

There were still details that baffled the mind. If Beringar had indeed turned a blind eye to Torold's hiding-place this evening, for what purpose? Granted he did not know at this moment where Godith was, and might choose to let one bird fly in order to secure its mate also. But now that Cadfael came to consider all that had passed there was no escaping the possibility, to put it no higher, that through-out, Beringar had been turning a similarly blind and sparkling eye to Godith's boyish disguise, and had had a very shrewd idea of where his missing bride was to be found. In that case, if he had known Godric was Godith, and that one of FitzAlan's men was in hiding in the old mill, then as soon as he had satisfied himself that Cadfael had recovered the treasure for him he could simply have gone in force and gathered in all three prizes, and delivered them to a presumably delighted and grateful king. If he had not done so, but chosen this furtive way, it must mean something different. As, for instance, that his intent was to secure Godith and Torold and duly hand them over for his reward, but despatch FitzAlan's gold, not back to Shrewsbury, but by his own men, or indeed in person, to his own home manor, for his own private use. In which case the horses had been moved not only to fool a simple old monk, but to transfer the treasure direct to Maesbury in complete secrecy, without having to go near Shrewsbury.

That, of course, was all supposing Beringar was not Nicholas Faintree's murderer. If he was, the plan differed in one important aspect. He would see to it that though Godith went back to bait the trap for her father, Torold Blund was taken, not alive, but dead. Dead, and therefore silent. A second murder to bury the first.

Altogether a grim prospect, thought Cadfael, surprisingly undisturbed by it. Except, of course, that it could all mean something very different. Could, and does! or my name is not Cadfael, and I'll never pick a fight with a clever young man again!

He went back to the herbarium, settled in his mind and ready for another restless night. Torold was awake and alert, quick to lift the bolt as soon as he was sure who came.

"Is it time yet? Can we get round to the house on foot?" He was on thorns until he could actually see and touch her, and know that she was safe and free, and had taken no harm.

"There are always ways. But it's neither dark enough nor quiet enough yet, so sit down and rest while you may, for you'll have a share of the weight on the way, until we get to the horses. I must go to the dortoir with the rest, and to my bed. Oh, never fret, I'll be back. Once we're in our own cells, leaving is no great problem. I'm next to the night-stairs, and the prior sleeps at the far end, and sleeps like the dead. And

have you forgotten the church has a parish door, on to the Foregate? The only door not within the walls. From there to Mistress Siward's house is only a short walk, and if it passes the gate house, do you think the porter takes account of every citizen abroad somewhat late?"

"So this girl Aline could very well have gone to Mass by that door, like the rest of the laity," Torold realised, marvelling.

"So she could, but then she would have no chance to speak to me, and besides, she chose to exert her privilege with Courcelle, and show the Flemings she was to be reckoned with, the clever girl. Oh, you have a fine girl of your own, young Torold, and I hope you'll be good to her, but this Aline is only just stretching her powers to find out what she's worth, and what she can do, and trust me, she'll make such another as our Godith yet."

Torold smiled in the warm darkness within the hut, sure even in his anxiety that there was but one Godric-Godith. "You said the porter was hardly likely to pay much attention to citizens making for home late," he reminded, "but he may very well have a sharp eye for any such in a Benedictine habit."

"Who said anything about Benedictine habits drifting abroad so late? *You*, young man, shall go and fetch Godith. The parish door is never closed, and with the gate house so close seldom needs to be. I'll let you out there when the time comes. Go to the last little house, beside the mill, and bring Godith and the boat down from the pond to where the water flows back into the brook, and I shall be there, waiting."

"The third house of the three on our side," whispered Torold, glowing even in the dark.

"I know it. I'll go!" The warmth of his gratitude and pleasure filled the hut, and set the herbal fragrances stirring headily, because it would be he, and no other, who would come to fetch Godith away, more wildly and wonderfully than in any mere runaway marriage. "And you'll be on the abbey bank, when we come down to the brook?"

"I will so, and go nowhere without me! And now lie down for an hour, or less, and leave the latch in case you sleep too soundly, and I'll come for you when all's quiet."

Brother Cadfael's plans worked smoothly. The day having been so rough, all men were glad to close the shutters, put out the lights, barricade themselves in from the night, and sleep. Torold was awake and waiting before Cadfael came for him. Through the gardens, through the small court between guest hall and abbot's lodging, into the cloister, and in through the south door of the church, they went together in such a silence and stillness as belonged neither to night nor day, only to this withdrawn world between services. They never exchanged a word until they were in the church, shoulder to shoulder under the great tower and pressed against the west door. Cadfael eased the huge door ajar, and listened. Peering carefully, he could see the abbey gates, closed and dark, but the wicket gallantly open. It made only a very small lancet of twilight in the night.

"All's still. Go now! I'll be at the brook."

The boy slid through the narrow opening, and swung lightly away from the door into the middle of the roadway, as though coming from the lanes about the horse-fair. Cadfael closed the door inch by inch in silence. Without haste he withdrew as he had come, and strolled under the solitary starlight through the garden and down the field, bearing to the right along the bank of the brook until he could go no further. Then he sat down in the grass and vetches and mothpasture of the bank to wait. The August night was warm and still, just enough breeze to rustle the bushes now and then, and make the trees sigh, and cover with slight sounds the slighter sounds made by careful and experienced men. Not that they would be followed tonight. No need! The one who might have been following was already in position at the end of the journey, and waiting for them.

Constance opened the door of the house, and was startled and silenced by the apparition of this young, secular person, instead of the monk she had expected. But Godith was there, intent and burning with impatience at her shoulder, and flew past her with a brief, wordless soundless cry, into his arms and on to his heart. She was Godric again, though for him she would never now be anyone but Godith, whom he had never yet seen in her own proper person. She clung to him, and laughed, and wept, hugged, reviled, threatened him all in a breath, felt tenderly at his swathed shoulder, demanded explanations and cancelled all her demands, finally lifted to him an assuaged face in sudden silence, and waited to be kissed. Stunned and enlightened, Torold kissed her.

"You must be Torold," said Aline from the background, so serenely that she must have known rather more about their relationship, by now, than he knew himself. "Close the door, Constance, all's well." She looked him over, with eyes alert to a young man's qualities by reason of certain recent experiences of her own, and thought well of him. "I knew Brother Cadfael would send. She wanted to go back as she came this morning, but I said no. He said he would come. I didn't know he would be sending you. But Cadfael's messenger is very welcome."

"She has told you about me?" enquired Torold, a little flushed at the thought.

"Nothing but what I needed to know. She is discretion itself, and so am I," said Aline demurely. She, too, was flushed and glittering, but with excitement and enjoyment of her own plotting, half-regretful that her share must end here. "If Brother Cadfael is waiting, we mustn't lose time. The farther you get by daybreak, the better. Here is the bundle Godith brought. Wait here within, until I see if everything is quiet below in the garden."

She slipped away into the soft darkness, and stood by the edge of the pond, listening intently. She was sure they had left no guard behind, for why should they, when they had searched everywhere, and taken all they had been sent to take? Yet there might still be someone stirring in the houses opposite. But all were in darkness, she thought even the shutters were closed, in spite of the warm night, for fear some solitary Fleming should return to help himself to what he could find, under cover of the day's official looting. Even the willow leaves hung motionless here, sheltered from the faint breeze that stirred the grasses along the river bank.

"Come!" she whispered, opening the door narrowly. "All's quiet. Follow where I step, the slope is rough." She had even thought to change her pale gown for a dark one since afternoon, to be shadowy among the shadows. Torold hoisted FitzAlan's treasury in its sacking shroud by the rope that secured it, and put off Godith firmly when she would have reached to share the weight with him.

Surprisingly, she yielded meekly, and went before him very quickly and quietly to where the boat rode on its short mooring, half-concealed by the stooping willow branches. Aline lay down at the edge of the bank, and leaned to draw the boat in and hold it steady, for there was a two-foot hollow of undercut soil between them and the water. Very quickly and happily this hitherto cloistered and dutiful daughter was learning to be mistress of her own decisions and exploiter of her own powers.

Godith slid down into the boat, and lent both arms to steady the sacking bundle down between the thwarts. The boat was meant for only two people at most, and settled low in the water when Torold also was aboard, but it was buoyant and sturdy, and would get them as far as they needed to go, as it had done once before.

Godith leaned and embraced Aline, who was still on her knees at the edge of the grass. It was too late for spoken thanks then, but Torold kissed the small, well-tended hand held out to him, and then she loosed the end of the mooring-rope, and tossed it aboard, and the boat slipped out softly from under the bank and drifted across in the circling eddies of the outflow, back towards the brook from which the pool had been drawn. The spill from the head-race of the mill caught them and brisked their pace like a gentle push, and Torold sat with paddle idle, and let the silent flow take them out from the pond. When Godith looked back, all she could see was the shape of the willow, and the unlighted house beyond.

Brother Cadfael rose from among the long grasses as Torold paddled the boat across to the abbey shore. "Well done!" he said in a whisper. "And no trouble? No one stirring?"

"No trouble. Now you're the guide."

Cadfael rocked the boat thoughtfully with one hand. "Put Godith and the load ashore opposite, and then fetch me. I may as well go dry-shod." And when they were all safely across to the other side of the brook, he hauled the boat out of the water into the grass, and Godith hurried to help him carry it into hiding in the nearest copse. Once in cover, they had leisure to draw breath and confer. The night was still and calm around them, and five minutes well spent here, as Cadfael said, might save them much labour thereafter.

"We may speak, but softly. And since no other eyes, I hope, are to see this burden of ours until you're well away to the west, I think we might with advantage open it and split the load again. The saddle-bags will be far easier to sling on our shoulders than this single lump."

"I can carry one pair," said Godith, eager at his elbow.

"So you can, for a short spell, perhaps," he said indulgently. He was busy disentangling the two pairs of linked bags from the sacks that had swathed them. They had straps comfortably broad for the shoulder, and the weights in them had been balanced in the first place for the horses. "I had thought we might save ourselves half a mile or so by making use of the river for the first part of the way," he said, "but with three of us and only this hazel-shell we should founder. And it's not so far we have to go, loaded—something over three miles, perhaps."

He shook one pair of bags into the most comfortable position over his shoulder, and

Torold took the other pair on his sound side. "I never carried goods to this value before in my life," said Cadfael as he set off, "and now I'm not even to see what's within."

"Bitter stuff to me," said Torold at his back, "it cost Nick his life, and I'm to have no chance to avenge him."

"You give thought to your own life and bear your own burdens," said Cadfael. "He will be avenged. Better you should look to the future, and leave Nick to me."

The ways by which he led his little convoy differed from those he had used in Beringar's company. Instead of crossing the brook and making directly for the grange beyond Pulley, he bore more strongly to the west, so that by the time they were as far south as the grange they were also a good mile west of it, nearer to Wales, and in somewhat thicker forest.

"How if we should be followed?" wondered Godith.

"We shall not be followed." He was so positive about it that she accepted the reassurance gladly, and asked nothing more. If Brother Cadfael said it, it was so. She had insisted on carrying Torold's load for half a mile or so, but he had taken it back from her at the first sign of quickening breath or faltering step.

A lace-work of sky showed paler between the branches ahead. They emerged cautiously into the edge of a broad forest ride that crossed their path on good turf at an oblique angle. Beyond it, their own track continued, a little more open to the night than up to this point.

"Now pay good heed," said Cadfael, halting them within cover, "for you have to find your way back without me to this spot. This ride that crosses us here is a fine, straight road the old Romans made. Eastward, here to our left, it would bring us to the Severn bridge at Atcham. Westward, to our right, it will take you two straight as an arrow for Pool and Wales, or if you find any obstacle on the way, you may bear further south at the end for the ford at Montgomery. Once you're on this, you can ride fast enough, though in parts it may be steep. Now we cross it here, and have another half-mile to go to the ford of the brook. So pay attention to the way."

Here the path was clearly better used, horses could travel it without great difficulty. The ford, when they reached it, was wide and smooth. "And here," said Cadfael, "we leave our loads. One tree among so many trees you might well lose, but one tree beside the only ford along the path, and you can't lose it."

"Leave them?" wondered Torold. "Why, are we not going straight to where the horses are? You said yourself we should not be followed tonight."

"Not followed, no." When you know where your quarry must come, and are sure of the night, you can be there waiting. "No, waste no more time, trust me and do as I say." And he let down his own half of the burden, and looked about him, in the dimness to which by now their eyes were accustomed, for the best and safest concealment. In the thicket of bushes close to the ford, on their right, there was a gnarled old tree, one side of it dead, and its lowest branch deep in the cover of the bushes. Cadfael slung his saddle-bags over it, and without another word Torold hoisted his own beside them, and drew back to assure himself that only those who had hidden here were likely ever to find. The full leafage covered all.

"Good lad!" said Cadfael contentedly. "Now, from here we bear round to the east some-

what, and this path we're on will join the more direct one I used before. For we must approach the grange from the right direction. It would never do for any curious person to suppose we'd been a mile nearer Wales."

Unburdened now, they drew together and went after him hand in hand, trusting as children. And now that they were drawing nearer to the actual possibility of flight, they had nothing at all to say, but clung to each other and believed that things would go right.

Their path joined the direct one only some minutes' walk from the small clearing where the stockade of the grange rose. The sky paled as the trees fell back. There was a small rush-light burning somewhere within the house, a tiny, broken gleam showed through the pales. All round them the night hung silent and placid.

Brother Anselm opened to them, so readily that surely some aggrieved traveller from Shrewsbury must have brought word even here of the day's upheaval, and alerted him to the possibility that anyone running from worse penalties might well take warning, and get out at once. He drew them within thankfully and in haste, and peered curiously at the two young fellows at Cadfael's back, as he closed the gate.

"I thought it! My thumbs pricked. I felt it must be tonight. Things grow very rough your way, so we've heard."

"Rough enough," admitted Cadfael, sighing. "I'd wish any friend well out of it. And most of all these two. Children, these good brothers have cared for your trust, and have it here safe for you. Anselm, this is Adeney's daughter, and this FitzAlan's squire. Where is Louis?"

"Saddling up," said Brother Anselm, "the moment he saw who came. We had it in mind the whole day that you'd have to hurry things. I've put food together, in case you came. Here's the scrip. It's ill to ride too far empty. And a flask of wine here within."

"Good! And these few things I brought," said Cadfael, emptying his own pouch. "They're medicines. Godith knows how to use them."

Godith and Torold listened and marvelled. The boy said, almost tongue-tied with wondering gratitude: "I'll go and help with the saddling." He drew his hand from Godith's and made for the stables, across the small untended court. This forest assart, unmanageable in such troubled times, would soon be forest again, these timber buildings, always modest enough, would moulder into the lush growth of successive summers. The Long Forest would swallow it without trace in three years, or four.

"Brother Anselm," said Godith, running an awed glance from head to foot of the giant, "I do thank you with all my heart, for both of us, for what you have done for us two—though I think it was really for Brother Cadfael here. He has been my master eight days now, and I understand. This and more I would do for him, if ever I might. I promise you Torold and I will never forget, and never debase what you've done for us."

"God love you, child," said Brother Anselm, charmed and amused, "you talk like a holy book. What should a decent man do, when a young woman's threatened, but see her safe out of her trouble? And her young man with her!"

Brother Louis came from the stables leading the roan Beringar had ridden when first these two horses of his were brought here by night. Torold followed with the black.

They shone active and ready in the faint light, excellently groomed and fed, and well rested.

"And the baggage," said Brother Anselm significantly. "That we have safe. For my own part I would have parted it into two, to balance it better on a beast, but I thought I had no right to open it, so it stays as you left it, in one. I should hoist it to the crupper with the lighter weight as rider, but as you think fit."

They were away, the pair of them, to haul out the sackbound bundle Cadfael had carried here some nights ago. It seemed there were some things they had not been told, just as there were things Torold and Godith had accepted without understanding. Anselm brought the burden from the house on his huge shoulders, and dumped it beside the saddled horses. "I brought thongs to buckle it to the saddle." They had indeed given some thought to this, they had fitted loops of cord to the rope bindings, and were threading their thongs into these when a blade sliced down through the plaited cords that held the latch of the gate behind them, and a clear, assured voice ordered sharply:

"Halt as you stand! Let no man move! Turn hither, all, and slowly, and keep your hands visible. For the lady's sake!"

Like men in a dream they turned as the voice commanded, staring with huge, wary eyes. The gate in the stockade stood wide open, lifted aside to the pales. In the open gateway stood Hugh Beringar, sword in hand; and over either shoulder leaned a bended long-bow, with a braced and competent eye and hand behind it; and both of them were aimed at Godith. The light was faint but steady. Those used to it here were well able to use it to shoot home.

"Admirable!" said Beringar approvingly. "You have understood me very well. Now stay as you are, and let no man move, while my third man closes the gates behind us."

Chapter Ten

They had all reacted according to their natures. Brother Anselm looked round cautiously for his cudgel, but it was out of reach, Brother Louis kept both hands in sight, as ordered, but the right one very near the slit seam of his gown, beneath which he kept his dagger. Godith, first stunned into incredulous dismay, very quickly revived into furious anger, though only the set whiteness of her face and the glitter of her eyes betrayed it. Brother Cadfael, with what appeared to be shocked resignation, sat down upon the sacking bundle, so that his skirts hid it from sight if it had not already been noted and judged of importance. Torold, resisting the instinct to grip the hilt of Cadfael's poniard at his belt, displayed empty hands, stared Beringar in the eye defiantly, and took two long, deliberate paces to place himself squarely between Godith and the two archers. Brother Cadfael admired, and smiled inwardly. Probably it had not occurred to the boy, in his devoted state, that there had been ample time for both arrows to find their target before his body intervened, had that been the intention.

"A very touching gesture," admitted Beringar generously, "but hardly effective. I doubt if the lady is any happier with the situation that way round. And since we're all sensible beings here, there's no need for pointless heroics. For that matter, Matthew here could put an arrow clean through the pair of you at this distance, which would benefit nobody, not even me. You may as well accept that for the moment I am giving the orders and calling the tune."

And so he was. However his men had held their hands when they might have taken his order against any movement all too literally, it remained true that none of them had the slightest chance of making an effective attack upon him and changing the reckoning. There were yards of ground between, and no dagger is ever going to outreach an arrow. Torold stretched an arm behind him to draw Godith close, but she would not endure it. She pulled back sharply to free herself, and eluding the hand that would have detained her, strode forward defiantly to confront Hugh Beringar.

"What manner of tune," she demanded, "for me? If I'm what you want, very well, here I am, what's your will with me? I suppose I still have lands of my own, worth securing? Do you mean to stand on your rights, and marry me for them? Even if my father is dispossessed, the king might let my lands and me go to one of his new captains! Am I worth that much to you? Or is it just a matter of buying Stephen's favour, by giving me to him as bait to lure better men back into his power?"

"Neither," said Beringar placidly. He was eyeing her braced shoulders and roused, contemptuous face with decided appreciation. "I admit, my dear, that I never felt so tempted to marry you before—you're greatly improved from the fat little girl I remember. But to judge by your face, you'd as soon marry the devil himself, and I have other plans, and so, I fancy, have you. No, provided everyone here acts like a sensible creature, we need not quarrel. And if it needs saying for your own comfort, Godith, I have no intention of setting the hounds on your champion's trail, either. Why should I bear malice against an honest opponent? Especially now I'm sure he finds favour in your eyes."

He was laughing at her, and she knew it, and took warning. It was not even malicious laughter, though she found it an offence. It was triumphant, but it was also light, teasing, almost affectionate. She drew back a step; she even cast one appealing glance at Brother Cadfael, but he was sitting slumped and apparently apathetic, his eyes on the ground. She looked up again, and more attentively, at Hugh Beringar, whose black eyes dwelt upon her with dispassionate admiration.

"I do believe," she said slowly, wondering, "that you mean it."

"Try me! You came here to find horses for your journey. There they are! You may mount and ride as soon as you please, you and the young squire here. No one will follow you. No one else knows you're here, only I and my men. But you'll ride the faster and safer if you lighten your loads of all but the necessaries of life," said Beringar sweetly. "That bundle Brother Cadfael is so negligently sitting on, as if he thought he'd found a convenient stone—that I'll keep, by way of a memento of you, my sweet Godith, when you're gone."

Godith had just enough self-control not to look again at Brother Cadfael when she heard this. She had enough to do keeping command of her own face, not to betray the lightning-stroke of understanding, and triumph, and laughter, and so, she knew, had Torold, a few paces behind her, and equally dazzled and enlightened. So that was why they had slung the saddlebags on the tree by the ford, a mile to the west, a mile on their way into Wales. This prize here they could surrender with joyful hearts, but never a glimmer of joy must show through to threaten the success. And now it lay with her to perfect the coup, and Brother Cadfael was leaving it to her. It was the greatest test she had ever faced, and it was vital to her self-esteem for ever. For this man fronting her was more than she had thought him, and suddenly it seemed that giving him up was almost as generous a gesture as this gesture of his, turning her loose to her happiness with another man and another cause, only distraining the small matter of gold for his pains. For two fine horses, and a free run into Wales! And a kind of blessing, too, secular but valued.

"You mean that," she said, not questioning, stating. "We may go!"

"And quickly, if I dare advise. The night is not old yet, but it matures fast. And you have some way to go."

"I have mistaken you," she said magnanimously. "I never knew you. You had a right to try for this prize. I hope you understand that we had also a right to fight for it. In a fair win and a fair defeat there should be no heart-burning. Agreed?"

"Agreed!" he said delightedly. "You are an opponent after my own heart, and I think your young squire had better take you hence, before I change my mind. As long as you leave the baggage..."

"No help for it, it's yours," said Brother Cadfael, rising reluctantly from his seat on guard. "You won it fairly, what else can I say?"

Beringar surveyed without disquiet the mound of sacking presented to view. He knew very well the shape of the hump Cadfael had carried here from Severn, he had no misgivings.

"Go, then, and good speed! You have some hours of darkness yet." And for the first time he looked at Torold, and took his time about studying him, for Torold had held his peace and let her have her head in circumstances he could not be expected to understand, and with admirable self-restraint. "I ask your pardon, I don't know your name."

"My name is Torold Blund, a squire of FitzAlan's."

"I'm sorry that we never knew each other. But not sorry that we never had ado in arms, I fear I should have met my overmatch." But he was very sunny about it, having got his way, and he was not really much in awe of Torold's longer reach, and greater height. "You

take good care of your treasure, Torold, I'll take care of mine."

Sobered and still, watching him with great eyes that still questioned, Godith said: "Kiss me and wish me well! As I do you!"

"With all my heart!" said Beringar, and turned her face up between his hands, and kissed her soundly. The kiss lasted long, perhaps to provoke Torold, but Torold watched and was not dismayed. These could have been brother and sister saying a fond but untroubled farewell. "Now mount, and good speed!"

She went first to Brother Cadfael, and asked his kiss also, with a frantic quiver in her voice and her face that no one else saw or heard, and that might have been of threatened tears, or of almost uncontrollable laughter, or of both together. The thanks she said to him and to the lay brothers were necessarily brief, being hampered by the same wild mixture of emotions. She had to escape quickly, before she betrayed herself. Torold went to hold her stirrup, but Brother Anselm hoisted her between his hands and set her lightly in the saddle. The stirrups were a little long for her, he bent to shorten them to her comfort, and then she saw him look up furtively and flash her a grin, and she knew that he, too, had fathomed what was going on, and shared her secret laughter. If he and his comrade had been let into the whole plot from the beginning, they might not have played their parts so convincingly; but they were very quick to pick up all the undercurrents.

Torold mounted Beringar's roan, and looked down from the saddle at the whole group within the stockade. The archers had unstrung their bows, and stood by looking on with idle interest and some amusement, while the third man opened the gate wide to let the travellers pass.

"Brother Cadfael, everything I owe to you. I shall not forget."

"If there's anything owing," said Cadfael comfortably, "you can repay it to Godith. And see you mind your ways with her until you bring her safe to her father," he added sternly. "She's in your care as a sacred charge, beware of taking any advantage."

Torold's smile flashed out brilliantly for an instant, and was gone; and the next moment so was Torold himself, and Godith after him, trotting out briskly through the open gate into the luminosity of the clearing, and thence into the shadowy spaces between the trees. They had but a little way to go to the wider path, and the ford of the brook, where the saddle-bags waited. Cadfael stood listening to the soft thudding of hooves in the turf, and the occasional rustling of leafy branches, until all sounds melted into the night's silence. When he stirred out of his attentive stillness, it was to find that every other soul there had been listening just as intently. They looked at one another, and for a moment had nothing to say.

"If she comes to her father a virgin," said Beringar then, "I'll never stake on man or woman again."

"It's my belief," said Cadfael, drily, "she'll come to her father a wife, and very proper, too. There are plenty of priests between here and Normandy. She'll have more trouble persuading Torold he has the right to take her, unapproved, but she'll have her own ways of convincing him."

"You know her better than I," said Beringar. "I hardly knew the girl at all! A pity!" he added thoughtfully.

"Yet I think you recognised her the first time you ever saw her with me in the great court."

"Oh, by sight, yes—I was not sure then, but within a couple of days I was. She's not so changed in looks, only fined into such a springy young fellow." He caught Cadfael's eye, and smiled. "Yes, I did come looking for her, but not to hand her over to any man's use. Nor that I wanted her for myself, but she was, as you said, a sacred charge upon me. I owed it to the alliance others made for us to see her into safety."

"I trust," said Cadfael, "that you have done so."

"I, too. And no hard feelings upon either side?"

"None. And no revenges. The game is over." He sounded, he realised suddenly, appropriately subdued and resigned, but it was only the pleasant weariness of relief.

"Then you'll ride back with me to the abbey, and keep me company on the way? I have two horses here. And these lads of mine have earned their sleep, and if your good brothers will give them house-room overnight, and feed them, they may make their way back at leisure tomorrow. To sweeten their welcome, there's two flasks of wine in my saddle-bags, and a pasty. I feared we might have a longer wait, though I was sure you'd come."

"I had a feeling," said Brother Louis, rubbing his hands with satisfaction, "for all the sudden alarm, that there was no real mischief in the wind tonight. And for two flasks of wine and a pasty we'll offer you beds with pleasure, and a game of tables if you've a mind for it. We get very little company here."

One of the archers led in from the night

Beringar's two remaining horses, the tall, rangy dapple-grey and the sturdy brown cob, and placidly lay brothers and men-at-arms together unloaded the food and drink, and at Beringar's orders made the unwieldy, sacking-wrapped bundle secure on the dapple's croup, well balanced and fastened with Brother Anselm's leather straps, provided with quite another end in view. "Not that I wouldn't trust it with you on the cob," Beringar assured Cadfael, "but this great brute will never even notice the weight. And his rider needs a hard hand, for he has a hard mouth and a contrary will, and I'm used to him. To tell truth, I love him. I parted with two better worth keeping, but this hellion is my match, and I wouldn't change him."

He could not better have expressed what Cadfael was thinking about him. This hellion is my match, and I wouldn't change him! He did his own spying, he gave away generously two valuable horses to discharge his debt to a bride he never really wanted, and he went to all manner of patient, devious shifts to get the girl safe and well out of his path, and lay hand upon the treasury, which was fair game, as she was not. Well, well, we live and learn in the book of our fellowmen!

They rode together, they two alone, by the same road as once before, and even more companionably than then. They went without haste, unwinding the longer way back, the way fitter for horses, the way they had first approached the grange. The night was warm, still and gentle, defying the stormy and ungentle times with its calm assertion of permanent stability.

"I am afraid," said Hugh Beringar with compunction, "you have missed Matins and Lauds, and the fault is mine. If I had not delayed everything, you might have been back for midnight. You and I should share whatever penance is due."

"You and I," said Cadfael cryptically, "share a penance already. Well, I could not wish for more stimulating company. We many compound my offence by riding at ease. It is not often a man gets such a night ride, and safely, and at peace."

Then they were silent for some way, and thought their own thoughts, but somewhere the threads tangled, for after a while Beringar said with assurance: "You will miss her." It was said with brisk but genuine sympathy. He had, after all, been observing and learning for some days.

"Like a fibre gone from my heart," owned Brother Cadfael without dismay, "but there'll be others will fill the place. She was a good girl, and a good lad, too, if you'll grant me the fancy. Quick to study, and a hard worker. I hope she'll make as good a wife. The young man's a fair match for her. You saw he favoured one shoulder? One of the king's archers did his best to slice the round of it off him, but with Godith's care now he'll do well enough. They'll reach France." And after a moment's thought he asked, with candid curiosity: "What would you have done if any one of us had challenged your orders and made a fight of it?"

Hugh Beringar laughed aloud. "I fancy I should have looked the world's fool, for of course my men knew better than to shoot. But the bow is a mighty powerful persuader, and after all, an unchancy fellow like me *might* be in earnest. Why, you never thought I'd harm the girl?"

Cadfael debated the wisdom of answering

that truthfully as yet, and temporised: "If I ever thought of it, I soon realised I was wrong. They could have killed before ever Torold stepped between. No, I soon gave up that error."

"And it does not surprise you that I knew what you had brought to the grange, and what you came to fetch tonight?"

"No revelation of your cunning can surprise me any longer," said Cadfael. "I conclude that you followed me from the river the night I brought it. Also that you had procured me to help you place the horses there for a dual purpose, to encourage me to transfer the treasure from wherever it was hidden, and to make it possible for those youngsters to escape, while the gold stayed here. The right hand duelling against the left, that fits you well. Why were you so sure it would be tonight?"

"Faith, if I'd been in your shoes *I* would have got them away with all the haste I could, at this favourable time, when search had been made and failed. You would have had to be a fool to let the chance slip. And as I have found long ago, you are no fool, Brother Cadfael."

"We have much in common," agreed Cadfael gravely. "But once you knew that lump you're carrying there was safe in the grange, why did you not simply remove it, and make sure of it? You could still have let the children depart without it, just as they've done now."

"And sleep in my bed while they rode away? And never make my peace with Godith, but let her go into France believing me her enemy, and capable of such meanness? No, that I could not stomach. I have my vanity. I wanted a clean end, and no grudges. I have my curiosity, too. I wanted to see this young

fellow who had taken her fancy. The treasure was safe enough until you chose to get them away, why should I be uneasy about it? And this way was far more satisfying."

"That," agreed Cadfael emphatically, "it certainly was."

They were at the edge of the forest, and the open road at Sutton, and were turning north towards St Giles, all in amicable ease, which seemed to surprise neither of them.

"This time," said Beringar, "we'll ride in at the gate house like orderly members of the household, even if the time is a little unusual. And if you have no objection, we may as well take this straight to your hut in the garden, and sit out the rest of the night, and see what we have here. I should like to see how Godith has been living in your care, and what skills she's been acquiring. I wonder how far they'll be by now?"

"Halfway to Pool, or beyond. Most of the way it's a good road. Yes, come and see for yourself. You went enquiring for her in the town, did you not? At Edric Flesher's. Petronilla had the worst opinion of your motives."

"She would," agreed Beringar, laughing. "No one would ever have been good enough for her chick, she hated me from the start. Ah, well, you'll be able to put her mind at rest now."

They had reached the silent Abbey Foregate, and rode between the darkened houses, the ring of hooves eerie in the stillness. A few uneasy inhabitants opened their shutters a crack to look out as they passed, but their appearance was so leisured and peaceful that no one could suspect them of harmful intent. The wary citizens went back to bed reassured. Over the high, enclosing wall the great church loomed on their left hand, and the narrow opening of the wicket showed in the dark bulk of the gate. The porter was a lay brother, a little surprised at being roused to let in two horsemen at such an hour, but satisfied, on recognising both of them, that they must have been employed on some legitimate errand, no great marvel in such troublous times. He was incurious and sleepy, and did not wait to see them cross to the stables, where they tended their horses first, as good grooms should, before repairing to the garden hut with their load.

Beringar grimaced when he hoisted it. "You carried this on your back all that way?" he demanded with raised brows.

"I did," said Cadfael truthfully, "and you witnessed it."

"Then I call that a noble effort. You would not care to shoulder it again these few paces?"

"I could not presume," said Cadfael. "It's in your charge now."

"I was afraid of that!" But he was in high good humour, having fulfilled his idea of himself, made his justification in Godith's eyes, and won the prize he wanted; and he had more sinew in his slenderness than anyone would have thought, for he lifted and carried the weight lightly enough the short way to the herbarium.

"I have flint and tinder here somewhere," said Cadfael, going first into the hut. "Wait till I make you a light, there are breakables all round us here." He found his box, and struck sparks into the coil of charred cloth, and lit the floating wick in his little dish of oil. The flame caught and steadied, and drew tall and still, shedding a gentle light on all the strange shapes of mortars and flasks and bottles, and the bunches of drying herbs that made the air aromatic.

"You are an alchemist," said Beringar, impressed and charmed. "I am not sure you are not a wizard." He set down his load in the middle of the floor, and looked about him with interest. "This is where she spent her nights?" He had observed the bed, still rumpled from Torold's spasmodic and unquiet sleep. "You did this for her. You must have found her out the very first day."

"So I did. It was not so difficult. I was a long time in the world. Will you taste my wine? It's made from pears, when the crop's good."

"Gladly! And drink to your better success—against all opponents but Hugh Beringar."

He was on his knees by then, unknotting the rope that bound his prize. One sack disgorged another, the second a third. It could not be said that he was feverish in his eagerness, or showed any particular greed, only a certain excited curiosity. Out of the third sack rolled a tight bundle of cloth, dark-coloured, that fell apart as it was freed from constriction, and shed two unmistakable sleeves across the earth floor. The white of a shirt showed among the tangle of dark colours, and uncurled to reveal three large, smooth stones, a coiled leather belt, a short dagger in a leather sheath. Last of all, out of the centre something hard and small and bright rolled and lay still, shedding yellow flashes as it moved, burning sullenly gold and silver when it lay still at Beringar's feet.

And that was all.

On his knees, he stared and stared, in mute incomprehension, his black brows almost elevated into his hair, his dark eyes round with astonishment and consternation. There was nothing more to be read, in a countenance for once speaking volubly, no recoil, no alarm, no guilt. He leaned forward, and with a sweep of his hand parted all those mysterious garments, spread them abroad, gaped at them, and fastened on the stones. His eyebrows danced, and came down to their normal level, his eyes blazing understanding; he cast one glittering glance at Cadfael, and then he began to laugh, a huge, genuine laughter that shook him where he knelt, and made the bunches of herbs bob and quiver over his head. A good, open, exuberant sound it was; it made Cadfael, even at this moment, shake and laugh with him.

"And I have been commiserating with you," gasped Beringar, wiping tears from his eyes with the back of his hand, like a child, "all this time, while you had this in store for me! What a fool I was, to think I could out-trick you, when I almost had your measure even then."

"Here, drink this down," urged Cadfael, offering the beaker he had filled. "To your own better success—with all opponents but Cadfael!"

Beringar took it, and drank heartily. "Well, you deserve that. You have the last laugh, but at least you lent it to me a while, and I shall never enjoy a better. What was it you did? How was it done? I swear I never took my eyes from you. You *did* draw up what that young man of yours had drowned there, I heard it rise, I heard the water run from it on the stone."

"So I did, and let it down again, but very softly. This one I had ready in the boat. The other Godith and her squire drew up as soon as you and I were well on our way."

"And have it with them now?" asked Beringar, momentarily serious.

"They have. By now, I hope, in Wales, where Owain Gwynedd's hand will be over them."

"So all the while you knew that I was watching and following you?"

"I knew you must, if you wanted to find your treasure. No one else could lead you to it. If you cannot shake off surveillance," said Brother Cadfael sensibly, "the only thing to do is make use of it."

"That you certainly did. My treasure!" echoed Beringar, and looked it over and laughed afresh. "Well, now I understand Godith better. In a fair win and a fair defeat, she said, there should be no heartburning! And there shall be none!" He looked again, more soberly, at the things spread before him on the earth floor, and after some frowning thought looked up just as intently at Cadfael. "The stones and the sacks, anything to make like for like," he said slowly, "that I understand. But why these? What are these things to do with me?"

"You recognise none of them—I know. They are nothing to do with you, happily for you and for me. These," said Cadfael, stooping to pick up and shake out shirt and hose and cotte, "are the clothes Nicholas Faintree was wearing when he was strangled by night, in a hut in the woods above Frankwell, and thrown among the executed under the castle wall, to cover up the deed."

"Your one man too many," said Beringar, low-voiced.

"The same. Torold Blund rode with him, but they were separated when this befell. The murderer was waiting also for him, but with the second one he failed. Torold won away with his charge."

"That part I know," said Beringar. "The last he said to you, and you to him, that evening in the mill, that I heard, but no more."

He looked long at the poor relics, the dark brown hose and russet cotte, a young squire's best. He looked up at Cadfael, and eyed him steadily, very far from laughter now. "I understand. You put these together to spring upon me when I was unprepared—when I looked for something very different. For me to see, and recoil from my own guilt. If this happened the night after the town fell, I had ridden out alone, as I recall. And I had been in the town the same afternoon, and to say all, yes, I did gather more than she bargained for from Petronilla. I knew this was in the wind, that there were two in Frankwell waiting for darkness before they rode. Though what I was listening for was a clue to Godith, and that I got, too. Yes, I see that I might well be suspect. But do I seem to you a man who would kill, and in so foul a fashion, just to secure the trash those children are carrying away with them into Wales?"

"Trash?" echoed Cadfael, mildly and thoughtfully.

"Oh, pleasant to have, and useful, I know. But once you have enough of it for your needs, the rest of it is trash. Can you eat it, wear it, ride it, keep off the rain and the cold with it, read it, play music on it, make love to it?"

"You can buy the favour of kings with it," suggested Cadfael, but very placidly.

"I have the king's favour. He blows too many ways as his advisers persuade him, but left alone he knows a man when he finds one. And he demands unbecoming services when he's angry and vengeful, but he despises those who run too servilely to perform, and never leave him time to think better of his vindictiveness. I was with him in his camp a part of that evening, he has accepted me to hold my

own castles and border for him, and raise the means and the men in my own way, which suits me very well. Yes, I would have liked, when such a chance offered, to secure FitzAlan's gold for him, but losing it is no great matter, and it was a good fight. So answer me, Cadfael, do I seem to you a man who would strangle his fellow-man from behind for money?"

"No! There were the circumstances that made it a possibility, but long ago I put that out of mind. You are no such man. You value yourself too high to value a trifle of gold above your self-esteem. I was as sure as man could well be, before I put it to the test tonight," said Cadfael, "that you wished Godith well out of her peril, and were nudging my elbow with the means to get her away. To try at the same time for the gold was fair dealing enough. No, you are not my man. There is not much," he allowed consideringly, "that I would put out of your scope, but killing by stealth is one thing I would never look for from you, now that I know you. Well, so you can't help me. There's nothing here to shake you, and nothing for you to recognise."

"Not recognise—no, not that." Beringar picked up the yellow topaz in its broken silver claw, and turned it thoughtfully in his hands. He rose, and held it to the lamp to examine it better. "I never saw it before. But for all that, my thumbs prick. This, after a fashion, I think I may know. I watched with Aline while she prepared her brother's body for burial. All his things she put together and brought them, I think, to you to be given as alms, all but the shirt that was stained with his death-sweat. She spoke of something that was not there, but should have been there—a dagger that was hereditary in her family, and went always to the eldest son when he came of age. As she described it to me, I do believe this may be the great stone that tipped the hilt." He looked up with furrowed brows. "Where did you find this? Not on your dead man!"

"Not on him, no. But trampled into the earth floor, where Torold had rolled and struggled with the murderer. And it does not belong to any dagger of Torold's. There is only one other who can have worn it."

"Are you saying," demanded Beringar, aghast, "that it was Aline's brother who slew Faintree? Has she to bear that, too?"

"You are forgetting, for once, your sense of time," said Brother Cadfael reassuringly. "Giles Siward was dead several hours before Nicholas Faintree was murdered. No, never fear, there's no guilt there can touch Aline. No, rather, whoever killed Nicholas Faintree had first robbed the body of Giles, and went to his ambush wearing the dagger he had contemptibly stolen."

Beringar sat down abruptly on Godith's bed, and held his head hard between his hands. "For God's sake, give me more wine, my mind no longer works." And when his beaker was refilled he drank thirstily, picked up the topaz again and sat weighing it in his hand. "Then we have some indication of the man you want. He was surely present through part, at any rate, of that grisly work done at the castle, for there, if we're right, he lifted the pretty piece of weaponry to which this thing belongs. But he left before the work ended, for it went on into the night, and by then, it seems, he was lurking in ambush on the other side Frankwell. How did he learn of their plans? May not one of those poor wretches have tried to buy his own life by betraying them? Your man was there when the killing

began, but left well before the end. Prestcote was there surely, Ten Heyt and his Flemings were there and did the work, Courcelle, I hear, fled the business as soon as he could, and took to the cleaner duties of scouring the town for FitzAlan, and small blame to him."

"Not all the Flemings," Cadfael pointed out, "speak English."

"But some do. And among those ninety-four surely more than half spoke French just as well. Any one of the Flemings might have taken the dagger. A valuable piece, and a dead man has no more need of it. Cadfael, I tell you, I feel as you do about this business, such a death must not go unavenged. Don't you think, since it can't be any further grief or shame to her, I might show this thing to Aline, and make certain whether it is or is not from the hilt she knew?"

"I think," said Cadfael, "that you may. And after chapter we'll meet again here, if you will. If, that is, I am not so loaded with penance at chapter that I vanish from men's sight for a week."

In the event, things turned out very differently. If his absence at Matins and Lauds had been noticed at all, it was clean forgotten before chapter, and no one, not even Prior Robert, ever cast it up at him or demanded penance. For after the former day's excitement and distress, another and more hopeful upheaval loomed. King Stephen with his new levies, his remounts and his confiscated provisions, was about to move south towards Worcester, to attempt inroads into the western stronghold of Earl Robert of Gloucester, the Empress Maud's half-brother and loyal champion. The vanguard of his army was to march the next day, and the king himself, with his personal guard, was moving today into Shrewsbury castle for two nights, to inspect and secure his defences there, before marching after the vanguard. He was well satisfied with the results of his foraging, and disposed to forget any remaining grudges, for he had invited to his table at the castle, this Tuesday evening, both Abbot Heribert and Prior Robert, and in the flurry of preparation minor sins were overlooked.

Cadfael repaired thankfully to his workshop, and lay down and slept on Godith's bed until Hugh Beringar came to wake him. Hugh had the topaz in his hand, and his face was grave and tired, but serene.

"It is hers. She took it in her hands gladly, knowing it for her own. I thought there could not be two such. Now I am going to the castle, for the king's party are already moving in there, and Ten Heyt and his Flemings will be with him. I mean to find the man, whoever he may be, who filched that dagger after Giles was dead. Then we shall know we are not far from your murderer. Cadfael, can you not get Abbot Heribert to bring you with him to the castle this evening? He must have an attendant, why not you? He turns to you willingly, if you ask, he'll jump at you. Then if I have anything to tell, you'll be close by."

Brother Cadfael yawned, groaned and kept his eyes open unwillingly on the young, dark face that leaned over him, a face of tight, bright lines now, fierce and bleak, a hunting face. He had won himself a formidable ally.

"A small, mild curse on you for waking me," he said, mumbling, "but I'll come."

"It was your own cause," Beringar reminded him, smiling.

"It *is* my cause. Now for the love of God, go away and let me sleep away dinner, and afternoon and all, you've cost me hours enough to shorten my life, you plague."

Hugh Beringar laughed, though it was a muted and burdened laugh this time, marked a cross lightly on Cadfael's broad brown forehead, and left him to his rest.

Chapter
Eleven

server for every plate was required at the king's supper. It was no problem to suggest to Abbot Heribert that the brother who had coped with the matter of the mass burial, and even talked with the king concerning the unlicensed death, should be on hand with him to be questioned at need. Prior Robert took with him his invariable toady and shadow, Brother Jerome, who would certainly be indefatigable with finger-bowl, napkin and pitcher throughout, a great deal more assiduous than Cadfael, whose mind might well be occupied elsewhere. They were old enemies, in so far as Brother Cadfael entertained enmities. He abhorred a sickly-pale tonsure.

The town was willing to put on a festival face, not so much in the king's honour as in celebration of the fact that the king was about to depart, but the effect was much the same. Edric Flesher had come down to the high street from his shop to watch the guests pass by, and Cadfael flashed him a ghost of a wink, by way of indication that they would have things to discuss later, things so satisfactory that they could well be deferred. He got a huge grin and a wave of a meaty hand in response, and knew his message had been received. Petronilla would weep for her lamb's departure, but rejoice for her safe delivery and apt escort. I must go there soon, he thought, as soon as this last duty is done.

Within the town gate Cadfael had seen the blind old man sitting almost proudly in Giles Siward's good cloth hose, holding out his palm for alms with a dignified gesture. At the high cross he saw the little old woman clasping by the hand her feeble-wit grandson with his dangling lip, and the fine brown cotte sat well on him, and gave him an air of rapt content by its very texture. Oh, Aline, you ought to give your own charity, and see what it confers, beyond food and clothing!

Where the causeway swept up from the street to the gate of the castle, the beggars who followed the king's camp had taken up new stations, hopeful and expectant, for the king's justiciar, Bishop Robert of Salisbury, had arrived to join his master, and brought a train of wealthy and important clerics with him. In the lee of the gate-house wall Lame Osbern's little trolley was drawn up, where he could beg comfortably without having to move. The worn wooden pattens he used for his callused knuckles lay tidily beside him on the trolley, on top of the folded black cloak he would not need until night fell. It was so folded that the bronze clasp at the neck showed up proudly against the black, the dragon of eternity with his tail in his mouth.

Cadfael let the others go on through the gates, and halted to say a word to the crippled man. "Well, how have you been since last I saw you by the king's guard-post? You have a better place here."

"I remember you," said Osbern, looking up at him with eyes remarkably clear and innocent, in a face otherwise as misshapen as his body. "You are the brother who brought me the cloak."

"And has it done you good service?"

"It has, and I have prayed for the lady, as you asked. But, brother, it troubles me, too. Surely the man who wore it before me is dead. Is it so?"

"He is," said Cadfael, "but that should not trouble you. The lady who sent it to you is his sister, and trust me, her giving blesses the gift. Wear it, and take comfort."

He would have walked on then, but a hasty hand caught at the skirt of his habit, and Osbern besought him pleadingly: "But, brother, I go in dread that I bear some guilt. For I saw the man, living, with this cloak about him, hale as I..."

"You *saw* him?" echoed Cadfael on a soundless breath, but the anxious voice had ridden over him and rushed on.

"It was in the night, and I was cold, and I thought to myself, I wish the good God would send me such a cloak to keep me warm! Brother, thought is also prayer! And no more than three days later God did indeed send me this very cloak. You dropped it into my arms! How can I be at peace? The young man gave me a groat that night, and asked me to say a prayer for him on the morrow, and so I did. But how if my first prayer made the second of none effect? How if I have prayed a man into his grave to get myself a cloak to wear?"

Cadfael stood gazing at him amazed and mute, feeling the chill of ice flow down his spine. The man was sane, clear of mind and eye, he knew very well what he was saying, and his trouble of heart was real and deep, and must be the first consideration, whatever else followed.

"Put all such thoughts out of your mind, friend," said Cadfael firmly, "for only the devil can have sent them. If God gave you the thing for which you wished, it was to save one morsel of good out of a great evil for which you are no way to blame. Surely your prayers for the former wearer are of aid even now to his soul. This young man was one of FitzAlan's garrison here, done to death after the castle fell, at the king's orders. You need have no fears, his death is not at your door, and no sacrifice of yours could have saved him."

Osbern's uplifted face eased and brightened, but still he shook his head, bewildered. "FitzAlan's man? But how could that be, when I saw him enter and leave the king's camp?"

"You saw him? You are sure? How do you know this is the same cloak?"

"Why, by this clasp at the throat. I saw it

clearly in the firelight when he gave me the groat."

He could not be mistaken, then, there surely were not two such designs exactly alike, and Cadfael himself had seen its match on the buckle of Giles Siward's sword-belt.

"When was it that you saw him?" he asked gently. "Tell me how it befell."

"It was the night before the assault, around midnight. I had my place then close to the guard-post for the sake of the fire, and I saw him come, not openly, but like a shadow, among the bushes. He stood when they challenged him, and asked to be taken to their officer, for he had something to tell, to the king's advantage. He kept his face hidden, but he was young. And afraid! But who was not afraid, then? They took him away within, and afterwards I saw him return, and they let him out. He said he had orders to go back, for there must be no suspicion. That was all I heard. He was in better heart then, not so frightened, so I asked him for alms, and he gave, and asked my prayers in return. Say some prayer for me tomorrow, he said—and on the morrow, you tell me, he died! This I'm sure of, when he left me he was not expecting to die."

"No," said Cadfael, sick with pity and grief for all poor, frightened, breakable men, "surely he was not. None of us knows the day. But pray for him you may, and your prayers will benefit his soul. Put off all thought that ever you did him harm, it is not so. You never wished him ill, God hears the heart. Never wished him any, never did him any."

He left Osbern reassured and comforted, but went on into the castle carrying with him the load of discomfort and depression the lame man had shed. So it always is, he thought, to relieve another you must burden yourself. And such a burden! He remembered in time that there was one more question he should have asked, the most urgent of all, and turned back to ask it.

"Do you know, friend, who was the officer of the guard, that night?"

Osbern shook his head. "I never saw him, he never came out himself. No, brother, that I can't tell you."

"Trouble no more," said Cadfael. "Now you have told it freely, and you know the cloak came to you with a blessing, not a bane. Enjoy it freely, as you deserve."

"Father Abbot," said Cadfael, seeking out Heribert in the courtyard, "if you have no need of me until you come to table, there is work here I have still to do, concerning Nicholas Faintree."

With King Stephen holding audience in the inner ward, and the great court teeming with clerics, bishops, the small nobility of the county, even an earl or so, there was no room, in any case, for the mere servitors, whose duties would begin when the feast began. The abbot had found a friend in the bishop of Salisbury, and readily dismissed Cadfael to whatever pursuit he chose. He went in search of Hugh Beringar with Osbern's story very heavy on his mind, and the last question still unanswered, though so many sad mysteries were now made plain. It was not a terrified prisoner with the rope already round his neck who had broken down and betrayed the secret of FitzAlan's plans for his treasury. No, that betrayal had taken place a day previously, when the issue of battle was still to be decided, and the thing had been done with forethought, to save a life it yet had failed to save. He came by stealth, and asked to be taken to the officer of the guard, for he had something to tell to the king's advantage! And when he left he told the guard he had orders to go back, so that there could be no suspicion, but then he was in better heart. Poor wretch, not for long!

By what means or on what pretext he had managed to get out of the castle—perhaps on pretence of reconnoitering the enemy's position? —certainly he had obeyed his instructions to return and keep all suspicion lulled. He had returned only to confront the death he had thought he was escaping.

Hugh Beringar came out and stood on the steps of the great hall, craning round him for one person among all that shifting throng. The black Benedictine habits showed here and there in strong contrast to the finery of lordlings in their best, but Cadfael was shorter than many of those about him, and saw the man he was seeking before he was himself seen. He began to weave his way towards him, and the keen black eyes sweeping the court beneath drawn brows lit upon him, and glittered. Beringar came down to take him by the arm and draw him away to a quieter place.

"Come away, come up on to the guard-walk, there'll be no one there but the sentry. How can we talk here?" And when they had mounted to the wall, he found a corner where no one could approach them without being seen, he said, eyeing Cadfael very earnestly: "You have news in your face. Tell it quickly, and I'll tell you mine."

Cadfael told the story as briefly as it had been told to him, and it was understood as readily. Beringar stood leaning against the merlon of the wall as though bracing his back for a dour defence. His face was bitter with dismay.

"Her brother! No escaping it, this can have been no other. He came by night out of the castle, by stealth, hiding his face, he spoke with the king's officer, and returned as he had come. So that there might be no suspicion! Oh, I am sick!" said Beringar savagely. "And all for nothing! His treason fell victim to one even worse. You don't know yet, Cadfael, you don't know all! But that of all people it should be *her brother!*"

"No help for it," said Cadfael, "it was he. In terror for his life, regretting an ill-judged alliance, he went hurrying to the besiegers to buy his life, in exchange—for what? Something of advantage to the king! That very evening they had held conference and planned the removal of FitzAlan's gold. That was how someone learned in good time of what Faintree and Torold carried, and the way they were to go. Someone who never passed that word on, as I think, to king or any, but acted upon it himself, and for his own gain. Why else should it end as it did? The young man, so says Osbern, went back under orders, relieved and less afraid."

"He had been promised his life," said Beringar bitterly, "and probably the king's favour, too, and a place about him, no wonder he went back the happier in that belief. But what was really intended was to send him back to be taken and slaughtered with the rest, to make sure he should not live to tell the tale. For listen, Cadfael, to what I got out of one of the Flemings who was in that day's murderous labour from first to last. He said that after Arnulf of Hesdin was hanged, Ten Heyt pointed out to the executioners a young man who was to be the next to go, and said the order came from above. And it was done. They found it a huge jest that he was dragged to his death incredulous, thinking at first, no doubt, they were putting up a pretence to remove him from the ranks, and then he saw it was black reality, and he screamed that they were mistaken, that he was not to die with the rest, that he had been promised his life, that they should send and ask—"

"Send and ask," said Brother Cadfael, "of Adam Courcelle."

"No—I learned no name . . . my man heard none. What makes you hit on that name in particular? He was not by but once, according to this man's account, he came but once to look at the bodies they had already cut down, and it was early, they would be but few. Then he went away to his work in the town, and was seen no more. Weak-stomached, they thought."

"And the dagger? Was Giles wearing it when they strung him up?"

"He was, for my man had an eye to the thing himself, but when he was relieved for a while, and came back to get it, it was already gone."

"Even to one with a great prize in view," said Cadfael sadly, "a small extra gain by the way may not come amiss."

They looked at each other mutely for a long moment. "But why do you say so certainly, Courcelle?"

"I am thinking," said Cadfael, "of the horror that fell upon him when Aline came to collect her dead, and he knew what he had done. If I had known, he said, if I had known, I would have saved him for you! No matter at what cost! God forgive me! he said,

but he meant: Aline, forgive me! With all his heart he meant it then, though I would not call that repentance. And he gave back, you'll remember, the cloak. I think, truly I do think, he would then have given back also the dagger, if he had dared. But he could not, it was already broken and incomplete. I wonder," said Cadfael, pondering, "I wonder what he has done with it now? A man who would take it from the dead in the first place would not part with it too easily, even for a girl's sake, and yet he never dare let her set eyes on it, and he is in earnest in courting her. Would he keep it, in hiding? Or get rid of it?"

"If you are right," said Beringar, still doubtful, "we need it, it is our proof. And yet, Cadfael, for God's sake, how are we to deal now? God knows I can find no good to say for one who tried to purchase his own safety so, when his fellows were at their last gasp. But neither you nor I can strip this matter bare, and do so wicked an injury to so innocent and honourable a lady. It's enough that she mourns for him. Let her at least go on thinking that he held by his mistaken choice faithfully to the end, and gave his life for it—not that he died craven, bleating that he was promised grace in return for so base a betrayal. She must not know, now or ever."

Brother Cadfael could not but agree. "But if we accuse him, and this comes to trial, surely everything will come out. That we cannot allow, and there lies our weakness."

"And our strength," said Beringar fiercely, "for neither can *he* allow it. He wants his advancement with the king, he wants offices, but he wants Aline—do you think I did not know it? Where would he stand with her if ever a breath of this reached her? No, he will be at least as anxious as we to keep the story for ever buried. Give him but a fair chance to settle the quarrel out of hand, and he'll jump at it."

"Your preoccupation," said Cadfael gently, "I understand, and sympathise with it. But you must also acknowledge mine. I have here another responsibility. Nicholas Faintree must not lie uneasy for want of justice."

"Trust me, and stand ready to back me in whatever I shall do this night at the king's table," said Hugh Beringar. "Justice he shall have, and vengeance, too, but let it be as I shall devise."

Cadfael went to his duty behind the abbot's chair in doubt and bewilderment, with no clear idea in his mind of what Beringar intended, and no conviction that without the broken dagger any secure case could be made against Courcelle. The Fleming had not seen him take it, what he had cried out to Aline over her brother's body, in manifest pain, was not evidence. And yet there had been vengeance and death in Hugh Beringar's face, as much for Aline Siward's sake as for Nicholas Faintree's. What mattered most in the world to him, at this moment, was that Aline should never know how her brother had disgraced his blood and his name, and in that cause Beringar would not scruple to spend not only Adam Courcelle's life, but also his own. And somehow, reflected Cadfael ruefully, I have become very much attached to that young man, and I should not like to see any ill befall him. I would rather this case went to law, even if we have to step carefully in drawing up our evidence, and leave out every word concerning Torold Blund and Godith Adeney.

But for that we need, we must have, proof positive that Giles Siward's dagger passed into the possession of Adam Courcelle, and preferably the dagger itself, into the bargain, to match with the piece of it I found on the scene of the murder. Otherwise he will simply lie and lie, deny everything, say he never saw the topaz or the dagger it came from, and has nothing to answer; and from the eminence of the position he has won with the king, he will be unassailable.

There were no ladies present that night, this was strictly a political and military occasion, but the great hall had been decked out with borrowed hangings, and was bright with torches. The king was in good humour, the garrison's provisions were assured, and those who had robbed for the royal supplies had done their work well. From his place behind Heribert at the king's high table Cadfael surveyed the full hall, and estimated that some five hundred guests were present. He looked for Beringar, and found him at a lower table, in his finery, very debonair and lively in conversation, as though he had no darker preoccupation. He was master of his face; even when he glanced briefly at Courcelle there was nothing in the look to attract attention, certainly nothing to give warning of any grave purpose.

Courcelle was at the high table, though crowded to its end by the visiting dignitaries. Big, vividly coloured and handsome, accomplished in arms, in good odour with the king, how strange that such a man should feel it necessary to grasp secretly at plunder, and by such degrading means! And yet, in this chaos of civil war, was it so strange after all? Where a king's favour could be toppled with the king, where barons were changing sides according as the fortunes changed, where even earls were turning to secure their own advantage rather than that of a cause that might collapse under their feet and leave them prisoner and ruined! Courcelle was merely a sign of the times; in a few years there would be duplicates of him in every corner of the realm.

I do not like the way I see England going, thought Cadfael with anxious foreboding, and above all I do not like what is about to happen, for as surely as God sees us, Hugh Beringar is set to sally forth on to a dubious field, half-armed.

He fretted through the long meal, hardly troubled by the demands of Abbot Heribert, who was always abstemious with wine, and ate very frugally. Cadfael served and poured, proffered the finger-bowl and napkin, and waiting with brooding resignation.

When the dishes were cleared away, musicians playing, and only the wine on the tables, the servitors in their turn might take their pick of what was left in the kitchens, and the cooks and scullions were already helping themselves and finding quiet corners to sit and eat. Cadfael collected a bread trencher and loaded it with broken meats, and took it out through the great court to Lame Osbern at the gate. There was a measure of wine to go with it. Why should not the poor rejoice for once at the king's cost, even if that cost was handed on down the hierarchies until it fell at last upon the poor themselves? Too often they paid, but never got their share of the rejoicing.

Cadfael was walking back to the hall when his eye fell upon a lad of about twelve, who was sitting in the torchlight on the inner side of the gate house, his back comfortably against the wall, carving his meat into smaller pieces with a narrow-bladed knife. Cadfael had seen him earlier, in the kitchen, gutting fish with the same knife, but he had not seen the haft of it, and would not have seen it now if the boy had not laid it down beside him on the ground while he ate.

Cadfael halted and gazed, motionless. It was no kitchen knife, but a well-made dagger, and its hilt was a slender shaft of silver, rounded to the hand, showing delicate lines of filigree-work, and glowing round the collar of the blade with small stones. The hilt ended in a twist of silver broken off short. It was hard to believe, but impossible not to believe. Perhaps thought really is prayer.

He spoke to the boy very softly and evenly; the unwitting means of justice must not be alarmed. "Child, where did you get so fine a knife as that?"

The boy looked up, untroubled, and smiled. When he had gulped down the mouthful with which his cheeks were bulging, he said cheerfully: "I found it. I didn't steal it."

"God forbid, lad, I never thought it. Where did you find it? And have you the sheath, too?"

It was lying beside him in the shadow, he patted it proudly. "I fished them out of the river. I had to dive, but I found them. They really are mine, father, the owner didn't want them, he threw them away. I suppose because this was broken. But it's the best knife for slitting fish I ever had."

So he threw them away! Not, however, simply because the jewelled hilt was broken.

"You saw him throw it into the river? Where was this, and when?"

"I was fishing under the castle, and a man

came down alone from the water-gate to the bank of the river, and threw it in, and went back to the castle. When he'd gone I dived in where I saw it fall, and I found it. It was early in the evening, the same night all the bodies were carried down to the abbey—a week ago, come tomorrow. It was the first day it was safe to go fishing there again."

Yes, it fitted well. That same afternoon Aline had taken Giles away to St Alkmund's, and left Courcelle stricken and wild with unavailing regrets, and in possession of a thing that might turn Aline against him for ever, if once she set eyes on it. And he had done the only, the obvious thing, consigned it to the river, never thinking that the avenging angel, in the shape of a fisherboy, would redeem it to confront him when most he believed himself safe.

"You did not know who this man was? What like was he? What age?" For there remained the lingering doubt; all he had to support his conviction was the memory of Courcelle's horrified face and broken voice, pleading his devotion over Giles Siward's body.

The child hoisted indifferent shoulders, unable to picture for another what he himself had seen clearly and memorably. "Just a man. I didn't know him. Not old like you, father, but quite old." But to him anyone of his father's generation would be old, though his father might be only a year or two past thirty.

"Would you know him if you saw him again? Could you point him out among many?"

"Of course!" said the boy almost scornfully. His eyes were young, bright, and very observant, if his tongue was none too fluent, of course he would know his man again.

"Sheathe your knife, child, and bring it, and come with me," said Cadfael with decision. "Oh, don't fret, no one will take your treasure from you, or if later you must give it up, you shall be handsomely paid for it. All I need is for you to tell again what you have told to me, and you shan't be the loser."

He knew, when he entered the hall with the boy beside him, a little apprehensive now but even more excited, that they came late. The music was stilled, and Hugh Beringar was on his feet and striding towards the dais on which the high table stood. They heard his voice raised, high and clear, as he mounted and stood before the king. "Your Grace, before you depart for Worcester, there is a matter on which I beg you'll hear me and do right. I demand justice on one here in this company, who has abused his position in your confidence. He has stolen from the dead, to the shame of his nobility, and he has committed murder, to the shame of his manhood. I stand on my charges, to prove them with my body. And here is my gage!"

Against his own doubts, he had accepted Cadfael's intuition, to the length of staking his life upon it. He leaned forward, and rolled something small and bright across the table, to clang softly against the king's cup. The silence that had fallen was abrupt and profound. All round the high table heads craned to follow the flash of yellow brilliance that swayed irregularly over the board, limping on its broken setting, and then were raised to stare again at the young man who had launched it. The king picked up the topaz and turned it in his large hands, his face blank with incomprehension at first, and then wary and brooding. He, too, looked long at Hugh Beringar. Cadfael, picking his way between the lower tables, drew the puzzled boy after him and kept his eyes upon Adam Courcelle, who sat at his end of the table stiff and aware. He had command of his face, he looked no more astonished or curious than any of those about him; only the taut hand gripping his drinking-horn betrayed his consternation. Or was even that imagined, to fit in with an opinion already formed? Cadfael was no longer sure of his own judgment, a state he found distressing and infuriating.

"You have bided your time to throw your thunderbolt," said the king at length, and looked up darkly at Beringar from the stone he was turning in his hands.

"I was loth to spoil your Grace's supper, but neither would I put off what should not be put off. Your Grace's justice is every honest man's right."

"You will need to explain much. What is this thing?"

"It is the tip of a dagger-hilt. The dagger to which it belongs is now by right the property of the lady Aline Siward, who has loyally brought all the resources of her house to your Grace's support. It was formerly in the possession of her brother Giles, who was among those who garrisoned this castle against your Grace, and have paid the price for it. I say that it was taken from his dead body, an act not unknown among the common soldiery, but unworthy of knight or gentleman. That is the first offence. The second is murder—that murder of which your Grace was told by Brother Cadfael, of the Benedictine house here in Shrewsbury, after the count of the dead was made. Your Grace and those who carried out your orders were used as a shield for one who strangled a man from behind, as your Grace will well remember."

"I do remember," said the king grimly. He was torn between displeasure at having to exert himself to listen and judge, when his natural indolence had wanted only a leisurely and thoughtless feast, and a mounting curiosity as to what lay behind all this. "What has this stone to do with that death?"

"Your Grace, Brother Cadfael is also present here, and will testify that he found the place where this murder was committed, and found there, broken off in the struggle and trodden into the ground, this stone. He will take oath, as I do, that the man who stole the dagger is the same who killed Nicholas Faintree, and that he left behind him, unnoticed, this proof of his guilt."

Cadfael was drawing nearer by then, but they were so intent on the closed scene above that no one noticed his approach. Courcelle was sitting back, relaxed and brightly interested, in his place, but what did that mean? Doubtless he saw very well the flaw in this; no need to argue against the claim that whoever stole the dagger slew the man, since no once could trace possession to him. The thing was at the bottom of the Severn, lost for ever. The theory could be allowed to stand, the crime condemned and deplored, provided no one could furnish a name, and proof to back it. Or, on the other hand, this could far more simply be the detachment of an innocent man!

"Therefore," said Hugh Beringar relentlessly, "I repeat those charges I have made here before your Grace. I appeal one among us here in this hall of theft and murder, and I offer proof with my body, to uphold my claim in combat upon the body of Adam Courcelle."

He had turned at the end to face the man he accused, who was on his feet with a leap, startled and shaken, as well he might be. Shock burned rapidly into incredulous anger and scorn. Just so would any innocent man look, suddenly confronted with an accusation so mad as to be laughable.

"Your Grace, this is either folly or villainy! How comes my name into such a diatribe? It may well be true that a dagger was stolen from a dead man, it may even be true that the same thief slew a man, and left this behind as witness. But as for how my name comes into such a tale, I leave it to Hugh Beringar to tell—if these are not simply the lies of an envious man. When did I ever see this sup-posed dagger? When was it ever in my pos-session? Where is it now? Has any ever seen me wear such a thing? Send, my lord, and search those soldier's belongings I have here, and if such a thing is found in any ward or lodging of mine, let me know of it!"

"Wait!" said the king imperiously, and looked from one face to the other with frowning brows. "This is indeed a matter that needs to be examined, and if these charges are made in malice there will be an account to pay. What Adam says is the nub of it. Is the monk indeed present? And does he confirm the finding of this broken ornament at the place where this killing befell? And that it came from that very dagger?"

"I brought Brother Cadfael here with me tonight," said the abbot, and looked about for him helplessly.

"I am here, Father Abbot," said Cadfael from below the dais, and advanced to be seen, his arms about the shoulders of the boy, now totally fascinated, all eyes and ears.

"Do you bear out what Beringar says?" demanded King Stephen. "You found this stone where the man was slain?"

"Yes, your Grace. Trampled into the earth, where plainly there had been a struggle, and two bodies rolling upon the ground."

"And whose word have we that it comes from a dagger once belonging to Mistress Siward's brother? Though I grant you it should be easy enough to recognise, once known."

"The word of Lady Aline herself. It has been shown to her, and she has recognised it."

"That is fair witness enough," said the king, "that whoever is the thief may well be the murderer, also. But why it should follow that either you or Beringar here suppose him to be Adam, that for my life I cannot see. There's never a thread to join him to the dagger or the deed. You might as well cast round here among us, and pick on Bishop Robert of Salisbury, or any one of the squires down below there. Or prick your knife-point into a list of us with eyes closed. Where is the logic?"

"I am glad," said Courcelle, darkly red and forcing a strained laughter, "that your Grace puts so firm a finger on the crux of the matter. With goodwill I can go along with this good brother to condemn a mean theft and a furtive killing, but, Beringar, beware how you connect me with either, or any other honest man. Follow your thread from this stone, by all means, if thread there is, but until you can trace this dagger into my hands, be careful how you toss challenges to mortal combat about you, young man, for they may be taken up, to your great consternation."

"My gage is now lying upon the table," said Hugh Beringar with implacable calm. "You have only to take it up. I have not withdrawn it."

"My lord king," said Cadfael, raising his voice to ride over the partisan whisperings and murmurings that were running like conflicting winds about the high table, "it is not the case that there is no witness to connect the dagger with any person. And for proof positive that stone and dagger belong together, here is the very weapon itself. I ask your Grace to match the two with your own hands."

He held up the dagger, and Beringar at the edge of the dais took it from him, staring like a man in a dream, and handed it in awed silence to the king. The boy's eyes followed it with possessive anxiety, Courcelle's with stricken and unbelieving horror, as if a drowned victim had risen to haunt him. Stephen looked at the thing with an eye appreciative of its workmanship, slid out the blade with rising curiosity, and fitted the topaz in its silver claw to the jagged edge of the hilt.

"No doubt but this belongs. You have all seen?" And he looked down at Cadfael. "Where, then, did you come by this?"

"Speak up, child," said Cadfael encouragingly, "and tell the king what you told to me."

The boy was rosy and shining with an excitement that had quite overridden his fear. He stood up and told his tale in a voice shrill with self-importance, but still in the simple words he had used to Cadfael, and there was no man there who could doubt he was telling the truth.

"... and I was by the bushes at the edge of the water, and he did not see me. But I saw him clearly. And as soon as he went away I dived in where it had fallen, and found it. I live by the river, I was born by it. My mother says I swam before I walked. I kept the knife, thinking no wrong, since he did not want it.

And that is the very knife, my lord, and may I have it back when you are done?"

The king was diverted for a moment from the gravity of the cause that now lay in his hands, to smile at the flushed and eager child with all the good-humour and charm his nature was meant to dispense, if he had not made an ambitious and hotly contested bid for a throne, and learned the rough ways that go with such contests.

"So our fish tonight was gutted with a jewelled knife, was it, boy? Princely indeed! And it was good fish, too. Did you catch it, as well as dress it?"

Bashfully the boy said that he had helped.

"Well, you have done your part very fitly. And now, did you know this man who threw away the knife?"

"No, my lord, I don't know his name. But I know him well enough when I see him."

"And do you see him? Here in this hall with us now?"

"Yes, my lord," said the child readily, and pointed a finger straight at Adam Courcelle. "That was the man."

All eyes turned upon Courcelle, the king's most dourly and thoughtfully of all, and there was a silence that lasted no more than a long-drawn breath, but seemed to shake the foundations of the hall, and stop every heart within its walls. Then Courcelle said, with arduous and angry calm: "Your Grace, this is utterly false. I never had the dagger, I could not well toss it into the river. I deny that ever I had the thing in my possession, or ever saw it until now."

"Are you saying," asked the king drily, "that the child lies? At whose instigation? Not Beringar's—it seems to me that he was as taken aback by this witness as I myself, or you. Am I to think the Benedictine order has procured the boy to put up such a story? And for what end?"

"I am saying, your Grace, that this is a foolish error. The boy may have seen what he says he saw, and got the dagger as he claims he got it, but he is mistaken in saying he saw me. I am not the man. I deny all that has been said against me."

"And I maintain it," said Hugh Beringar. "And I ask that it be put to the proof."

The king crashed a fist upon the table so that the boards danced, and cups rocked and spilled wine. "There is something here to be probed, and I cannot let it pass now without probing it." He turned again to the boy, and reined in his exasperation to ask more gently: "Think and look carefully, now, and say again: are you certain this is the man you saw? If you have any doubt, say so. It is no sin to be mistaken. You may have seen some other man of like build or colour. But if you are sure, say that also, without fear."

"I am sure," said the boy, trembling but adamant. "I know what I saw."

The king leaned back in his great chair, and thumped his closed fists on the arms, and pondered. He looked at Hugh Beringar with grim displeasure: "It seems you have hung a millstone round my neck, when most I need to be free and to move fast. I cannot now wipe out what has been said, I must delve deeper. Either this case goes to the long processes of court law—no, not for you nor any will I now delay my going one day beyond the morrow's morrow! I have made my plans, I cannot afford to change them."

"There need be no delay," said Beringar, "if your Grace countenances trial by combat. I have appealed Adam Courcelle of murder, I

repeat that charge. If he accepts, I am ready to meet him without any ceremony or preparations. Your Grace may see the outcome tomorrow, and march on the following day, freed of this burden."

Cadfael, during these exchanges, had not taken his eyes from Courcelle's face, and marked with foreboding the signs of gradually recovered assurance. The faint sweat that had broken on his lip and brow dried, the stare of desperation cooled into calculation; he even began to smile. Since he was now cornered, and there were two ways out, one by long examination and questioning, one by simple battle, he was beginning to see in this alternative his own salvation. Cadfael could follow the measuring, narrowed glance that studied Hugh Beringar from head to foot, and understood the thoughts behind the eyes. Here was a younger man, lighter in weight, half a head shorter, much less in reach, inexperienced, over-confident, an easy victim. It should not be any problem to put him out of the world; and that done, Courcelle had nothing to fear. The judgment of heaven would have spoken, no one thereafter would point a finger at him, and Aline would be still within his reach, innocent of his dealings with her brother, and effectively separated from a too-engaging rival, without any blame to Courcelle, the wrongly accused. Oh, no, it was not so grim a situation, after all. It should work out very well.

He reached out along the table, picked up the topaz, and rolled it contemptuously back towards Beringar, to be retrieved and retained.

"Let it be so, your Grace. I accept battle, tomorrow, without formality, without need for practice. Your Grace shall march the following day," And I with you, his confident countenance completed.

"So be it!" said the king grimly. "Since you're bent on robbing me of one good man, between you, I suppose I may as well find and keep the better of the two. Tomorrow, then, at nine of the clock, after Mass. Not here within the wards, but in the open—the meadow outside the town gate, between road and river, will do well. Prestcote, you and Willem marshal the lists. See to it! And we'll have no horses put at risk," he said practically. "On foot, and with swords!"

Hugh Beringar bowed acquiescence. Courcelle said: "Agreed!" and smiled, thinking how much longer a reach and stronger a wrist he had for sword-play.

"Á l'outrance!" said the king with a vicious snap, and rose from the table to put an end to a sullied evening's entertainment.

Chapter Twelve

On the way back through the streets of the town, dark but not quite silent, somehow uneasily astir as if rats ran in a deserted house, Hugh Beringar on his rawboned grey drew alongside Brother Cadfael and walked his mount for some few minutes at their foot-pace, ignoring Brother Jerome's close proximity and attentive ears as though they had not existed. In front, Abbot Heribert and Prior Robert conversed in low and harried tones, concerned for one life at stake, but unable to intervene. Two young men at bitter enmity had declared for a death. Once both contestants had accepted the odds, there was no retreating; he who lost had been judged by heaven. If he survived the sword, the gallows waited for him.

"You may call me every kind of fool," said Beringar accommodatingly, "if it will give you any ease." His voice had still its light, teasing intonation, but Cadfael was not deceived.

"It is not for me, of all men," he said, "to blame, or pity—or even regret what you have done."

"As a monk?" asked the mild voice, the smile in it perceptible to an attentive ear.

"As a man! Devil take you!"

"Brother Cadfael," said Hugh heartily, "I do love you. You know very well you would have done the same in my place."

"I would not! Not on the mere guess of an old fool I hardly knew! How if I had been wrong?"

"Ah, but you were not wrong! He is the man—doubly a murderer, for he delivered her poor coward brother to his death just as vilely as he throttled Faintree. Mind, never a word to Aline about this until all's over—one way or the other."

"Never a word, unless she speak the first. Do you think the news is not blown abroad all through this town by now?"

"I know it is, but I pray she is deep asleep long ago, and will not go forth to hear this or any news until she goes to High Mass at ten. By which time, who knows, we may have the answer to everything."

"And you," said Brother Cadfael acidly, because of the pain he felt, that must have some outlet, "will you now spend the night on your knees in vigil, and wear yourself out before ever you draw in the field?"

"I am not such a fool as all that," said Hugh reprovingly, and shook a finger at his friend. "For shame, Cadfael! You are a monk, and cannot trust God to see right done? I shall go to bed and sleep well, and rise fresh to the trial. And now I suppose you will insist on being my deputy and advocate to heaven?"

"No," said Cadfael grudgingly, "I shall sleep, and get up only when the bell rings for me. Am I to have less faith than an impudent heathen like you?"

"That's my Cadfael! Still," conceded Beringar, "you may whisper a word or two to God on my behalf at Matins and Lauds, if you'll be so kind. If he turns a deaf ear to you, small use the rest of us wearing out our knee-bones." And he leaned from his tall horse to lay a light hand for an instant on Cadfael's broad tonsure, like a playful benediction, and then set spurs to his horse and trotted ahead, passing the abbot with a respectful reverence, to vanish into the curving descent of the Wyle.

Brother Cadfael presented himself before the abbot immediately after Prime. It did not seem that Heribert was much surprised to see him, or to hear the request he put forward.

"Father Abbot, I stand with this young man Hugh Beringar in this cause. The probing that brought to light the evidence on which his charge rests, that was my doing. And even if he has chosen to take the cause into his own hands, refusing me any perilous part in it, I am not absolved. I pray leave to go and stand trial with him as best I may. Whether I am of help to him or not, I must be there. I cannot turn my back at this pass on my friend who has spoken for me."

"I am much exercised in mind, also," admitted the abbot, sighing. "In spite of what the king has said, I can only pray that this trial need not be pressed to the death." And I, thought Cadfael ruefully, dare not even pray for that, since the whole object of this wager is to stop a mouth for ever. "Tell me," said Heribert, "is it certain that the man Courcelle killed that poor lad we have buried in the church?"

"Father, it is certain. Only he had the dagger, only he can have left the broken part behind him. There is here a clear contest of right and wrong."

"Go, then," said the abbot. "You are excused all duties until this matter is ended." For such duels had been known to last the day long, until neither party could well see, or stand, or strike, so that in the end one or the other fell and could not rise, and simply bled to death where he lay. And if weapons were broken, they must still fight, with hands, teeth and feet, until one or the other broke and cried for quarter; though few ever did, since that meant defeat, the judgment of heaven convicting, and the gallows waiting, an even more shameful death. A bitter business, though Cadfael, kilting his habit and going out heavily from the gate house, not worthy of being reverenced as the verdict of God. In this case there was a certain appropriateness about it, however, and the divine utterance might yet be heard in it. If, he thought, I have as much faith as he? I wonder if he did indeed sleep well! And strangely, he could believe it. His own sleep had been fitful and troubled.

Giles Siward's dagger, complete with its lopped topaz, he had brought back with him and left in his cell, promising the anxious fisher-boy either restoration or fair reward, but it was not yet time to speak to Aline in the matter. That must wait the issue of the day. If all went well, Hugh Beringar himself should restore it to her. If not—no, he would not consider any such possibility.

The trouble with me, he thought unhappily, is that I have been about the world long enough to know that God's plans for us, however infallibly good, may not take the form that we expect and demand. And I find an immense potential for rebellion in this old heart, if God, for no matter what perfect end, choose to take Hugh Beringar out of this world and leave Adam Courcelle in it.

Outside the northern gate of Shrewsbury the Castle Foregate housed a tight little suburb of houses and shops, but it ended very soon, and gave place to meadows on either side the road. The river twined serpentine coils on both sides, beyond the fields, and in the first level meadow on the left the king's marshals had drawn up a large square of clear ground, fenced in on every side by a line of Flemings with lances held crosswise, to keep back any inquisitive spectator who might encroach in his excitement, and to prevent flight by either contestant. Where the ground rose slightly, outside the square, a great chair had been placed for the king, and the space about it was kept vacant for the nobility, but on the other three sides there was already a great press of people. The word had run

through Shrewsbury like the wind through leaves. The strangest thing was the quietness. Every soul about the square of lances was certainly talking, but in such hushed undertones that the sum of all those voices was no louder than the absorbed buzzing of a hive of bees in sunshine.

The slanting light of morning cast long but delicate shadows across the grass, and the sky above was thinly veiled with haze. Cadfael lingered where guards held a path clear for the procession approaching from the castle, a brightness of steel and sheen of gay colours bursting suddenly out of the dim archway of the gate. King Stephen, big, flaxen-haired, handsome, resigned now to the necessity that threatened to rob him of one of his officers, but none the better pleased for that, and not disposed to allow any concessions that would prolong the contest. To judge by his face, there would be no pauses for rest, and no limitation imposed upon the possible savagery. He wanted it over. All the knights and barons and clerics who streamed after him to his presidential chair were carrying themselves with the utmost discretion, quick to take their lead from him.

The two contestants appeared as the royal train drew aside. No shields, Cadfael noted, and no mail, only the simple protection of leather. Yes, the king wanted a quick end, none of your day-long hacking and avoiding until neither party could lift hand. On the morrow the main army would leave to follow the vanguard, no matter which of these two lay dead, and Stephen had details yet to be settled before they marched. Beringar first, the accuser, went to kneel to the king and do him reverence, and did so briskly, springing up vigorously from his knee and turning to where the ranks of lances parted to let him into the arena. He caught sight of Cadfael then, standing a little apart. In a face tight, grave and mature, still the black eyes smiled.

"I knew," he said, "that you would not fail me."

"See to it," said Cadfael morosely, "that you do not fail me."

"No dread," said Hugh. "I'm shriven white as a March lamb." His voice was even and reflective. "I shall never be readier. And your arm will be seconding mine."

At every stroke, thought Cadfael helplessly, and doubted that all these tranquil years since he took the cowl had really made any transformation in a spirit once turbulent, insubordinate and incorrigibly rash. He could feel his blood rising, as though it was he who must enter the lists.

Courcelle rose from his knee and followed his accuser into the square. They took station at opposite corners, and Prestcote, with his marshal's truncheon raised, stood between them and looked to the king to give the signal. A herald was crying aloud the charge, the name of the challenger, and the refutation uttered by the accused. The crowd swayed, with a sound like a great, long-drawn sigh, that rippled all round the field. Cadfael could see Hugh's face clearly, and now there was no smiling, it was bleak, intent and still, eyes fixed steadily upon his opponent.

The king surveyed the scene, and lifted his hand. The truncheon fell and Prestcote drew aside to the edge of the square as the contestants advanced to meet each other.

At first sight, the contrast was bitter. Courcelle was half as big again, half as old again, with height and reach and weight all

on his side, and there was no questioning his skill and experience. His fiery colouring and towering size made Beringar look no more than a lean, lightweight boy, and though that lightness might be expected to lend him speed and agility, within seconds it was clear that Courcelle also was very fast and adroit on his feet. At the first clash of steel on steel, Cadfael felt his own arm and wrist bracing and turning the stroke, and swung aside with the very same motion Beringar made to slide out of danger; the turn brought him about, with the arch of the town gate full in view.

Out of the black hollow a girl came darting like a swallow, all swift black and white and a flying cloud of gold hair. She was running, very fleetly and purposefully, with her skirts caught up in her hands almost to the knee, and well behind her, out of breath but making what haste she could, came another young woman. Constance was wasting much of what breath she still had in calling after her mistress imploringly to stop, to come away, not to go near; but Aline made never a sound, only ran towards where two gallants of hers were newly launched on a determined attempt to kill each other. She looked neither to right nor left, but only craned to see over the heads of the crowd. Cadfael hastened to meet her, and she recognised him with a gasp, and flung herself into his arms.

"Brother Cadfael, what is this? What has he done? And you knew, you knew, and you never warned me! If Constance had not gone into town to buy flour, I should never have known…"

"You should not be here," said Cadfael, holding her quivering and panting on his heart. "What can you do? I promised him not to tell you, he did not wish it. You should not look on at this."

"But I will!" she said with passion. "Do you think I'll go tamely away and leave him now? Only tell me," she begged, "is it true what they're saying—that he charged Adam with murdering that young man? And that Giles's dagger was the proof?"

"It is true," said Cadfael. She was staring over his shoulder into the arena, where the swords clashed, and hissed and clashed again, and her amethyst eyes were immense and wild.

"And the charge—that also is true?"

"That also."

"Oh, God!" she said, gazing in fearful fascination. "And he is so slight...how can he endure it? Half the other's size...and he dared try to solve it this way! Oh, Brother Cadfael, how could you let him?"

At least now, thought Cadfael, curiously eased, I know which of those two is "he" to her, without need of a name. I never was sure until now, and perhaps neither was she. "If ever you succeed," he said, "in preventing Hugh Beringar from doing whatever he's set his mind on doing, then come to me and tell me how you managed it. Though I doubt it would not work for me! He chose this way, girl, and he had his reasons, good reasons. And you and I must abide it, as he must."

"But we are three," she said vehemently. "If we stand with him, we *must* give him strength. I can pray and I can watch, and I will. Bring me nearer—come with me! I must see!"

She was thrusting impetuously through towards the lances when Cadfael held her back by the arm. "I think," he said, "better if *he* does not see *you*. Not now!"

Aline uttered something that sounded like a very brief and bitter laugh. "He would not see me now," she said, "unless I ran between the swords, and so I would, if they'd let me—No!" She took that back instantly, with a dry sob. "No, I would not do so to him. I know better than that. All I can do is watch, and keep silence."

The fate of women in a world of fighting men, he thought wryly, but for all that, it is not so passive a part as it sounds. So he drew her to a slightly raised place where she could see, without disturbing, with the glittering gold sheen of her unloosed hair in the sun, the deadly concentration of Hugh Beringar. Who had blood on the tip of his sword by then, though from a mere graze on Courcelle's cheek, and blood on his own left sleeve below the leather.

"He is hurt," she said in a mourning whisper, and crammed half her small fist in her mouth to stop a cry, biting hard on her knuckles to ensure the silence she had promised.

"It's nothing," said Cadfael sturdily. "And he is the faster. See there, that parry! Slight he might seem, but there's steel in that wrist. What he wills to do, he'll do. And he has truth weighting his hand."

"I love him," said Aline in a soft, deliberate whisper, releasing her bitten hand for a moment. "I did not know until now, but I do love him!"

"So do I, girl," said Cadfael, "so do I!"

They had been two full hours in the arena, with never a break for breath, and the sun was high and hot, and they suffered, but both went with relentless care, conserving their strength, and now, when their eyes met at close quarters over the braced swords, there was no personal grudge between them, only an inflexible purpose, on the one side to prove truth, on the other to disprove it, and on either side by the only means left, by killing. They had found out by then, if they had been in doubt, that for all the obvious advantages on one side, in this contest they were very evenly matched, equal in skill, almost equal in speed, the weight of truth holding a balance true between them. Both bled from minor wounds. There was blood here and there in the grass.

It was almost noon when Beringar, pressing hard, drove his opponent back with a sudden lunge, and saw his foot slip in blood-stained turf, thinned by the hot, dry summer. Courcelle, parrying, felt himself falling, and threw up his arm, and Hugh's following stroke took the sword almost out of his hand, shivered edge to edge, leaving him sprawled on one hip, and clutching only a bladeless hilt. The steel fell far aside, and lay useless.

Beringar at once drew back, leaving his foe to rise unthreatened. He rested his point against the ground, and looked towards Prestcote, who in turn was looking for guidance to the king's chair.

"Fight on!" said the king flatly. His displeasure had not abated.

Beringar leaned his point into the turf and gazed, wiping sweat from brow and lip. Courcelle raised himself slowly, looked at the useless hilt in his hand, and heaved desperate breath before hurling the thing from him in fury. Beringar looked from him to the king, frowning, and drew off two or three more paces while he considered. The king made no further move, apart from gesturing dourly that they should continue. Beringar took three rapid strides to the rim of the square, tossed his sword beneath the levelled lances,

and set hand slowly to draw the dagger at his belt.

Courcelle was slow to understand, but blazed into renewed confidence when he realised the gift that was offered to him.

"Well, well!" said King Stephen under his breath. "Who knows but I may have been mistaken in the best man, after all?"

With nothing but daggers now, they must come to grips. Length of reach is valuable, even with daggers, and the poniard that Courcelle drew from its sheath at his hip was longer than the decorative toy Hugh Beringar held. King Stephen revived into active interest, and shed his natural irritation at being forced into this encounter.

"He is mad!" moaned Aline at Cadfael's shoulder, leaning against him with lips drawn back and nostrils flaring, like any of her fighting forebears. "He had licence to kill at leisure. Oh, he is stark mad. And I love him!"

The fearful dance continued, and the sun at its zenith shortened the shadows of the two duelists until they advanced, retreated, side-stepped on a black disc cast by their own bodies, while the full heat beat pitilessly on their heads, and within their leather harness they ran with sweat. Beringar was on the defensive now, his weapon being the shorter and lighter, and Courcelle was pressing hard, aware that he held the advantage. Only Beringar's quickness of hand and eye saved him from repeated slashes that might well have killed, and his speed and agility still enabled him at every assault to spring back out of range. But he was tiring at last; his judgment was less precise and confident, his movement less alert and steady. And Courcelle, whether he had got his second wind or simply gathered all his powers in one desperate effort, to make an end, seemed to have recovered his earlier force and fire. Blood ran on Hugh's right hand, fouled his hilt and made it slippery in his palm. The tatters of Courcelle's left sleeve fluttered at the edge of his vision, a distraction that troubled his concentration. He had tried several darting attacks, and drawn blood in his turn, but length of blade and length of arm told terribly against him. Doggedly he set himself to husband his own strength, by constant retreat if necessary, until Courcelle's frenzied attacks began to flag, as they must as last.

"Oh, God!" moaned Aline almost inaudibly. "He was too generous, he has given his life away...The man is playing with him!"

"No man," said Cadfael firmly, "plays with Hugh Beringar with impunity. He is still the fresher of the two. This is a wild spurt to end it, he cannot maintain it long."

Step by step Hugh gave back, but at each attack only so far as to elude the blade, and step by step, in a series of vehement rushes, Courcelle pursued and drove him. It seemed that he was trying to pen him into a corner of the square, where he would have to make a stand, but at the last moment the attacker's judgment flagged or Hugh's agility swung him clear of the trap, for the renewed pursuit continued along the line of lancers, Beringar unable to break out again into the centre of the arena, Courcelle unable to get through the sustained defence, or prevent this lame progress that seemed likely to end in another corner.

The Flemings stood like rocks, and let battle, like a slow tide, flow painfully along their immovable ranks. And halfway along the side of the square Courcelle suddenly drew back one long, rapid step instead of pursuing, and tossing his poniard from him in the grass, stooped with a hoarse cry of triumph, and reached beneath the levelled lances, to rise again brandishing the sword Hugh Beringar had discarded as a grace to him, more than an hour previously.

Hugh had not even realised that they had come to that very place, much less that he had been deliberately driven here for this purpose. Somewhere in the crowd he heard a woman shriek. Courcelle was in the act of straightening up, the sword in his hand, his eyes, under the broad, streaming brow half-mad with exultation. But he was still somewhat off-balance when Hugh launched himself upon him in a tigerish leap. A second later would have been too late. As the sword swung upward, he flung his whole weight against Courcelle's breast, locked his right arm, dagger and all, about his enemy's body, and caught the threatening sword-arm by the wrist in his left hand. For a moment they heaved and strained, then they went down together heavily in the turf, and rolled and wrenched in a deadlocked struggle at the feet of the indifferent guards.

Aline clenched her teeth hard against a second cry, and covered her eyes, but the next moment as resolutely uncovered them. "No, I will see all, I must...I will bear it! He shall not be ashamed of me! Oh, Cadfael...oh, Cadfael...What is happening? I can't see..."

"Courcelle snatched the sword, but he had no time to strike. Wait, one of them is rising..."

Two had fallen together, only one arose, and he stood half-stunned and wondering. For his enemy had fallen limp and still under him, and relaxed straining arms nervelessly into the grass; and there he lay now, open-eyed to the glare of the sun, and a slow stream of red was flowing sluggishly from under him, and forming a dark pool about him on the trampled ground.

Hugh Beringar looked from the gathering blood to the dagger he still gripped in his right hand, and shook his head in bewilderment, for he was very tired, and weak now with this abrupt and inexplicable ending, and there was barely a drop of fresh blood on his blade, and the sword lay loosely clasped still in Courcelle's right hand, innocent of his death. And yet he had his death; his life was ebbing out fast into the thick grass. So what manner of ominous miracle was this, that killed and left both weapons unstained?

Hugh stooped, and raised the inert body by the left shoulder, turning it to see where the blood issued; and there, driven deep through the leather jerkin, was the dead man's own poniard, which he had flung away to grasp at the sword. By the look of it the hilt had lodged downwards in thick grass against the solidly braced boot of one of the Flemings. Hugh's onslaught had flung the owner headlong upon his discarded blade, and their rolling, heaving struggle had driven it home.

I did not kill him, after all, though Beringar. His own cunning killed him. And whether he was glad or sorry he was too drained to know. Cadfael would be satisfied, at least; Nicholas Faintree was avenged, he had justice in full. His murderer had been accused publicly, and publicly the charge had been justified by heaven. And his murderer was dead; that failing breath was already spent.

Beringar reached down and picked up his sword, which rose unresisting out of the convicted hand. He turned slowly, and raised it in salute to the king, and walked, limping now and dropping a few trickles of blood from stiffening cuts in hand and forearm, out of the square of lances, which opened silently to let him go free.

Two or three paces he took across the sward towards the king's chair, and Aline flew into his arms, and clasped him with a possessive fervour that shook him fully alive again. Her gold hair streamed about his shoulders and breast, she lifted to him a rapt, exultant and exhausted face, the image of his own, she called him by his name: "Hugh...Hugh..." and fingered with aching tenderness the oozing wounds that showed in his cheek and hand and wrist.

"Why did you not tell me? Why? Why? Oh, you have made me die so many times! Now we are both alive again...Kiss me!"

He kissed her, and she remained real, passionate and unquestionably his. She continued to caress, and fret, and fawn.

"Hush, love," he said, eased and restored, "or go on scolding, for if you turn tender to me now I'm a lost man. I can't afford to droop yet, the king's waiting. Now, if you're my true lady, lend me your arm to lean on, and come and stand by me and prop me up, like a good wife, or I may fall flat at his feet."

"Am I your true lady?" demanded Aline, like all women wanting guarantees before witnesses.

"Surely! Too late to think better of it now, my heart!"

She was beside him, clasped firmly in his arm, when he came before the king. "Your Grace," said Hugh, condescending out of some exalted private place scarcely flawed by weariness and wounds, "I trust I have proven my case against a murderer, and have your Grace's countenance and approval."

"Your opponent," said Stephen, "proved

your case for you, all too well." He eyed them thoughtfully, disarmed and diverted by this unexpected apparition of entwined lovers. "But what you have proved may also be your gain. You have robbed me, young man, of an able deputy sheriff of this shire, whatever else he may have been, and however foul a fighter. I may well take reprisal by drafting you into the vacancy you've created. Without prejudice to your own castles and your rights of garrison on our behalf. What do you say?"

"With your Grace's leave," said Beringar, straight-faced, "I must first take counsel with my bride."

"Whatever is pleasing to my lord," said Aline, equally demurely, "is also pleasing to me."

Well, well, though Brother Cadfael, looking on with interest, I doubt if troth was ever plighted more publicly. They had better invite the whole of Shrewsbury to the wedding.

Brother Cadfael walked across to the guest hall before Compline, and took with him not only a pot of his goose-grass salve for Hugh Beringar's numerous minor grazes, but also Giles Siward's dagger, with its topaz finial carefully restored.

"Brother Oswald is a skilled silversmith, this is his gift and mine to your lady. Give it to her yourself. But ask her—as I know she will—to deal generously by the boy who fished it out of the river. So much you will have to tell her. For the rest, for her brother's part, yes, silence, now and always. For her he was only one of the many who chose the unlucky side, and died for it."

Beringar took the repaired dagger in his hand, and looked at it long and somberly. "Yet this is not justice," he said slowly. "You

and I between us have forced into the light the truth of one man's sins, and covered up the truth of another's." This night, for all his gains, he was very grave and a little sad, and not only because all his wounds were stiffening, and all his misused muscles groaning at every movement. The recoil from triumph had him fixing honest eyes on the countenance of failure, the fate he had escaped. "Is justice due only to the blameless? If he had not been so visited and tempted, he might never have found himself mired to the neck in so much infamy."

"We deal with what is," said Cadfael. "Leave what might have been to eyes that can see it plain. You take what's lawfully and honourably won, and value and enjoy it. You have that right. Here are you, deputy sheriff of Salop, in royal favour, affianced to as fine a girl as heart could wish, and the one you set your mind on from the moment you saw her. Be sure I noticed! And if you're stiff and sore in every bone tomorrow—and, lad, you will be! —what's a little disciplinary pain to a young man in your high feather?"

"I wonder," said Hugh, brightening, "where the other two are by now."

"Within reach of the Welsh coast, waiting for a ship to carry them coastwise round to France. They'll do well enough." As between Stephen and Maud, Cadfael felt no allegiance; but these young creatures, though two of them held for Maud and two for Stephen, surely belonged to a future and an England delivered from the wounds of civil war, beyond this present anarchy.

"As for justice," said Brother Cadfael thoughtfully, "it is but half the tale." He would say a prayer at Compline for the repose of Nicholas Faintree, a clean young man of mind and life, surely now assuaged and at rest. But he would also say a prayer for the soul of Adam Courcelle, dead in his guilt; for every untimely death, every man cut down in his vigour and strength without time for repentance and reparation, is one corpse too many. "No need," said Cadfael, "for you ever to look over your shoulder, or feel any compunction. You did the work that fell to you, and did it well. God disposes all. From the highest to the lowest extreme of a man's scope, wherever justice and retribution can reach him, so can grace."